In the Quiet Fields

Peter Beacham

In the Quiet Fields

pb PUBLISHING

First published in Great Britain by pb PUBLISHING 2024.

ISBN 978-1-3999-7741-8

Editor:
Shannon Roberts

Copy Editor:
Richard Crangle

Design and production:
Topics – The Creative Partnership, Exeter.

Typeset in Adobe Garamond Pro. 11/14pt.

Front cover illustration: *(Untitled) Devon Landscape*, Robert Organ, oil on canvas, 36" x 23", 1993.

Printed in UK.

Contents

Jeffrey Stride painting.
Sketch by Robert Organ.

In Memoriam

Robert Organ

1933 – 2023

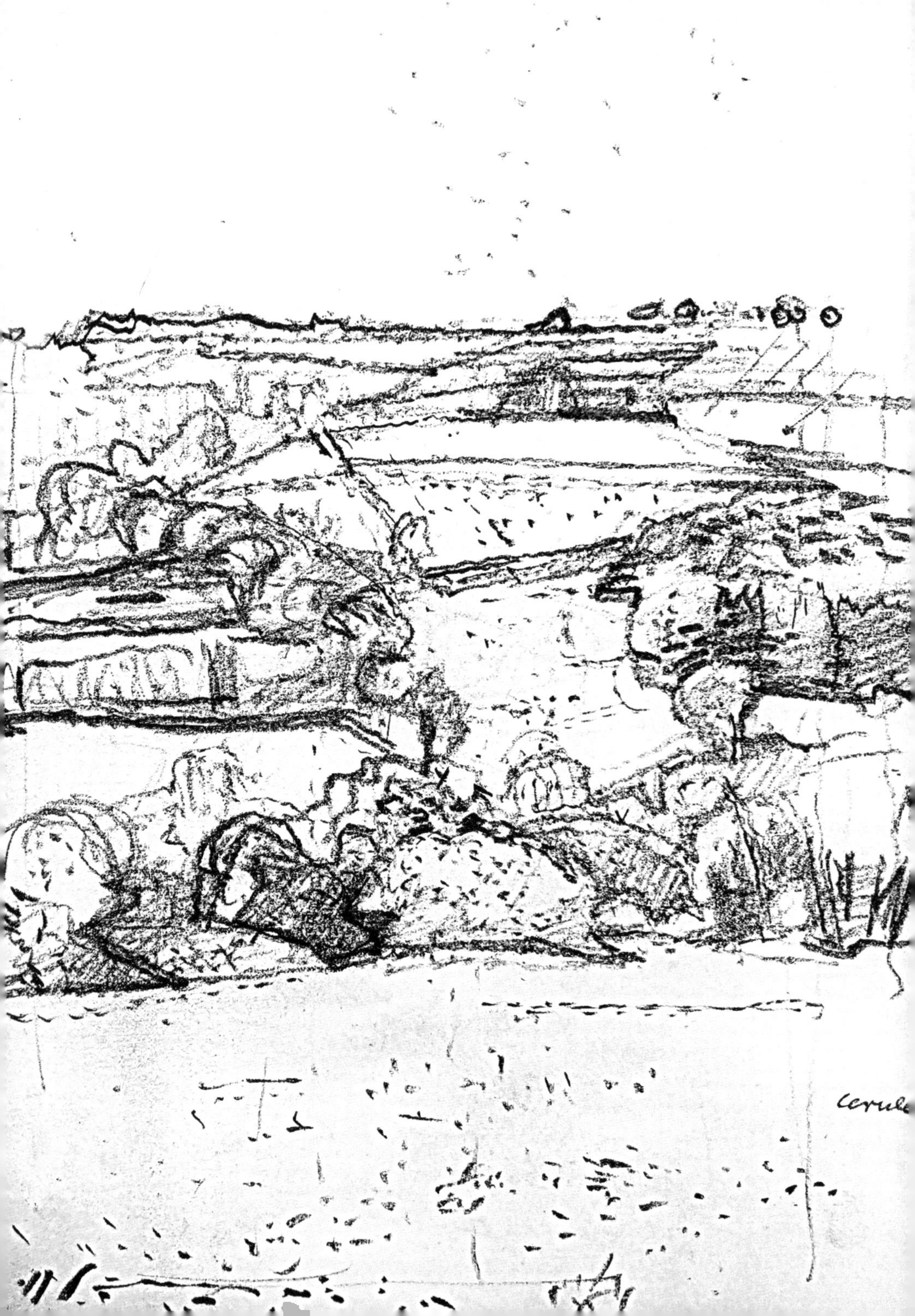
cerule

I never saw a man in all my days –
One whom the calm of quietness pervades –
Who gave not woods and fields his hearty praise
And felt a happiness in Summer shades.
There I meet common thoughts, that all may read
Who love the quiet fields....'

JOHN CLARE

1967

ONE

15th February 1967

8.15pm

Somewhere in the remote reaches of the West Country, the yellow headlights of the last bus to Michaelchurch shone through the heavy sheets of rain. A fierce Atlantic gale had been blowing all day and the driver, Les Trebilcock, was on high alert. He was an old hand at navigating these narrow lanes, but this was the worst storm he'd seen all winter, flood or fallen tree likely round every corner.

A faint scatter of lights came into view. Les nursed the bus with its ancient gearbox up a steep hill and into the dimly lit streets of the small country town, finally coming to a halt in the modest Market Square. After the grumble of the engine died away, Les clambered out of his cab and hurried round to the passenger door to find Percy Burden, the conductor, counting his meagre takings.

'Don't mind telling you, mate, glad that one's over. Suppose weren't much for you to do tonight – anyone left on board?'

'Just going to check now – must say, Les, you did proper job to get us through that lot.'

Percy ambled towards the back of the bus. There hadn't been more than a handful of passengers, mostly regulars who'd already got off. But come to think of it, there'd been that young man in the posh suit, the one who'd got on at the station. Percy couldn't recollect him leaving at any of the previous stops.

As he approached the back seats, he heard loud snoring. He grinned – that was him all right, nice looking lad, all floppy hair like the Beatles, and out like a light. His suit wasn't looking so smart now.

Percy cleared his throat loudly, then bent over and tapped the fellow on the shoulder.

'Sorry sir, you'll 'ave to wake up now.'

The young man slowly opened his eyes, rubbing them and blinking in the glare of the light bulb above.

'Oh, yes… sorry, I must have fallen asleep.'

'Not to worry, you're 'ere where you'm said you wanted to be – Michaelchurch.'

'Yes, of course, I'll get out of your way.'

'No 'urry young man. You're not from down 'ere perhaps?'

The passenger picked up his overnight bag, still blinking. 'No, it's my first visit.'

'Well, 'ope you've not far to go – not much of a night to be 'angin' about outside. You be careful how you go, now.'

'I will,' the young man said as he moved towards the front of the bus. 'Thank you.'

Jonathan stepped out of the warm interior of the bus and into terra incognita.

God, it was cold, and very wet. How long had he been asleep? He shook his head to try to wake himself up properly. So far this had been the journey from hell. The train from London was delayed, he'd missed several connections, and now here he was, hours later than planned, a complete stranger in the dark of a foul winter night in a small town in the far west of England.

What to do?

Everything was shut and there was no sign of life – even the bus had disappeared now. He remembered the farmer's wife saying that the B&B was a bit remote. Well, nothing for it now but to find a telephone.

15 February 1967, 8.15pm

He searched for a familiar red kiosk, and squinted in the gloom as he saw a figure stepping out of a doorway, hurrying through the downpour towards a Land Rover parked nearby. He quickened his pace and called out.

'Hello there!'

The stranger turned. 'Can I help you?'

'Please. Could you tell me where the nearest telephone is?'

'There's one just round the corner near the post office,' the stranger replied. 'Why, are you in a spot of trouble?'

'I suppose I am. I've booked bed and breakfast at a farm near here – not exactly sure where – and was going to walk, but I'd expected to be here a lot earlier, and I'm not sure how I'm going to find my way in the dark. I need to call the farm and tell them what's happened. Or perhaps there's a local taxi service?'

'Which farm are you looking for?'

'Hall Farm.'

'Oh, the Northcotts' place! Well, you certainly don't want to be walking anywhere on a night like this – not without waterproofs, or in those town shoes of yours. The lanes will be a mud bath. The good news is I'm a vet on call to the next farm; I could take you most of the way. Jump in – we're getting soaked and there's a lambing ewe in trouble.'

'Thanks,' Jonathan said, scrambling into the Land Rover's passenger seat. 'That'll save my life.'

As soon as the doors closed, they rumbled through the flooded lanes at speed, wheels throwing up a shower of mud.

Sorry,' the young man said, holding up an awkward hand. 'I'm Jonathan Lane.'

'Pleased to meet you, Jonathan – I'm Jim Jewell. Down here on business?'

'More like a bit of a break.'

'Not the best time of the year for a holiday,' Jim said, shooting him a curious sidelong look, 'not in this part of the world. Been down here over thirty years and still can't get over how different it is from where I was brought up – in the middle of Brum. Two things the locals say – 'The grass never stops growing and it never stops raining.' And I can tell you from experience, both are true.'

'Well, it certainly seems wet.' Jonathan peered out of the window, but could see little save the driving rain that streaked along the glass. 'I don't know the West Country at all, I'm afraid. I'm from London – but you'd probably guessed that already?'

Jim laughed. 'Pretty much – we're used to getting togged up to go out in this sort of weather.'

'Yes, I didn't exactly plan for this. Still… at least it'll be memorable, and I'll get a breath of fresh air.'

'You'll certainly find plenty of that. And the Northcotts will give you a warm welcome. They're clients of mine too, great people.'

'That's good to hear. I could do with a bite and a comfortable bed.'

'Then you've definitely made the right choice of billet at Hall.'

Eventually the vet pulled up at a crossroads and came to a stop, in what seemed to Jonathan like the middle of nowhere.

'Sorry I can't take you all the way,' Jim said, 'but I really need to get on. Hall's not far up that lane on our left, but you'll need to watch your step – it's a bit rough in places. Tell you what, I've got some spare kit in the back. Let me fetch it out.'

Jim Jewell was a big man, and Jonathan slipped easily into his borrowed rainwear and over-sized boots. He picked up the powerful torch he'd also been offered and climbed out.

'You've been really kind Jim,' he said, raising his voice above the hammer of the downpour. 'Thank you.'

'No problem. It's what we do in this part of the world – you never know when you're going to need a hand yourself! I'll pick my gear up from the Northcotts when I'm next there. Now, must be on my way, good to meet you!'

'You too, and thanks again.'

15 February 1967, 8.15pm

Jonathan watched the Land Rover's red tail lights disappear into the dark, adjusted his eyes to the torchlight, then turned his steps up the sodden lane.

TWO

15th February 1967

9.10pm

The lane seemed more like a stream bed than a metalled road, and even where it rose to higher ground was full of potholes, with deep mud at the verges. In the dark with rain still sheeting down, it seemed to run quite a bit further than Jim had suggested – so the sight of lighted windows came as a great relief.

As instructed, Jonathan found the door from the yard. His arrival had been announced by the barking of a dog, and the door was quickly opened. A woman – in her early forties, perhaps, and with a pleasant open face – greeted him with a wide smile.

'Hello!' She took in her guest's bedraggled appearance. 'You must be Mr Lane. Do please come in, you must be soaked to the skin – it's a horrible night out there. I'm Anna Northcott. We spoke on the phone when you booked the room. We were beginning to wonder what had happened to you.'

'I'm really sorry,' he said, shedding his raincoat, 'my train was delayed about an hour and a half at Paddington, and then the bus had to divert because of flooding.'

'It's we who should apologise. If we'd known you weren't coming under your own steam, we could have picked you up from the town.'

He glanced down. 'I'd better take these boots off, they're very muddy. I've got some shoes in my bag.'

'Oh, don't worry – we live with mud all the time.'

She ushered him in to a room full of gumboots and damp coats. The only furniture was a wooden bench opposite an old kitchen range giving out waves of welcome heat.

'If you'd like to take your wet stuff off in here, it'll be dry by morning – we keep the range going all night. Then come on through to the kitchen and warm up properly.'

Jonathan hung his coat on a peg, sat on the bench, and breathed a deep sigh of relief. He changed back into what the vet had called his 'town shoes', then ventured into the farmhouse kitchen.

'Can't tell you how good it is to be here at last,' he said as he pulled up a chair at the wide, weathered wooden table. 'I hadn't really counted on getting here after dark, and certainly hadn't bargained for this awful weather. But had a bit of luck when I hitched a lift with your vet – he lent me the waterproofs, and the torch.'

'Oh, Jim Jewell? That's typical, nothing ever too much trouble. Just as well you ran into him, it's not a night to negotiate our lanes for the first time. My husband Ted's around somewhere, I'll go and find him.'

At that moment a door off the kitchen opened. The man who entered was of that slight but wiry build which comes from a life of demanding physical activity.

'Oh, here he is,' said Anna. 'Ted, this is Jonathan Lane.'

'It's good to meet you, Ted,' said Jonathan, rising and advancing a few steps towards the farmer. 'It's very kind of you to put me up in the off-season.'

Ted looked to be a few years older than his wife, with thoughtful brown eyes and dark curly hair tinged with grey. He flashed a ready, shy smile.

'You're most welcome Jonathan, we're open for business anytime,' Ted said. 'Please make yourself at home.'

'I expect you're hungry,' Anna said. 'I've got your supper ready but it'll take a few minutes to finish off. Ted could show you to your room if you like, and you can settle in before you come down and join us.'

Ted led him through a narrow passage along the back of the house, up a handsome staircase, and along a landing off which he was shown into a room with massive curved beams rising up to arches in the ceiling. A log fire crackled in the huge fireplace and a four-poster bed stood invitingly against the end wall, with thick curtains shutting out the winter night.

It looked like heaven.

'Will this do?' said Ted, slightly hesitant. 'You've got a bathroom to yourself in the room next door on the landing.'

'It's marvellous,' said Jonathan, his nightmare of a day already fast receding. 'I couldn't wish for anything better.'

'Glad you like it. It's funny, but some folk can't cope with all this space, all these beams. They think this plasterwork over the fireplace is a bit weird too,' Ted said, going to the overmantel and pointing out some of its more exotic features – mermaids, kraken, and other strange sea-creatures.

'It's wonderful,' Jonathan said, peering at the plaster. 'I've never seen anything like it!'

'We think it's an amazing room, best in the house.' There was a note of pride in Ted's tone. 'The roof's over five hundred years old apparently, and the plasterwork's late seventeenth century, back when this was the great chamber of an important house.'

'It's amazing – I'll feel like a king in that huge bed!'

'Well, you enjoy it.' Ted reached for a couple of logs from the basket beside the fireplace and set them carefully on the flames. 'Now, if you've got all you need, I'll leave you to make yourself at home and we'll see you downstairs as soon as you like.'

Between the splendid room, warm slippers, and the even warmer welcome, Jonathan felt instantly at home. After a quick wash, he hung up his damp and crumpled suit, changed into a spare shirt and trousers he'd brought, and made his way downstairs again. He was keen to rejoin his hosts but even keener for some supper.

The cottage pie and vegetables followed by apple pie and custard, washed down with some local cider, seemed like a feast. Despite his weariness, Jonathan was captivated by his host's talk of life on the farm.

'It's not easy,' Ted said, after a lengthy description of the farmer's lot. 'Takes a lot to keep it going day after day, month after month, year after year.'

Anna caught Jonathan stifling a yawn and flashed him a quick, knowing smile.

'So what we're really saying is, it's a hard life, and you'd not do it if you didn't love it,' she said. 'You wouldn't believe the hours we put in – which is why we need go to bed early and get up early.' This last remark was delivered along with a rather pointed look to her husband.

'It's a complete way of life,' Ted said. 'You just have to accept that it demands your total commitment. You can't give up on the animals or the crops, whatever the weather. You'll always be looking out for them.'

'Ted,' Anna said. 'We don't want Jonathan thinking farmers are all the world's biggest moaners, do we?'

'To be honest, I know next to nothing about farming,' Jonathan said. 'Or much of anything to do with the countryside for that matter. I'm afraid I've led an almost totally urban existence. I'd be keen to learn though!'

'Well, we'd be pleased to show you a bit more tomorrow, wouldn't we?' said Anna. 'Depending of course what you're planning to do. Pity you're only stopping over for the one night!' She seemed about to add something, then shook her head a little. 'And on the subject of the night,' she continued, 'we've got to be up by four to start the milking, so we're usually earlier than this to bed.'

'I'm so sorry, I was so interested in what you were telling me I'd forgotten the time. Please forgive me.'

'Nothing to forgive,' said Ted, 'we quite enjoy an audience, as you can probably tell! Now, there're just a couple of things you need to know before you disappear. The most important is we don't have mains electric, so ours comes from a generator – it's a noisy old beast but pretty reliable.

We switch it off when we go to bed, and on when we get up. The thing to remember is it starts up whenever you throw a switch, so if you turn on a light in the middle of the night you'll wake the whole house as the old girl gets going! That's why there's an oil lamp and some candles in your room.'

'Just as well you told me that,' Jonathan said. 'Well, I'll say goodnight then, and thank you for making me feel so welcome.'

'Goodnight Jonathan, sleep well,' said Anna. 'Oh, the other thing we need to mention – we don't usually do breakfast until we've finished milking, if that's alright with you.'

'Perfectly, I don't need to be away early.'

Exhausted by the journey, Jonathan clambered up the stairs and into the welcoming embrace of the four-poster, where he fell asleep in seconds.

After he'd gone and Ted and Anna tidied up, they also found their way to bed.

'What a sweetie!' Anna murmured as they settled down for the night. 'He seemed so grateful for everything – must be a bit of a stranger to home comforts.'

'He took a bit of a shine to you, love.' As he switched off the last light, the generator rumbled down into silence.

Anna snorted. 'Probably reminded him of his mum more like.'

Ted chuckled as he threw an arm across her waist. 'Bit of a mystery man, though – what on earth's he doing down here in the middle of February, and wearing a suit and tie too!'

'Was dying to ask him, but I know what you'd think – Anna being nosey again.'

'Go on, have a guess.'

'Oh, I don't know. That kind of shyness – and that arty woollen tie he had on – could he be an art teacher going for a job at the new comprehensive?'

'Could be – he's certainly a good listener.'

Even in the dark, the smile in her voice was clear. 'He had to be, with you in such talkative form, love! He's so dishy he'd have all the girls swooning over him, though.'

'Let's see what we can find out over breakfast, shall we?'

THREE
16th February 1967

Chug … chug … chug … chug-chug-chugchugchughCHUG –

What the hell is that?

Jonathan fumbled for his watch as he struggled towards semi-consciousness. When he finally grabbed it and shone the torch on its face, he saw it was almost half-past four.

Oh, it's that bloody generator…

Flicking off the torch and dropping his watch back on the bedside table, he shut his eyes. The hum of the generator soon lulled him back to sleep.

He woke again as dawn broke, about half-seven. As he slowly came to, he contemplated his lot from the warmth of the stately bed.

He'd surprised himself by coming this far, having nearly called the whole thing off at Paddington. The promise of a good lunch in the dining car had eventually lured him on board and, as he'd observed the ever-changing landscape from his window seat, he'd persuaded himself that, yes, he really was ready for a bit of an adventure.

It was only when he looked at his watch once more that he realised he'd been musing a bit too long. He rose and made his way to the window, where he pulled back the curtains. Arriving in the dark at a strange house makes the first look out of the window in the morning one of life's great excitements.

He was not disappointed.

16th February 1967

The storm of the previous evening had worn itself out. Just outside his window was a small paddock, and on the other side of it, a hedge bank rising up. Covering the bank was a mass of pure white snowdrops shining in the bright, low winter sun. There was something about their unassuming cheerfulness in the dullness of the winter hedgerow which quickened his spirits.

He washed and dressed, then retraced his route down to the farmhouse kitchen. It was a haven of warmth that winter morning, heated by a large range occupying a cavernous fireplace that spanned almost the whole length of the end wall. There was no-one about, so he warmed himself by standing with his back to the range while he took in the scene.

At the opposite end of the large high-ceilinged room was a dark oak screen of massive uprights and recessed panels. Against it was set a table of monumental proportions, home to piles of paper and farming magazines but with ample space left to seat a family and guests. The wall between was taken up with a long granite mullioned window through which the morning sun flooded onto a couple of well-worn leather chairs, presently occupied by cats resting after their nocturnal exertions. The other wall housed a floor-to-ceiling dresser displaying a cornucopia of crockery, family memorabilia, and a number of books – the latter intrigued him, as there was a lot of poetry among them. The room had a comfortable, lived-in character and, if the old beams above his head were anything to go by, seemed to have been like that for centuries.

The door from the yard banged open and a breathless Anna hurried into the kitchen.

'Sorry Jonathan,' she said as she passed him on her way into the hall. 'We're running a bit late I'm afraid, we've got a problem with one of the cows and I'm just going to give Jim Jewell a ring to get him out. Please, take a seat over there and I'll get us some breakfast in a minute. Ted will be in shortly.'

Jonathan had been too exhausted to notice last evening, but when Anna grabbed a pan and set it on the range, he saw what a good-looking woman she was, with piercing blue eyes and that healthy bloom of people who spend a lot of time out of doors.

'Morning, Jonathan.' Ted appeared, looking like a man for whom the day had started some hours previously. 'Sleep well? Sometimes people from town say they can't because it's too quiet.'

'Slept like a log, thanks. Glad you warned about the generator though! It gave me a start when it fired up but once it got going I was back to sleep in no time.'

'That's good then, we'll soon get you used to life on the farm!'

Ted had been washing his hands very thoroughly, and now came over to join Jonathan at the table. Anna brought a large teapot and filled their huge mugs to the brim.

'Thirsty work, milking,' said Ted, drinking deeply. 'I hope you're hungry, Anna prides herself on giving our guests such a good breakfast they don't need to eat for the rest of the day!'

'Sounds wonderful to me,' Jonathan said. 'I live on my own so breakfast is usually just a bowl of cereal.'

'Well, I hope this won't disappoint you,' Anna said as she brought plates of bacon and eggs, sausage, mushrooms, tomatoes and fried bread. 'Come on, just tuck in!'

Silence reigned for a minute or so as Jonathan complied. Once everyone had taken the edge off their appetite, though, he spoke.

'I was looking out of my bedroom window earlier and thinking how lovely it all looked. I've never stayed anywhere like this before.'

Ted flashed a quick, proud smile.

'Hall's been in my family for over a century,' he said. 'My great grandfather bought it for pennies from the Tremaine estate, the big landowners round here. The farm was a lot larger then, but over the years land and cottages had to be sold off to pay death duties, though it's still above average for this part of the world. It came to me by chance – I was a geography teacher at the local school at the time, just over twenty years ago. My old uncle who'd been farming here died suddenly, before he'd put his affairs in order. His wife had died a few years before. They had a son but he was killed in the last war. It all took a fair time, but after the lawyers finally unravelled his affairs, they declared me next of kin.'

Jonathan smiled. 'Was that a blessing or a curse?'

Ted and Anna both laughed, though he noticed Ted at least had a touch of anxiety in his eyes.

'We weren't at all sure at first,' said Ted. 'By the time we finally took it over it was in a bit of a state, I can tell you. We've had to work hard to get it back together, haven't we, love?'

'We certainly have,' Anna said. 'We've gradually built it up into a medium-sized mixed farm centred round a pretty successful dairy herd we've bred ourselves. Milk's been good for us, so far. We sell it locally, mostly to the dairies in Broadhaven – there's a new ice cream factory there, which is another good market for us.'

'Where's Broadhaven? I feel so ignorant about this part of the world.'

'Oh, sorry, we keep forgetting!' Anna said. 'It's a large seaside resort about ten miles away. To be honest, it's seen better days, but the beaches are amazing, and that means big caravan and camping parks, so there's a good demand for our produce in the summer.'

'You must be doing very well then.'

Again, he thought he spotted a touch of worry – or maybe weariness – behind the smiles.

'We do all right, especially with the B&B, and we've been expanding that recently,' Ted said. 'Partly to make use of some of the spare rooms we've got here.'

'You won't have realised yet what a huge old pile this is,' Anna said.

'I'm afraid parts of it are in a pretty poor state,' said Ted. 'My uncle did a bit of research when he took it on and discovered it was a grand house a few centuries ago – as your room shows – when it was part of the Tremaine estate. It was actually called The Hall in some of the old documents from that period. But it used to belong to one of the great mediaeval monasteries before the Dissolution.'

'Really?' Jonathan sat up straighter, ignoring his plate for the moment. 'I take a bit of an interest in monastic sites.'

'The mediaeval house was pulled around to make it into a smart gentry residence, but since then it's gradually slid down the social scale,' Ted said. 'A process of 'genteel decay' as one of our visitors put it! We do our best to keep the old place together, but there's an awful lot of it. Sometimes we feel we're losing the battle.' Ted sighed. 'But we love it here, and we'd like to hand it on to our children eventually.'

'Are they keen to take it on?'

'They're as passionate about it as we are.' As she spoke, Anna rose and went to refill the teapot from the kettle on the range. 'In fact our daughter's at Cirencester Agricultural College and our boy's just started reading agriculture at the University of Reading, so between the four of us we've quite an investment in the future of farming.'

Jonathan sat quietly for a moment, taking in once more the high beams and the warmth of the range. What a thing, to raise a family here.

'It must be a great incentive for you,' he said.

'It is,' said Anna, 'but we're going to have to make some big decisions soon. This year we're aiming to expand our holiday business with a caravan and camping site, if the council will let us. It's a lovely spot we've got here and we want more people to enjoy it.'

'It's a pity you're not here for longer,' said Ted, 'because after our talk last evening we were saying we thought you'd be very interested to see the rest of the farm. Our land goes right down to the sea, and there are wonderful coastal walks, some lovely little secluded beaches… some of our guests come back year after year. We'd love to show it all to you.'

Jonathan was moved by their rootedness, their love for this small piece of the world and their stewardship over it. But then, this was the kind of place you could fall in love with – it was hard to feel such a sense of pride for his small, impersonal London flat.

'I'd love to come back,' he said. 'If I have the opportunity.' Which – depending on how his morning went – he very well might.

'You'll be very welcome anytime,' said Ted, 'the more visitors the better as far as we're concerned!'

'Tell you what,' Anna said, 'why don't you come down for a few days in late summer if you can, for the Michaelchurch show at the end of August? It's the highlight of our year, and a lot of fun.'

'Or, if you fancy a winter break,' Ted said, 'come in early November for our carnival? There's a procession of floats which some of the locals work on all year, not to mention the fireworks!'

'They both sound marvellous.' He glanced at the large grandfather clock just visible through the door into the hall. 'I've come down for an interview in the town this morning, so when I come back will rather depend on how I get on, I suppose.'

'Goodness, what time's your interview?' Anna said. 'We've been talking for ages.'

'It's at eleven.'

'I could give you a lift,' said Ted. 'I've got an appointment with the bank manager at eleven – worse luck.'

'Well, it's quarter past ten already,' Anna said. 'I'm rather intrigued what job you might be going for – perhaps you'd drop us a line to let us know how it all went?'

Jonathan wanted to answer Anna directly, but something held him back.

'Of course I will,' he said with a smile. 'Honestly, I'm fascinated by your set-up here – I've dreamed of living in the country since I was a boy.'

So it was with some reluctance he collected his things from his room, allowed himself a farewell look out of the window at those snowdrops, thanked Anna, then climbed into the passenger side of Ted's old Land Rover.

FOUR

16th February 1967

Mid-morning

The return to town felt much quicker by daylight than the uncertain journey of the previous evening. To Jonathan's disappointment the steeply banked lanes prevented any wider views of the countryside – he still had that childhood longing to glimpse the sea – though even more masses of snowdrops in the hedge banks sustained the promise of that pale morning.

The road rose steadily towards Michaelchurch, which occupied a hill-top site well above the valley that led down to the farm and the coast. It was one of those old market towns which had the air of having gone quietly to sleep ever since their zenith in the previous century. Some more recent post-war housing washed around the approaches, but they soon left that behind, driving through narrow streets between much older buildings until they reached the Market Square, where the bus had dropped Jonathan off the night before.

Ted parked and the two of them went on chatting – longer than was wise, given that Jonathan still didn't know exactly where he was heading. Ted explained the layout of the town, essentially four main streets: West Street by which they'd arrived, East Street straight ahead, South Street to the right, and Fore Street (the main street) to the left, by the parish church.

Realising they were about to go their separate ways, Jonathan suddenly felt guilty. He'd said so little of himself, and his hosts had been so easy and open with him.

'Ted, I hope you might be able to tell me where to find the place I'm going for my interview – it's an architectural firm by the name of Atherton & Green – they're in South Street, I think.'

Ted laughed.

'You'll certainly enjoy your interview, then – more than I shall mine anyway! Atherton & Green are an interesting bunch, a bit off the wall for this part of the world, some folk say. Anna had you down as an art teacher going for a post at our local secondary school – pretty near miss I'd say, she'll be chuffed by that.'

Jonathan smiled. 'I'm looking for something out of the ordinary myself. Anyway, I suppose we'd both better get going. I do hope I can come and visit you and Anna again, whatever happens today.'

'So do I – and best of luck with the interview. Let us know how you got on, won't you?'

'I certainly will.'

They got out of the car and shook hands.

'Good luck with your Mr Money Man, Ted. And thanks again for all your and Anna's kindness, it's been such a help.'

Jonathan watched as Ted walked like a reluctant schoolboy towards the stern classical facade of his bank, leaving him to his own date with destiny.

It was only a short step to South Street and a couple of hundred yards further to a sign on the iron railings of a forecourt: 'Atherton & Green Architects'. The building looked like an old chapel, its front a competent essay in the Gothic Revival style, nicely proportioned and faced in honey-coloured sandstone with good architectural details in granite. It intrigued Jonathan more than a little that architects who advertised themselves as modernists would choose such a building as their office.

The answer was obvious immediately when he stepped inside. The interior was spacious, light and airy, and simply but beautifully furnished:

clearly a statement of the practice's intent. The reception area rose to the full height of the building and was backed by a wide flight of metal stairs to a mezzanine floor above. Roof lights gave plenty of northern light and the internal partitions were also glazed. He noted a baby grand piano to one side of the reception desk and the sound of classical music permeating the space. A friendly spaniel waddled up and sniffed him enthusiastically.

'Hello, are you Mr Lane?' The voice came from a young woman who'd just appeared at the top of the stairs. 'I'm Emma.'

'Hello, yes, I'm Jonathan Lane. Good to meet you, Emma.'

She descended the stairs and offered her hand. 'Please, have a seat and I'll get you a coffee or tea, whichever you'd like.'

'I'd love a coffee, thank you.'

'We arranged 11.00, didn't we? I'll tell them you're here. They're having a meeting about one of our schemes at the moment but they won't be long – we're pretty good at time-keeping.'

He sat and drank his coffee. He'd only taken a few sips when a diminutive woman, elegantly dressed in a black kaftan, glided along the balcony and down the stairs towards him.

'Hello, you must be Mr Lane.' The voice was gracious but direct. 'May I call you Jonathan? We're quite informal round here.'

'Yes, of course.' Jonathan found himself straightening his shoulders as he rose from the sofa to shake her outstretched hand.

'I'm Caroline Atherton,' she said. 'I'm really pleased to meet you; thank you for coming all this way to see us.'

Caroline! Jonathan was momentarily taken aback. Why on earth had he assumed C. Atherton would be a Charles, or a Christopher, or even a Crispin? It never crossed his mind it would be a woman.

God, I hope she hasn't picked up on that – she looks sharp as a needle!

'Come on through to our practice meeting room so we can talk. Do take a seat, and I'll make us another coffee – between you and me, our Emma doesn't make it quite strong enough for my liking.'

When she returned – with a large coffee pot and a plate of biscuits – she sat herself down not opposite but beside him, fixing him with a forensic gaze through her black-rimmed spectacles.

'Now, I don't like formal interviews – they never get to grips with what really matters, which isn't just a question of 'Is this person up to the job?' but 'Could I bear working with them?' So, you and I will chat. I'll talk and ask you a few questions first, then you can talk and ask me anything you like.'

'That sounds good to me.'

'Excellent. First, let me tell you a bit about the practice. I set it up when I moved down from London over fifteen years ago – didn't expect I'd ever do that, but it's what happens when you fall in love, and my husband's family have lived in these parts forever. I'd been quite happy working for one of the larger modernist firms on major projects – in fact, the very same outfit you're with at the moment – which is one of the reasons I was interested in your application.'

'Coming down here and starting up this sort of practice must have been quite a challenge then,' Jonathan remarked. At least, that was in line with all the metropolitan chatter, that rural England might as well be like living in the Dark Ages.

'It's certainly proved to be,' she said. 'I began on my own, from a room in our house. I soon discovered people down here are pretty conservative, not least in their views about what a building should look like. Don't get me wrong – as an observer I'm catholic in my architectural tastes, but as a practitioner I want to make contributions of our own time. I had to go along with what people were used to for a while. Then I got a few commissions for small projects where I could work in my preferred style – a couple of private houses, an extension to the cottage hospital in Broadhaven, a new library and a classroom block at the local secondary school. Things like that got me going.'

She'd risen to pull out some photographs from a filing cabinet behind her; now she spread them out on the table before them.

'Great photographs,' Jonathan said. 'Modern architecture looks so good in black-and-white.'

'That's absolutely true, at least in the hands of a decent photographer! We've got an excellent local woman who's so good with light and shade, textures and surfaces.'

'But you also do more traditional work, from what I saw in the brochure you sent?'

'Yes indeed. I realised I couldn't just survive on such jobs. So I asked Tony Green, who you'll meet later on, whether he'd be interested in going into partnership with me – he'd had a long-established practice specialising in the repair and adaptation of old buildings. It turned out he was fed up with being a sole practitioner, so we joined forces ten years ago – and I have to say the two streams of work have turned out to complement each other rather well.'

'I was rather taken with his jobs,' Jonathan said, warming to the conversation. 'Some very clean-lined conversions of old buildings to new uses, like this office.'

'That's where the practice has been doing well, picking up on the continuity of what's around us, rather than old and new pitted against each other.'

'I'm all for that.' He appreciated her matter-of-fact approach. 'There's so much needless destruction going on in our cities at the moment – I see it every day in London.'

She offered the coffee pot, and he poured himself another cup.

'The developer's wrecking ball hasn't reached this part of the world just yet, thank goodness,' she said as she followed suit and topped up her own coffee. 'But they'll eventually find a way in. The sands are shifting down here too, even if it isn't quite as obvious yet as it is in urban England. Which is why I see our practice as so important – we can show how to adapt and change and modernise without ruining what gives the area its unique character. Does that make any sense to you?'

'It makes complete sense, and it's very refreshing. I suppose I'd been puzzled how your practice could make its way in an area like this.'

'When you get under its skin, this part of the world isn't as backward looking as it first appears. Once folk understand what you're trying to do to improve things for them, they'll get behind you.'

'I think it's exciting you can practise modernism down here.' He was beginning to think he might have a real chance.

'Don't get carried away just yet!' said Caroline. 'Now, I realise I've been going on a bit – I was keen to set out our manifesto, as it were. So why don't I stop there and let you do the talking? As I said earlier, you can ask anything you like.'

She rose once more and walked over to the window, giving Jonathan a few moments to consider his response.

'I suppose the one question I'd like to ask is what I might be working on if you invited me to join the practice.'

'Good question.' Leaning back on her palms on the edge of the desk, she continued. 'You'd be mainly on our public sector projects, through which I'm hoping to expand the practice. Luckily for us, the County Council's Architect's Department is keen to promote modernism in its public building programme, and there's so much work to be done they outsource increasing amounts of it to private practice. And believe it or not, there are already several ambitious housing schemes to bring London and Birmingham overspill down to expand towns like Barnstaple and Bodmin!' Jonathan couldn't help but feel caught up in her passion for her work. 'I'm in the final stages of negotiating a council housing scheme myself – not a huge one like those you'll have worked on, but quite a significant project for this part of the country. If you came, I'd be thinking of you taking the lead on it.'

'That would be just up my street.'

'But you might also want to try your hand at some of our repair and conversion jobs with Tony,' she said, 'to expand your experience. After decades of rural depopulation – with young people moving to the cities because there's no work – people with money are beginning to move down here for the way of life. So we're getting an increasing number of commissions for the remodelling of older properties… as well as for the odd new private house which might also interest you.'

'That sounds like a great opportunity as well, I'd be very interested'.

'Good.' She paused, took off her glasses, cleaned them, and put them back on. 'But I've got off track again. Now go on, tell me about yourself and I'll do the listening.'

Jonathan knew this was the crunch. If he talked about a fresh start, it would sound like he'd made a hash of his career thus far. Instead, he talked about wanting to broaden his experience by working in a different part of the country and in a smaller practice. He made much of his lifelong interest in design and was pleased to see Caroline taking a thoughtful look through the sketch books he'd been asked to bring along: unusually, they hadn't asked for a portfolio of previous work. And, in view of what she'd already told him, he put deliberate stress on how much he'd enjoyed working on social housing projects in London.

'And your practice gave you a good reference too,' said Caroline, 'one I actually believe for once – I still know a few people there, including Alice who wrote it!' He noticed that her gaze had grown ever more intense. 'But there's one thing I wanted to clear up, if you don't mind. Before you worked for them, there's a gap of a couple of years in your C.V. – what were you up to then?'

This was the question he'd been dreading, but he'd carefully rehearsed his response. 'Oh, sorry, I should have explained. I needed to take some time out, so I went travelling.'

Caroline paused, and for a moment he was worried he'd spoken too casually. He was relieved when she continued.

'I did much the same at about your stage, before I met my husband,' she said. 'In many ways it sorted me out. Look, I think it's time to ask Tony to come down so you two can have a chat. I'll join you a bit later.'

Tony Green was an older man, rather more genial than Caroline.

'Hello old chap,' Tony said, offering a hand. He had one of those lived-in faces and the air of someone who, having seen it all before, was content to look at life with a wry smile. 'Meet the practice dinosaur. I'm Tony, and you're Jonathan I believe. Delighted to meet you.'

Jonathan instantly rose to return the handshake. 'Hello Tony, I'm delighted to meet you too.'

'Please do sit down, old thing. Have a couple of these biscuits – I'll have a couple too. I expect The Boss was grilling you so hard she forgot to offer you one!'

'Oh, not at all – it was a very good conversation, we both got a little caught up I think.'

'Only joking. Anyway, I'm bound to ask, in all seriousness: what on earth brings you to the edge of the civilised world, eh?'

Jonathan laughed. 'Sense of adventure, I suppose. I've never been down this way before so it's all new to me. And I was very intrigued by the job advert – it seems such an unusual set-up, modernism and tradition together. From what's in the brochure and what Caroline's told me it seems very successful.'

'Oh yes – it's been terrific, working with Caroline, she's full of energy and ideas. All these bright young folk she's got in to the office as well, they're such fun to work with – specially for an old 'un like me.'

'Bit unusual for a practice in this part of the world too – I gather they're mostly one-man bands,' said Jonathan. A little self-consciously, he added, 'with an emphasis on the 'man' bit.'

Tony nodded, slowly.

'You're absolutely right. Caroline's been a welcome breath of fresh air. As you've no doubt guessed, she won't stand for any nonsense – she's ruffled the feathers of plenty of the male peacocks who've been strutting around unchallenged here for far too long. All power to her elbow is what I say!'

'I do rather warm to her style.'

Tony rose and rummaged through a plan chest in the corner for a moment, pulling out some drawings and watercolour perspectives. He began arranging them in front of Jonathan.

'Good. Now, you're interested in modernism obviously, but what about this sort of stuff I do? Messing around with existing buildings, repairing crumbling wrecks, finding a way to give an old heap a new lease of life? Take a look at some of these little jobs I've done over the years.'

Jonathan lifted a few and studied them. 'They're beautifully drawn.'

'I think good draughtsmanship is the key to good design, don't you?'

'I do, and I quite enjoy sketching myself – these colour-washed ones are exquisite. To answer your question directly, dealing with old buildings isn't something I've ever thought about before. But the more I think about it, the more I think I'd like to have a go.'

'That's good to hear,' Tony said with a chuckle, 'because at my stage of life I feel it's time I started handing on such bits of wisdom I've gained. You'd find it a lot of fun too – it's surprising what you learn about your fellow human beings when you're fiddling around with their houses. I love it!'

'Yes, I think I can imagine,' said Jonathan. 'All a bit different from the housing schemes I'm working on in London.' Then, rather quickly, he added, 'but a change is what I'm after, so that's just as well.'

'I bet. I'm sure you'd miss the buzz of the city, but this is a wonderful place to live and work. Wonderful scenery too – moors behind us, sea in front of us – and there's more culture around than you'd think. I play in a little jazz quartet we've been running for a few years now.'

'Is the baby grand in the foyer yours, then?'

'Yes, a little indulgence of mine. I play it when I feel we need a little livening up, though my instrument is double bass.'

The conversation continued amiably for some time until Caroline rejoined them, listening in the doorway for a moment. Eventually she intervened.

'It sounds as though you two have had a good chat. I think this would be a good moment for Jonathan to come on upstairs and meet the rest of the team. We've got a sandwich lunch for us all – we believe it's important to let you see them and they you.'

The rest of the day seemed to go well enough. Jonathan got on well with everyone, though he guessed that Caroline would have the final say on his hire.

'I'll be in touch as soon as I can,' she said as they parted. 'I'm assuming you're still interested?'

'I certainly am,' he said, hoping he didn't sound too keen – though he doubted he was able to hide that very well.

FIVE

17th February 1967

Though Jonathan woke the next morning back in London in his small flat south of the river, his head and heart were still in the far west. The place had taken on the allure of a foreign country, somewhere he could start life all over again. Try as he did to temper his enthusiasm, and knowing other candidates must be in the running for the same job, for the first few days he was like a coiled spring: whenever the phone rang or the post came he was up, and whenever it turned out to be nothing, he'd console himself by counting his present blessings.

His living room looked out over the life and buildings which composed the inner London suburbs; endlessly fascinating to observe. He loved its mix of cultures and its warm humanity, enriched in recent decades by the arrival of a thriving West Indian community with their spicy food and vibrant music. People here hadn't got much, but they didn't complain, they just got on with it – and they accepted each other, whatever.

Did he really want to swap all that for a place where he'd be treated with suspicion years after moving in? A place where even mains electricity or water wasn't a given?

Jonathan stood at the window in the early dark of the winter evening, watching the maze of lights and streams of traffic, listening to the muffled rumble of the underground trains. He loved his life in London, his work and his friends… but at heart he felt restless, increasingly aware it was time to move on.

Here he was at the start of his fourth decade, still searching for something or someone to build his life around. But even his most daring experiment – the two years he'd spent in a Benedictine monastery, the gap in his C.V. Caroline had mentioned – even that hadn't brought him any peace of mind. There was much about monastic life which appealed to him, not least its structure and the discipline of daily worship, prayer and contemplation. Yet there was also such a lot he simply couldn't live with, namely the baffling dualities of belief, not to mention that the monks could be as driven by petty feuds and rivalries as any secular co-worker.

Before he'd left, he'd sought guidance from the Abbot, one day after Vespers when he couldn't hold the contradictions in his head together any longer.

Abbot Christopher, an astute and kindly man in late middle age, had welcomed Jonathan into his gracious sitting room and offered him a gin and tonic. 'I've found it generally does the trick,' the Abbot said, 'when one has something weighing on the mind.'

Once he'd mixed them both a drink, he settled in.

'Now, Jonathan, how may I be of assistance?'

'May I come straight to the point, Father Abbot?'

'That's usually for the best.'

'I've thought long and hard about this before asking to see you… to put it plainly, the fact is I'm struggling with my vocation.'

There was a long pause, and more than one sip from his glass, before the Abbot spoke.

'That's not as unusual as you probably think. We all struggle with our vocation, at least from time to time, some of us constantly – would it shock you to know I'm in the latter camp?'

'I suppose it would.'

'Well, it shouldn't. You've simply discovered what all monastics realise sooner or later – we don't escape the contradictions of the human condition when we enter the monastery. If anything, our vocation forces us to face up to them more honestly.'

'It's not that I don't want to commit,' Jonathan said, staring into the cool clarity of his own drink. 'But more and more obstacles crowd in to stop me.'

'May I ask what kind of obstacles?'

'It's mostly all this... well, theology.' He returned the Abbot's amused smile with a wry look of his own. 'It's not that I don't enjoy it intellectually – in fact I find the challenge of it very stimulating. But that's not the same as being able to assent to it, to believe it, to have faith in it... is it?'

'No, it isn't. In the end, our faith has to spring from a life lived, not books or church doctrines – or even, wonderful as it can be, the liturgy. Our faith must be an affirmation of our experience of God's grace and love, practised by us, broken fragments of humanity that we are.'

They spoke for some time, and in due course the Abbot refreshed their glasses.

'I feel such a fraud, Father.' If it weren't for the glass in his hand, he'd have felt he was at confession. 'I'm so full of doubt.'

The Abbot let his words hang in the air before responding.

'The great figures of all religions have struggled with that one, Jonathan. Doubt is vital to the life of faith – we should never stop facing up to the challenges it poses because, properly understood, it means we never stop searching.'

Jonathan was, in turn, silent for a few beats. 'I suppose I was, well... naive to expect to find any certainty.'

'No, not naive. It's a common enough assumption about the religious life. There are certainties to be discovered, but not the sort one might imagine. And we religious have no monopoly on wisdom.'

'I find that rather liberating.'

'So you should. I always remember that, as we were told to turn over the examination paper for our theology finals at Oxford, one of my fellow students stood up and said very loudly 'THERE ARE NO ANSWERS!' – and he's gone on to be a wise priest and distinguished theologian!'

Jonathan smiled.

'Look, you're not the first novice to come to this point,' the Abbot said, 'and you certainly won't be the last... let's just be quiet and silently prayerful for a few minutes. Perhaps you'd agree we've shared enough words for now?'

'I'd find a time of quiet very helpful now, Father.'

It was in the silence which followed that Jonathan gradually came to feel a serenity, a peace which had so long eluded him. Though reluctant to break that serenity, it gave him the strength to put the question he'd dreaded asking.

'Father Abbot, can I ask for your guidance?'

'Of course you may. Though you might not want to hear it just now, or perhaps not want to follow it. But what I have to say to you is said with love and care for you, always remember that.'

'You have my word.'

'Then try to hear this. From what I've seen and know of you, I think you are one of our most promising novices.

'That said… perhaps you might consider whether you're yet ready to commit to the monastic life. Return to the world for a while, with my blessing. And of course, if and when the time comes, you find your way back, the door will always be open to you. But don't rush into a decision. Think on what I've suggested and pray about it. And feel free to talk further with me at any time.'

It was on such terms six months later that he'd left the monastery, open-minded about the future, and seeing himself 'a work in progress', as the Abbot had put it. He'd found the courage to restart his architectural career back in London, which he'd broken off so abruptly to enter the monastery, and to rekindle some of his old friendships.

Those who knew him best assumed he'd 'lost his faith', that cliché often carelessly employed when observing another's spiritual struggle, without realising the hurt it causes. Jonathan understood their confusion and tried, without much success, to explain the opposite was true. His faith in the church may have taken a hit, his prayer-life may have dissolved into the ether, but his time in the monastery had only fired up his conviction that 'God so loved the world….'

As he'd told Caroline, he'd found great satisfaction in his work on rehousing schemes for deprived parts of inner London. Or he had, until he'd begun to have doubts about the wisdom of clearing away whole communities and sticking people in giant slabs of concrete. Worse, there was now a whiff of scandal, rumours of corruption in major public sector developments. What had been the scaffolding for his attempt to rejoin the world had become unstable, even treacherous.

He needed to seek out fresh fields, which was why the job at Atherton & Green had sounded so compelling. But having gone so long with no word, that prospect seemed to have diminished to a vanishing point. After an interminably wet, cold weekend he decided to end the agony and call Caroline himself.

Just as he was screwing up the courage to do so, however, the phone rang.

'Hello Jonathan, Caroline Atherton here. Look, I'm sorry to have been so slow in getting back to you. The thing is, we've decided you might fit rather well into our little set-up down here, so I'm ringing to offer you the job… Jonathan? … Hello, are you still there?'

'Yes, sorry! I'm a bit surprised, that's all,' he said. 'I'd rather given up and assumed you'd found someone else.'

'Quite the reverse. Now,' she continued in her brusque way, 'can you give me an answer immediately or do you need some time to think it over?'

'I don't need any more time Caroline – I'm thrilled at the prospect of working with you all and I'm delighted to accept.'

'Good. Now, we'll talk about your salary and then you can tell me when you might be able to start.'

SIX

Early April 1967

Only a few weeks later, Atherton & Green's new assistant was installed at his drawing board.

He found the practice a congenial workplace. Caroline's crisp command was tempered by Tony's more relaxed approach, and everyone seemed to get on most of the time – not always the case in a small outfit. Tony particularly delighted in teasing the two young draughtsmen, Mike and Chris, about their unrequited passion for the vivacious but unavailable Emma, who was going out with the heir to a prosperous local haulage business.

Stuck to find a place to stay, Jonathan had asked the Northcotts whether he could base himself at the farm as a paying guest. Since the summer holiday season was some way off, they readily agreed, and for a little extra offered to provide him evening meals, as long as he didn't mind eating in the kitchen with them. So it was to all three's mutual pleasure that he found himself back in the room he'd occupied on his first visit.

He was thrilled to be living in the countryside. Brought up in Eastbourne where his family had run a small hotel not far from the sea front, he'd gone to a well-regarded art school in the town and then on to architectural school in London. Even the monastery had been in a London suburb. So he was spellbound as he watched the country spring unfold.

The snowdrops which had captivated him were long vanished, but thousands of primroses lit up the deep lanes as the hedgerows quickened to life. He started by walking the couple of miles between farm and office – walking in London had always been one of his pleasures, with so many architectural riches to be enjoyed once the eye had been trained to look up. That discipline served him well as he relished the sights, sounds and scents of his new world. He was fascinated by the simple things: the frenetic activity of nesting birds; the myriad shades of fresh green as trees and hedgerows burst into leaf; the slow, mysterious unfurling of the ferns' croziers; and the pungent, sometimes overwhelming aroma of wild garlic in the woods. All around, he could practically feel the pulse of late spring.

However, following one too many breathless and sometimes mud-spattered arrivals at the office, Caroline produced an old bicycle for him. This led to new excitements, like gliding home in the evening, a gentle downhill slope all the way. And there was deep pleasure at the end of each day in Ted and Anna's company over supper. He learned a great deal about the realities of life on the farm, a necessary tempering of his inclination to believe he'd wandered into the Elysian Fields. His picture of the countryside had, until now, been drawn from the Romantic poets – and while the journeys of Wordsworth and Coleridge in the West Country now took on special significance for him, it was John Clare's poetry of the fields, woods, and seasons in Northamptonshire which he began to understand for the first time.

He was, gradually, making the shift from an observer of rural life to an enthusiastic participant. No longer did he feel like a passenger on a country train, looking out of the window as he ambled between villages and small towns on a sleepy summer afternoon.

It was a shock when he'd first helped Ted in castrating piglets. On a regular basis he now found himself part of the burial party for the casualties of livestock farming, and always noted Ted's stoicism on the days he sent stock to the abattoir.

He never forgot the day he returned home to find no Sam to greet him – Ted had shot the dog that morning after he'd found it worrying sheep on a neighbouring farm.

Ted's willingness to take him on expeditions beyond the farm gate helped too. Farm sales were a source of fascination, not just because of what was up for grabs, but on account of the farmers themselves. Most of all, he relished the occasional visit to the town's livestock market, held every Wednesday near the old station below the town. He would take half a day off, unpaid – standing at the ringside, surrounded by farmers in their flat caps and gumboots, he was totally absorbed, and felt as if he'd been granted rare access to the heart of the community.

'What's he saying?' he'd once dared ask Ted as the auctioneer rattled through the sale of livestock in staccato bursts of bidding he could hardly parse.

'Quiet,' said Ted sharply, 'I need to concentrate on these prices.'

'Sorry,' Jonathan mumbled. A new bit of etiquette: nothing must interrupt the sacred ritual.

After the market closed and Ted completed his business with the auctioneer, Jonathan ventured another question as they walked towards the Land Rover.

'Did you do all right today?'

'Not bad, I suppose,' Ted said. 'Got a fair price for those heifers I put in – in fact, it was good enough for me to buy you a pint to celebrate.'

They adjourned to the Railway Inn, crowded with other farmers. Jonathan was amused: the terse reticence of the ring had been replaced by warm conviviality between men who'd been bidding fiercely against each other only an hour or so earlier.

'If you want to know what makes us farmers tick,' Ted told him as they settled in for their pint, 'there's no better time and place than after market at the Railway.'

◆

On their way home Ted opened up about the financial challenges facing them.

'We've got to find new ways to substantially increase the farm's income, realise more of the potential of our set-up. Can't put my finger on just what at the moment though.'

'Any idea what other farmers are doing? I guess many of you are in the same boat.'

'We're off to see a few places trying something a bit different soon. Anna's got high hopes we'll pick up some ideas, but I'm not so sure. One sure thing – whatever it might be will cost money, money we haven't got.'

'I'll ask around a bit too. The practice has quite a few of the bigger farmers in the wider area on our books – see what I can pick up.'

'I'm sure you've realised we'll be glad of any help we can get Jonathan – we really value your friendship already, you know.'

'And me yours Ted – and Anna's too. If I'm honest, I was at a bit of a low ebb when I landed on your doorstep – being here has helped me begin to open up new perspectives.'

'So we're a mutual help group then!'

'I guess so!'

SEVEN

Late April 1967

As Caroline promised, Jonathan's first job was the public housing project she'd won through a national architectural competition. Government ministers wanted this to showcase what public housing could achieve in rural England; consequently Caroline felt it was vital in building the profile of the practice.

Jonathan felt flattered, if a little daunted, to be entrusted with it. He'd been inspired by the drawings and model which had won Caroline the commission.

'Such a refreshing change from the mass housing I've been doing in London,' he told her, 'all high density and often high rise. I got more and more uncomfortable about making people live in monoliths.'

'Well, it's certainly a world away from that,' said Caroline, 'though it's not without its own challenges. It's over in Broadhaven; I guess you've never been?'

'No, but I've heard it mentioned a lot since I've been down here – and I've got an image of it in my head from the posters in the waiting room at Paddington. Looks quite a classy sort of place.'

'Well, I'm afraid it's rather faded since its glory days in the 1920s. Look, I've arranged for us to go over to meet our clients this afternoon and see the site – if you haven't got any appointments this morning, why don't we start off soon so we can have a look round and catch a spot of lunch beforehand?'

'That sounds ideal.'

The approach to Broadhaven was unremarkable, the roads lined with the bungalows and semi-detached houses of the inter- and post-war periods typical of twentieth-century English suburbs. But as they reached the sea front, the town itself was suddenly revealed.

'How stunning!' Jonathan said as he got his first glimpse of white surf breaking endlessly over miles of golden sand.

'It's quite magical, isn't it? Thrills me every time I see it – looks perfect on a day like this. Mind you, it won't feel quite so idyllic when we get out of the car!'

A stiff north-westerly breeze was racing clouds across the spring-blue sky, shafts of light and spots of shade chasing each other across the sea, the beaches, and further inland. Caroline and Jonathan had to shout to hear each other as they walked along the promenade.

'It's certainly bracing,' said Jonathan, 'but I'm used to that – I was brought up on the seafront at Eastbourne.'

'If you'll allow me, this is rather different – the Atlantic coast, not the Channel,' Caroline replied. 'There's nothing between us and America!'

'But it's a marvellous spot,' he said. 'I can see what would have made it such a major resort.'

'Its Victorian promoters saw it as an English version of a European spa – look at this grand promenade, those luxuriant public gardens, and the monster hotels behind.'

'Have we got time to take a look at the town?'

'Let's take a look down here around the harbour first – it started as a fishing port, you know. A few day boats still go out – you can get good fresh fish from those stalls on the quay.'

They turned inland and were soon walking past a string of large hotels whose peeling stucco suggested they'd seen better days.

'Why is it all looking so forlorn?'

'Well, there was a time when you could step on a train at Waterloo and get off here – the Atlantic Coast Express, it was called. But cheap air fights and guaranteed sun are putting paid to the British seaside resort, I'm afraid. So when British Railways, in their infinite wisdom, closed the branch line, it was all over for Broadhaven.'

Soon they were at the town centre. The main street still had a gracious air, tall stone, brick and terracotta-tiled facades above pretty shopfronts with curved glass bay windows, glazed lettering and Art Deco ironwork. There were several banks, vying with each other in architectural ambition, and three Nonconformist chapels of impressive scale, if not entirely convincing Classical or Gothic pedigree. A vast barn of a late Victorian parish church, complete with soaring spire, attempted to dominate the skyline from its elevated site on the hill behind. But Jonathan could sense the joie-de-vivre was missing – the carnival had clearly long since left town.

They had lunch surrounded by the faded grandeur of the town's one remaining department store.

'There's a lot of deprivation,' Caroline said, 'far more than summer visitors ever realise. The holiday trade used to offer well paid jobs in the season, enough to tide people over during the winter. Nowadays there are quite a few pockets of poor housing because landlords haven't had the cash to keep them up.'

'Is poor housing what this housing project is trying to address?'

'Partly. But it's also about pioneering a partnership between our local council and the government, who are considering the possibility of decanting London or Birmingham overspill down here.'

'Won't that only worsen the unemployment problem?'

'Well, the idea is to bring jobs too – 'light industry' they call it. There are plans for a couple of industrial estates not far from our site.'

'How's that going down with the locals?'

'It's the usual story – some are all for it, others dead agin it.' Caroline pursed her lips. 'It's causing quite a bit of division in the community, and making the locals even more suspicious about development – they fear being taken over by newcomers.'

In other words, the project wouldn't get an easy ride. Jonathan wasn't terribly surprised.

After lunch they headed towards the town hall, set in the public gardens back from the promenade. It was an architectural expression of the self-confidence of the late Victorian and Edwardian town, in Neo-Gothic country house style, boasting a ponderous clock tower as its centrepiece. A grand sweep of steps led into a cavernous marbled entrance hall, where a uniformed attendant greeted them and asked how he could help.

'We're here for an appointment with the Housing Project Officer,' said Caroline.

'Very well, madam, please carry on,' he said.

Caroline guided them through a warren of dingy corridors and offices. They stopped outside a door with an improvised notice pinned to it which read 'Housing Project Office.' Caroline knocked, and a friendly-sounding female voice called them in.

'Hello Naomi,' said Caroline, 'here's my new colleague, Jonathan Lane. Jonathan, meet Naomi Walters, the project officer for our scheme.'

'So pleased to meet you Jonathan.' Naomi got up from behind her desk and came round so they could shake hands.

'Delighted to meet you,' said Jonathan, immediately at ease with her.

'You'll be working closely together,' said Caroline, 'so it's important you get on.'

'I'm sure we will,' said Naomi firmly.

'Absolutely,' said Jonathan with equal conviction.

'Please, do take a seat. These battered old chairs aren't the most comfortable I'm afraid, but they're all the council could find.' As she spoke, Naomi moved over to a large-scale map on the wall. 'Now, I'm sure Caroline will have outlined the general picture, but would it help if I gave you a bit of background from my perspective?'

'That'd be great.'

'Essentially, our job is to turn Caroline's concept into a viable scheme. It's got to be good quality housing across the range, from young working families through to the elderly, so we achieve a good social mix. It's also pioneering the idea of creating a traffic-free environment with a good pedestrian network, generous landscaping, a parade of shops and recreational areas – a modern version of the garden city suburb. And, as you'll see, it must take full advantage of a wonderful site.'

She tapped the map, pointing to the location of the site. It was just on the outskirts of the town, but not too far from the sea. Jonathan got up to take a closer look.

'It looks as if it's a prime location for what's planned. It seems such an unusual opportunity for this part of the world.'

'It is. I ought to explain I'm on secondment from Whitehall for three years to see the project through. It's a bit of a test to see whether by local and central government working together we can radically improve public housing provision. If we can, our template could be applied at much larger scale all over the country. So there's a lot hanging on it.'

'I can't wait to get started.'

'Good. We'd better go and see the site!'

All three walked about half a mile to the edge of the town, down towards gently sloping fields with mature hedgerows and trees giving into a wooded valley sheltered from the sea.

'This is it,' said Naomi as they walked the site. 'Great, isn't it?'

'It certainly is,' said Jonathan. 'I can see why your scheme won, Caroline, it works with all the natural features – the contours, the field pattern and tree cover.'

'I only did a few sketches really!' Caroline smiled. 'There's a lot of hard work ahead for you to make all this happen.'

'I hope you like a challenge,' said Naomi. 'What do you know about the background of the project?'

'Well, I'm used to politics getting mixed up with housing schemes in London,' said Jonathan, 'but I guess this is a bit different.'

'Yes and no. It's unusual – the original idea came from representatives of the local community – leading figures from business, residents' groups, churches and chapels – who were concerned the town was going downhill and the area was turning inward on itself. They saw the need for an initiative which would open things up, bring in fresh thinking.'

'That does sounds unusual – and a breath of fresh air,' said Jonathan.

'It is, and it's the reason why London took such an interest when the council approached Whitehall about the possibility of part-funding it.'

'Which they are doing, I understand,' said Jonathan.

'They are, and very generously. We've had an advisory group which has proved invaluable in keeping people together, though I sense tensions could develop when we get into cost and contracts.'

'Maybe we should leave it there for today,' said Caroline, 'I'm sure Jonathan will be a great help to you with all that, but for the moment I'd like him to concentrate on working up the scheme.'

'Of course,' said Naomi, 'but I hope, Jonathan, you've found it useful to appreciate what a rare opportunity this is for all of us.'

'I certainly do!'

He felt a surge of energy to be in on the ground floor of such a project. His friends in London had warned him he'd be going into voluntary exile, a true backwater – but with everything he'd seen and heard today, nothing could be further from the truth.

EIGHT

Early May 1967

Tony and Jonathan were, by then, in the habit of an after-work drink at The Castle, the most convivial of the former coaching inns and the best of the town's small hotels. It had a smart red-brick front which the Georgians had tacked on to the mediaeval house behind. Run by the Kennall family for a couple of generations, it had a comfortable, unpretentious character. The menu was hearty farmhouse fare and the rooms were always clean, even if the plumbing was unpredictable. Cheek-by-jowl with the castle, it was the meeting place of choice for Michaelchurch society. To Jonathan's pleasure, Jim Jewell was a regular as well – he'd turned out to be one of Tony's best friends, of roughly similar age, someone who also liked keeping up with what was going on.

It was one such evening when Tony and Jonathan had settled comfortably into their regular corner, waiting for Jim to join them, that Tony lit his pipe and took a few puffs to get it going.

'That's better,' he said contentedly. 'I'm full of admiration for dear Caroline, as we all are, but I do find her prohibition on smoking in the office a bit of a sore trial. Sorry, I've never asked – you don't smoke, do you?'

'No, never have.' Jonathan smiled as his thoughts went back briefly to the monastery, where even the most apparently abstemious of monks could be found dragging desperately on a fag while lurking in a remote corner of the monastery garden.

'But you don't mind my pipe, I hope?'

'My dear Tony, of course I don't. Anyway, you'd never go into a pub if you minded tobacco smoke – look at the blue haze in here already this evening!'

'Rather comforting isn't it? I've always found it so.' He settled back into his chair and took a long draught from his pint.

'Don't take this amiss, old thing, but before Jim gets here, I wonder if we could touch on your transport arrangements.'

Jonathan flashed him a polite but puzzled look. 'Not sure what you mean.'

'Oh, just that it might be good if you got yourself some wheels. I mean, just something reliable, nothing too flash – wouldn't suit our image.'

Understanding and a wry smile dawned. 'I'm guessing a country lane bike doesn't quite fit the image either?'

Tony beamed. 'Precisely. Nothing wrong with it, of course – charming, in fact. But you can't deny it's not reliable – and you simply can't keep taking the bus out to work sites, can you?'

Jonathan nodded. 'I've been thinking I ought to get a car, but to be perfectly honest I haven't got the funds at the moment.'

Tony leaned towards him and lowered his voice.

'Tell you what then, why don't I lend you a few quid for a couple of months or so? I'd quite enjoy coming with you to try out a few motors – know a bit about them from my army days, and if you don't mind me saying, you don't look like the kind of fellow who enjoys getting his head under the bonnet.'

'You're absolutely right – I never had the need, living in London.'

'Suppose not – but you can't really do without one in the country in our line of work. You can drive, can't you?'

'The one bonus of doing National Service – army trucks and jeeps, mostly on endless journeys from Aldershot to Salisbury Plain and back again!'

'So you wouldn't be averse to my little proposal?' Tony leaned back, eyeing Jonathan over the rim of his pint glass.

'I had clocked the odd raised eyebrow from Caroline,' Jonathan said. 'I don't want to embarrass the office. If you're sure about a temporary loan – it's very kind of you and I promise I'll pay you back as soon as possible.'

'Don't worry about that, just pleased to help. Someone did the same for me when I was starting out – and you'd be surprised what it does for your image, especially with the ladies!' He chuckled.

'Well, that alone would make it worth doing,' Jonathan said with a slight flush. 'Much as I enjoy your and Jim's company, I'm beginning to miss the female of the species quite badly!'

'Good looking young fellow like you won't have any trouble on that score!'

'If only it was that simple, Tony,' said Jonathan with an audible sigh.

'Sorry, didn't mean to pry,' Tony said quietly.

'It's all right – let's just say there was a girl, once a very special girl, or so I thought. But it didn't work out…'

'Then all the more reason to get you back on the road – in more ways than one, old thing! Why don't we take a look at what Sam Dingle's got knocking around at the moment? He runs that bit of a tip of a garage on the main road, but he knows his stuff and you might be able to pick up a bargain.'

'I had noticed he's got some interesting motors on the forecourt, but never been in.'

'Time you did then.'

◈

So, on a Saturday morning soon afterwards, Jonathan and Tony met at the office and walked down to Sam Dingle's premises.

'Take your lead from me,' Tony said as they crossed the lot towards the garage office. 'Old Sam's got a good eye for motors but he's got an equally good eye for making a bob or two.'

'I'm completely in your hands Tony. As I told you, I know bugger all about cars. And I haven't driven since my national service days.'

'Well, let's see what he's got. That's if we can find him in all this chaos.'

'I 'eard that Mr Green, I did,' said a voice from underneath a car. "Tisn't chaos, 'tis all in order so I knows where everything's to.' The proprietor crawled out from an inspection pit covered in oil and grease. 'Sorry, I'm in a bit of a pickle – that bloody thing just practically blew up on me, it did.'

'Hello Sam, just joking, old thing. This is my new colleague, Mr Lane. He's looking for a motor – nothing too posh, just a reliable means of getting him around for site visits and that sort of thing. Thought we'd take a dekko at what bargains you might tempt him with.'

'Pleased to meet you Mr Lane, but us best not shake 'ands with this grease an' all. So you don't want anything a bit sporty-like, what a young man might be goin' for? 'Cos I've got a nice little MG TD over there, only done a shade shy of 5,000.'

'Well, that could be just what I'm after!' said Jonathan, having not spotted Tony's shaking head. 'How much is it?'

'Only £400 to you, Mr Lane.'

'Ah, I'm afraid that's a bit out of my price range, Sam.' Jonathan realised he and Tony hadn't discussed the size of the loan on offer. 'I'm looking more in the £200 to £300 range.' He glanced at Tony while saying this and was pleased to see him nod his head approvingly.

'Ah, I see. Well now, there's this Rover over here. Nice condition, belonged to a gent who came down on 'oliday last summer an' snuffed it, poor bugger, while he was taking some girl for a spin – 'eart attack. Likely got all 'ot an' bothered, if you take me meaning!' This was said with a wide grin and exaggerated wink. 'Dented 'im a bit where 'e went off the road 'e did, but I've put 'im back together and 'e's right as rain. Only £300.'

As Sam made his pitch, Tony had been surveying the lot, and pointed something out. 'What's that over there?'

'Ah yes, she's a good 'un, Mr Green. 1959 Volvo. Built like tanks they are. Belonged to a farmer who 'ardly ever used it – only got 3,000 on the clock. Yours for £250.'

'Can we try her out, Sam?'

'Course you can – I'll go get the keys.'

Jonathan climbed into the driver's seat and Tony into the passenger's side. He laid his hands on the steering wheel, but hesitated when it came time to turn the key.

'God, I'm a bit nervous Tony.'

'Come on, old thing, it's only a car. You'll be fine!'

Starting her up, Jonathan edged his way slowly out of the forecourt onto the open road.

'She sounds very smooth,' Tony said as Jonathan accelerated cautiously through the gears. 'How does she feel to you?'

'Feels great. I can see myself in this. Shall we just go on for a couple of miles along the main road, then come back through the lanes?'

'Good idea, see how she handles around those tight corners.'

There was one anxious moment when they met a tractor, but all went well. As they neared the garage, Tony hardly needed to ask:

'Shall we settle on her then? I think we can persuade Sam to knock a few quid off for cash – and a tank of four-star of course!'

So Jonathan acquired his pride and joy, a red Volvo Estate in immaculate condition, with pristine leather seats because the farmer never carried any passengers. He persuaded himself it delivered the desired semblance of professional dignity and reliability as he purred along the country lanes.

More than that, though, Tony's ready generosity cemented their easy friendship. Jonathan quickly realised just how much the older man enjoyed acting as mentor to the younger people in the office. Since the death of his wife a few years earlier, Tony was never in a hurry to go home. Though he never talked about it much, Jonathan gathered he felt lucky to have come out of the last war alive. He observed the world through thick half-moon glasses with a hint of a smile always playing over his face, as if he was determined to enjoy the rest of his life, and try to ensure others did as well.

NINE
Mid-May 1967

As their friendship with Jonathan grew, Ted and Anna felt comfortable in frequently rehearsing their concerns about the future.

From what Jonathan had overheard when Ted and Anna spoke with George and Annie Webber from the neighbouring farm, it was a shared dilemma. Jonathan was always amused to see them standing together in the yard: George a gentle giant of a man, dwarfing the wiry Ted.

'Ted's been a mate of mine since we were boys,' George told Jonathan at their first meeting. 'Farming can be a solitary business, you need to have someone you know will understand your worries. We've got much the same sized farm as this, but our house is a modest set-up, not like this huge old place here. Mind you, I'm not sure which of us has the better options for the future. Ted tells me he's even having problems about setting up this camping and caravan site they want.'

'It's getting ridiculous,' Ted grumbled. 'Just when we thought we'd finally got the OK, another council bloke turns up who starts prattling on about the possible effect of our site on the protected monument, or some such.'

'That's a new one on me,' Jonathan said. 'What do you think he meant?'

'All I know is this house has got some kind of preservation order on it, God help us – I wouldn't mind if that meant they'd help prop up the old ruin, but they won't of course. But the camp site's way down from here and completely out of view of the house.'

'Tell you what, I'll have a word with Tony in the office about it – he's an old hand on such stuff. I'm sure we'll be able to sort something out. But it'd help if I'd seen the site for myself.'

'That would be great' Anna said, rather quickly. 'Are you free next Saturday?'

'All day, name your time.'

It was mid-morning when the three of them set off across the fields Jonathan could see from his window. It had been a sea-fog shrouded week, but the wind had picked up overnight and cleared the air so their world was visible once more. The farmstead's first builders had chosen the site well: a relatively sheltered spot a few fields back from the ocean. Behind, the land rose towards the moors, appearing like mountains as they reared up to ragged peaks against a skyline of towering clouds, looking every bit as mysterious as earlier travellers and topographers had described them. This was exposed coastal country, and the farmstead was hunkered down against Atlantic gales – even the hedgerow trees bowed over like crouching beasts in obeisance to the prevailing westerlies.

They walked in early spring sunshine down through the orchard below the house, where ancient apple trees grown to craggy sculptures were swathed in clouds of pink-white blossom, with the orchard floor grazed by contented-looking sheep.

'It's mostly cider apples,' Ted said. 'Back in my uncle's day, most West Country farms made their own cider – it was part of the farm worker's wages.'

'Is it the apple blossom giving that heavenly scent?' Jonathan breathed it in deeply. 'It's intoxicating!'

'It is,' Ted replied. 'It's difficult to believe now because so many orchards have been grubbed up, but they were once a West Country tourist attraction in their own right. Coachloads would come from the Midlands just to visit them in blossom time.'

A gate at the far end gave into a gently sloping meadow which ran south towards what, judging from the salt-laden air now filling their lungs, promised to be the sea. Sure enough, just a few yards further on, Jonathan caught his first glimpse of the ocean stretching to the horizon. Sheltered by the orchard above and protected by hedgerow trees either side, this was the Northcotts' proposed camping site. It looked a heavenly place to spend a couple of weeks in the summer months.

'Well, here we are,' Ted said, exuding the sense of a man proud to be steward of such a glorious corner of the world.

'What a perfect spot,' Jonathan said. 'I'd book to come anytime!'

'We'll need to do a bit of levelling for the pitches,' Ted said, 'but essentially we'd offer it as it is. As you see it's completely hidden from the farm, so what that council fellow was going on about I don't understand.'

'We're beginning to wonder whether the council's got another agenda,' Anna said. 'One of the long-standing councillors we know says the newer councillors haven't got a clue about farming. They see the future as developing the area big time.'

'There's a lot of talk about development,' said Jonathan. 'But I can't see why a few tents and caravans down here, so secluded from the farmhouse, should cause any problems.'

'That's good to hear,' said Anna. 'So can we leave it to you to sort out? And if we can, how much do we owe you?' This last remark, Jonathan noted, sounded anxious.

'You can, and you owe me absolutely nothing, Anna.'

'That's wonderful, isn't it, Ted?' To his relief, she was positively glowing once more. 'Look, have you got a bit more time? We could walk on down to the sea – we'd like to show you something a bit special.'

'I'd love to. I can't possibly miss out on reaching the sea on a morning like this.'

They hiked out of the field onto a grassy track which ran between tall banks topped by overgrown hedges. It led gently downhill, and whenever they passed a field gate Ted or Anna would name the field, point out which were the unimproved hay meadows with abundant wild flowers, or name the breed of livestock grazing the pasture. Their love of the land was infectious.

'I love the tapestry of these fields,' Jonathan said, 'not so much green as dappled, with all the colours of grasses and flowers woven together.'

'It's because the fields have always been permanent pasture,' Anna said.

'We're always being told to plough them up by the men from the Ministry.' Ted shook his head. 'Make the land more productive, they say, reseed with modern varieties, put some nitrogen on, grass will grow stronger. Well, we're not having that – we don't want all this miracle of nature mowed over with boring fields of 'nitrogen green' grass.'

They walked on, and quite suddenly emerged onto the seashore. It was high tide, and they stood on the water's edge gazing at the sea, its steel blue dappled with green and grey under a sky of fair-weather clouds. A chill breeze flecked the waves with white horses, and they strode along the shore towards the cliff which gave the beach some shelter. They scrambled up a steep path through gorse and last year's rust-red bracken to a point perhaps fifty feet above.

Anna, who'd been leading the way, stopped.

'Take a look at this, Jonathan,' she said quietly.

There, built into the rock face, was a simple arch. It gave into a small stone-vaulted chamber filled by a pool of cold, clear water which flowed out under the front into a little stone-lined rill before disappearing underground. The pool was continually refreshed by a spring in the rear wall, the sound of gently falling water blending with the wash of waves from down below.

Jonathan had never seen anything like it, but sensed it was a place of great significance for the Northcotts. They'd not spoken a word, as if they wanted the place to work its magic on him – and it had. He felt moved to a kind of reverence – the serenity, the spiritual power of this place was palpable. When he finally broke the silence he spoke very softly.

'It's a well, isn't it? But what on earth is it doing here?'

'You're right' Anna said, her low tones matching his. 'It is a well, of course – our very own *holy well*.'

'I've always been intrigued by holy places,' he murmured, 'and what exactly makes them so. I do remember reading about holy wells. Aren't they connected with all those legends about the Celtic saints?'

'Yes, and you'll find quite a few of them in this part of the world. This one's dedicated to St Nectan. According to his legend, he sailed over from Wales to the West Country in the fifth or sixth century. He's supposed to have set up an oratory nearby but the archaeologists found only the faintest traces of another building some years ago and that's since fallen into the sea as the cliff eroded.'

'Is there a connection between the well and your farm?'

'Ted's uncle found a reference to 'a holy well that doth much benefit the house' in his researches – it clearly added status to Hall, at least in the eyes of the abbey who owned it before the Dissolution. We think there's something very special about the atmosphere here – we often come down if we need to think things over.'

Jonathan was mesmerised by the trickling water. 'I can see why.'

'You don't have to buy all that stuff about the Celtic saints, either,' Ted said. 'You can easily appreciate a spot like this, knowing it's been hallowed by generations of use.'

'I like that,' said Jonathan, sitting down and breathing in its atmosphere. After a while, he asked tentatively, 'Would it be OK for me to come here from time to time?'

'Come any time you like,' said Ted. 'It's more or less on the public footpath anyway, but people still have to seek it out. It's surprising how many of our guests do. They often tell us it was one of the high points of their holiday.'

Then, suddenly, 'Do you say your prayers, Jonathan?'

'I'm afraid I've rather fallen out of the habit.'

'Me too. Anna does, don't you love, but just coming here, being quiet and still for a few minutes, is as near as I'm likely to get.'

'Well, who knows – maybe it will be the same for me.'

Eventually they wandered on along the cliff top path, back through fields open to the cutting breeze. Even on a decent spring day, it came as a relief to turn inland and make their way back to the shelter of the farmhouse.

The well soon became Jonathan's special space, its utter simplicity appealing to him as surely as the embellished altar and reredos in the abbey church had once done. It prompted a stirring of his profound, though long-suppressed, curiosity. In the monastery he'd been urged to consider a 'journey of the soul', but could never quite imagine what that might look like.

As the evenings drew out, he often took a walk to the well after his return from work. No amount of scepticism about the legends of the Celtic saints diminished his conviction that this was, as Ted put it, a place hallowed by centuries of use. He even sensed this might be somewhere, one day, he could be brought to his knees again.

TEN
Late May 1967

'Fancy a guided tour of our little town by yours truly one evening?' Tony offered. 'I've had the chance to get to know a bit of its secret history over the years.'

'I'd like that,' said Jonathan, 'I've been thinking it's about time I got to know more about my home turf.'

'How about Wednesday next week? We could finish a bit early, and as it's market day, all the hostelries will be open – we might take the odd half-pint to refresh us on our perambulation – and we could end up at The Castle for a pint and supper on me?'

'It's a deal.'

◈

It was a fine early summer evening when they walked out of the office into the warm sunshine.

'Let's start with the castle,' Tony suggested. 'It was quite a major fortification in mediaeval times – even in ruins, it's still pretty impressive. Look at how it dominates the skyline.'

'I've been meaning to go up the tower for ages – I bet it's worth it, you must be able to see for miles,' said Jonathan.

'The view's stunning,' said Tony. 'Mind you, it's quite a pull up there – at least for an old 'un like me. I'll take my time, but you go on and I'll see you at the top.'

Jonathan took him up on it, quickly climbing up the steps to the small viewing platform at the highest point of the tower. It was a breathtaking, achingly lovely view, the whole town and all the outlying countryside arrayed before him.

'Isn't... it... grand?' said a breathless Tony when he finally joined Jonathan on the platform a few minutes later. 'You can see why they chose this place for a castle.'

'And you get a great sense of how the old town grew around it,' said Jonathan. 'And the church, and all those narrow little streets, how they open up into Market Square.'

'Yes, it's still mediaeval in plan,' said Tony. 'If you turn round this way, though, and look over there, you can see how the coming of the railway at the end of the last century brought new development below the old town.'

'I see it,' he said, turning just as Tony suggested, 'the railway station, goods yard, livestock market and abattoir, the old dairy and brewery – not forgetting The Railway Inn, of course! I've been there a few times on market day with Ted.'

'Not a bad boozer, top place for the farmers on market day. All in all, a proper little Victorian suburb, isn't it?' said Tony. 'That was when the livestock market moved down from the Square, where it had been for centuries…'

They stood together, silently, for a while, savouring the panorama.

'It is wonderful,' Jonathan said slowly. Then, with a tinge of melancholy in his voice, 'but if we're honest Tony, we're looking at the end of centuries of continuity, a world about to be in flux. A world which can't go on as it is because it so desperately needs new investment – of energy and imagination as much as money.'

'You may well be right, old thing, only time will tell… Look, when you're ready, why don't we make our gentle descent – and perhaps reward our mountaineering achievements with a swift half?'

'Excellent plan!'

They adjourned to The White Hart in Market Square.

'This place isn't what it was, I'm afraid,' said Tony under his breath. 'It was the premier inn of the town, as you can see from that grand carriage entrance into this courtyard. But when the railway came…'

'But they still pull a good pint,' Jonathan said, supping his beer. All this talk about the railway had set his thoughts down an odd path – what would the motorway do, when it eventually made its way here? 'Now, tell me a bit more about the town.'

'Well, here's a thumbnail history then. From the seventeenth century, Michaelchurch thrived on the coaching trade. It's the reason why we're so generously endowed with hostelries – for which I, for one, am eternally grateful! Then in the last century it became a bit of a boom town when tin mining was at its peak round here – that's all gone too now, of course.'

'So that's why there are so many banks,' said Jonathan. 'Must've been pretty prosperous.'

'Yes, it was, and it's that history which produced its delightful 'mongrel' architectural character. Drink up and I'll show you what I mean.'

They stepped into the Square, stopping outside a grand-looking brick house of the eighteenth century.

'Now,' said Tony, 'here's a good example. Look at this nice early Georgian front – you'd never know it hides a mediaeval courtyard house behind.'

'You're right – impossible to tell from here!'

'There's lots of that sort of disguise all over the town – buildings centuries older than they appear. And then look over there, at that seventeenth-century timber-framed house – there are a few of those around the town, the ones the tourists always take photos of. I like the way they're all jumbled up with eighteenth-century brick houses and a lot of nineteenth-century commercial buildings – some of them are quite showy, aren't they?'

'They're fun, aren't they – even if sometimes not very architecturally correct!'

'Don't say it too loudly in the office, but who cares about architectural purity if a building's such a treat to the eye!'

After an exhaustive exploration of the old town, Tony suggested it was time to repair to The Castle for more serious refreshment.

'It's always been a rather a self-sufficient sort of place,' he told Jonathan over a fish and chip supper. 'Folk don't have much cause to venture further afield.'

'It meets all my needs. Do you know, I've even treated myself to a linen jacket and Panama hat for the summer from Lee's.'

'Well done that man! I look forward to seeing you sporting it in the office – we could do with someone to raise the sartorial standards of the male contingent, given the elegant way The Boss presents herself – and Emma too, in a rather modern way!'

'I'll have to work up the courage to do that. On a more practical note, where's the best place to get some gumboots? – I've ruined a couple of pairs of shoes already in mucky farmyards.'

'Ah, you'll need to make the acquaintance of 'Citizen Pen' then, won't you?'

'I've heard the name – isn't that Horace Penhaligan, of Penhaligan's Stores?'

'The very same. But don't be fooled into thinking he's just a simple shopkeeper – though of course that's just what he wants you to think. He's chairman of the council, been mayor several times, and he's a magistrate. Not much goes on around here without our Horace being involved in some way or other.'

Jonathan chuckled. 'Can't wait to meet him – I'll call in for some boots tomorrow.'

'I'll be interested to see what you make of him!'

'And while we're on the subject of local knowledge, Tony, have you come across a new man at the council who is giving Ted and Anna a bit of a hard time over their new camping site – something to do with Hall being a 'protected monument', or some such preservation business?'

'Ah yes, indeed I have. Name of Manners, *Doctor* Manners – don't miss out the Doctor bit! I'll get us the other half and I'll fill you in on him.'

◈

Penhaligan's Stores was an imposing building with a spectacular front in red and yellow terracotta, a shock to the eye in the centre of a mostly slate-grey town. Glazed tile lettering between the ground and first floors proudly proclaimed 'IRONMONGERS AND GENERAL GOODS,' and its window displays were a cornucopia of hardware, farming implements, cooking utensils, crockery, electrical goods, pocket knives, binoculars, maps, walking sticks, work clothes and footwear. 'The Stores', as it was always known, was the first and last resort for all the farmers of the area.

Jonathan was intrigued. Tony's advice had always been sound, and his warning not to take Penhaligan at face value captured Jonathan's curiosity.

'Mornin' sir!' An ample figure with a genial voice approached him as he entered. 'What might you be lookin' for? 'Tis a bit of a maze in 'ere till you knows yur way round.'

Jonathan assumed this must be the man himself. 'Yes, it is a bit, isn't it? I'm after some gumboots.'

'Ah, they be in our boot department up them stairs, over there in the corner – best come with 'ee since our Ivy 'ain't come in yet, an' its terrible quiet in 'ere anyways this morning. Come this way, up 'ere.'

Jonathan followed him up the stairs and was soon fitted out with a stout pair of Argylls – 'farmers' favourite,' the shopkeeper assured him.

As they headed back down to settle up, Penhaligan eyed him. 'You visiting, young man?'

'No, I'm new down here. I work at Atherton & Green.'

'Ah, you'm an artichect then.'

'Yes, that's right.'

'Well, 'spect our paths'll cross then. I'm Penhaligan – 'Orace to most folks – Chairman of the council – see quite a bit of your lot's stuff come to the planning committee, we do.'

'Pleased to meet you Mr Penhaligan, I'm Jonathan Lane. And yes indeed, I expect we shall see more of each other.'

'Ted Northcott's been telling me the future of the market now looks quite secure – been a relief to him and the rest of the farmers. They were getting really worried it might go bust, I take it.'

Penhaligan wrapped the boots and dropped them in a bag. 'Let's 'ope so, young man.'

'I understand you got some financial backing from the council which saved it.'

''Tis only what I always does, boy,' said Penhaligan with a smile. 'You'm no doubt learning, nothing 'appens round here by 'isself. An' someone's got to keep an eye out for them farmers – stubborn lot sometimes, an' not so clever at getting 'emselves in order on somethin' like the market.'

He wasn't entirely sure that was true – Ted was quite clever, not to mention he'd been fired up about it when he told Jonathan. Still, it seemed rude to cross him.

'It's good they've got you behind them,' Jonathan said.

'Not that I gets much thanks, mind,' said Penhaligan. 'Folk thinks I got 'other interests', as they puts it. I takes no notice, just carry on doin' my job, I does.'

ELEVEN

Early June 1967

Surprisingly, perhaps, the churches of the area had shown resilience to the rising winds of change. The far south-west had been a stronghold of 'The Old Dissent', and the Quakers had a plain but dignified meeting house not far from the town centre. Nonconformity had later become the *de facto* established religion of this part of the world, and its numerous chapels were not just a feature of the landscape but a force in the cultural life of the area. A few had closed in the last ten years – Atherton & Green occupied one, of course – but Methodism was still a force to be reckoned with, as borne out by the dearth of pubs in some parts of the countryside.

By far the largest place of worship in the area was the parish church of St Michael and All Angels, after which the town took its name. It stood right in the centre of town, just off the Square, and its handsome mediaeval tower surmounted by a stubby but sturdy spire was a landmark for miles around. Its peal of eight bells was renowned. Its band of devoted ringers, and frequent visiting teams from other towers, sent its plangent music rolling out across the town, through every lane and over parish fields. The body of the church had been rebuilt in the mid-nineteenth century by a West Country pioneer of the Gothic Revival, of which it was regarded as an early masterpiece.

The parish was of the High Anglican tradition, and the cassock-clad figure of its rector, Father Leo Colchester, was a familiar sight in the town. Father Leo had come to Michaelchurch more than twenty years before and had long since earned respect as a hard-working parish priest. He saw it as his job to care for all his parishioners, whether or not they ever darkened the doors of his church, and he was active in the life of the community. He lived alone in the vast rectory which lay secluded in heavily wooded grounds beside the church, but always made himself available to anyone in need.

Tony Green was the church architect; he and Father Leo had become good friends, the rector frequently dropping by the office to discuss the latest necessary repairs. It was during one such visit that Tony waved Jonathan over to him.

'Got a bit of time for something different this morning, old thing?'

'Sure – what sort of different?'

'We've got water in the ringing chamber of the church tower – the ringers are kicking up about it.'

'I'm afraid I wouldn't be much use to you, Tony – I've no experience of that kind of thing.'

'Then I think it's high time you got some. You may have noticed it rains a lot down here, so dealing with wet walls is, whether you like it or not, part of what we do.' This was said with a smile. 'Come on downstairs and I'll introduce you to Father Leo. Then we'll go over to the church together and look at the problem.'

Jonathan hesitated. He'd not gone to church since leaving the monastery – he'd even given up church-crawling, previously one of his favourite activities. He'd also been avoiding the rector for much the same reason. Still – this was work, so he squared his shoulders and followed Tony down the steps.

'Leo,' Tony began, 'this is my new colleague Jonathan Lane – I don't think you've met?'

'Hello, Jonathan,' said the rector, with a disarming smile. 'No, we haven't, though I've seen you around. It's a bit later than I'd have wished, but may I offer you a warm welcome to Michaelchurch? I hope you're settling in well?'

'Thank you, Father.' Jonathan found himself naturally reverting to the customary form of address. 'Everyone's been very kind and I'm already beginning to feel very much at home.'

As they walked the short distance to the church, Jonathan found himself being gently quizzed. The rector's close-cropped grey hair and ascetic features gave him an austere appearance, but he had a ready smile, and Jonathan warmed to him quickly.

'You're probably familiar with our church I imagine? It's a little jewel of the Gothic Revival. You've no doubt explored it already, and perhaps even read about it in the textbooks on the period?'

'I have to confess I haven't, Father, which is very remiss of me.'

'Then there's no time like the present to put that right. We can spare a few minutes to show Jonathan around, can't we Tony?'

'Of course,' said Tony, clearly amused by his colleague's little embarrassment.

They stepped into the church, dim and swathed in shadows.

'Wait here a moment,' the rector said, 'while I go and switch all the lights on.'

He disappeared into the gloom at the back of the church. As they heard a long sequence of switches being thrown, the richness of the interior was gradually revealed, cast in a warm yellow glow.

Every surface bore some decorative mark: a tracery, stencilling, some patterned tiles. A rood screen ran right across the nave and the north and south aisles, magnificently carved and richly done in gold and green and red and blue.

'Goodness, Father, it does rather take your breath away doesn't it?' Jonathan gasped when the rector returned.

'A ravishing example of High Victorian taste, expertly done,' Father Leo said proudly.

'It's superb, and very difficult to believe it's not mediaeval, it's so well done.'

'There's more through here in the chancel,' the rector said, leading the way through the screen. 'Look at the way the light in here is slightly darker because of these lovely Morris & Co. windows. It gives this part of the church a more mysterious ambience, doesn't it? And the way in which the ceiling is painted to represent the starlit heavens.'

Jonathan lifted his eyes and saw painted stars shining out from a deep azure blue backdrop. Various details led the eye directly down towards the sanctuary, with an exquisite golden altar.

'It's a masterpiece, isn't it? Who was the architect?'

'It was one of the Seddings – we're not entirely sure which one. You'll certainly know J.D. Sedding, the architect of Holy Trinity, Sloane Street?'

'It's one of my favourite churches!'

'Well then, you'll certainly feel at home here, though I think this was more likely to have been completed by his nephew, E.H. Sedding.'

'It's marvellous.' By now, Jonathan was thoroughly transported back to his days in the monastery, much influenced by the sweet aroma of incense lingering in the air – he fancied he could even hear Father Richard's voice remarking on the *odour of sanctity* as he sniffed the air after High Mass. As at the holy well, he momentarily longed for that spiritual world from which he'd exiled himself for so long.

He realised the rector was still enthusing.

'The architect designed everything down to the last detail, you know. I don't know whether you'd be interested but we've still got the original drawings. You'd be very welcome to come over to the rectory sometime and have a look at them – they're beautifully done.'

A stab of feeling, melancholy maybe, struck him straight to the heart. 'I'll certainly take you up on that if I may, Father.'

'Gentlemen,' Tony said, 'sorry to interrupt, but do you think perhaps we'd better go and look at the problem with the tower?'

TWELVE

Mid-June 1967

Now the country lanes were in their early summer glory. Bluebells and foxgloves had long since vanished, but now there were clouds of cow parsley, red campion and honeysuckle in the hedge banks, while drifts of meadowsweet floated in the roadside ditches. This was the moment, Jonathan thought as he threaded the Volvo through the lanes overflowing with colour, when it would be good to stop the clock. Dreamily enjoying this paradise, he'd made not even the most perfunctory attempt to find alternative accommodation. But the peak holiday season was approaching.

'It's time for me to move on, I suppose.' He broached this, reluctantly, over dinner with Ted and Anna. His room would command a premium rate, and he well knew they could use the income.

'Actually, Ted and I have been giving that a bit of thought,' Anna said, as always the one to take the lead. You may think it's a non-starter – and we won't be offended if you do – but it might just be something to suit all of us.'

'I'm intrigued,' Jonathan said, slightly hesitant. He worried, sometimes, that he'd imposed a little too much on their kindness.

'Well, we've probably bored you silly with our worries about the future,' said Anna.

'And we're fed up with more and more regulations every year,' said Ted. 'They're trying to make us use 'modern framing methods' – by which they mean chemical fertilisers, not good honest dung; sprays to kill every so-called pest and God knows how many of the good insects; sow new varieties of cereal which won't stand up to the rigours of our weather; replace our tried and tested breeds with new strains of livestock – '

'Some of our neighbours have sold up already,' Anna said. 'Some of our best friends too. It all looks idyllic to our summer visitors, but...'

'It's one of the main topics at the Castle,' said Jonathan. 'Jim Jewell has some pretty sad stories.'

'But we don't want to get dragged down and just give up,' said Ted. 'To put it bluntly, we've decided we'll need to really up our game way beyond and above our bed and breakfast trade – and the camping site – if we're going to survive at all. By the way, have you got anywhere with what that council bloke was on about? It's getting late for us to get the work done if we're going to have the site open this summer.'

'I think I have,' said Jonathan. 'Tony did a bit of digging; he says your man – a Dr Manners apparently – is a new breed of official who's keen to see people aren't bashing protected monuments around too much.'

'Oh God, not more red tape,' Ted said. 'Why can't the council leave us alone?'

'Well, the good news is that it seems to have been a case of a new boy's over-enthusiasm. So there's nothing for you to worry about and you should get the all-clear next week.'

'That's a relief, thanks for sorting it out,' said Anna. 'But Ted's right – if we're going to be more restricted about what we can do, it could kill our big idea stone dead.'

'I think you're getting ahead of me – I don't even know what this big idea of yours is yet!'

'Let me get us another glass of cider,' said Ted. 'This is an important moment.'

He went out to the store room, returned with another bottle and refilled their glasses.

'Since we built the new yard and sheds a few years ago,' Anna said as she took a sip of cider, 'we've not used the old farm buildings, and they're in pretty bad shape. So – here's the crazy idea – we're beginning to wonder whether we might be able to renovate, turn them into a kind of rural studies centre – and perhaps even use the derelict ranges of this house as part of it.'

'You'll have to forgive my ignorance but what is a 'rural studies centre'?'

'They're a government initiative to let city children live in the countryside to learn about rural life,' Anna said.

'We've been to see a farm in Dorset where they've done it, and were pretty impressed,' said Ted. 'There's some generous funding available for setting them up and running them. We've got a stunning location here, within reach of the sea and the moors, which would be an eye-opener for these youngsters.'

'It sounds an ambitious project!' said Jonathan. 'Forgive me for asking, but how might you fund it? It surely can't all come from the public purse?'

'No, it'll cost us – but we've made some initial soundings,' said Ted. 'Oddly enough, this all started the day you came for your interview – you won't remember, but I had a meeting with our bank manager that morning.'

'I do remember!' Jonathan said. 'And I recall you weren't looking forward to it.'

'True, I wasn't. But to my surprise old Waring the bank manager turned out to be all for some bold new investment. He suggested a generous loan from the bank would be available to add to what we could expect by way of government grants.'

'Honestly, I've rarely seen you so fired up,' Anna said with a smile. 'It started us thinking seriously that something might be possible.'

'It sounds promising.' Jonathan said. 'But I'm a bit mystified about the connection between all that and my need to move on.'

'Have a bit more cider,' said Ted, nudging the bottle in Jonathan's direction. 'We might as well finish the bottle now.'

'And it'll help me get to the important bit,' said Anna, laughing. 'Here's our other crazy idea. We need some inspiration – someone to sketch out possibilities, do some sounding out with the locals, the council, find out more about these grants. But we can't afford architects' fees just now. So we were wondering whether you'd consider helping us out in your spare time – and in return we'd offer you the use of a house we've got down in the valley, rent free.'

'It's a bit remote – you've probably never seen it – and doesn't have much in the way of modern facilities,' Ted said, holding up a cautionary hand. 'It's the mill house of an old watermill, very much part of life here until the last war – I remember helping my uncle with it when I was a lad. I'm afraid we've rather neglected it over the years, so the mill's a bit sad these days, but we've kept the house in good order – we've even managed to let it from time to time. But its remoteness doesn't appeal to that many people – we thought it might suit you, though.'

'I quite enjoy the Spartan life!' he replied, with a broad smile. 'I mean, I find it very comfortable here, positively luxurious compared to some places I've lived. So I rather relish the possibility of living in a remote old mill house!'

'So you'll give our idea some thought?' Anna asked anxiously.

'Yes, of course. I'll need to run the deal past the office though. I wouldn't want them to think I was moonlighting so early on in my time down here.'

'We'd expect that,' said Ted. 'And, if the project turned out to be a goer, we'd happily employ Atherton & Green to see the job through.'

'That'd certainly make it attractive to Caroline and Tony. Tell you what, why don't I have a proper look at the whole farm? As you say, I've never been inside most of the buildings. Then I can put my thinking cap on and give you my initial thoughts about the possibilities. And I can't wait to see this old mill!'

'So why don't we start tomorrow evening?' Anna asked eagerly. 'It's light till about ten now so we could go to the mill after supper, and then, in the next week or so, whenever you've got a free hour or two, we can look round the buildings here.'

The following evening the three of them set off. It was not the most propitious weather: the heavens opened in frequent, heavy showers, making the steep track to the mill a fast-flowing stream only navigable thanks to the Land Rover. They made their way down the side of the valley, its steep banks stuffed with luxuriant ferns falling like cascades of green water, then along the side of a small watercourse. Eventually they came to a group of ivy-clad buildings on level ground just above the stream. In the bright sunshine between the showers, it was a magical world of shining, aqueous green. Jonathan fell in love with it immediately – on that early summer evening, the decades of benign neglect only intensified his sense of wonder.

'Well, here it is,' said Ted as he turned the huge old key to the door of the mill house. 'Come on in.'

They went into a passage which ran straight through to the back door. On either side were doors into the two main rooms of the house. Ted opened one of them.

'Let's look in here first,' he suggested, 'it was the hub of the house when Frank Basset, the last miller, and his wife lived here in the '40s.'

The room was spacious but plain, its only feature a large old range built into a floor-to-ceiling recess in the side wall.

'Shall I explain the domestic side of things?' Anna asked. 'It isn't that obvious without the furniture.'

'Yes, please,' Jonathan said. 'Is this the kitchen as well as the living room?'

'Sort of,' Anna replied. 'If you come through here, it's easier to see how it all works.'

She led Jonathan through a door at the back of the room.

'This was the scullery, washroom and cold store. We've kept most of the features, but modernised a bit and put in this small bathroom so we could let it out.'

'Looks very well appointed to me,' said Jonathan.

'Glad you think so,' Ted said. 'The people who've stayed here seem to like it well enough.'

'But I'm still not sure about the cooking arrangements,' said Jonathan.

'Sorry, I got distracted,' Anna said. 'I know it sounds a bit quirky but, like in the farmhouse, everything here depends on the range in the main room – that's where all the heat and hot water come from.'

'So you prepare food in this back room but cook in the front room on the range?'

'I'm afraid so,' Ted said apologetically. 'It's a bit old fashioned, I know.'

Jonathan paused to let his eyes roam over the whole scene. Immediately, he could imagine living here, perhaps with a dog – and, if he ever met her, with a woman of his dreams.

'I think it's terrific – what a wonderfully snug arrangement!'

'Shall we show you the other room across the passage which used to be the parlour in Frank Basset's day?' said Anna.

'Yes, please, this is all looking wonderful!' His enthusiasm increased with every new prospect.

The parlour was a more modest room with a plain fireplace, and cupboards and shelves built into the recesses either side.

'This would make an ideal study, wouldn't it?' Jonathan said. 'I could set up a drawing board in here so I could work from home.'

'Glad you like it. You ought to see upstairs,' Anna said.

The tour continued as they showed him two decent-sized bedrooms on the first floor and another two rooms in the attic, all with views out over the mill and valley. When they finally emerged from the house, he was eager to explore further.

'Can I see the mill?'

'Not sure about that.' Ted looked a little dubious. 'It's in a very poor state – floorboards gone in places, and the stairs missing a few treads.'

'But we could just poke our noses in, couldn't we?' Anna gave him a pleading look.

'I suppose so, but only if you go very carefully and follow me, step by step.'

'I'm quite used to building sites, you know,' Jonathan said. 'I'll be careful where I step.'

'Of course – come on then.'

Ted led them cautiously out of the house and into the main floor of the mill.

'Wow!' said Jonathan, 'looks as if Frank Basset just walked out!'

It was a poignant still-life of a vanished age, dusty sacks still hanging from the walls, a myriad array of gearing, pulleys, belts and levers ascending and descending through the floors – and centre-stage, the vast mill stones, a monumental presence even in their silent stillness.

'We'll come back another time to see the rest,' Ted said, clearly anxious to curtail any further exploration that evening.

'Is there still a waterwheel?' Jonathan asked excitedly, 'I've always wanted to see one.'

'There is,' Ted said, 'it's on the other side – but it's really dangerous, so promise me you won't try and get too close.'

They went round to the back of the mill and there, to Jonathan's delight, was the huge water wheel. Its gaunt iron frame was still intact, though its wooden paddles had almost all rotted and fallen off into the bottom of the wheel-pit, now full of debris and ferns. A slow trickle of water, struggling through a weed-choked leat, was all that survived of the watercourse which once provided power for the mill.

'I'm completely hooked,' Jonathan said as they walked back to the Land Rover in the deepening twilight. 'I'll take it!'

'That's wonderful, isn't it, Ted?' said Anna. 'You could move in anytime you want.'

'Yes, I'd be very happy with that,' Ted agreed. 'But of course, to keep our bargain, tomorrow night we'll need to start looking at the farm!'

THIRTEEN
Mid-June – Early July 1967

Next evening they began exploring the disused ranges behind the farmhouse, room by room.

'Sorry about all this junk, Jonathan,' Ted told him as he hoisted up another stack of dining chairs and shifted them to one side. 'My uncle started the rot by piling stuff up in here – he never threw anything away.'

'And you've carried on the family tradition love, haven't you!' Anna laughed as she chipped in, grappling with an iron implement whose purpose was a complete mystery to Jonathan.

'Don't worry about it,' said Jonathan. 'I'm used to seeing through all the flotsam and jetsam. I'm no expert, but even I can see your uncle was dead right about Hall being a posh mediaeval house – built around a courtyard plan, with the east, south and west ranges the top-notch accommodation and the kitchen and service rooms in the north range.'

'Is that good or bad news for us?' Ted shot Anna an anxious look.

'It's good news, Ted, honest it is,' said Jonathan. 'For instance, this room's dark, but only because the original windows have been blocked – we can simply un-block them. Look over there behind that old bedstead – it's a lovely moulded stone fireplace. If I shine the torch up here, you can see the ceiling beams are beautifully carved. And in the room we've just been through I noticed there was some plasterwork – rather the worse for wear, but eminently saveable. There seems to be lots of that sort of thing.'

'Sounds expensive,' Ted said beneath his breath.

'I wouldn't look at it like that,' said Jonathan. 'You've got original features which give the place great character. I'm not sure how this could work as part of the studies centre just yet – we can puzzle that out in due course – but for now you should regard it all as a potential asset.'

'I suppose so,' Ted said. 'What do you think, love?'

'I think Jonathan's right,' Anna said. 'Let's stay positive.'

Once Jonathan had completed his survey of the old house, he turned to the disused farm buildings. They were the product of later nineteenth-century zeal for agricultural improvement common on large estates in that period. Sited some distance from the old house, the substantial and well-built structures were arranged around a spacious yard. The centrepiece was a large stone-walled threshing barn, its vast double doors either side of the still-intact oak threshing floor. The long flanking ranges in brick and slate were the usual specialist buildings needed on the farm in those days – cattle-shelters and stables with haylofts above, cart sheds, a dairy and a root house. It looked ideal for conversion to a studies centre: the great barn for dining and communal activities, the other structures for teaching rooms, dormitories and other facilities. Jonathan assured the Northcotts there was plenty of potential for them to realise their vision.

'Well,' said Caroline – when Jonathan found a moment to talk to her and Tony about the project – 'I'll say this for the Northcotts, they certainly don't lack ambition. A project like that's going to cost an arm and a leg. Where on earth are they going to find that sort of money?'

'I've done a bit of research of my own,' Jonathan said. 'They're becoming quite a thing, these rural studies centres. Local councils often take on the running of them as part of their role as education authorities. And Ted was right about the bank – it's prepared to make the Northcotts substantial loans against the security of the farm. The bank manager sees considerable development potential in Hall.'

'I'm not entirely convinced,' said Caroline, 'but I think it's worth giving it a fair wind – on the basis that you'll be doing all the preparatory work free of charge in exchange for your accommodation, and the practice only gets involved if the project proves to be a goer. What do you think Tony?'

'I couldn't have put it better myself. It certainly won't be plain sailing – the council's attitude has swung about quite a bit, lately. They only seem interested in promoting large-scale development, and there's almost no interest in helping the small hoteliers, local businesses, and farmers carry on as they've always done.'

'I'm a realist,' said Jonathan. 'And I'd be a fool not to anticipate a bumpy ride. But at the very least it would let me try my hand at your kind of work, Tony – and learn from you, too.'

'Then we must let you give it a go,' said Caroline, 'mustn't we?'

'We must indeed,' Tony replied. Then, turning away from Caroline and winking at Jonathan, he added sotto voce, 'and I'd be happy to lend an informal hand too – out of office hours of course!'

FOURTEEN

Late July 1967

He moved in almost immediately.

The more time Jonathan spent in the mill house, the more he knew it was what he'd been looking for, perhaps unconsciously, ever since he'd left the monastery. A little more than half a mile from the farmhouse, without mains electricity or water, no telephone, and with an even noisier generator than the one at Hall, its seclusion and simplicity appealed to him. There was even a large neglected kitchen garden with a few old fruit trees to the south side of the house, which promised a degree of self-sufficiency if brought back into cultivation.

'Are you still keen on it?' Anna asked when she called to see how he was settling in. 'It's a bit primitive.'

'It'll do me fine,' Jonathan told her. 'Honestly, I feel lucky to be here.'

'I'm so pleased. You know we really didn't want to lose you.' Standing there in the middle of the parlour, she gave him an almost shy smile. 'You've become part of the family.' Her sharp blue eyes roamed the bare space. 'When you get your furniture down from London I'm sure it'll soon feel like home.'

'I'm afraid I sold all my stuff when I went travelling.' He dissembled without a flicker of conscience. 'So I'll have to start all over again.'

'Why don't you come with me down to some of the local auctions?' she said. 'Ted can't stand them, but I love them. It's amazing what bargains you can find.'

'That sounds great, if you can spare the time.'

The auction rooms were a cornucopia of objects: some of obvious use, many more of dubious use or taste and, it had to be admitted, a lot of junk. Jonathan was surprised to find he enjoyed it, though. Anna would take his arm and guide him round, suggesting what he might bid on before the sale got underway – he soon found she had a special eye for 'mixed lots', and pointed him towards more than a few bargains.

He also couldn't deny he got a frisson of excitement when he and Anna brushed against each other, as when she leaned over during the auction, whispering when to bid and when to stop.

She was only being friendly, he knew. But...

God, I need a girl!

Anna also enjoyed their expeditions. Now the children were away, she'd more time for herself, an unaccustomed luxury for a farmer's wife. Her forte was looking after people, as the success of their B&B business demonstrated, and it felt natural to help Jonathan set up home, though she was careful not to be seen as mothering him.

She continued to ponder what made him tick. He was affable, but curiously reticent if one tried to get too close – a perceptive observer rather than the life of the party. She wondered what really went on underneath that mass of floppy fair hair. And what about his love life? After all, he was quite a looker – it was a bit odd he hadn't met someone yet, though by all accounts he'd set some hearts racing. And judging from the way she'd sometimes caught him glancing at her, he wasn't uninterested in the opposite sex.

But I'm not going to object to that – should be flattered really!

He shared her interest in painting and drawing, too – that kind of thing didn't light Ted's fire. All in all, she was glad he'd moved no further than the mill house – with more of their friends selling up every day, she couldn't bear to lose another rare friendship.

Jonathan enjoyed living independently again. He soon got back into his old routine of shopping and cooking for himself – after a battle with the old range, which seemed to have a mind of its own. It wasn't all plain sailing, though. Living next to the mill and all its disused outbuildings meant his nearest neighbours were the resident rodents, and they were keen to pop by uninvited. At first he tolerated their presence – the 'live and let live' approach of the novice countryman – but when his food started disappearing, he rapidly changed tack and acquired a couple of kittens, who gradually got things under control.

But it was a minor irritation in the face of so many delights. He was determined to start growing some vegetables in the old garden, an activity he'd fallen for when working in the monastery. Here, he got a bit of unexpected help from Len Moyse, Ted's right-hand man on the farm, who lived with his wife, Daisy, in a cottage just up the lane. They kept a close eye on comings and goings around the farm, Daisy also being Anna's right-hand woman when it came to running the B&B in the summer.

Jonathan and Len bumped into each other in the farmyard one evening while he was collecting his milk.

''ow you'm be getting on down at that there old mill, young man?' Len asked.

'OK, thanks, Len – settling in nicely.'

'Back in the day, old Fred used to get some fine produce out o' that garden of yours, 'e did.'

'Ah, funny you should mention that – I could do with a bit of your wisdom.'

''appy to 'elp if I can.'

'I'm thinking of getting the vegetable garden back into some kind of order so I can grow a few crops.'

'Reckon you'm be needin' a hand gettin' it in shape then.'

'That would be great Len, if you can spare the time.'

'You'm best be getting' on with it, summer soon slips by. Only got to ask, you 'ave.'

'How are you fixed on Saturday? Forecast says it'll be fine and warm.'

'Be down after I've 'ad me breakfast, 'bout 9.00? You got any gardenin' tools?'

'Not many, I picked up a fork and spade at one of the auctions I've been to.'

'Better bring some of me own down then – us'll need more than a fork an' a spade to sort that patch out, bin nothing done to it for years.'

Sharp at 9.00 on Saturday morning, Len arrived on the tractor.

'Morning Len!' Jonathan's eyes went wide as they roamed over the tractor. 'I thought you were bringing a few tools, not this beast.'

''Ere,' Len said, 'I've 'ad an idea, see – put it to the boss an' all – better if I can plough and till the ground 'stead of goin' over it by 'and. 'Tis all brambles and scrub anyway. Save us days of work. But you're gonna 'elp by lighting up a bonfire of all the stuff I clears.'

By late afternoon the ground had been cleared, smoke was rising from a huge bonfire, and the two of them were enjoying a glass or two of cider as they surveyed their work.

'Looks a picture, Len.'

'So it does. Good soil too, been worked for generations. Used to 'elp the boss's uncle down 'ere when I were a little 'un.'

'Did you help in the mill as well?'

Len grinned. 'Course, that were the excitin' bit! Got to know 'ow all them pulleys and belts and things worked. Kept clear of the water wheel though – bloody dangerous old bugger. Saw one man slip and fall into wheel pit, crushed to death.'

'God – how terrible.'

'You'd be surprised 'ow many accidents I've seen down 'ere.'

'I bet. Do you think you could explain to me how the machinery used to work sometime? I'd love to understand how it all goes together.'

'Be pleased to – only pity is we can't run the wheel no longer, 'cos we ain't got no water power with the leat all blocked up an' the wheel rotted out.'

'Well, there's a project for the future – the restoration of the water wheel and the leat!'

◈

With the garden in good order, Jonathan was able to start planting up. It gave him great satisfaction to wander around his patch morning and evening, watching his seedlings emerge, tend the plants as they developed, hoe between the neat rows, and water them as necessary. He was settling into country life at last.

All the while, he was getting to know an ever-widening circle of people, learning what kept the community together and what threatened to pull it apart. There was no city anonymity here – everybody knew each other in a small town. He relished the tales of quiet heroism, of folk caring for each other against almost impossible odds, as well as of the tragi-comedies of the human condition. There was plenty of less savoury gossip too: personal and professional rivalries, slights imagined or real, who owed money to the bank and who was stinking rich despite appearances, loyalties and betrayals, infidelities ancient and modern, incest and adultery, the alcoholics and the secret drinkers, the shady dealers and the outright crooks – the list of indictable offences seemed endless.

As summer faded into autumn, he began to keep the range on overnight to help with the damp. Exploration of his new surroundings had made him realise how water-permeated the whole valley was. He'd soon found the dry, overgrown millpond which stored the water to turn the waterwheel when milling was going on, and had subsequently traced the course of the leat which fed the pond back to where it took off from the river higher up the valley.

One evening he'd sat on the hillside above the mill, rejoicing in the quietude and listening to birdsong and the sound of gently running water. He'd thought how different the scene was compared to just a few decades ago – indeed, in Ted and Len's memory – when it would have been alive with activity. Carts and wagons would have carried in grain to be milled and borne flour away in sacks; water would have rushed beneath the mill race as the waterwheel turned; the deep rumble of the millstones would have reverberated around the valley; dogs would be barking and cats ratting.

For a moment, he saw all those people and their secret histories alive again.

Now the summer visitors were gone, Ted and Anna were keen to know how he was getting on with the scheme for the future of the farm. He'd been so busy on the drawings for the Broadhaven project, and so relishing his new life at the mill, he'd fallen behind on that score. So he buckled down to work in the evenings in the parlour, on the drawing board he'd acquired during one of his excursions with Anna. Sometimes he let his imagination wander into dreams of owning the mill and making it truly his own. But for now, as he looked up from his drawings to glance out of the window over the valley before dusk turned to dark, he just reflected on his good fortune in landing up in such a place.

FIFTEEN
September 1967

The Broadhaven project was now absorbing much of Jonathan's attention, not only because of the amount of office time required. At his meetings with Naomi Walters he'd picked up on her concern that the political mood music was changing.

'I'm getting a bit worried,' she told him. 'When I first arrived the coverage was all so positive – the council was proud to be midwife to a pioneering initiative. But since the *Gazette* started in with all this criticism, I've detected nervousness among some of the councillors.'

'That regular columnist of theirs – *Beachcomber* – certainly seems to have it in for us.' Jonathan was leafing through yesterday's copy, which had been sitting on Naomi's desk when he arrived. 'Always ranting on about the locals not wanting it.'

'That's the point – it's become quite a hostile little campaign.' She leaned in over his shoulder. 'Have you seen this week's headline? '*HOUSES WHERE YOU CAN'T PARK YOUR CAR OUTSIDE YOUR OWN FRONT DOOR!*' That's the last thing Whitehall will want to see – if this project doesn't have popular support, it'll kill their plan to use us as a pilot for similar schemes round the country.'

Jonathan sighed. 'Dear oh dear. Welcome to the late twentieth century, citizens of Broadhaven, eh.'

'I've heard councillors going on about it being too 'modern'. I think there's going to be serious trouble.'

'What sort of trouble?'

Naomi got up and leaned out of the door, peering up and down the corridor before she withdrew, shut the door, and lowered her voice.

'There's a lot going on under the surface – including a protest group to 'protect the area's special character from further development.''

'That's crazy!' He could understand the concerns, but he'd seen how dire things were by now, even for people like the Northcotts. 'This area needs new investment desperately.'

'Of course it does. Most councillors are still all for it. But there are a few, as you'll know from London, who'll climb on any passing bandwagon if they think it'll win votes. I'm struggling to see any pattern yet, but there'll be one, you can bet on it.'

'God, it's all pretty depressing.' He threw the paper back down on the desk and rubbed his temples. 'I came down here to get away from this kind of rubbish.'

'We've got to stay strong – too much hanging on it. Whitehall wants me to manage the local scenario as best I can, and I'll need your help.'

'You've got it, of course – what can I do?'

Naomi thought for a few moments before she answered. 'With all your local contacts, do you think you might help me track down who *Beachcomber* is? We need to know what – or who – is behind all this incoming flak.'

'I'll ask around and see what I can find.'

'Good. Now I'm afraid there's one more 'little local difficulty' I need to share with you, in complete confidence. Let's step out of the office and get a bit of air, shall we?'

As soon as they were clear of the town hall, Naomi drew in a deep breath, her shoulders slouching as she let it all out.

'Sorry about the cloak-and-dagger stuff. But 'walls have ears', as they say, and I can't risk being overheard.'

'It's that serious?' said Jonathan.

'To be blunt, it's potential dynamite. I was talking to Walter Johnson, the town clerk?'

'... and?'

'I'd said we'd have to be particularly scrupulous about the tendering process, given the scrutiny it's bound to get from London. He's mentioned more than once how 'things are done a bit differently down here' but this time ... he told me, 'but of course you wouldn't have realised that, because you're only on secondment, aren't you?'' Naomi wrapped her arms around herself. 'It sounded like a hint to watch my step.'

Jonathan stopped in his tracks. 'That's not so much a hint as a thinly veiled threat. I must tell Caroline about this.'

'No, you mustn't! We need to keep this between ourselves at the moment.'

Jonathan frowned. 'She's in charge of the scheme, Naomi, for God's sake – don't you think she's a right to know?'

'Let's keep walking,' Naomi said, softly.

With a growing unease, he followed her a few more steps.

'There's ... an unwritten part of my brief from London – even Caroline doesn't know this – to find out how things operate in this part of the world,' she said slowly. 'Government needs to be sure the processes are all above board, especially if huge sums of public money are to be put into future projects managed by small local councils.'

Jonathan hesitated. This could put him in an awkward position.

'Well, thanks for letting me in on that. I have to say it puts quite a different perspective on your role in this project. But it's going to be tricky for me to keep all this from Caroline. If it all blows up, I can see me losing my job – and my professional reputation with it.'

'I do know that – and I appreciate the risks we're both taking.' Her expression was solemn. 'I can only say you need to trust me, if you feel you can.'

Again, Jonathan took his time before replying. He'd got to know Naomi well, and felt she was someone of integrity. True, she'd been keeping this from him… but she was coming clean now, and asking for his help, too.

'You must realise I'm going out on a limb, Naomi – but alright. I'll do as you ask, because I do trust you.'

'Thanks, Jonathan.' She looked relieved. 'It means a lot to me to have your support just now. I promise I'll keep you closely informed. Now, I suppose I'd better get back to the office and tackle one or two other annoying matters, if you don't mind.'

'Of course – and I ought to get back too.'

Jonathan had been shaken by what he'd heard, and rather than return directly to the office, headed towards the old town to mull things over.

He walked to the end of the harbour wall and sat down to contemplate the incoming tide. He was worried about what he might've got himself into, keeping so many of Naomi's secrets. But, watching as the harbour slowly filled and the boats refloated on their moorings, he felt a sense of acceptance descend. He could no more escape life's realities by coming to a remote part of the south-west than he'd been able to by entering a monastery.

He was walking back past some fishermen's net stores when he saw a young woman with a striking head of brown hair falling down to her waist. As they passed each other, their eyes met and they exchanged a smile.

What a stunner! – well above my pay grade though.

But it changed his mood, and for a moment he forgot all about the low politics of Broadhaven. Ever since he'd had that disastrous break-up at architectural school, he'd never come to terms with the raw reality that it had rocked him to his foundations – and had made him steer clear of women.

Now, though – he felt he was beginning to come to terms with his past, and with a place of his own, and a job he enjoyed – maybe he was ready to try again.

SIXTEEN
Late Autumn 1967

It was late autumn by the time Jonathan completed his outline scheme for Hall. Tony's old-hand wisdom had been immensely valuable, helping to point his young apprentice in the right direction. He'd even done some watercolour perspectives for Jonathan to show the Northcotts – 'they'll understand it all so much better if they can imagine how it'll look.' They showed the disused farmyard buildings transformed into a studies centre focused around the great threshing barn, full of new life, with children learning, eating, and generally enjoying themselves.

His scheme was an immediate hit with Ted and Anna.

'It's so exciting!' Anna said. 'We've had our own ideas, but this takes it all to a different level. Makes me want to get on with it straight away, doesn't it you, Ted?'

'Certainly does. It looks a great scheme,' Ted said. 'Like Anna says, we couldn't visualise it as you've done.'

'I'm glad you're pleased. But that's the easy part – making it happen is the real test, for all of us.'

'We know we're in for the long haul,' Anna said. 'We'll try to be patient, I promise. What happens next?'

'Tony thinks – before I start drawing up detailed plans – it'd be wise to test the water with the council, and a few other people who'd be useful to have on side. It's better to prepare the ground and not spring surprises. That way you can flush out any problems.'

'You think there'll be problems?' Ted's smile had slipped away, leaving him anxious once again.

'We simply won't know till I've taken soundings.'

'I can see that's sensible,' said Anna. 'Are you really able to do that for us informally, or is this the moment we need to start paying you?'

'Not just yet,' Jonathan said. 'Let me see what I can find.'

It was not only Tony's wisdom, but his own experience in Broadhaven, which convinced Jonathan he should go carefully. He decided to start with the rector, who surely must know a thing or two about sounding out local opinion.

'Hello Jonathan, it's me again I'm afraid,' he'd said as they bumped into each other in the office foyer one morning. Father Leo had become an ever more frequent visitor to the office lately.

'Always pleased to see you, Father,' Jonathan said. 'Tony tells me you've made some exciting discoveries now you've stripped the old render off the tower.'

'Ah yes, we have. A blocked Norman door and window in the lower stages of the tower, no less – so it's much older than we thought, by about three centuries. You must come and take a look.'

'I certainly will – Tony's probably told you I'm up to my ears in this housing project over at Broadhaven.'

'Ah, yes, I can imagine – and you've got that nasty little campaign in the *Gazette* to deal with too. Well, if you need a distraction, why don't you come over to the rectory after work one evening? We could combine a quick scramble up the scaffolding with a drink, and I could show you those plans of the church I mentioned too.'

'That sounds wonderful.'

'Then shall we say next Wednesday about five?'

It was the perfect opportunity to sound the rector out on the Northcotts' project – and a chance to see whether the rector could throw any light on the identity of *Beachcomber*.

They met at the church, where Jonathan found the rector wearing some rather comically ill-fitting overalls.

'The builders thought I was a danger to myself clambering around in my cassock, so they lent me these,' he said, looking sheepish. 'But I think they make me more of a liability than ever!'

Jonathan did his best not to laugh. 'Oh, I don't know – you look quite the part, Father!'

'Come and look at this,' he said, leading Jonathan to the west face of the tower where the Norman doorway had been uncovered. 'Late twelfth century they say, as is the window above.'

Together, they scrambled up onto the scaffolding for a better view.

'They're both remarkably well preserved,' said Jonathan as he examined them.

'Yes they are – they've been covered up since the tower was heightened in the fifteenth century. Tony's suggested we open them up to improve ventilation of the tower. Now, if you've seen enough, let's repair to the rectory for some refreshment.'

He led the way through the churchyard to the gate into the rectory garden. The house was sequestered from public view behind thickets of overgrown laurel and rhododendron through which the path wound towards the front of the house, all steeply pitched gables, polychrome brickwork and pointed-arched windows.

'Designed by the same hand as the church – one of the Seddings,' Leo said. 'Please come in.'

They passed through a gracious entrance hall, from the rear of which a staircase rose elegantly to the upper floor, and the rector led him to a large, high-ceilinged reception room. It was less richly furnished than it probably had been in the past. The centrepiece was a sofa and three leather chairs, all of which had seen better days, gathered around an elaborate Gothic fireplace. An enormous Edwardian bookcase, a large table and an ungainly sideboard, set off by a faded but beautiful red Persian carpet, completed the furnishing. The odd ensemble gave it a homely character.

At the rector's invitation, he sank comfortably into one of the leather chairs.

'Now, I'll just get out of these overalls and fetch us some drinks. Would a whiskey and ginger hit the spot?'

'It certainly would.'

Father Leo rumbled off into the distance, and Jonathan, hearing his footsteps receding for ages, began to realise what a huge pile the rectory was.

'Sorry to have been so long,' Father Leo said, returning in clerical gear and bearing generous measures. 'It's a day's journey to the kitchen. Well, here's to your happy residence among us.' He raised his glass to Jonathan's. 'Would you care for one of these?' he continued, offering a packet of Woodbines.

'No thank you, Father, I don't actually smoke.'

'Ah, very wise of you, I'm sure. But you won't mind if I do?'

'No, of course not.'

'I feel I can allow myself this small vice in the privacy of this great barn.'

'It certainly is quite a place, if you don't mind me saying. It's almost on the minor country house scale.'

'I don't mind at all – I say it myself all the time, not least to the Archdeacon and Bishop. It's crazy – there are over twenty rooms all told. I live in a couple of rooms near the front door so visitors don't have to tramp through the rest, which I can't possibly afford to heat on my stipend.'

'It does rather seem to belong to another age, Father.'

'Exactly so. By the way, please feel free to call me Leo – I'm happy with Father, as you've probably picked up, but there's really no need on my account.'

'If that's all right, I will.'

'Excellent. Now, as you were rightly implying, this place was built when the rector did indeed live more like the minor gentry than almost all his parishioners. What must people think who come knocking on my door from the little terraced houses in the town asking about baptisms, weddings and funerals? No wonder the church seems irrelevant to the lives of most people.'

'But that's quite a recent development, surely?'

'Not down here.' Jonathan sensed Leo was warming to his theme, so he sat back, nursing his drink as he continued. 'I'm sure you've read of the West Country's long history of fierce independence, including religious dissent. So, when the mining industry boomed in the eighteenth and nineteenth centuries, it was the 'dissenters' who swept the board.'

'You mean the Quakers, Baptists and Methodists?'

'Yes, but particularly the latter. John Wesley was hugely successful down here and the Bible Christian branch of Methodism was really strong. That's why you see so many chapels with those evocative Old Testament names – Bethel, Mount Sion, Providence, and so on.'

'But then, why all the Gothic Revival churches like yours down here?'

'It was the established church's attempt at a fightback – offer richness, colour, beauty, even mystery with clouds of incense – as a contrast to the drabness of ordinary life.'

'Did it work?'

Leo lit another cigarette and took a couple of sips of his whiskey before he replied.

'To a certain extent,' he said eventually. 'But in the countryside we've always struggled with the image of the C of E as being for the elite – the landed gentry, the squire, rich farmers and all that. We've rarely lived up to our dream of being for the deprived and the poor – it was different, of course, in the cities, where we did have more success with working people.'

'I must admit I've been struck by the deprivation down here. It's not what I'd expected – I suppose I'd seen poverty as an urban problem. When Caroline first asked me to take on the Broadhaven project, I wasn't sure why it was needed – but I certainly do see that now.'

'So many people who come on holiday down here don't realise that.

And affluent incomers don't particularly want their rural utopian fantasy spoiled by the facts.'

'I was surprised how much opposition there is to the housing project.' He was sensing a useful ally. 'The *Gazette* – and particularly their *Beachcomber* column – are getting to be quite a headache for us. Do you know, by any chance, who might be behind the campaign?'

'I have my suspicions.'

'Sorry Father, I don't want to trespass into matters that you might feel are confidential.'

'It's all right, Jonathan, I have quite a stake in your project as Chairman of the advisory committee behind its setting up. When we held a public meeting to publicise what we were trying to achieve, it was generally good-natured except for one man who made a nasty, hostile little speech against the whole concept – I made some discreet enquiries and found out he was a well-known former Fleet Street journalist by the name of Harry Humphries who'd retired down here recently. My money's on him.'

'I see. So it's possible he pens all this stuff.'

'I'd say it's more than likely. The *Gazette* has taken a much more strident tone since his arrival.'

'Well, you did well to get the project going then, given there was that kind of looming opposition.'

'I think we created the initial impetus – and then luckily the government came along wanting a pilot project. I guess you work closely with Naomi Walters? She's an exceptionally talented young woman.'

'Yes, she's my main contact. So perceptive – not much gets past her. And she shares our concerns about social deprivation.'

'She certainly does… But enough of all that – you came for an architectural treat!'

Leo went to fetch the architect's drawings from his study. When he returned, he spread them on the table behind them. To Jonathan's apprehension, he then lit what must have been his fourth cigarette, leaning over as he enthused over their remarkable quality, apparently unaware of cigarette ash drifting over them. Jonathan was suitably impressed by their draughtsmanship but, anxious for the safety of the drawings, eventually steered the conversation away from the table and back to their comfortable chairs and life in Michaelchurch.

'You might be surprised to know I'd always served in inner-city parishes before I came here,' said Leo.

'Why such a change?'

'Because I felt rural and urban England were losing touch and wanted to do something about it. I tried to make this sprawling pile into a kind of retreat house for hard-pressed urban families who needed a break – but that was considered far too risky by the diocese.'

'Pity, it would have been a great use for it.'

'I thought of developing part of the rectory garden for housing locals too, but that was rebuffed as well. They didn't want people in the large houses near the rectory screaming blue murder about their property being devalued...' Ruefully, the rector shook his head. 'Sorry. You came for a relaxing drink, not a lecture on the shortcomings of the C of E!'

'On the contrary,' Jonathan said, spotting his chance, 'this is actually rather relevant to something I'd like to run past you.'

'How intriguing,' Leo said, brows rising. 'Do go on.'

'You know the Northcotts over at Hall?'

'I do, they're good people.'

'Well, they're thinking of developing their disused farm buildings into a rural studies centre for city children – I have their go-ahead to run the plans past you.'

'Let me refresh our drinks and you can tell me all about it.'

Leo ambled off to the kitchen again and returned with refilled glasses, lighting up yet another Woodbine as he eased back in his chair. As Jonathan explained Ted and Anna's vision, though, he began to lean in, and by the time Jonathan was wrapping up, the rector was literally on the edge of his seat.

'Music to my ears, every word,' Leo said. 'It would bring new life to the area. I imagine there'd be some jobs in it, too – more and more young people are leaving us because there's no work here.'

'So when the scheme goes public, could Ted and Anna count on your support?'

'Of course they could – and it would be whole-hearted.'

'My sense is they'll probably need it.'

Leo drew deeply on his cigarette, clouds of tobacco smoke ascending to the lofty ceiling.

'Yes, I think they will. You'll know that some people get upset by the prospect of change. For locals, it's because the world they've always known is disappearing before their eyes – whatever its shortcomings, they'd prefer the old certainty to an uncertain future. I can empathise with that, honestly. What I find more difficult is the newcomers who want to pull up the drawbridge now they've secured their bit of Eden.'

'But do you think the Northcotts could count on some support, at least?"

'Oh yes – they're well thought of and do a lot for the community. Anna's the one who comes to church, and I've always found Ted a sympathetic character, though he only puts in an occasional appearance. But you've got to expect opposition too – I can see the idea of city children being brought into this community not going down well in some quarters.'

'I'm sure you're right. But they'll be pleased they can count on your support.'

'They certainly can, and not just moral support. I've maintained contacts with my urban colleagues – and I can see collaboration between them and the Northcotts if this project comes off. If you'll allow me one perhaps rather predictable observation, I see their vision as offering real possibilities for the nurturing of the soul.'

Jonathan couldn't help but think of all the ways the place had nurtured him. 'I'd like to think that too.'

As soon as he got to the office in the morning, he called Naomi.

'I've got a promising lead on *Beachcomber*.'

'Great, Jonathan – please fill me in, I could do with a bit of good news right now.'

'I was talking to Father Leo Colchester last evening – I didn't realise you knew each other, but he thinks very highly of you – he suggests it is probably a retired journalist called Harry Humphries.'

'That's very interesting. I remember now that Father Leo warned me about him during the hand-over period when I first arrived. Even more to the point, Walter Johnson has mentioned more than once that Humphries is someone not to offend. Curious, don't you think?'

'Very.'

'Well, we'll keep a close eye on him from now on.'

SEVENTEEN
December 1967

From the moment of their first encounter, Jonathan had always had the greatest respect for Caroline Atherton. Since he'd started working in the practice, everything he'd seen and heard about her confirmed his first impression – that her authority stemmed from the high regard of others rather than her place as the senior partner in the practice.

But almost everything else about her remained a mystery.

He only knew she lived with her husband a few miles away in a house at Tremaine, a place he'd never had cause to visit. The office never talked about her personal life, and she gave every impression that she wasn't very curious about what the rest of them got up to outside work either – Jonathan assumed she wanted to keep her professional and home life completely separate. So he was surprised when one day she asked whether he was free the following weekend.

'I was wondering whether you might be able to join us for lunch this Sunday. It's been months since you arrived, and Oliver and I have never asked you over for a meal, which we feel rather bad about. Can you come?'

'I'd love to, thank you.'

'Good, we've got someone else coming who I think you'll enjoy meeting – and hasn't been in the area long either.'

'I'll look forward to that very much. Where are you and what time would you like me to come?'

'Oh, we're easy to find. Tremaine's a tiny place, so just drive to the centre and ask, everyone knows where we live. Come about 12.30. And we're very free and easy, dress like tramps when we're at home!'

That Sunday, as he made yet another wrong turn and found he was embarked on a long diversion, he cursed he hadn't bought a new map of the area. The tatty old Ordnance Survey map he'd borrowed from the office was so worn at the folds he couldn't make out how the maze of lanes worked. Bounded by great hedge banks, he felt he was in a tunnel most of the time, with no decent viewpoints to check his whereabouts. And it didn't help that the previous night's heavy rain had left water all over the road and mud everywhere.

Why on earth did you bother to wash the car this morning? You ought to know by now that car washing in the country's one of life's futile gestures.

So he was a little later than planned when a roadside sign, almost obscured by a fallen branch, announced he'd reached Tremaine. It appeared a modest enough place, no more than a few cottages grouped around an ancient church, except that every house was painted in the same colours, with yellow-ochre lime-washed walls and maroon paintwork – the tell-tale sign of an estate village. He pulled in and got out of the car when he spotted a man clearing leaves from a blocked drain.

'Sorry to bother you, but I wonder if you could tell which is the Athertons' house, please?'

'Ah, you mean Tremaine Manor,' the man replied, looking up from his work as if he was glad of a break. 'It's easy. Just carry on down here and you'll see the entrance gates on the other side of the church, then follow the drive through the park till you reach the house.'

A manor, reached from an estate village through its own park? No wonder Caroline had suggested it was easy to find.

Passing through entrance piers and ornate ironwork gates in need of repair, the drive wound its way through ancient parkland whose air of benign neglect only enhanced its serenity in Jonathan's eyes. It led on, down past a wide lake on the valley floor, then up towards a large and ancient grey house set against steeply rising woods. Finally it gave onto a gravelled forecourt in front of the house where a couple of battered old cars, one of which he recognised as Caroline's Mini, the other a venerable Rover saloon, were parked.

So this was Tremaine.

Jonathan got out of the car and took in the scene. What a place! He could now see the house sprawled generously to the side which had been hidden from view as he drove up. Formal gardens spread to both sides and on below into the valley. He looked for an obvious entrance somewhere in the long facade but, unsure where to make for, was relieved to see Caroline coming across the forecourt to meet him.

'Jonathan, how clever of you to find us, welcome to Tremaine.'

'Hello Caroline, sorry I'm late – I came by what the guidebooks call the scenic route.'

'Oh, it doesn't matter. We're pretty relaxed round here about most things.'

'I didn't realise Tremaine was the name of the house as well as the village.'

'Well, we don't go on about it. It's Oliver's ancestral pile,' Caroline said with amusement. 'His baronetcy goes back over four hundred years and his family have lived here most of that time. Back then, the estate was vast, but nowadays it's much reduced. In fact we struggle to keep it all going, as you'll see. We like to think what it lacks in 'mod cons' it makes up for in character.'

'I'd no idea,' he said, trying to find words to cover his surprise.

Caroline noted his slight embarrassment.

'I'm sorry, Jonathan, I'm sure you've picked up from the office that I try my best to keep my professional and private worlds apart,' she said in her matter-of-fact manner. 'It wouldn't help the reputation of the practice much if it was primarily seen as being the plaything of Lady Caroline, if you see what I mean – people would think architecture was something I amused myself with, rather than being my passion, not to mention our primary source of income. Now, you must be getting cold, so come on in and meet Oliver and have a drink – our other guest hasn't arrived yet either.'

Caroline led him through a tall, gabled entrance porch into a wide passage with walls of ancient oak panelling and a decorated plaster ceiling.

'Wonderful!' Jonathan said as he feasted his eyes on the craftsmanship.

'This is the old part of the house – we're told it dates from the late fourteenth century. Come on in here, the great hall – the roof was put up in the 1380s, according to the experts.'

She'd ushered him into a huge room open to the roof and lit by a magnificent full height bay window, its hundreds of panes of old glass filtering the pale winter sunlight. The heirlooms of centuries furnished the room, with three enormous sofas gathered around a great chimneypiece, from which a fire of what looked to Jonathan like small tree-trunks threw out welcome heat. From one of the sofas a man of modest height, slim and dapper, rose to greet him.

'Jonathan, I'm Oliver Atherton.' He had an upright and dignified bearing as he crossed the floor to shake Jonathan's hand. 'Pleased to meet you at last, Caroline's told me a lot about you.'

'Hello Oliver, delighted to meet you too – and to see Tremaine, it looks marvellous.'

'We think so. But it can strike a little chill in winter, so come and have a seat by the fire and warm up. We only use the great hall when we have guests. Let me get you a drink – we usually indulge in a gin and tonic before Sunday lunch, if that would appeal?'

'It would indeed.'

Jonathan sank into one of the sofas, falling somewhat further back than was strictly compatible with dignity. Drinks arrived, courtesy of Oliver, and the conversation turned to the house.

'Nothing very pure about it, as you modernists might say,' Oliver said with a wry glance towards his wife, 'but we rather like its mongrel character

– and, of course, because it's been in the family such a long time we invest it with all kinds of personal history. If you could bear it I'll give you a tour after lunch – you might at least enjoy taking a peek at some of the more interesting parts.' He said all this in a diffident manner, as if it might be an imposition rather than the rare privilege it seemed to his guest.

'I'd like that very much, thank you.'

They were interrupted by the sound of a car screeching to a stop on the gravel of the forecourt.

'Ah,' said Caroline with a smile, 'that'll be our other guest.'

She went out to greet the new arrival, and shortly afterwards ushered a young woman into the room, who was talking so animatedly to her hostess she seemed at first oblivious to the two men. She was wearing an eye-catchingly short mini dress – daringly short, thought Jonathan, for this part of the world, suddenly conscious of how much he missed one of contemporary London's delights – and she tossed her mane of long brown hair quite wildly over one shoulder as she spoke.

Caroline interrupted her flow to do the introductions.

'Sophie, this is Jonathan Lane, my relatively new colleague. Jonathan, this is Sophie Ryder, a friend of mine who moved down from London like yourself.'

In a flash, he realised he'd seen her before – the stunner he'd been eyeballing down by the harbour in Broadhaven.

'Hello Jonathan – and Oliver too – I'm so sorry, I'm afraid I was rather caught up talking with Caroline, please forgive me.' With that she embraced Oliver and kissed him on both cheeks.

'Let me get you a drink Sophie – we're all on gin and tonics, if that would suit you?'

'It most certainly would, thank you. Now…'

She turned and advanced towards Jonathan. Much to his surprise, and delight, she embraced him as well, planting an air-kiss on either cheek. He was already slightly in awe of this display of supreme self-confidence, and very aware she was in total command of the situation.

'So,' she continued with a broad smile and huge brown eyes which managed to convey intimacy alongside serious intent, 'we're both newcomers – is that the only reason why we haven't met before?'

'Well actually… we have, sort of…'

Before he got any further, Oliver returned with Sophie's drink, ushered her to a seat and offered her a cigarette from a silver cigarette case. She took one, allowed Oliver to light it for her, and drew on it extravagantly.

'If you'll excuse us,' said Oliver, 'Caroline and I have a few finishing touches to put to our lunch.'

'Of course,' said Sophie, 'it'll give me a chance to interrogate Jonathan!'

Jonathan was thrilled, though he tried to look as much at his ease as possible.

'What I really want to know is,' she continued when the others had left the room, 'are you intending to put down roots here in the deep west, or are you just a bird of passage?'

'Ah, no… I mean, I'm not intending to go anywhere…' He'd been distracted by Sophie's figure, now displayed to great effect on the sofa into which she'd leaned back theatrically, drink in one hand, cigarette in the other. 'In fact… I'm feeling very settled already. How about you?'

'Oh, I love it down here. I feel I've started a new life – and would you believe, I'm doing so in Broadhaven, of all places!'

'I'm looking after a new housing scheme there.'

'Yes, I've heard a lot about it from Caroline – and of course the local paper's been full of the ructions they say it's causing. But I think it sounds very much needed. It was quite a shock to see how run-down the town is – not the classy resort it once was, is it?'

'No, it surprised me a bit as well.' Her directness inspired him to issue a sudden invitation. 'If you'd be interested, and ever have a moment, I'd be pleased to show you over the site sometime and explain my design.'

'I've lots of moments at present, and I'd very much like to see what you're up to. Drop me a note – I'm down by the harbour, Caroline will give you my address. I'm trying to set myself up as a sculptor but it's proving a struggle. I may have to go and work in a bar or something next summer the way things are going.'

'That's nonsense, Sophie!' said Caroline, coming back into the room. 'She's a very promising new talent Jonathan, there's a freshness about her work – as you'll see when you come, as I hope you will, to her first solo exhibition in a couple of months? I'm helping her to set herself up.'

'Where's your show going to be?' said Jonathan.

'Broadhaven!' Sophie replied. 'Caroline thinks I should be a new name in a new place, don't you?'

'I'm hoping it'll have more impact that way – a bit risky, of course, but better than trying to persuade one of those stuffy galleries up in Bath or Bristol or down at Newlyn or St Ives to give her space – they'd charge the earth and she'd still not get a show of her own.'

'Let's be honest, Broadhaven's not a place which springs to mind when you think of artistic innovation, is it!' Sophie laughed. 'But if you want to change the world you've got to start somewhere, so why not there? Anyway, I'm getting quite fond of the place already.'

Just then Oliver re-appeared in the doorway.

'Lunch is ready, if you'd like to come through to the dining room.'

They followed him across the entrance passage into a panelled room with a wonderfully ornate plasterwork ceiling of leaves, fruit and flowers – though for once Jonathan was less interested in the room than the guest with whom he shared a table.

When he'd mentioned his invitation to Tremaine to Tony, all the elder architect had said was that cooking was Oliver's forte. So it proved, over a Sunday feast taken at leisurely pace on into the afternoon – onion soup with croutons; roast beef and Yorkshire pudding, roast potatoes and parsnips, creamed leeks and horseradish sauce; apple pie and custard; fresh fruit; and finally cheese and biscuits. Three different wines complemented the courses.

'We don't eat like this all the time!' Oliver assured his guests as they showered him with praise. 'But we do make a bit of an effort once in a while when we've got special guests.'

They retired to the great hall for coffee, and eventually Oliver repeated his offer of a tour of the house. Jonathan secretly hoped Sophie would join them, but –

'Would you mind terribly if I missed out on that, Oliver? Caroline gave me the grand tour last time I was here and, to be perfectly honest, I need more of her wisdom on the design of my exhibition.'

'Of course,' said Oliver. 'Well, Jonathan, we'd better make a start while the light's still OK, I think.'

The interior of the house proved as labyrinthine as the exterior had promised. The extensive wing Jonathan noticed on arrival turned out to be a suite of elegant eighteenth-century rooms, though Oliver told him they were hardly ever used now. Jonathan counted three fine staircases of different periods, a couple of internal courtyards, and a large number of service rooms at the rear, including a cavernous Victorian kitchen.

Oliver stuck to the things he thought might interest his guest, but allowed ample time for Jonathan to drink in the atmosphere and ask questions. He said very little about himself, besides a fleeting reference to having spent time in the diplomatic service. For all Jonathan knew he'd spent a lifetime in espionage.

When they talked about the changes needed to make old houses fit for modern living, Jonathan took the opportunity to sound him out about the Northcotts' project.

'Do you know Hall, where I live? The other side of Michaelchurch, near the sea?'

'Hall. Let me see, it certainly rings a bell. Yes, of course, the Northcotts' place. Another ancient pile, not quite as sprawling as this, but full of interest – sadly not in such good nick these days, I understand. Pity. Used to be part of the Tremaine estate at one time.'

Jonathan did, now that he'd mentioned it, remember Ted saying something of the sort. 'They've got plans to turn the disused farm buildings into a studies centre for city children.'

'Good for them! That's exactly the kind of new venture we need in this area. I'd be all for it, if that's what you're asking.'

A little embarrassed to have made himself so transparent, Jonathan nodded. 'It would mean a great deal to them if they could count on your support.'

'Of course – and I'm afraid they'll certainly need all the friends they can muster. I'm sure others will have warned you, but it seems there's always controversy when it comes to doing things differently.'

'I'm only too aware – I've been having quite a torrid time over in Broadhaven.'

For a fleeting moment, Oliver looked slightly pained. 'Please forgive me, I should have remembered – between you and me, the hostility has quite upset Caroline.'

When they returned to the welcome warmth of the great hall, Caroline was serving tea, over which Jonathan found himself the subject of further questioning by Sophie.

'So Jonathan, I imagine you'll be living in some sleek architectural box – not that I've seen much of that round here, except for Caroline's little masterpieces!'

'Well no, actually, quite the opposite – I'm renting part of an old water mill.'

'How exciting! I insist you invite me over to see it!'

Jonathan felt his heart pounding.

'I'd love to… just tell me when you're free.'

'Tell you what, I'll ring you at the office and we'll fix something – and don't forget you're going to show me your project!'

'Of course, I'll look forward to either – or better still, both!'

'Now, thank you all for such a fun Sunday – and a delicious lunch, Oliver, I don't think I'm going to have to eat for a week! I'd better be going – it's dark already.'

'Any chance I could follow you as far as Michaelchurch?' Jonathan asked. 'I got a bit lost on the way here and don't fancy my chances of finding my way back through the lanes the way I came.'

'Of course – I'll show you a route via the better roads.'

It was a bit more of an adventure than he expected. Sophie had a little sports car, an Austin Healey Sprite, and she didn't hang around. Jonathan struggled to keep up, constantly on the verge of losing her tail lights around the corners – all of which she took at truly alarming speed.

Thank God, she's pulled in.

'Here's where I leave you,' she shouted through her window.

'Michaelchurch's that right turn over there. See you soon I hope!'

And blowing him a kiss, she drove off into the night.

'What a girl!' he said out loud as he turned his car towards Michaelchurch, still driving at Sophie speed.

Slow down man, for God's sake, don't kill yourself before you've even had a date with her!

Still, he was grinning. He could just about believe she might fancy him.

1968

cliff top warm burnt sienna to greener cool -

Upper cliffs ethereal yellow buff naples. Cool[illegible] tend towards yellow staining

½ tones purple grey -

EIGHTEEN
February and March 1968

Though she occupied his thoughts almost constantly, Jonathan didn't hear from Sophie – and nor, for that matter, did she hear from him.

Christmas came and went, and when the New Year was no longer new, he began to wonder if Sophie Ryder was just a figment of his imagination. Had he misread the signals? Perhaps she'd just showed polite interest in a fellow guest. Or maybe she was the coquettish sort, in which case he'd steer well clear.

The impasse was broken by his invitation to Sophie's private show, though disappointingly it came from Caroline. He had the distinct impression as she handed it to him it wasn't so much an invitation as a royal command.

'You will be there won't you, Jonathan? It's an important moment for her – and me and Oliver too. She's become something of a surrogate daughter, so I'd like a good turn out from the office.'

'Of course, wouldn't dream of missing it!' He was aiming for enthusiastic without revealing that wild horses wouldn't keep him away.

'Good. We thought the two of you got on well when you came for lunch. She was rather taken actually, thought there was a hint of mystery about you.'

Jonathan breathed an inner sigh of relief. 'At least she thought there was something more to discover.'

'Honestly, Jonathan, don't be so feeble!' Caroline laughed. 'Come on, she's worth a try!'

Caroline's light-hearted directness hit home. He hadn't always been so feeble, as she put it – in truth it was quite the reverse in his student days. But then there'd been Judith. He'd invested so much in their relationship, and without warning…

If he'd learned one thing about himself in the monastery, it was that the collapse of their relationship had broken him. With Judith, he'd known exactly who he was – without her, he hadn't a clue. He' been left in pieces, and only now, years later, did he feel like trying to get himself together again.

Realizing Caroline was eyeing him in that penetrating way she had, he cleared his throat.

'I'll do better next time, I promise,' he assured her.

She gave him a firm, approving nod. 'I should jolly well hope so!'

The private view happened on a cold, wet evening in late March, one of those days when winter's sullenness made the promise of spring feel impossibly distant. That didn't stop a good crowd getting over to Broadhaven. Wine flowed freely, with Tony's jazz quartet providing just the right background music. Caroline had seemingly called up all her friends in the art world, as well as many of her wealthier clients. There were a good number of locals, including Leo, Jim, and Ted and Anna, to whom Jonathan proudly introduced Sophie. And Sophie brought her own colourful circle of fellow artists to give the occasion a distinctly Bohemian air – a heady mix of interesting aromas filled the air, and even the more staid guests loosened up as the evening wore on.

Sophie's work looked stunning in the old sail loft above the harbour she'd hired for the evening, the roughly-hewn roof beams, warm brick walls, and wooden planked floor providing the perfect ambience. As

Caroline had hinted, her sculpture was certainly full of promise, to Jonathan's eye: simple forms, mostly in wood, but a few smaller pieces in bronze – 'so expensive a material and process,' Sophie told him, 'I've had to take out a mortgage to pay for the casting!' Her inspiration, she said, came from the sea-worn rocks of the local shores as well as the granite tors of the moors. He was particularly captivated by a figure sculpture that played with the young human form in sensuously smooth curves with utter purity. Here, Jonathan thought, was someone who had a profound understanding of the human body, and through her acuity of observation had captured something of its sweet beauty and its transience.

Afterwards, Caroline and Oliver hosted a celebratory supper in a little restaurant near the harbour. Jonathan spent most of it in a state of mild delirium as he found himself seated next to Sophie. He soon realised she was on a high and ready to take on all comers, especially him.

'I'm disappointed, Mr Lane.' She gave him a wide grin. 'I've been expecting that invitation you promised!'

'Oh gosh…' He stumbled over his words with sheer excitement. '…I'm sorry Sophie, I've been meaning to… I promise I have!'

'I've been dying to see you again! And you haven't even tracked me down at my studio, though I bet you've been to Broadhaven more than once since we met, haven't you?'

'I have, of course,' he said, fumbling for an excuse. 'But I suppose I was hoping you'd call me – you did say you would.'

She laughed. 'Yes, I did, but I've been so busy getting things ready for this show – well, fair enough, we're quits I suppose! But from now on, I'm free to come whenever you want – that's assuming you still want me to of course? And the evenings are getting much lighter now the clocks are going forward. Go on, be brave, Jonathan – fix a date now!'

'Tell you what, they say the weather's on the turn after next week – more like spring then,' he said. 'If you came over on the Saturday or Sunday of the week after next, we could go for a walk along the coast? And I could offer lunch or supper, or even both!'

This last remark was a little rash given his limited culinary skills and cooking facilities, but what the hell? She'd challenged him to be brave.

'It's a deal!' she said, clinking glasses with him as they held each other's gaze.

NINETEEN
Early April 1968

Though his head was now full of Sophie Ryder, Jonathan had plenty to distract him, at least during daylight. He'd put in a lot of extra hours getting the documents ready for the housing project to go out to tender. When they met at Naomi Walters' office to hand them over, he found her uncharacteristically downbeat.

'Honestly Jonathan, I'm really struggling.'

'Going out to tender's never much fun, is it?' said Jonathan, hoping her demeanour was down to weariness with the process.

She hesitated.

'It's a bit more than that, I'm afraid. I'm bothered about the way the council wants to handle the tender process.'

'How do you mean?'

'Walter Johnson's pressing me to come up with a short list of potential contractors – a list which only includes firms the council's used before, even though I can prove they're always the most expensive.'

His brows drew together sharply. 'That's surely a bit out of order.'

Naomi lowered her voice and leaned closer.

'Given his previous attempts to intimidate me, it's definitely out of order.'

Anxiety he thought he'd tamped down began to rise up once more. 'That's worrying. I've not said a word to Caroline, but I ought to brief her now, surely? Especially if there's any doubt of proper process – she won't want the practice associated with anything underhanded.'

'It's a lot to ask of you, but please hold off a bit longer. I've been looking at the council's contracts over the years and found a consistent pattern of the same contractors always getting the jobs.'

'Surely there can't have been that many jobs going out to tender in a small council like this?'

'You'd be surprised. That great surge of public building we've seen across the country in the last few years – new schools, libraries, police and fire stations, courts – it all adds up to millions of pounds worth of work, even down here.'

'So you think it's not all been above board?'

'Don't get me wrong. Most of the councillors – and the officers – are people of great integrity, committed to public service. But you know what they say – 'it only takes one bad apple' – and if that person's in a powerful position, things can get pretty murky over time. I don't want anything to go wrong with our project – it should be such a shining example of how good public sector housing can be! But, as you can probably imagine, I'm sailing pretty close to the wind.'

'So am I, Naomi.' He realised he was drumming his fingers ceaselessly against the arm of his chair. 'I'm really not sure I can, or should, keep this from Caroline.'

'Please bear with me. We're so near getting the project on site, and anyway, Johnson doesn't hold all the cards. The council's committed their part of the budget and Whitehall's given it the go-ahead, confirmed their share of the funding. So it's all systems go – all being well, and the tender process proceeding as it should, we'll have this scheme on site by early summer. And I'm not easily intimidated – don't forget, ultimately I report to London, not Johnson.'

Jonathan thought hard about his response – he was now exposed to even greater risk. But he admired Naomi's determination, and had implicit faith in her.

'OK, I'll go along with you. I suppose we're in the same boat, I just hope the engine doesn't explode and wreck us both.'

Leaving the town hall, he needed to get things in perspective, and so once again headed for the harbour and the sea.

Bloody hell, what have I got myself into? Can't even tell Tony, and there's no-one else I'd trust.

He found himself meandering along the old fish quay, with fish-cellars carved out of the cliff behind. On the spur of the moment, he realised he must be near Sophie's place – hadn't she said she'd rented a studio on the ground floor with a small one-bedroom flat above?

He looked around for a likely candidate. Most of the cellars were shut up, but then he saw one with the doors open and a light on inside. He peered through the door – and there was Sophie, hard at work at her bench in clouds of dust.

She glanced up to see him standing in the doorway.

'Well, hello Jonathan Lane, so you've finally made it to my lair!'

'Hello Sophie – better late than never I suppose!'

'Come in – welcome to the studio and workshop of Sophie Ryder, aspiring sculptor!'

'It looks just the right sort of place for you.'

'It's a bit basic but all I can afford at the moment. Here, sit yourself down.' She blew the dust off an old chair. 'I need a break – shall I make us a pot of tea?'

'Thanks, I could do with a cup – just finished a meeting over at the town hall about the housing project.'

They exchanged glances and smiles as the tea brewed, discreetly sizing each other up. She thought him quite dishy with his mop of blonde hair dishevelled by the sea breeze. He found her highly attractive in her work gear – heavy apron, face covered in dust, hair tied up under a cap.

'Look,' he said, 'you know you challenged me to be brave.'

'And so you are, by coming to see me here!'

'Yes… well… I want to be braver still.'

'Go on then!'

'I don't want to wait to see you again so I've come with a firm proposition – why don't you come over for the day this Saturday?'

'That's the sort of proposition I like to hear – I'd love to!'

'As you said last time, it's a deal then!'

And, at least in this moment, Jonathan's spirits soared.

TWENTY
Mid April 1968

It was warm and bright as Sophie swung the Sprite into the yard at Hall – Jonathan had suggested they meet there so he could guide her down to the mill. Ted and Anna were unloading some supplies from the back of the Land Rover, and readily agreed that it would be just fine to show Sophie around.

She was instantly taken with the rambling old house as Jonathan led her through the disused parts.

'Just think how many lives have been lived here,' she murmured. 'Countless loves and losses, births and deaths, the daily round, over the centuries. Wouldn't it be wonderful if we could go back and hear something of their stories!'

It was a pleasure, hearing his own sentiments fall so easily from her lips. 'I often try to work out how these rooms were used – it helps me think how I could bring the house back to life.'

'Ah, the architect-creator – you're not getting a bit above yourself, are you?!'

'I hope not,' he replied with a wide grin, 'but I know what you mean. I think sometimes we kid ourselves we know what's best for the world, not to mention our poor clients – 'For architecture, among all the arts, is the one that most boldly tries to reproduce in its rhythm the order of the universe, which the ancients called *kosmos*'.'

The delight on her face was undeniable. 'I suppose it's not that different from me having the cheek to try to fashion forms inspired by the rocks on the seashore or the moors, imagining I can improve on nature.'

In the end they were so absorbed in exploring the house and the farm they only had time for a short walk down to the sea and back, after which she followed him back down to the mill house for what he called 'a scratch supper.' Of course he'd planned and prepared meticulously – spaghetti Bolognese, the one dish which he'd perfected cooking for himself in London, with a bottle of Chianti on which he'd splashed out to make the right impression, served with fresh fruit and cheese. It was a lot more sumptuous than his usual modest snacks. Over dinner they talked at length about their mutual passions for art and landscape, searching each other out, every discovery reinforcing his impression that they had a great deal in common. In fact he was tempted, at one point, to move in for a passionate kiss… but courage failed him.

It wasn't just a question of being gun-shy, either. Even on such a perfect evening, he found himself unable to quite shake his worries over the Broadhaven project. Caroline had put so much trust in him – even introduced him to Sophie! – and here he was, withholding vital information on the project.

Why is life so bloody complicated?

Sophie seemed to sense his reticence, and so settled for a warm hug and peck on the cheek, along with a fervently expressed desire she should come over again very soon.

◈

On the way home, she puzzled over it: how buttoned-up, even distracted, Jonathan had seemed. Surprising, after he'd called in at her studio. She'd got the impression that he couldn't wait to get going, but the second they were alone together…

She confided in Caroline.

'Honestly,' she told her over the phone, 'that Jonathan Lane of yours is proving a bit of a closed book.'

'Well, I could have told you that from what I've seen of him in the office – inclined to put up the shutters when people get too close. You'll have to work hard to unlock that one, I've always thought – but probably worth the effort, don't you think?'

'Oh God yes – I'm nuts about him! But it's like we're doing a slow waltz to a string quartet when I want to do a mad jive to loud jazz!'

'If you want to know what I think – '

'You know I do, or I wouldn't have called!'

'I bet he's never come across anyone like you before. I'd say he's absolutely smitten, but hasn't got a clue how to handle you.'

'God, I only wish he would handle me!'

'You like a challenge, don't you?'

'I do – and our elusive Mr Lane is going to find he's been rumbled at last!'

Sophie returned to the mill house a couple of days later. As she and Jonathan walked the coastal path at dusk, she stopped and turned to face him.

'Where do you come from, Jonathan Lane?'

'How do you mean? I've told you what there is about me. Not much of interest really.'

'Oh for God's sake, don't be so silly – you know exactly what I mean! I'm not asking for your C.V.! I'm asking who Jonathan Lane really is.'

'Sophie…' He cleared his throat. 'You must have realised by now I'm not much good at that sort of stuff.'

'Well, it's high time you tried harder, don't you think? They say practice makes perfect you know.'

She put out her hands, and he took a few tentative steps closer, until they were holding each other at arm's length. She fixed him with an intense gaze.

'I'm asking because you matter to me – and I'm going to be bold and say I believe I matter to you too. Now, why don't you start by just telling me the kind of things you turn over in your head in the wee small hours?'

There was a long pause which she refused to be the first to break, studying him closely.

'I find it difficult to open up about myself,' he said eventually. 'But you're right, Sophie, I'm mad about you… really… you mean so much to me already, and we've really only just met. But something gets in the way of me being how I want to be with you… that's partly work, which is worrying me a lot just now… but, if I'm honest, it's about personal stuff as well.'

Sophie let this hang in the air a few more moments, then:

'Well, Mystery Man, are you going to say a bit more, or is that it?'

'All right – not about work, but I suppose I can tell you about the other stuff.'

'It might help if you did.'

'OK… Well, it's nothing that hasn't happened forever. Usual scenario, really… I once fell head over heels for a girl, Judith.'

As the last light went cold and faded, it was difficult to see his face – but she could certainly hear the tautness in his tone.

'I thought she was the one, for life… but she dumped me, very suddenly. Almost overnight in fact. I was shattered... couldn't bear the hurt I suppose.'

He fell silent. Down along the shore, the waves filled the silence, gently washing up against the sand and rolling back with a whisper.

'But that was a long time ago,' he said. 'Now, with you… I'm beginning to believe it could be different.'

She squeezed his hands, palms warm against hers.

'Thank you,' she said. 'I know it cost you a lot to say that. I've always thought there might be a lot of hurt in you – as there is in me, probably in all of us. And it's only natural to develop armour to protect ourselves. The problem is, sometimes the armour's so thick no-one can ever pierce it.'

He loosed his hands from hers, taking a few steps away to gaze at the sea.

'I'd like to be break out of it, I really would. But I don't know how.' She let him be for a minute or two, then went over and put her arms round him from behind, whispering in his ear.

'You could start by realising I'm the same as you, at least in terms of having been hurt, several times over in my case, by loving someone and eventually realising they didn't love me back – not as much as I wanted, or expected.'

He turned and opened his arms to bring her close, and they spoke softly, their heads resting side by side.

'I don't know what makes me say this,' said Jonathan, 'but I feel you're probably better at coping with all that than I am.'

'Maybe it's just coping differently,' said Sophie. 'All I've learned is that, after each heartbreak, I eventually decide to try again. I've opted for taking the risks, rather than shutting out the possibilities.'

She felt him draw in a deep breath. 'I think that's where I am too.'

'So what are you going to do about it?'

He released himself from their embrace and held her once again at arm's length, looking deeply into her eyes.

'How do you mean?'

'Well… I think you lost a lot of your self-belief over that Judith, but I'm presumptuous enough to believe you might recover it, if you let yourself go with me.'

He loved her blunt but honest analysis. And something in him which had been fast-bound for years burst free. He was smiling broadly, almost laughing.

'You must know I want to let myself go with you – to make love with you, desperately. You've no idea what a relief it is to say that!'

'It's just lovely you can say that!'

They stood looking at each other, and they hugged again. To his own surprise, he did feel free, more than he had in years.

'I don't want to break this spell,' Jonathan said eventually, 'so would you understand if we stop there this evening?'

'I don't want to, but I understand. And do you know why? Because there's the same searching in me as there is in you. We could be soul mates.'

'That would be wonderful.'

Then, for the first time, they fell into a long, passionate embrace.

TWENTY-ONE
Late April 1968

Not long after, on a soft spring evening, they walked through the old orchard down to the sea, along the shoreline and up the cliff path towards the holy well.

'I've got a special treat for you,' said Jonathan.

'Can I guess?'

'You can try, but I don't think you'll be able to, even with your vivid imagination!'

He'd stopped and was pointing ahead.

'Follow this path up till you come to a little stream with stepping stones across it. But don't cross it – instead turn right inland alongside it.'

'You're not coming with me?'

'I want you to discover it for yourself.'

She laughed. 'You make it sound like a treasure hunt.'

'I suppose it is, in a way,' he said. 'Off you go! I'll see you there in a few minutes.'

When he arrived he found her sitting on the grassy bank in front of the well, lost in contemplation. He wasn't sure she was quite aware he'd joined her, but finally she spoke, slowly and quietly.

'I love the way the little structure belongs to the living rock behind it… the stone-vaulted roof makes it like a cave… and that clear pool's always being secretly refreshed.'

She paused for a while.

'This is such a special place.'

'It's a holy well,' he said. 'It goes back centuries.'

'What a blessing, having this right on your doorstep.'

'Doubly blessed I can share it with you.'

They remained in amiable silence while the evening shadows lengthened, the air cooled, and the world closed down for another night.

In the dusk of that summer evening they walked back to the mill house without a word. As they walked, Sophie reached for his hand, gripping firmly and squeezing it. She knew this was a special moment, of Jonathan reaching the end of a long exile from human intimacy. She wanted him passionately – and was certain he felt the same.

But not tonight. She sensed that too – that to wait a little longer would make things so much more fulfilling, for both of them.

They didn't part hands until they got back to the mill. Their embrace was longer and more intimate this time, their lips lingering on each other's until, by mutually reluctant consent, Sophie thanked him for 'an unforgettable evening', and drove off at her customary ill-advised speed up the track.

Sophie came back the very next night. The weather was unseasonably chilly and Jonathan had kept the range on all day to keep the house warm.

They walked, but it was rain-soaked. When they got back he offered Sophie some towels which had been warming above the range while he went upstairs to change. When he came down he found her sitting in a chair in front of the open range, clad only in one of inadequate towels, with her long legs and wet hair glistening in the firelight.

'Sorry,' he said, rather awkwardly, 'do you need another towel?'

'Not really.' She gave him a slight smile. 'It's just that my clothes are so damp I can't bear to put them back on yet. I thought I could dry them over the range while we have supper.'

He poured some wine, and they sat at table to eat baked potatoes with a chopped ham and cheese topping and lots of butter, before returning to sit in front of the range, basking in its warm glow. As they talked, they looked at each other with ever increasing affection. She thought how good he looked with his tousled wet hair, and so relaxed. He was captivated by her body and her face, shining with health in the heat of the fire.

'You know the other evening, how we said we were both searching?' he said, getting up and refilling their glasses.

'Of course I do – why, have you discovered what it was you're looking for?'

'I think I'm on the right track.' He handed back her glass. 'I want to tell you something I've kept to myself for far too long, which might help you make some sense of me.'

'You sound awfully serious.'

'It is serious – but it's not heavy, if that's what you're thinking. In fact you might think it's just weird, or hilarious – or both.'

"Curiouser and curiouser' – go on, tell me.'

'A few years ago I thought I knew what I wanted to do with my life. So I entered a monastery as a novice to 'test my vocation', as the religious put it.'

He was still standing and watching her carefully. She was looking back at him wide-eyed.

'Go on,' she said gently.

'I was there for nearly two years, but couldn't stay the course. So I left and returned to architecture. But I guess part of me has never left the abbey, which is why, until I met you, I was so tentative about letting myself go with anyone. Meeting you has changed all that.'

Sophie looked across the hearth – then rose and threw herself into his arms, nearly losing her towel in the process.

'You dear, dear man!'

They held each other tight for ages. Sophie spoke first.

'Well,' she announced, 'I'm certainly not going home tonight. It's not often you get lucky with a monk!'

They both fell about laughing.

'I want you to stay, believe me,' Jonathan said. 'I've wanted it ever since we met at Tremaine.'

'Me too.'

'I'll just go upstairs and tidy up a bit – '

'God, Jonathan, don't you think you've teased me long enough?'

He almost laughed. 'Just stay down here in the warm. I really won't be long.'

His bedroom boasted a large brass bedstead Anna had persuaded him to buy at one of the auctions. He put on some clean sheets and made it look comfortable and inviting. Just for a moment, he had a flash of self-doubt.

But, going downstairs again, it vanished the second he saw her.

'It's all ready.'

'I want you now!'

She rose and moved close to him, her eyes smiling, her lips slightly open, her almost naked body pressed against his. She kissed him softly but briefly on the lips, then slipped away up the stairs, aware his eyes were following her every move, turning and smiling and letting the towel drop away completely as she reached the top of the stairs.

He watched her go, aching with desire. He hurriedly put more fuel in the range to keep it in overnight, and bounded upstairs. She was lying on her side, looking towards the door.

'You've been far too long, darling!' she murmured. 'Come and join me in this lovely bed of yours.'

She reached out her arms to him and this time they kissed long and deeply, with him drawing himself up next to her as they slid down to lie side by side.

'Oh for goodness sake, get into bed with me, these sheets and blankets are coming between us,' she laughed. 'And take those clothes off!'

He did as she commanded. Her body was warm and welcoming and infinitely desirable. Wordlessly now they fell into each other, hungrily but tenderly, their vulnerabilities exposed, their couplings passionate, thrilling, and comforting in equal measure. All their anxieties and inhibitions dissolved in the joy of their togetherness as they cried out at the unexpected delights of each other. They laughed too as their lovemaking was accompanied by a veritable percussion of rattles, creaks and shudders of the old bedstead. They were liberated, almost childlike in their playfulness.

The night passed in a blur of intense lovemaking punctuated by periods of gentle dozing in the warmth of the other's body until, at dawn, they finally lay exhausted and sank into blissful oblivion.

Jonathan woke after the deepest sleep he'd had in years, and reached out dreamily, his eyes still closed, to find Sophie. But the bed was empty. He started into life and raced downstairs, to find her gone, but a note on the kitchen table.

'Darling, please don't think badly of me, but I've had to rush away early because I've just realised I have to finish off a piece I promised to a client by close of play today. But please, please, please, can we reprise our lovemaking soon? S XXX'

He read it several times, delirious with the joy of new love, rubbing his eyes to convince himself he wasn't having some sort of fantasy.

Did all that really happen?

He reprised the events of the last twenty-four hours in his head over and over again. Yes, it had, and he was in love with the most amazing woman he'd ever met.

God, look at the time – nearly ten o'clock – Caroline'll kill me!

He gulped down a cup of strong coffee and drove off at Sophie speed to the office.

TWENTY-TWO
Early May 1968

Within a couple of weeks Sophie had moved into the mill house, an arrangement warmly endorsed by Ted and Anna. That Sophie was fascinated by their vision for Hall fuelled Jonathan's determination to get on with the plans, and he started working feverishly on a detailed scheme he could show to potential funders.

But there were puzzling gaps in his survey. The old granary, on the first floor of the south wing of the farmhouse and accessed by an external stone stair, was a particular mystery. He'd already noticed its fine arched roof and guessed it must have been one of the most important rooms in the mediaeval house. But its conversion to a granary had completely hidden its walls behind timber grain bins, making further investigation into its original purpose impossible. He explained to Ted and Anna he'd have to strip out the bins so he could have a proper look at what, from the outside, looked like blocked-up windows, and they'd agreed readily.

He asked Sophie whether she'd be interested in helping.

'Fancy some detective work in the old granary?'

'What are we looking for?'

'We need to strip off some of the timber cladding so I can see the walls behind. Better get togged up, though – it'll be filthy work I'm afraid.'

She laughed. 'Darling, can I just remind you I'm the one whose working days are spent in clouds of dust while you're cossetted in your smart office!'

They started by dragging away a couple of bins from the far end of the granary. The wall behind turned out to be a rough, uneven surface covered with cobwebs and the dust of ages.

Sophie blew a stray strand of hair out of her dusty face. 'Not much to see, is there?'

'Doesn't look very promising, but let's give it bit of a brush.'

They gently removed some of the surface debris, and with the aid of a stronger light they were able to see the outlines of several former openings – blocked to keep vermin out of the grain no doubt. One such opening caught Jonathan's eye – it was narrower and taller than the others, and had an arched head. Near the top, the masonry looked precarious.

'It's a very unusual shape,' he said, squinting in the dim light. 'Definitely not a window, there's no evidence of any opening like that outside.'

'So what could it could be?'

'Don't know yet. I'll go and get a ladder so we can reach the top. And I'd better ask Ted and Anna whether they'd mind us doing a bit of poking around.'

Sophie was practically squirming with excitement. 'Just don't be too long, I can't wait!'

Jonathan bumped into Anna and Ted in the yard.

'We were just coming to see how you were getting on,' said Anna, 'we don't want to miss anything.'

'Well, I think we've made some kind of discovery, but I'm not sure what. Come on up – we need a ladder and your go-ahead to do a bit more investigation.'

'Go ahead,' said Ted, 'but don't go too mad.'

Together they climbed the steps to the granary where Sophie was waiting. She'd done a bit more cleaning-up, and the wall surface was more visible now, along with the outline of the blocked opening.

'Hello Sophie, he's recruited you to the workforce now, has he?' Ted laughed. 'Well, we certainly need all the help we can get. Now, what is it you think you've found? All I can see is a bit of rough old wall.'

'It's this blocked opening,' said Jonathan.

'Why's that special? Isn't it just another bit of farmer's bodging-up?'

'This one's a curious shape – look, it's tall and narrow and with what looks like an arched top. I can't think what it's for – it's quite different from the other blockings, which were windows.'

'How do we find out more?' Anna said.

'As I'm sure you can see,' Jonathan said, pointing, 'the top stones look pretty wobbly. What I'd like to do is very carefully tease out one or two so we can see whether there's anything behind which might give us more of a clue.'

'Go on,' said Ted, 'we're as keen as you are. Always been a bit of a mystery, this granary, with its fancy roof.'

Aware he'd raised expectations, Jonathan climbed the ladder to the top of the arch. Close up, the stonework was in worse condition than he'd thought, near collapse. He came down.

'I think we should move the ladder to a more stable location,' he said, 'and it'd be best if everyone took a few steps back, out of harm's way. Sophie, could you hold the torch for me, and point it just at the top – ' he indicated the peak of the arch ' – so I'll have both my hands free?'

More gingerly this time, he ascended, while the Northcotts watched with wide eyes and Sophie shone the torch steadily at the spot he'd pointed out. He identified three stones right at the top of the arch which were just resting on each other, all the mortar long since crumbled into dust.

He reached out and felt around the topmost stone. To his relief, it was free and lifted out easily with a bit of wiggling. Taking it to the ground and returning twice more to remove the other two stones, he was then able to take the torch back up and shine it into the newly revealed recess.

What he saw was the head of a mediaeval arch with beautifully carved stone tracery which seemed to be the front to a plastered niche behind. What could it be? His knowledge of mediaeval architecture was rudimentary, but he sensed this was a major find.

'Well, come on,' Sophie called up. 'Don't keep us in suspense – what is it?'

'It's remarkable' he replied as he climbed down. 'It's a lovely arched head to a recess – must be mediaeval. But I've no idea what it's for – and it'll need a lot more careful investigation before we can be sure how much survives.'

'Can we all go up and have a look?' asked Anna excitedly.

'Of course, but don't touch the masonry – it's all loose near the top.'

Anna went first, followed by Sophie, with Ted last. As each of them shone the torch into the opening they let out little cries of surprise, Ted's the more measured.

'I'm all for getting the whole blocking cleared out now!' Anna said.

'So am I!' Sophie chimed in.

'Hold on,' said Ted, 'let's not get too carried away. Jonathan's warned us it's pretty dangerous – I'd rather nobody get crushed by a pile of rocks just because we were in a hurry!'

Jonathan wiped some of the grime off his forehead and shot Ted a grateful nod. 'Quite right. I wouldn't be happy with us pushing on just now. And to be honest, I'm out of my comfort zone about what might turn out to be quite an important mediaeval feature – I think we need some expert advice before we do anything else.'

'Good idea,' Ted said, clearly relieved at the excuse for a pause. 'Tell you what, why don't we ask Leo? He's a bit of an expert and he'll not cost us anything either. And he's not 'official' so we won't get held up by anyone.'

Jonathan went to see Leo at the rectory the following morning on his way to work. The rector was intrigued and agreed to come over to Hall that very evening. They all gathered in the granary as Leo climbed up to make his own inspection of the evidence.

When he finally descended, he had a thoughtful look.

'You've made an extraordinary find,' he said. 'As you thought Jonathan, it's clearly an arched head of late mediaeval date – I would think late fifteenth century. It's of remarkable quality, and well preserved.'

'What is it, and what on earth's it for?' asked Anna eagerly.

'It looks like the head of a recess, because the void behind it retains its original plaster. But what it's for is a mystery. The best way to start finding out would be to remove the rest of the rubble infill.'

'If you agree,' Jonathan told Ted and Anna, 'I'll get a couple of boards to support the lower part of the infill while I take more of the upper part down.'

'Go ahead,' Ted said. 'We should get on with it, at least we'll know then what we're dealing with.'

With the support in place, Jonathan began to tease out more rubble from the top of the infill. It was a slow process but the stones came out easily enough, the mortar holding it together little more than dry sand. The tracery was now clearly visible and, after an hour's patient work and with Sophie's help, the whole recess was revealed. Though there was murmured conversation during the unblocking, they awaited Leo's verdict with a mixture of impatience and excitement.

When he finally he spoke, they hung on his every word. 'I can't quite believe what I'm seeing,' he said quietly but confidently, 'but I'm pretty sure what you've discovered is an image niche.'

'What on earth's that?' Anna said.

'It's a recess in a religious building where a figure of the Blessed Virgin Mary or one of the saints might be placed.'

'So what's an image niche doing here?' Anna said.

'I don't know for certain,' Leo said slowly, 'but I've been looking at the fine mediaeval roof in here, and can you see how it gets more elaborate towards this end – the timbers are more richly moulded and the bosses at the intersections are larger and more elaborately carved too. And I think this is the east end of the granary, isn't it?'

'Yes it is,' Ted said 'because the front of the house – the bit we live in – faces east, and this south wing runs back west from it. Is that significant?'

'It is,' Leo said, 'because if you put all the evidence together – the position and orientation of this room in the mediaeval house, its roof being more sumptuously decorated at the east end, and this niche being near the east end as well – it all points to this having once been the chapel to the old house.'

'That's amazing!' Anna said, 'we never thought this place would have had a chapel. Your uncle never discovered anything about a chapel in his researches, Ted, did he?'

'No, but then he wouldn't have been looking for one,' Ted said – with a note of anxiety lurking in his voice. 'Can we do anything else to prove your theory, Leo?'

'We can see whether there are any other features like this up here,' said Leo. 'That means stripping out the rest of the bins and boarding. And I could take a look in the diocesan record office to see whether there's any mention of a licence for a chapel at Hall in the mediaeval bishops' registers.' He tilted his head, curiously. Clearly, he'd picked up on Ted's worry. 'If that's perfectly all right with you, of course.'

'I swear I'm as excited as the rest of you,' Ted said, 'It's just… we've had so many problems with the council. I'm worried this might create difficulties for us – you know, all the experts coming in and telling us it's so important we can't touch it, or we must do something very expensive to repair it but not be able to use it. At best it might delay things, at worst it could scupper us – and just when we'd started making progress.'

Jonathan caught Sophie's eye – her lips were parted, but he shook his head, just once.

'I can understand how you feel,' Leo said. 'I'm constantly being told what I can or can't do by the diocesan experts. But I genuinely think this discovery might actually help rather than hinder.'

'I don't see how,' said Ted.

'Because it adds to the importance of the building – surviving domestic chapels of this date are very rare. It will have to be kept for posterity. And keeping it going has to mean finding a new use for it – there are more than enough 'monuments' just standing around looking gloomy.'

'I'm with Leo, Ted, on that line of thought,' Jonathan said, finally perceiving his opening. 'I'd even dare to hope we might get funding for its repair.'

Ted looked reassured by this, so Anna weighed in.

'I think we should be really positive about this,' she said. 'You never know, it might even inspire us in some way. What do you think the next steps are, Jonathan?'

'We should do what Leo suggests – a bit more investigation, get an expert we can trust to be discreet to look at the niche and anything else we find.'

Sophie – whose attention had wandered back to the niche, over the beams, and the space in general – finally chimed in.

'I think this space has got a wonderful serenity about it,' she said softly, 'which people would find very attractive.'

'It does have a peaceful feel,' Leo said. 'If we're right about it having been the chapel, just think how many prayers must have been said here over the centuries.'

At that, Jonathan was pleased to see, Ted's frozen anxiety seemed to thaw a little. For his own part, Jonathan had been thinking the same, and how very much it reminded him of the holy well – hallowed by use.

'Well, it's been a most interesting evening,' Leo said. 'Thank you so much for inviting me over. Haven't enjoyed myself so much for ages! But if you would excuse me, there are a few tasks I need to tackle before the end of the day.'

'Thank you for coming, Leo, it was me you've got to blame for getting you over,' Ted replied with a warm smile. 'I'm taken with those words, and yours too Sophie – I promise we'll give this a lot of thought. I'm inspired too, you know, just takes me a bit longer than the rest of you to get there!'

TWENTY-THREE

May 1968

Anna was well aware of Ted's sensitivity. Years of farming had made him wary of sudden changes of tack – his family crest, if he had one, would surely have read 'hasten slowly'. Somehow, she knew she'd need to navigate a course between Ted's caution – he'd already been obsessing over costs – and everyone else's enthusiasm, including her own.

The best option would be to ask Jonathan to soft-pedal on the granary for a while, but that wasn't going to be easy, now the rest of them had got the bit between their teeth.

It took a few days before an opportunity arose for her to catch him without either Ted or Sophie around. But one morning she was in the lane when he drove past on his way to work. She hailed him down.

'Have you got a moment?'

'Yes, of course.' He switched off the Volvo's engine and leaned out of the window.

'It's about the granary.'

'Ah, sorry, I'm afraid I haven't done anything more about that since Leo's visit.' He looked distinctly guilty. 'This Broadhaven housing's taking up all my time at the moment.'

'Maybe that's just as well, from my point of view anyway.' At his puzzled expression, she continued.

'It's just that, I'm sure you'll have realised, we need to be extra careful, you know… making sure Ted's on board about any more 'poking around.'

To her relief, Jonathan gave her a nod of understanding as he leaned on the window. 'I got the sense when Leo was here that we needed to tread a bit carefully.'

'If we can do that, he'll be all for it in the end.' She bit her lip. 'But there's something else – something to keep between the two of us.'

'You have my word, Anna.'

He got out of the car and came to stand alongside her in the lane.

'I'm a bit bothered about him, Jonathan.' Her tone was steady, but serious. 'He's been struggling with some of the heavier jobs around the farm. Then about two months ago he had a dizzy spell while he was working in the cliff fields. It's been the devil's own job to get him to see Dr Colville, but he did eventually, a couple of weeks ago. He was sent for tests at the hospital last week and we're waiting for the results.'

Jonathan paused before replying.

'I'm so sorry to hear that. You'll both be on tenterhooks till you know something, but it's got to be the sensible thing to do.'

She turned away as she spoke, feeling her throat begin to tighten as her eyes went suddenly bleary.

'It may turn out just to be him overdoing it. But he's worrying himself silly – all the worst possible outcomes of course…'

Jonathan put an arm around her shoulder.

'I can imagine. Men are hopeless about medical stuff – we either ignore the symptoms, or assume we're at death's door.' A little awkwardly, he patted her shoulder. 'And us all getting so excited about the granary won't have helped. Is there anything I can do?'

'I hate to say it, but I think it best if we put a brake on the granary for a bit.'

He took his arm away and waited for her to dry her eyes and face him.

‘Message received,’ he said, with a slight smile. ‘But you do want me to continue with the rest of the project?’

‘Yes, that’s really important.’

‘Good.’ He laid a hand on the door of the Volvo. ‘Well… I’d better get off to the office I suppose.’

‘Thank you, Jonathan. I knew you’d understand.’

He got back into the car. Anna waved him on his way and walked back to the house, breathing a deep sigh of relief.

◈

But they’d both reckoned without Father Leo’s enthusiasm. There was hardly anything which gave him more pleasure in his spare time than historical research. He was a familiar figure in the diocesan record office, a miraculous survivor of a bygone age. Housed in a wing of the old bishop’s palace, the bookish aroma of the search room was to be treated with as much reverence as incense at the altar.

The office was presided over by the diminutive figure of Miss Audrey Elkins, who’d been the archivist for longer than anyone could remember. She was a recognised authority on mediaeval ecclesiastical history, and an expert on the mediaeval bishops’ registers.

‘Hello Father,’ she said, glancing up from her desk as Leo stepped through the door. ‘It’s a pleasure to see you again.’

‘Likewise, Miss Elkins, you know how much I always appreciate your help with my little researches.’

‘I wouldn’t say they were little, Father!’ She beamed. ‘You’ve made some important discoveries over the years. How might I help you today?’

‘Well, I may be on to quite something this time. I think I’ve come across a previously unknown mediaeval domestic chapel.’

‘That would be remarkable. Where is it, if I may ask?’

‘At a farm called Hall, near Michaelchurch. Great rambling old pile of a place. And pretty remote too. We’ve discovered what looks like an image niche in a first-floor room which has been used as a granary for at least a century.’

'About what date do you think it is?'

'From the tracery, I'm putting it at late fifteenth century.'

'So you're after the bishop's registers for that period?'

'Precisely. If we could find a bishop's licence for saying Mass at Hall at that time, it would clinch the argument, wouldn't it?'

'It would certainly take you a giant stride towards proving it. If you give me a few minutes, I'll go to the strongroom and find the relevant volumes. We may be in luck, they're complete and particularly full of detail for that period.'

It was no hardship for Leo to amuse himself perusing some of the leather-bound volumes around him as Miss Elkins went on her mission. She returned looking triumphant and carrying a heavy document case.

'I've found it! Let's lay it out over here and see what we can find.' She dropped it on the reading table with a bit of a thump. 'Late fifteenth century you say. So let's start at 1450 and work through to 1500.'

They both leaned over the table, straining to scrutinise the fine lines of handwritten text, Miss Elkins deciphering the more obscure references and phrases in mediaeval Latin. Just when Leo's eyes were beginning to feel the strain, Miss Elkins suddenly straightened up.

'Here it is, Father – a licence to celebrate Mass in a chapel at Hall, dedicated to St Mary Magdalene. And it's dated May 1477.'

'That's wonderful, Miss Elkins!' He winced a little as he straightened up after so long stooped over the register. 'I can't thank you enough. It'll make a huge difference to the people at Hall to know this.'

'Well Father, I'm glad to be of help to you. Now, after all that excitement, and if you can spare a few minutes, I think you should come into my office and we'll celebrate with a cup of tea and a biscuit.

I've got a couple of things I'd value your thoughts on.'

Though he could hardly contain his excitement, Leo knew he

mustn't rush the Northcotts. It was late afternoon when he got back to Michaelchurch, and he went straight over to the office to see if he could catch Jonathan.

'Hello Emma,' Leo called out as he opened the front door of Atherton & Green.

'Oh, hello Father Leo, I was just about to shut up shop. Are you looking for Tony?'

'I'm after Jonathan actually.'

'You're in luck, he's still here. Why don't you go on up?'

He found Jonathan at work at his drawing board, one pencil in hand and another absently tucked behind his ear. At the sound of the rector's footsteps he lifted his head.

'Leo, good to see you – to what do I owe this pleasure?'

'I'm the bearer of some exciting news. I've just come back from the diocesan record office, and I've found a clear entry in the bishops' registers to a chapel at Hall. And there's a date – 1477 – and a dedication too, to St Mary Magdalene!'

'Brilliant, Leo – well done! I can't thank you enough.'

'That said,' Leo continued, 'I appreciate it might not be what Ted wants to hear at present. I thought I'd best sound you out before I shared the news.'

Jonathan nodded. 'He is a bit low just now. But Anna's sure he'll come round, given time – I appreciate you letting me know first. In the meantime, is there anything else we could be doing?'

'We'll still need some expert help at some point, to stabilise the image niche – and look for any further evidence of the chapel.'

For a moment, Jonathan looked almost as pensive as Ted. 'To borrow a phrase from our mutual friend, 'that sounds expensive."

'Leave it with me,' Leo said. 'I've got a contact in the British Museum who owes me a favour. I'll see whether I get us some advice, gratis.'

'That would be great, thanks so much. I'll keep you posted on how things are with the Northcotts – and Leo? … best to hold off getting anyone on site till I tip you the wink.'

TWENTY-FOUR

June 1968

About a fortnight later, as Jonathan was collecting some milk and eggs from the farm dairy, Anna called out from the kitchen door, a sunny smile on her face.

'Jonathan!' She stepped out into the yard. 'Good news – the results of Ted's hospital tests. He's got what they call a 'chronic but treatable' heart condition. It explains why he's been feeling so tired. They're hopeful once they've sorted out the right medication he'll be feeling much better.'

'That's terrific Anna. Such a relief – I bet that's cheered him up!'

'Certainly has – seems to have revitalised him!'

Jonathan shifted his pail of eggs from one hand to the other. 'So, do you think he's ready to talk about the granary, or shall I hold off for a bit longer?'

'That's why I wanted to catch you. He's raring to go! Why don't you and Sophie come over for supper tomorrow evening, if you're free?'

'I'll check with her, but I'm sure we'd love to.'

They were amazed to see the change in Ted. When they told him about Leo's discovery in the archives, he bubbled with enthusiasm.

'Good old Leo! Now look, I've been doing a lot of thinking recently, and I've come up with an idea about the future of the granary. But you've both been so brilliant I wanted your thoughts.' Ted topped them all up on a round of cider. 'Do you think the granary could work as part of the study centre?'

'What have you got in mind?'

'Up to now we've been planning to repair the back ranges of the house, including the granary, and convert them to holiday cottages. But I've realised we're going to have enough on our plate building the study centre – we'll be too stretched financially to do both at the moment. And anyway, I can't see us being allowed to make the granary part of a holiday let.'

This was not quite what Jonathan was expecting.

'Sorry Ted, you've lost me. I understand the financial issues of course – but are you saying you want to shelve the work on the back ranges?'

'No, not at all. I was thinking, why can't we make the granary into some kind of communal space for the studies centre? A bit apart from the hurly-burly of the rest, somewhere students and teachers could find a bit of peace and quiet? The idea came from what Sophie and Leo said about it having a peaceful atmosphere. I've been going up there on my own, and I'm convinced, yes, it really does have a special feel.'

There was a pause before anyone responded. Eventually it was Jonathan who spoke, slowly, as he thought through the implications.

'I think you've hit on the best possible solution, Ted. You're right about needing to rethink what we do with the granary now we've established its likely significance. We need more expert advice, and I'm convinced once the experts have seen it, they'll be as excited as we are. They'll be dead keen to find a use for it of the sort you've got in mind – and that'll increase the chances of getting funds to repair it.'

'So, next steps?' Ted really did have the bit between his teeth.

'Leo thinks he's got a friend who can help – for no charge, if I understood him right.'

Leo's friend at the British Museum, it turned out, was a specialist on mediaeval domestic chapels: Professor Gwyneth Evans. Within a few weeks Leo phoned to say she was staying with him and he'd like to bring her over to Hall. She was a large lady with an intense gaze through her wire-framed glasses, very Welsh, passionately interested in her subject and mustard keen to get on with her investigation.

'I hope we haven't got you here under false pretences, Professor,' Jonathan said as they climbed the steps to the granary.

'I'm sure not,' she said, 'Leo has an instinct, and I've never known him not to have found something of interest – so I always come running when he calls!'

She spent some time at the top of the ladder, teasing off some of the loose lime wash from the tracery of the arched head and inside the niche with surgical precision.

'This is very exciting,' she called down. 'It is certainly an image niche. It would have been coloured originally – I've found some tiny patches of red, green and gold as the background for the figure.'

'It's all a bit crumbly,' Ted said, 'can we save it?'

'It's in remarkable condition, given it's nearly five hundred years old – blocking it in seems to have done it a favour!'

'Is there more to discover up here?'

'It would be well worth getting a conservator to come and have a proper look when the other openings are unblocked – and consolidate the niche.'

'Can you recommend someone?' Ted asked. 'We're keen to get on now – we don't want to delay things.'

'It shouldn't hold up anything,' the professor said. 'And I know someone who could come more or less straight away – one of my most promising students, Esther Gracie, who's looking for work experience of exactly this kind.'

'Would she be expensive?' Anna said, with a sideways glance at Ted.

'If you could put her up here on the farm, I can get the Museum to pay her other expenses because it's an essential part of her training.'

'I'm sure we can find room for her,' said Anna. 'Or would she like to camp, if the weather's good? We've got a lovely campsite just below the orchard with glimpses of the sea.'

'That sounds just up Esther's street. I'll get on to her straight away.'

The professor was as good as her word and Esther Gracie arrived a week later. She seemed schoolgirl-like with her slender figure and shy demeanour, but worked with great enthusiasm. Jonathan and Sophie dropped in on her every evening, and often invited her to join them for supper. Since Esther was particularly interested in sculpture, Sophie invited her to her studio to watch her at work.

Esther painstakingly investigated the other blocked openings and made another significant discovery. In the south wall, near its junction with the east wall, was another much more modest niche with a stone bowl housed in it and a drain in its base. Everyone came together one evening to take a look.

'It's a piscina, for the washing of the holy vessels for Mass, I think – isn't that right Father?' she asked Leo.

'It is indeed. It's exactly where you'd expect it to be – to the right of altar – and indisputable evidence this was the chapel.'

'That's wonderful!' Ted rubbed his hands together with almost childlike enthusiasm. 'What better than to have a place where the washing up was done in a room we want to use as a communal space!'

'I can't quite believe it,' Anna said with a smile of equal delight. 'It feels like fortune's shining on us for once!'

'We can't thank you enough, Esther – and you too, Leo, of course,' Ted said. 'We'll have quite a party when we've got the project going!'

TWENTY-FIVE

July 1968

Ted's enthusiasm for the granary quickly morphed into the zeal of the convert. He got Jonathan to write a piece for the *Gazette*, inviting people to see their discoveries, which attracted a number of visitors to the farm. Colonel Hughes, one of Leo's churchwardens and a respected local historian, was particularly gracious, admitting he'd never discovered any mention of a chapel at Hall in his researches.

Horace Penhaligan turned up too – Ted thought it worth giving him a personal tour of the whole farmstead as well as the granary. Penhaligan took an unusual interest in the whole site, so the Northcotts offered him a cup of tea and some cake when they returned to the farmhouse.

'Fine old place you'm got 'ere, Ted, Anna. Always thought so, I 'ave,' said Penhaligan, supping his tea appreciatively.

'Thanks, Horace,' Ted said. 'We're very lucky to have it.'

'I should say so. This chapel business's real special though.'

'We're hoping it'll be a real asset for us,' said Anna.

'Goin' to cost a fair bit to put 'im right though, I'm thinking?'

'Yes, but it's an important part of our project now,' Ted said. 'We'll be coming to talk to the council about it all soon.'

'Look forward to that – could do a lot with this place, with the right scheme of course. What this area needs is serious money comin' in to turn us round.'

'We've got Atherton & Green on the job, so we're hoping to come up with something special,' said Anna.

'I knows you 'ave – got to know Mr Lane a bit, 'e's always comin' in the store for somethin' or other. 'E tells me 'e's working up a big old project – you got the funds for it?'

'We hope to get a fair bit of funding,' Anna said, a little more reserved now, 'but that depends on getting it through the council.'

'Ah, mustn't say too much then, me being Chairman an' all. Better be off now.'

'That went well,' Anna said, once he'd gone – though her tone was cautious.

'He made the right noises,' Ted said. 'But strange him asking about funding – none of his business really, is it?'

'You never know with Horace, so many irons in the fire.' Anna sighed. 'We'll just have to hope he's on our side when the plans come up before the council.'

Among the many visitors, the only one who put Ted's back up was Richard Forrester, a young property developer who'd not long arrived in the area and already earned a reputation as quite an operator. Good looking with an easy charm, people took to him immediately.

'Mrs Northcott, I don't think I've had the pleasure.' He offered Anna a firm handshake. 'I'm Richard Forrester – Ricky to my friends.'

'Pleased to meet you Mr Forrester,' Anna said. 'I hope you like our little discoveries?'

'They're very interesting, very interesting indeed. What a wonderful old place you've got here, bags of potential.'

'We certainly think so.'

'I don't want to appear presumptuous, but you might be interested to know I'm acting for some major developers from London who are looking for suitable properties in this area.'

'Why would I be interested?'

'Because this is just the sort of place they're looking for.'

'Well, I'm sorry to disappoint you, but we've plans of our own.'

'What a pity!' Forrester said. 'They'd be prepared to offer a very large sum to secure it, much more than its market value.'

Anna frowned. 'Why would they do that?'

'Because they'd want to help realise its potential – to develop the whole farm into a premier holiday village. It's the coming thing.'

Anna felt her cheeks flush. 'It may well be, Mr Forrester, but it's not the scheme for us.'

Ted was furious when Anna told him – as much for Forrester's effrontery in approaching Anna without him as for assuming they'd be interested in selling up.

'The bloody nerve,' he muttered, as they were washing up in the kitchen.

'Do you think we should mention it to Jonathan?'

Ted waved the plate he was drying, with a little too much energy. 'Why mention it if we're not interested?' With a huff, he set the dish in the rack. 'No, he has enough on his plate. Best let him get on with it.'

Tony Green suggested it might be wise to invite the man from the council with whom they'd had a run-in over the campsite, just to smooth things over. Ted wasn't exactly relishing the prospect, but agreed it was sensible – and also agreed to let Jonathan do most of the talking.

It was a serious-looking young man who arrived at the farmhouse door, and Jonathan, as promised, handled the introductions.

'Dr Julian Manners, I believe you've met Mr Northcott,' he said.

'Ah yes, I've had the pleasure.' He was a short man with an unexpectedly deep voice, and spoke with exaggerated slowness. 'But not of meeting you, Mrs Northcott, or indeed you, Mr Lane, though we've spoken on the phone.'

Anna and Jonathan had to suppress their smiles at his heavy tweeds with waistcoat on a very warm day, not to mention what Jim Jewell would undoubtedly call 'town shoes'. A gold Hunter pocket watch on a gold chain across his chest, immaculately groomed hair and a goatee beard completed the ensemble.

After a round of handshakes, he continued. 'Now, I'm given to understand you have something of interest to show me?'

Ted was already frowning.

'We think so,' said Jonathan, stepping in quickly. 'I don't believe you saw the house or farm buildings on your previous visit about the campsite, Dr Manners, so would you like to take a look at those first?'

'If you don't mind,' Dr Manners said, 'I always like to begin with the matter in hand – this supposed mediaeval chapel you told me about on the phone. I'm a bit of an authority on mediaeval ecclesiastical architecture,' he added. 'I may be able to confirm your hunches.'

Jonathan noticed Ted rolling his eyes, as did Anna – who shot her husband a look of stern warning.

'Of course, we wouldn't want to waste your time,' Jonathan said.

'Let's go straight up to the granary, then.'

He led the little party round the house, up the broad stone steps, and into the granary. Since the windows had been unblocked, a warm light filtered in.

'You'll see the first thing which caught our attention is the fine mediaeval roof,' said Jonathan.

'Ah, yes, let me get a look.' Dr Manners reached a hand into his jacket. 'You wouldn't object to my pipe? I find it aids my analysis.'

'Not unless you intend to set the place on fire,' Ted said.

'I promise to take the greatest of care, Mr Northcott,' said Manners, a little coolly. 'I am exceptionally conscious of my responsibilities.'

He produced a tobacco tin and pipe, and made quite the ceremony of filling and lighting it, before he began puffing away leisurely while staring upwards, peering at the roof.

'Late fifteenth century from the look of it,' he announced eventually. 'It's a very good example, and I see it gets more elaborate at the far end?'

'Yes, and that's significant,' Jonathan said, 'because it's the east end where we've made our discoveries. Come and take a look.' He led him through towards the ladder, which was at this point a fixture. 'Here's the image niche, and on the opposite wall over there is the piscina.'

Manners produced a small notebook; Jonathan saw he was making accomplished sketches of some details as he undertook a lengthy investigation of all the visible evidence. The others waited in respectful, though in Ted's case grudging, silence until he was ready to deliver his verdict.

'It does indeed look very much like a chapel. As I said, my specialism is ecclesiastical architecture of this period, so I'm very interested indeed.' He paused to adjust his spectacles. 'Surviving domestic chapels of this date are rare, except in great houses, of course.'

'So we were given to understand,' said Ted, despite a pleading, shushing motion from Anna. 'By someone from the British Museum.'

'May I ask who?'

'Professor Gwyneth Evans,' Jonathan said. 'She also found us a specialist who did some initial consolidation of our finds.'

'Professor Evans is one of the top people in my field,' Manners said, his tone suddenly much warmer. 'I've never had the good fortune to meet her, but I've learned so much from what she's published. You've done well to find her – may I ask how?'

'She's an old friend of Father Leo Colchester – the rector of Michaelchurch,' Jonathan said. 'He's the one that tracked down a date of 1477 for the chapel's licencing, and its dedication to St Mary Magdalene, in the bishop's registers for the period.'

'Ah yes, I've met him – quite an expert on local ecclesiastical history, I understand! Well, that is exceptionally interesting.'

Ted had taken to pacing around the other end of the granary, but returned now seemingly at the end of his tether.

'Look,' he said, 'I know all this historical stuff's fascinating, but what matters to us is the future. Can we talk about what we might do with this part of our house?'

'Of course, Mr Northcott,' said Manners. 'I'm afraid I got a bit carried away. Please allow me to congratulate you on your discoveries – it makes this house very special indeed. And you're absolutely right, now you've identified it, the question is, what are you going to do with it?'

While not exactly warming to Manners, Ted seemed to relent at the change in tone.

'Why don't we go to the house and talk about it over a cup of tea?' he said, as Anna gave an encouraging nod. 'If you have time.'

'Thank you, Mr Northcott,' Manners said with a courteous little nod. 'A cup of tea would be most welcome.'

They reassembled in the farmhouse kitchen, with Manners taking great interest in its period features. They sat round the table, tucking into slices of Anna's farmhouse fruit cake, which did a great deal to soften Manners' somewhat stiff demeanour into something more amenable, not to mention pacifying a great deal of Ted's hostility. Sensing this, Jonathan seized the moment.

'Given what we now know about its history, Dr Manners, Mr and Mrs Northcott think the old granary should play a significant role in the rural studies centre we talked about when I phoned about this meeting.'

'I certainly agree it's important enough to warrant careful repair and conservation,' Dr Manners said as he sipped his tea. 'And these days we're keen to encourage appropriate use rather than letting a building just sit there. That way, it stands a better chance of surviving long-term. May I ask what kind of role you see it playing?'

'I'll let Mr and Mrs Northcott explain,' said Jonathan.

'We think it has a special atmosphere,' Ted said, 'which would make it ideal as a quiet space set apart from the main centre – but available to children and teachers – as a peaceful retreat if you like. And we'd make it clear we see this facility as an integral part of the enterprise.'

'That sounds most appropriate,' said Manners. 'It would maintain continuity with its mediaeval function – and such a low-key use might mean it's eligible for public funding towards its repair.' Carefully, he dabbed his lips with a napkin. 'I'd be happy to help point you in the right direction.'

'That would be very welcome,' said Jonathan. 'In light of that... do you feel you'll be able to support us if we go ahead and work up a detailed scheme for the whole site? In consultation with you, of course.'

'As you're probably aware, some of the councillors seem to have taken against such developments recently – '

Ted's expression darkened.

' – but I've had a preliminary word with my colleagues in the office, and they seem happy in principle with your proposal,' he continued – either missing or graciously ignoring Ted's sour turn. 'Speaking of which, I'd very much like to see the old farm buildings while I'm here, if that's possible.'

'Mr and Mrs Northcott would be pleased to show you round.'

Tea finished, the four of them embarked on a tour of the whole farmstead. Somewhat to their surprise, Manners showed appreciation of its history and sympathy to their cause. Still, when he'd gone, they all breathed a sigh of relief.

'I thought it went well,' said Jonathan, as they all returned to the farmhouse kitchen.

'Much better than I expected,' said Ted. 'Didn't take to him at first, but he thawed out eventually – thanks to your cake, Anna!'

'Oh, it was more than that,' said Anna. 'He seemed genuinely interested, not just in the chapel but in our project.'

'I think he is,' said Jonathan. 'He could be an important ally. And given how the political dynamics are down here these days – as I've learned in Broadhaven – we must expect a few bumps in the road.'

'God help us,' said Ted. 'But, for once, I'm going to be the optimist on the basis of this afternoon's encounter with Dr Manners!'

TWENTY-SIX

Early August 1968

Though the Northcotts' enthusiasm to push ahead had provided a distraction, Jonathan's worries about the Broadhaven housing project continued to haunt him. It had finally got on site the previous month, and there was a flurry of meetings as his plans began to translate into road layouts, building plots and foundations.

He and Naomi had agreed a pattern of Monday morning site visits, and that first Monday of August was particularly significant: Naomi was taking a fortnight's leave from the end of the week.

They met at the site office, and as soon as he opened the door he noticed she wasn't her usual cheery self.

'Bet you can't wait to get away,' he said. 'Don't worry – it's all under control.'

She put her finger to her lips and came over to whisper in his ear.

'Let's walk the site.'

A familiar feeling of dread crept over him, and it seemed his legs were made of lead as they stepped out into the fresh summer air.

They reached the high point of the site, which offered a grandstand view of all the construction activity: diggers excavating soil, building materials being unloaded, gangs of men sending up clouds of dust everywhere.

'Exciting, isn't it?' said Naomi, though she looked anything but.

'We've both worked so hard to get it to this point.'

'We're a good team, you and me.'

'We are indeed.' She paused for a moment, her gaze shifting up from the site and out towards the sea. 'But sadly, that can't continue.'

'What do you mean?'

She turned and faced him.

'My secondment's been terminated, with immediate effect – I was told by Walter Johnson when I turned up at the town hall this morning.'

He was momentarily dumbfounded, his worst fears realised. Eventually he found some words.

'Naomi… I'm astonished, and so sorry for you.'

She nodded, but motioned for him to keep walking with her.

'I don't trust anyone anymore,' she said. 'I'm not even supposed to be here, but I wanted to see you, not just to say goodbye but to tell you something which you must promise to keep to yourself.'

More secrets. 'Of course I will.'

'I understand why they want rid of me. As you know, I've been putting together all the evidence I can find in the council records about the awarding of contracts and other financial matters – the use of 'undue influence' to give council contracts to certain favoured firms, over an extended period. In plain English, I've got evidence of long-term fraud and corruption.'

'I don't know what to say – '

'Don't say anything – to *anybody*,' she said. 'This is really serious stuff.'

'But I don't understand why you've been pushed out just now?'

'I've been rumbled by Johnson. He's complained to my bosses in Whitehall that I'd been 'going beyond my brief' – asked one too many questions.'

'That's scandalous – Caroline will be livid, and she'll make a stink about it, I promise – not least because, of course, she'll be terrified the practice could be drawn into a scandal – '

She held up a hand to stall him, looking pained. 'I know this is going to sound weird, but… I need to ask you not to tell Caroline.'

'Naomi, surely now – '

'Just say I've been recalled to London suddenly because I'm needed for another big job – I was only ever on secondment so it'll sound quite plausible.'

'But what about the corruption you've uncovered? It can't all just be swept under the carpet, for God's sake!'

'I know it's difficult for you, Jonathan, but we've got to stay calm about this. As I say, I've got all the evidence – copied from the council files – and I'm taking it all with me. I can assure you this isn't the end of the matter, far from it.' She looked grim. 'The best help you can give me is to stay alert to what's happening down here, make notes and keep a diary of anything which seems suspicious – especially anything about *Beachcomber*.'

'You have my word, I will. But what do I do with anything I find without you here?'

'Keep it to yourself for now. My bosses always knew this was a possibility, so they're OK with Johnson's decision – it simply means I'll continue working on all this from London. We've got other people working on similar lines in other councils, and at some stage we'll be ready to bring it all together. And, to answer your specific question, someone from London will be in touch with you at the appropriate moment.'

They'd looped back along the path and were now near the site office.

'I'm going to say goodbye now.' Naomi smiled. 'It's been great working with you – and maybe we'll meet again in better circumstances.'

'I'm going to miss you such a lot.' Not just because he'd enjoyed working with her, either – what was he to do, on his own, with all the secrets he was keeping?

'And I'll miss you,' she said. 'But it'll go well under your supervision, the shining example of modern public housing we always knew it would be.'

She turned and walked away.

More shaken than he cared to admit, Jonathan performed the bare minimum of tasks he needed to tick off for the day, then drove back to the office via a familiar pub where he consoled himself with a stiff drink.

That evening he shared what he could with Sophie, explaining Naomi's sudden departure as the result of an urgent recall to London, but not holding back about increasing tensions with the town hall.

'I'm pretty shaken up by all this, Soph, I really am,' he said.

'I'm not surprised, darling – but from what you've said, you must have known something might blow up. Naomi sounded pretty high-voltage – I can well imagine she might have sent a few shocks round the town hall circuit board.'

'I suppose so. I only hope her replacement is someone I can work with.'

'I guess you'll just have to bear with whoever it is – at least it's mostly in your court now the project's on site.'

'That's true on the technical side, but the council's in overall control so I've still got to deal with Johnson, the little tinpot dictator.'

'Try not to let it take over your life, darling.' She came over to settle on the arm of his chair, putting her arms round his shoulders. 'There's such a lot of good stuff going on too – not least, us!'

'You're right, love.' He turned to press a kiss to her long dark hair. 'I promise I'll try to not let it spoil this wonderful summer of ours.'

'Good. Now go and open that nice bottle of white I saw in the pantry, and we'll drink to that!'

TWENTY-SEVEN

Late August 1968

'You two doing anything this weekend?' Anna asked Sophie as she dropped by to deliver a parcel to the mill house early one evening.

'Nothing planned yet,' Sophie said. 'I'm hoping Jonathan won't have to work again – he seems more preoccupied with that Broadhaven scheme than ever.'

'Why don't you make him take a break – on Saturday – so you can both come to the Show?'

'The Show?' Sophie wrinkled her nose, bemused.

'*THE Show*, of course!' said Anna, throwing her arms wide. 'The *MICHAELCHURCH* Show, one of the highlights of our year!'

'Oh yes, I've seen the posters in the town – but isn't it just a flower and veg show?'

'Sophie!' Anna gently swatted at her with the dish-towel she held. 'Don't say that around here! It's the main event, not just for us farmers, but the whole community. It's great fun – you'd both enjoy it, I promise. Fancy a cuppa?'

'Yes please, I've got time for a quick one.'

Anna made them two mugs and they sat down at the long kitchen table.

'So, how do I sell this to Jonathan?' Sophie said, blowing a cloud of steam off the surface of her cup.

'Well, the centrepiece is the show ring,' said Anna, 'where we can show off our livestock – it means a lot if we get a prize for one of our animals, a bit of recognition for all our hard work breeding them.'

'I know nothing about farming,' Sophie said with a laugh, 'so I'd certainly learn a lot.'

'And there's so much more – show jumping, sheep and gun dog trials, displays of farm machinery old and new, demonstrations of local crafts – '

'Now that, I'd be very interested in!'

' – food and drink producers offering tasting sessions of their wares – and the best cream teas in the West Country, enjoyed to the music of the town's silver band in the main marquee!'

'Right,' said Sophie, 'I'm hooked – Jonathan will love all that!'

'He's got quite the garden now,' Anna said. 'Tell him he should put something in the flower and veg show, try his chances at a prize!'

The Show was held in a large field on the northern edge of the town, on a fine hot Saturday. It looked like a mediaeval battle encampment with a cluster of large and small marquees and more modest tents set up at varying distances around the ring. Apart from the hedgerow trees, there wasn't a lot of shade, which meant long queues for a cool draught from the beer and cider tents, further fuelling the convivial atmosphere.

Jonathan and Sophie spent some time exploring the displays and demonstrations before starting to sample the food and drink stalls, finally taking their ease on a couple of straw bales in the cider tent.

'Glad you strong-armed me into this,' said Jonathan. 'Everyone seems so relaxed.'

'Including us, I hope! I'm certainly taking a liking to this farmhouse cider – looks odd, being so cloudy, but it's delicious.'

'Good, isn't it? I think it's made by George and Annie Webber. It's just won a prize too.'

'What's good too is seeing you so relaxed – you need to be off duty more often.'

'I am trying, Soph.'

At that moment the ample figure of Horace Penhaligan loomed up, glass in hand, sporting his Chairman's chain of office. He sank down, heavily, on an adjacent bale.

''ello young man. Mind if I joins you?'

'Of course. Good to see you. May I introduce you to Sophie Ryder? Sophie, this is Mr Penhaligan, of the famous Stores of that name.'

'Pleased to meet you Miss. I'm 'Orace to most folk.'

'And I'm pleased to meet you, Horace,' Sophie said graciously. 'Jonathan's told me a lot about you.'

'All good, I 'opes,' said Penhaligan with a genial smile. 'You're not from round 'ere then? – not seen you in my Stores.'

'I'm working in Broadhaven – but I'm living with Jonathan at the old mill house at Hall.'

'Well, good to see you both 'ere – 'tis the place to meet everyone. You'm stopping fur the livestock judging and prize givin' I 'opes? Some of the best beasts in the far west. Them cups and rosettes are right sought after in these parts, they are.'

'We certainly will be,' said Jonathan, 'when does it start?'

'Judgin' goes on all afternoon, presentations at teatime. So, you'll be needin' some more of George and Annie's cider no doubt? – I'll be getting' you some, then.'

'That's kind of you Horace, yes please,' said Sophie.

'Proper job,' said Penhaligan, rumbling off towards the bar.

Jonathan and Sophie had arranged to meet Ted and Anna near four o'clock for a cream tea in the big marquee. It was an impressive sight: in the background, the silver band was playing a selection of old favourites, its music muffled by the buzz of conversation on the long tables set up end to end and laden with jugs of local wild flowers. It seemed all Michaelchurch was there, mingling with visiting holiday makers, everyone tucking enthusiastically into their scones with jam and clotted cream. Mugs of tea were being dispensed from huge urns and served by the ladies of the Women's Institute.

'Isn't this great?' Ted said. 'Shows off the farming community at its best.'

'We're loving every minute,' Sophie said, leaning into Jonathan's side as they sat shoulder to shoulder. 'And I've just had the privilege of being bought a drink by 'Citizen Pen' himself!'

'Never misses a trick, does Horace,' Anna said. 'But then, a bit of liquid refreshment always helps oil the wheels. Must have been the same at harvest time in the old days after all that back-breaking work of getting the crops in – no wonder people let their hair down at the harvest supper after a few drinks!'

At that moment the loudspeaker boomed.

'LADIES AND GENTLEMEN, THE LIVESTOCK JUDGING WILL SHORTLY BE COMPLETED. THEN, FOR FIVE O'CLOCK SHARP, WE INVITE YOU TO GATHER ROUND THE SHOWRING FOR THE PRESENTATIONS!'

'Better finish our tea and get over there,' Ted said. 'We've got a couple of cows in with a chance of the dairy cup. Len's looking after them.'

'I'll just finish that last bit of cake if no-one else wants it,' Jonathan said, 'then I wanted to take a quick look at the old tractors en route – Tony said he was going to be here with his old Massey Ferguson.'

He and Sophie made their way to the tractor enclosure where they found Tony, in flat cap and overalls, proudly explaining the workings of his venerable workhorse to a group of enthusiasts.

'Hello old things!' He threw them both a smile and a quick wave. 'Isn't this old girl a real beauty? I saw her in George Webber's shed years ago, rusting away, so I asked him if I could buy it. He said he'd be pleased if I could take it off his hands, gratis – so I did, and have had many happy hours doing her up!'

'She looks a picture, Tony,' said Jonathan, 'is she in for a prize?'

'Actually, I'm rather chuffed,' Tony said, hooking his thumbs in the straps of his overalls. 'She's been awarded a rosette as 'highly commended' in the restoration category. Not bad for an old 'un, eh!'

'For both 'old 'uns', I'd say!' Sophie winked.

Tony laughed. 'It is rather, isn't it? Funny how, as you go on, it's life little triumphs which bring one such unalloyed joy!'

'THE PRESENTATIONS ARE ABOUT TO COMMENCE!' boomed the loudspeaker.

They watched from the ringside as one by one the cups, plates, and rosettes were awarded by a dapper little man in country tweeds, who had a word with each of the proud recipients.

'Who's that doing all the glad-handing?' said Jonathan to Tony, who'd just returned with his rosette.

'Ah, so you've not made the acquaintance of Harry Humphries then?'

'So that's Humphries is it? No, I haven't ever seen him before, but I've been told by Leo he's most likely to be behind all that hateful stuff in the *Gazette*.'

'That would fit. I think he's best described as a prize example of a 'veteran Fleet Street hack!' He was a columnist with one of the nationals for decades – The *Herald*, I think it was – and rabble-rousing is his stock-in-trade. Now he's retired down here, he likes to think of himself as a bit of a celebrity. So he'll be in his element doing the honours today.'

'God, I think he's poison, Tony,' said Jonathan.

'You take the words out of my mouth, old thing, Tony said in low tones. 'Too full of spite for me.'

'AND NOW THE CUP FOR THE BEST DAIRY COW IN SHOW – TED AND ANNA NORTHCOTT OF HALL!' intoned the sonorous announcer.

'They'll be thrilled!' Sophie whispered.

'Tell you what,' said Tony, 'let's find Ted and Anna, and I'll stand you all a pint in the beer tent – after all, we've got a lot to celebrate!'

TWENTY-EIGHT

September 1968

If Nigel Ashman was a little dull compared to Naomi, his predecessor, at least he was diligent and competent, and he and Jonathan quickly formed a good working relationship. The housing scheme soon began to take shape on Jonathan's innovative layout, which gave pedestrians priority over the car. The controversy over its design seemed to have died down at last.

As late summer faded into early autumn, life at Hall was pleasant. With Ted's return to good health, the new camping site doing excellent business, and their plans for the future taking shape, the Northcotts felt a corner had been turned. Jonathan and Sophie had been joined in the mill house by a lively cocker spaniel, Cadoc, named after another of the Celtic saints – the dog struck up a close bond with Ted, accompanying him round the farm on the days when Jonathan couldn't take him to the office or out on site.

Now that Sophie's sculpture was getting wider recognition with commissions from further afield, she was away for days at a time – and on the rare occasions they were together, she found Jonathan often preoccupied with work. She knew him well enough to cut him some slack on that count, because she thought it might one day be the other way round. Even so, it was frustrating because things had gone so well between them over the summer. A certain reticence began to creep in, and she held back from making too many assumptions about their future.

For Jonathan's part, he could see he wasn't giving her the attention she deserved – but felt unable to do anything about it until he was clear of the murky world Naomi had let him in on. He adored Sophie and longed to tell her how much he was in love with her – but then, he'd recall she never used the language of love herself, or talked about their future any more than a few days or weeks ahead. Perhaps the best he could do for the present was enjoy what there was, without making long-term plans.

Jonathan had now completed most of the drawings for the Northcotts' scheme. Knowing he needed Tony's wisdom on how best to proceed – Tony was a veteran at steering tricky projects through to completion – he approached him in the office first thing on a Monday morning.

'Time for a drink this evening, Tony?'

'You hardly need to ask, old thing, only too pleased to oblige.'

After work they made their way over to The Castle where they found Arthur Kennall presiding at the bar – Monday evenings were quiet so Arthur never bothered to get bar staff in on those nights, preferring to make an appearance himself and keep up with the local gossip.

'Evening Tony, Jonathan – your usual, gentlemen?'

'Yes please, Arthur,' Jonathan said, 'and this one's on me, Tony.'

'How are things going with the Northcotts' place, if you don't mind me asking?' Arthur enquired as he fetched their drinks. 'It's gone a bit quiet since all that excitement about the chapel.'

'It's been slow old progress I'm afraid,' Jonathan said. 'But I'm hoping we'll be able to say something public soon.'

'I hope so,' Arthur replied. 'We need some fresh ideas. I wish them well, whatever they do with that vast old place.'

'Thanks. They'll be pleased to know they can count on your support. They're buzzing with ideas, I assure you.'

'That's good to hear. Now, I'd better let you and Tony get on – and I do believe I've got another customer. What can I get you, sir?' With that he ambled over to the other end of the bar while Tony and Jonathan found themselves a quiet table.

'Need a bit of help Tony,' Jonathan said as he settled himself. 'About how to play the game on the Hall project, in fact. Now Broadhaven seems to be going smoothly, at least for the moment, I don't want to run straight into another local row.'

'Tricky, isn't it?' There was a long pause for thought as Tony drew on his pipe. 'It's worth remembering nobody around here's ever seen anything like your plans for Hall – the usual solution when a farm's not making ends meet is to sell up. If you think about it, what you're proposing is quite radical.'

'How do you mean?'

'Well, you know how people down here are about strangers. It's not just the locals – you can sort of understand that – but newcomers too, they're often the worst offenders. This studies centre of yours will be bringing a lot of outsiders in.'

Leo, Jonathan now recalled, had said much the same thing.

'But they're mostly going to be children or young people, for God's sake,' Jonathan said. 'And they're only visitors, here for a week or so at a time.'

'That won't matter. And to make it worse, they'll be kids from the cities, won't they?'

'Why should that make matters worse?'

'Come on, don't be so naive – look at the mischief some people made about your housing scheme. So think how they'll feel about seeing all those black and brown faces – a pretty rare sight down here I think you'll agree.'

Jonathan frowned. 'You're probably right. So how can we reassure people?'

'Gently does it,' Tony said. 'I suggest we give the project a bit of a public airing.'

'Not sure Ted would fancy that. He got mightily pissed-off when one or two who came to see the chapel voiced some less than charitable ideas about the studies centre.'

Tony drew on his pipe for a while, the fragrant blue smoke filling the air between them with a slight haze.

'Yes, but the overwhelming reaction was very positive, wasn't it? We'll have to help him over the hurdles… What about an open evening, hosted by the practice, when we could present our scheme to the locals? As a way of sounding out opinion, before we put in an application to the council.'

'Is that wise at this stage?'

'I think so. For one thing it always looks good if you're as open as possible – what irks people is the suspicion of a stitch-up. I think the best way of keeping Ted upbeat is for us to demonstrate we've got the community behind us.'

'But what if they're not?'

'Then at least we'll know what – and who – we're up against. You never know with these things, as I've learned the hard way. People can be as nice as pie to your face, and then you'll find they've said quite the opposite to others. That's one of the downsides of small-town life for you, I'm afraid.'

'You're making me nervous.'

'Don't be – and don't show any sign of nervousness to the Northcotts. It's a good scheme and your job is to show your belief in it, get out there and sell it – then build it.'

'I do believe in it, passionately. I'm convinced it will be good for the area, new jobs and opportunities for local businesses – as well as demonstrating how farmers can diversify and bring new investment in.'

'That's the perfect line to take – we'll need to stress the benefits for the community. After that we can show your pretty pictures of the old farmyard buildings and the old chapel restored – as Arthur's just reminded us, that's created a lot of interest. Ted wanting to show it off like he did was a stroke of publicity genius.'

'All right, I think you've persuaded me. So how do we play it? Do we get someone like Penhaligan or Leo to chair it, then ask the Northcotts to speak and field questions?'

Tony shook his head. 'Let me get us the other half and I'll explain.'

Tony ambled off to the bar, leaving Jonathan wondering what he had in mind. When he returned, he refilled and lit his pipe before he continued.

'As to your suggestions… apart from the fact he'd be in an invidious position as Chairman of the council, Horace doesn't always – let's just put it like this – live up to the image of a 'simple local businessman.' He's a politician, and you don't get to be Chairman for years without being a world-class wheeler and dealer.'

'What about Leo, then?'

'We'll need him to speak up for the project – you said he's very much in favour of it and, because he's widely respected, he'd be a powerful advocate. As for Ted and Anna, it's better they don't speak – we don't want Ted sounding off if someone says something stupid, which they will.'

'So who does that leave us?'

'It must be our show as a practice, as Ted and Anna's representatives. I'm not much of a chair but Caroline is a natural, so I suggest we ask her to do the honours.'

'That makes sense.'

'And of course you're our main man to do the presentation and answer questions. You know the project better than anyone, and not just the technical stuff – you'll be its best advocate.'

'I'm not sure I feel as confident of my abilities as you do. But I'll give it a go.'

'Good man.'

TWENTY-NINE

October 1968

Tony's suggestions found favour all round, but it wasn't until a late October evening that the hall of the local school was packed for what Atherton & Green had publicised as 'an opportunity to hear about an exciting new development for the area.' To the dismay of Ted and Anna, the *Gazette* had run it on their front page under the banner headline *CULTURE CLASH OVER FUTURE OF ANCIENT MONASTERY*, a statement not even tangentially in touch with the facts.

Tony was sanguine, saying only that the publicity might at least guarantee a good turnout. But as he cast his eyes over the sea of faces, he began to have second thoughts. Sure, there were the usual suspects... but there were a number of faces he didn't recognise, with placards saying 'Save Our Rural Way of Life'. There was also, he noted, a reporter from Plymouth for the *Western Morning News*, an indication of growing interest in a story already something of a regional *cause célèbre*. Several local councillors had turned out too, including Horace Penhaligan, who was deep in talk with the placard holders.

Tony had agreed to take notes of the meeting and was sitting next to Jonathan with Caroline at the table on the stage.

'A word in season, old thing,' he whispered to Jonathan. 'There's likely to be some fun and games this evening from the look of who's here.'

'God, Tony, I'm nervous enough already.'

'Don't be – just keep your cool, even if you're provoked. We can rely on Caroline to keep an orderly house.'

And as she stood up a few moments later, Caroline duly took command.

'I'm Caroline Atherton, of Atherton & Green Architects, and I'm chairing this event. So may I warmly welcome you, on behalf of our clients, Mr and Mrs Northcott of Hall. This evening is an opportunity to explain our plans for an exciting new phase in the long history of their farm, one of the oldest and most interesting in the area.'

Jonathan sensed an air of anticipation in the audience – the *Gazette* had certainly aroused local curiosity, if nothing else.

'I'd like to introduce my colleague, Jonathan Lane, the job architect, who will give a presentation of our proposals, and then it's over to you for questions and discussion. I want to stress, we're keen to hear your views, which we'll take into account before we prepare our final scheme to go before the council.'

Jonathan cleared his throat and rose from his chair as Caroline resumed her seat.

He showed drawings of the farm buildings as they looked currently, followed by plans and sketches of how it would look if the scheme went ahead. He heard murmurs of approval when he mentioned the possibility of new jobs at the studies centre, but there were some muted groans about the idea of bringing children from urban areas.

Then Caroline opened up the floor to the audience.

At first there were mild-mannered questions easy enough for Jonathan to field – 'Would the scheme result in a lot more traffic on narrow lanes?' – 'Will the character of the old farm buildings be kept?' – 'Will it be possible for other people to use the facilities of the centre when it's not being used by schools?'

There was special interest in the future of 'the old chapel,' as most people now called the granary – the idea of it as a communal space, set apart from the studies centre, went down well, especially if it could be used by local residents some of the time.

Then one of the placard-carriers rose to his feet.

'Yes,' Caroline said, 'the gentleman in the third row. Just to remind you, please give your name before you ask your question so we can attribute your views correctly in the record.'

'I'm Harry Humphries,' he began confidently as if he was used to public speaking, 'and my wife and I have recently moved to this area. We came here because it's unspoilt, untouched by the horrors of modern life, especially with all these people flooding into our cities from foreign parts. Now to me, this 'rural studies centre' sounds like nothing so much as a hostel for youth from our inner cities. It will ruin our peace and quiet. There could well be hooliganism, drunken louts roaming wild in the town centre, smashing things up – '

The speaker's derisive caricature was loudly applauded by the placard-carrying group with cries of 'Well said!' and 'Hear, hear!', though there were also counter-shouts of 'Sit down!' and somewhat fruitier ripostes.

'That's beginning to turn into a speech,' Caroline said firmly. 'I'm going to stop you there and ask Mr Lane to respond.'

Though he'd heard the speaker identify himself, for a moment it didn't click that this this was *Beachcomber* of the *Gazette*! Slightly wrong-footed, he paused before he replied, allowing Humphries to get up again.

'See what I mean? He can't answer that basic question, can he? This is an ill-thought out scheme which I hope the council will turn down flat – '

'Please resume your seat,' Caroline said crisply, 'and allow Mr Lane to answer your question.'

This time Jonathan was ready.

'I understand your concerns Mr Humphries,' he began, 'and can appreciate that you and possibly others here might be apprehensive. But our scheme's been very carefully thought through with all the relevant parties. It's most certainly not a 'hostel', but an exciting educational venture for the wellbeing of young people, and it's a national initiative supported and part-funded by both central government and the local council – you can rest assured it will be very carefully managed and monitored by them.'

This brought a ripple of applause. Jonathan felt emboldened.

'And it's surely got to be right to help children appreciate how food is put on their plates, and how that's connected to the very way of life we all value so much?'

This produced a loud snort from one of the protesters, but was otherwise received with another round of warm applause. Sensing it was politic to move on, Caroline asked for other questions.

It was Richard Forrester who spoke next.

'My name is Richard Forrester, and like the previous questioner, I too have only come to this area recently. But I'd like to offer a different perspective. I think most people here – though obviously not everyone, as we've just heard – will appreciate the worthy aims of this project which Mr Lane set out very clearly in his presentation and just underlined in his response. Atherton & Green's clients are, as we know, people who are deeply rooted and well regarded in the area, and rightly so – they are models of the best farming practice.'

It was said with apparently genuine admiration, and went down well with the audience who murmured their agreement.

'I've moved down here not just for the way of life the area offers in such a wonderful part of the world, but also because I'd like to help ensure its well-being and prosperity for the future.'

'My God,' whispered Tony in Jonathan's ear, 'you've got to admit our friend's got quite a way with words!'

'Yes indeed,' Jonathan murmured, 'but I bet we can guess what's coming next.'

'It's likely many farms will go out of traditional use in the next few years,' Forrester continued, 'so we need to think about what's best to do with them. One model, of course, is what Atherton & Green are suggesting, and I'm all for it. But, of course, not every farm can become a studies centre. What we need is development which will open up major new employment opportunities. So I want to suggest an alternative which could help revitalise the whole area.'

'Mr Forrester, with the greatest respect,' said Caroline, 'this is also turning into a speech – what's your question?'

'My apologies, madam chairman, I'll be brief. It is simply this – why shouldn't farms which aren't viable any more be developed into holiday villages, with all the facilities the modern visitor wants? That way we'd attract people who will want to make a substantial investment in our area – and we all know how much that's needed.'

This was greeted with applause from most of the audience, but groans from the placard-carriers.

'Thank you, Mr Forrester. You make some interesting points. But we're here this evening to discuss the specific proposals for Hall, rather than the general economic future of the area,' Caroline said. 'Incidentally, it would also be helpful if questioners declared any special interests – I believe, for example, you're a property developer yourself, are you not?'

Richard Forrester stood immediately. 'My apologies, madam chairman, I should have said that, of course.'

'Thank you, Mr Forrester, I'll ask Mr Lane for his comments.'

Jonathan was disconcerted both by Forrester's graciousness and his seizing of the moral high ground.

'I share Mr Forrester's concern about the future,' he said. 'And I ought to make it clear again, our proposals represent a major investment in the area which will create good jobs – and year-round ones too. I also agree there is a case for providing good modern holiday accommodation and facilities, but, in the right places.'

He paused for a moment, noticing the audience were very attentive now – his next words would carry a lot of weight. Rather to his surprise, the grilling he'd got had boosted his confidence and he now spoke with real passion.

'But we also have to be careful development doesn't destroy the very things which attract people to come here – our landscape, the fields, trees, and hedgerows; those familiar clusters of isolated farmstead buildings hidden down deep lanes; our strong sense of our own identity and culture formed from a way of life which has gone on here for centuries. Our project will involve my clients *continuing to* farm their land – the working farm is central to their whole concept of the studies centre, because we want young people to learn that it's farming which shapes and sustains the landscape we all love.'

This powerful defence of the life of the area drew loud applause.

'If I'm allowed a supplementary, madam chairman?' Forrester asked.

'Very briefly, please, Mr Forrester.'

'I just wanted to say I'm in complete agreement with Mr Lane about that. I was simply putting the case for more substantial investment to revive the area.'

Forrester knew he had made his point and looked well-satisfied with his evening's work.

'Let's move on,' said Caroline. 'Who'd like to be next?'

'I'm Sophie Ryder,' a strong voice announced from the back of the hall. 'I'm a newcomer too and some of what I've heard this evening saddens me. I mean, we've no right to put up 'keep out' notices just because we're lucky enough to have found such a wonderful part of the world and think we can keep it for ourselves. We need to share it, and giving some less fortunate kids a chance to live here for a short time is the least we can do.'

She spoke from the heart, and was rewarded with appreciative applause which drowned out the shouts of 'Nonsense!' from some of the protestors. Jonathan glowed with pride in her.

'If I may?' That was Father Leo, who'd been sitting patiently in the front row.

'Of course, Father Leo, I'm sure we'd all be interested in your views,' said Caroline.

The rector rose. 'I'm Leo Colchester, rector of Michaelchurch, and I want to strongly support what we've just heard – '

'Then you're a disgrace to your cloth!' shouted one of the protesters.

'PLEASE,' Caroline said, loudly, 'I'm not having Father Leo – or anyone else for that matter – subjected to that kind of abuse! We shall all treat each other with respect, whatever our differences of opinion. Rector, please continue.'

The volatile atmosphere took a little time to settle before Leo felt it right to continue.

'Hear me out, my friend', he said calmly. 'Our part of the world is in decline – indeed, it's suffered significant depopulation in recent decades. Mr Forrester is right: we desperately need new investment, projects which allow us to build confidence in ourselves again, keep our young people here instead of running off to our towns and cities looking for jobs. This venture at Hall is a glimpse of what we should be looking for. It does mean change, but keeps the best of what we have while it moves us towards the future. And, most excitingly for me, it promises to forge links with our cities – I came to this parish from ministry in tough inner-city parishes, and it saddens me to see rural and urban England grow further and further apart – '

'WE'RE NOT!' shouted one of the protesters. 'That's why we moved down here, to get away from the nightmare our cities are!'

This was loudly applauded and accompanied by stamping of feet. Caroline pleaded for quiet, but the protesters shouted her down. Above the din, a burly, red-faced man who seemed to have the ear of the mob got up and motioned his followers to desist, allowing him the opportunity to speak before Caroline could intervene.

'I'm Major Monty Malthouse,' he barked, 'and I'm proud to be the spokesperson for our protest group here this evening. I want to make it clear we're not just objecting to this mad idea, but to what the council is foisting on us at a much bigger scale, bringing thousands of people from the worst parts of London down here into huge new housing estates like that expensive and ill-conceived housing scheme in Broadhaven – '

'That's enough, Major,' Caroline said, looking rather fierce, 'as I said earlier we're not here to debate such broader issues. Please resume your seat.'

And, evidently surprised to be given orders, the Major sat down.

'If there is any repeat of this discourteous behaviour I shall have no option but to close the meeting.' Caroline cast a sharp look about the room. 'Now, before he was so rudely interrupted, Father Leo was speaking and I'm going to ask him to resume. Rector, you will be heard respectfully this time.'

Leo rose slowly and turned to face the protesters directly.

'What I've just heard truly distresses me. How can we be so uncharitable?' He paused. 'We're so blessed – things aren't perfect, I know, and there's deprivation here too – but not on anything like the scale of our cities. People there have so little in comparison to us. I pray we can find it in our hearts to share something of our good fortune.'

This brought some sullen muttering from the protestors.

'And, as far as the proposals we're discussing this evening, I just want to say I've got clergy colleagues who'd give anything to bring children from their very deprived neighbourhoods to have the kind of experience this venture promises to offer.'

Sensing other voices needed to be heard, Caroline asked for further comments, resulting in a mixed bag which included some supportive contributions from the more thoughtful locals, including the younger section of the audience, who seemed firmly on the side of the plans for the studies centre.

The evening eventually came to a close, and to Jonathan's surprise Tony seemed entirely cheerful about it.

'Well done! What excitement, eh? Michaelchurch hasn't seen anything like that since a man from the water board was here to explain the need for a reservoir – you'd have thought he was proposing to flood the place!'

'Not sure that's much comfort, Tony,' Jonathan said. 'Humphries was up to his old tricks again. He really is a stirrer, isn't he?'

'You've got to admit he's good at it.'

'God, we need him like a hole in the head.'

'Are you talking about Mr Humphries?' said Caroline as she joined the conversation. 'You did very well out there, Jonathan – well done.'

'Not as well as you, I'm afraid.'

'I was just doing my job.'

'Well, I'm just very grateful you were in the chair. But shouldn't we be worried? What will Penhaligan have made of it?'

'He'll no doubt have found it very useful – to whatever agenda he's trying to push through the council at the moment.'

'Even all that hostility to large scale development?'

'He's a wily old bird is Horace,' said Tony. 'He'll find a way of using it to his advantage, I'm sure.'

'So you don't think it'll hurt our prospects?' He honestly didn't see how it wouldn't.

'I doubt it,' Caroline said. 'Those protesters are well-organised and hooked up to the *Gazette*. But the council must look at each and every proposal on its merits. We must show we're sensitive to any reasonable concerns but let's not get disheartened – remember just how much support there was for our project out there tonight.'

Sophie appeared at his side, throwing her arms round him. 'I think you did splendidly, darling.'

'You were magnificent!' Jonathan returned her embrace. 'Have you seen the Northcotts? I wondered how Ted had taken all that nonsense in there.'

'Ted was pretty upset,' said Sophie, 'so Anna thought it best if they left immediately – before Ted gave them a piece of his mind!'

'Probably wise,' Jonathan said. 'I just need to thank a few people, and then we'd better get back and have a word with them.'

Back at the farm with Ted, Anna and Sophie, Jonathan mulled over the evening's events. His fears about Ted proved well founded – the man refused to cheer up even after they rehearsed all the positives, then declared himself too exhausted to stay up any longer and shuffled off to bed.

After he'd gone, Anna opened up.

'You'll have worked out by now he's easily discouraged. It was only to be expected, really, but Ted won't have seen it like that. He'll only remember the negatives and now he'll be down about the whole thing. We'll have to be patient until he shifts into forward gear again. And it couldn't have happened at a worst time.'

'What do you mean?' said Jonathan.

'You won't have heard,' Anna said softly. 'It's been kept very quiet.' She drew in a steadying breath, palms pressed flat against the table. 'It's George Webber.'

'I've met him quite a few times,' Jonathan said, wondering what on earth could have cast such a heavy pall over Anna – her eyes were damp with tears now. 'What's happened?"

'Two nights ago, Annie couldn't find him at supper time.' The next breath she took was uneven. 'She went out to call him in – ' Anna dropped her head into her hands. 'She found him hanging from one of the beams in the barn. He'd – he'd jumped off the loft.'

'Dear God!' Sophie's eyes were wide as they met Jonathan's.

For his own part, he felt a horrible numbness. All he could think of were those mugs of cider he and Sophie shared at the fair, made by George and his wife.

'Anna,' he said quietly. 'Why didn't' you say? If we'd known – '

She was shaking her head. 'Ted didn't want to postpone it,' she said, running the back of her hand across her cheeks, wiping away the tears.

'That was very brave,' Sophie ventured, laying a hand on Anna's shoulder. 'Going ahead and dealing with all that nonsense.'

'We farmers are tough old beasts. We needed to go ahead.'

'I'm sure you need to be with Ted, so we'll be off now,' Sophie said. 'Unless there's anything we can possibly do?'

'That's kind of you, but there really isn't,' said Anna.

'We're here for you both, anytime, for anything,' said Jonathan.

'Thank you. Your friendship means so much to both of us, though

Ted won't be able to say that, dear man that he is. We'll need to give him some time, then I'm sure he'll get the protests in perspective. And I almost forgot to thank you, Jonathan, for what you did for us this evening – and you too, Sophie. Please thank Caroline for us too, won't you? I didn't have a chance to do that.'

'Of course I shall. Now, Anna, as Sophie says, we must leave you to get some rest, you must be exhausted.'

THIRTY
Early November 1968

Though he'd given Jonathan every encouragement, Tony harboured serious doubts about the Hall project. He'd seen many a good scheme come to grief on the rocks of cost, planning consent, or clients changing their minds… and it was this latter possibility he was most concerned over, particularly after Richard Forrester's remarks. What if the developer managed to sweet-talk the Northcotts out of their studies centre, with the prospect of making a mint on selling up for a holiday village?

He didn't want to believe this, and certainly had no intention of saying anything to Jonathan. But like a persistent itch, the worry wouldn't quite go away.

A few days after the meeting, he'd made his way to The Castle to ruminate over a pint and found Jim Jewell already installed at the bar.

'Hello Tony, what can I get you?'

'Good to see you Jim, pint of my usual, please.'

'Coming up. Why don't you settle yourself over at our table and I'll bring it over.'

Tony had lit his pipe by the time Jim arrived with his beer and was puffing away thoughtfully.

'Mind if we talk a bit of shop?' he asked.

'You know me – it's one of the delights of coming in here.'

'Too right. Just wondered how you thought our little exercise in 'public consultation' went the other night?'

Jim paused to take a few sips from his pint.

'Pretty well, all things considered. Caroline and Jonathan did a great job dealing with some of the stroppy customers. I found it all fascinating – not least because of what we learned about this protest group.'

'It's useful to know where they're coming from,' Tony said. 'I just hope the Northcotts' project doesn't get gunned down in a skirmish of the bigger campaign they're waging.'

'Ted and Anna have a lot of support,' said Jim. 'And it's a damn good scheme too, deserves to succeed.' After another contemplative sip, he added, 'I had no idea Leo came here from the smoke.'

'I know – he's nothing like that old scoundrel Humphries.'

'He's got some pretty poisonous views, hasn't he?'

'He's a snake in the grass, that one. What do you suppose his game is… beyond just causing trouble, I mean?'

'Heaven only knows, but there'll be something underhanded going on.'

Tony drew on his pipe, wondering exactly what that might be. Drawing a blank, he returned to his main theme.

'What do you make of Richard Forrester?'

'Pretty little speech, wasn't it?' said Jim. 'I can't make up my mind about him. He's so affable, gets on with everyone – and he's certainly got the gift of the gab. But he's a developer, isn't he? He made his money in the City apparently, so he must be a pretty smooth operator. I think he might be looking to make a packet down here from folk he sees as easy pickings.'

'You take the words out of my mouth, Jim. Though he might not have reckoned on farmers being pretty savvy about the development value of their land.'

'No, that's certainly true.'

For a while, both men were quiet, taken with their own lines of thought.

'Any idea who else he's spoken to?' Tony said. 'Forrester, I mean.'

'You know how farmers are – keep themselves to themselves, men of few words, and very tight-lipped about money – especially to their vet!' said Jim. 'But from what little I've gathered, someone – whether it's Forrester or not I don't know – has been sounding out quite a few folk about whether they'd be prepared to sell up.'

'I thought that might be the case. I'm quite surprised the Northcotts haven't been approached.'

'We don't know whether they have or not, do we?'

That took Tony well aback. Surely Jonathan would have said something? 'Do you really think there're others scouting around like Forrester?'

The two men had been talking quietly, but now Jim lowered his voice further and leant over the table, hands wrapped around his pint glass.

'Yes, I do. Before you came in, Arthur Kennall was telling me he's had a couple of what he thought were property developers from up country staying here at The Castle. They were about as different from our friend Forrester as could be – brash, loud-mouthed, splashing their money about, and asking all kinds of questions about nearby farms. He didn't take to them at all, nor did most of the regulars.'

'God help us. Who'd ever have thought our backwoods part of the world would become a playground for property speculators!'

'I don't think it's quite got to that just yet, Tony!'

'Still.' Tony exhaled heavily. 'Time I retired, maybe.'

'Nonsense, you've got years in you yet.'

'Come on – drink up and I'll get the other half. Then we can change the subject.'

THIRTY-ONE
December 1968

Ted realised he'd withdrawn into his shell. But as he went about his work on the farm, he'd been mulling things over. It wasn't fair, he knew, to Jonathan and Sophie… and least of all to Anna. Somehow he had to dig himself out of the pit he'd fallen into.

Early one December afternoon he was inspecting the coastal fields when he spotted Jonathan and Cadoc walking along the path near the sea. Knowing it was high time he broke his self-imposed seclusion, Ted steered the tractor over towards them.

'Hello Jonathan!' He had to shout to be heard over the din of the tractor's engine. 'You're not usually home after lunch.'

'Hello Ted, good to see you. No, I had a site meeting which turned out shorter than I expected, so Cadoc's having an extra walk – he deserves one, been in the car most of the morning.'

Ted switched off the engine, but remained seated as the engine chugged slowly down to silence. 'You could have left him with me.'

'Didn't think it through, did I?'

There was a pause as both men listened to all the little sounds of the fields now audible. Ted cleared his throat. 'You got a moment?'

'Always!'

But it was several seconds before Ted spoke, gazing out over the sea.

'Whenever I come up here, I feel I can see forever.'

'Balm for the soul, isn't it?'

'Is that what it is?' Then he sighed. 'Sorry, didn't mean to be rude. I just don't get what people mean by 'soul'.' Almost irresistibly, his line of sight was drawn away from Jonathan and out across the waves. 'Anna does, I think. Goes off quietly to early service every Sunday, then just gets on with life. But church… all those weird things you're supposed to hold in your head, the things you're supposed to say… it all makes me want to run in the opposite direction.'

Jonathan smiled. 'Maybe the rest of us are too used to using words like 'soul' as a sort of shorthand.'

Ted raised a hand, pointing.

'See that bit of cliff over there? Apparently it's an Iron Age burial site. And the marvellous thing about it is, as the cliff erodes, the remains slowly tumble down into the sea. We return to what we came from.' He inhaled the scent of salt and cut grass. 'It's that kind of thing which moves me.'

Jonathan kept quiet as they both continued contemplating sea and sky. 'Sorry I've been out of circulation,' Ted said eventually. 'I've been pretty down, but I've done a lot of thinking. The troublemakers at our open evening didn't help, but... the real body-blow was George going like he did.'

'Sophie and I were so sorry to hear about it. He seemed such a lovely man.'

'He was, one of the very best. And the more I've thought about it, the more I've realised how heavily Anna and I have come to be burdened by Hall, just like George and Annie were on their farm. All the problems we face, trying to find a way forward… it often feels like things are crushing us, making us prisoners of our own circumstances.'

'Even as an outsider, I can see how you could see things that way.'

'I've been agonising about what to do for ages. If we sold up to Forrester we'd get a damn good price – I don't take to the man, but that's what he told Anna. In a single stroke we'd be completely free.'

Jonathan's face went still. 'Surely you're not….?'

He shook his head. 'No, we're not selling up. But I've come to realise how much the chapel's changed my thinking. It's given shape to a kind of vision I've had.'

'A vision?'

Ted climbed down off the tractor and leaned against a gatepost. His thumbs were hooked in his pockets, and he had a thoughtful expression.

'Not a blinding light or anything – though it did come out of the blue, one day last summer. It was something one of our B&B guests said. They were Asian, from Birmingham – the man had his own small business in the Jewellery Quarter – and they lived in a terraced house with no garden. Their children had never seen fields, woods, lanes, hedges… let alone sand and sea, before. When Anna asked them what they'd miss most, the wife said 'The healing this place has brought to all of us."

'It's brought me more than you'll ever know.'

Ted smiled, then – that rare, shy smile he'd offered Jonathan on his first night. 'I don't know about that… but it's what convinced me we should share our experience – give people the chance to 'heal', just by walking through the fields and woods, to hear birdsong… watch water running in a small stream.'

'Like John Clare?'

Ted's eyes lit up. 'You know him?'

'I do. I used to read him a lot – but I now realise I didn't begin to understand him until I came to live here.'

'Every one of his lines speaks to my daily life… the voice of the true countryman. He didn't just observe nature; he walked it, breathed it, lived it. The hay meadow, 'the happy bird' – there's so much love for what surrounded him in every line.' There was a long pause before he continued. 'Don't think I've found religion. I've had a lifetime of healthy scepticism. But I've come to see the granary as a special place, a hallowed place. And I've thought about its dedication, you know, to Mary Magdalene, the one who anointed the feet of Jesus.'

Sensing there was more to come, Jonathan held back. Ted could be a talkative man, but he'd never, as long as Jonathan had known him, opened up so much on something like this – matters of the soul, though certainly Ted himself wouldn't have put it that way.

'So I've had an idea,' Ted said, 'which you may think is mad, but I want your view on it. I've told Anna – and she's all for it.' A pause. 'I think we should put something back in the image niche, something which could represent that healing.'

Jonathan took some time before finding the words.

'I think it's a great idea. And it rings very true.'

'Good. That's why I'm so committed to offering the opportunity to be part of our world, of sleeping under the stars in a dark sky, in a space to dream dreams – to greet the dawn and realise there's milking and a day of hard graft to follow.'

'Ted, we can make it happen. But I have to ask you. Are you really giving me the go-ahead?'

'I most certainly am.' Shoving off from the gatepost, he began to mount the tractor once again. 'It's such an important moment for all of us, I didn't want it to just come out. But yes, Anna and I are completely agreed, we must press ahead – and we're going to prove all those doomsayers wrong!'

'That's brilliant news. I'll put our application in next week!'

1969

THIRTY-TWO

January and early February 1969

No sooner had the Northcotts' scheme been submitted than the *Gazette* resumed hostilities.

The protesters' antics had provided good copy, and now the paper became their mouthpiece. A string of columns by *Beachcomber* excoriated plans for inner-city overspill and the new motorway as threats to the West Country's traditional way of life – and now lumped the rural studies centre in with the Broadhaven housing scheme as precursors of this new Dark Age.

The critical coverage generated a number of formal objections to the proposals for Hall and, feeling rather overwhelmed, Jonathan asked Tony to go over to Broadhaven with him to take a look at them.

'God, Tony, nearly thirty of them – seems an awful lot.'

'Only to be expected, given the way the local rag's been dancing to the protesters' tune. Let's have a quick scan through them – half each – then compare notes.'

They spent the next half hour reading, Tony quietly, Jonathan letting out frequent groans. Eventually, the elder architect set his stack aside.

'Finished, old thing?'

Jonathan practically flung his down on the table. 'Yes, and bloody depressing it's been too.'

'Let's go have a pint and a pastie, chew the cud.'

They repaired to a pub overlooking the harbour. It was winter-empty, and the view of the wind-whipped ocean out of the window struck Jonathan as rather melancholy.

'Mornin' gents, what can I get you?' asked the barman, seemingly pleased his boredom had been relieved.

'Two pints of best bitter and a couple of pasties, please,' said Tony.

'You'm not in a 'urry I 'ope, sir? Them pasties take 'bout twenty minutes 'cos they're home-made and we bake 'em to order.'

'Not at all,' said a delighted Tony, 'we'll have our pints over by that fire – and might even squeeze in another when the food comes!'

They settled themselves down either side of the hearth.

'It's not as bad as it looks,' Tony observed as they supped their beer. 'Were all yours variations on the same theme?'

'Yes, they were,' Jonathan said. 'Could've all been ghost-written by *Beachcomber*.'

'Mine too – which tells me the whole thing's been orchestrated. Question is, are the objections valid?'

'What do you mean?'

'They can only be considered if they relate to the application under consideration. In my view, they'll almost all be ruled out of order because, for all the huffing and puffing about overspill and the motorway, those issues are completely irrelevant to whether or not there should be a rural studies centre at Hall.'

'Surely there'll be hell to pay if the objectors don't get a hearing?'

At this point the pasties arrived, courtesy of the barman.

'There you be, gents. Best pasties in the sou'west – 'nother beer to go with 'em?'

'Rather,' said Tony.

Once their glasses were replenished and pasties consumed, Tony continued.

'Trust me, I'm an old hand at this game. No doubt the protestors will stage some sort of show – probably when your scheme's considered at a council meeting – but it won't get them anywhere. The plain fact is there's no show-stoppers here – the council officers are bound to recommend approval.'

'Why do you say that?'

'Because your plans tick all their boxes: finding new uses for redundant buildings, restoring the chapel, bringing new jobs and investment into the area, all council priorities. We can expect some hot air from one or two when the scheme comes to committee, but we'll win the day.'

'I hope you're right, Tony.'

A fortnight later Atherton & Green were notified that the council wanted a site inspection.

'More bad news,' said Jonathan as he showed the letter to Tony.

'Just the opposite, I think!' Tony clapped a bewildered Jonathan on the back. 'I'll bet what's happened is the officers have recommended approval, but because one or more of our councillor friends have made a stink, the legal eagles will have suggested a site inspection so the committee can see for themselves.'

'Is that really a good thing? You know how officialdom can make Ted go off the handle.'

'It's really in the Northcotts' best interests. The committee loves getting out and about, and they'll see for themselves what a wonderful place it is, what a great rural studies centre it'll make, and most important, get a sense of what genuine people Ted and Anna are. So, get them to offer the councillors a cup of tea and a slice of Anna's cake afterwards – always goes down well!'

The committee arrived in the early afternoon of a bright but bitterly cold January day, and a fine lunch seemed to have put most of the members in good humour. The only odd note was the presence of Horace Penhaligan.

'What's he doing here?' whispered Ted to Jonathan as the committee climbed out of the council minibus. 'He's not a member of the planning committee, is he?'

'No, he's not. He's probably invited himself along as Chairman of the council to 'observe' – but he won't be allowed to speak.'

'Seems a rum do to me,' Ted grumbled.

Jonathan welcomed the delegation, introducing them to Ted and Anna, and Tony who Jonathan wanted there for moral support.

'With your agreement, Madam Chairman,' he said, 'I suggest we look at the disused farm buildings first, which will be the new rural studies centre, then the ranges behind the farmhouse including the old chapel, and we'll end up at the farmhouse itself.'

'Perfect, Mr Lane,' said Madam Chairman, a jolly lady who seemed (as Tony suggested) very pleased to be out and about. 'We're very interested to see your farm and hear your exciting proposals, Mr and Mrs Northcott, after all we've read about them!'

The tour went well, most of the councillors clearly taken with the farm's long history and impressive survival. While they were in the granary, Madam Chairman asked Dr Manners to give his views.

'Dear God,' whispered Ted to Anna, 'this could be our life-or-death moment.'

'It'll be fine, love,' she whispered back, 'remember how he came round to our side last time he was here.'

And indeed Manners proved an enthusiastic supporter of the project.

'I can't over-emphasise the historical significance of Hall,' he said. 'It's not just another old farmhouse but a major mediaeval house which, as I've tried to demonstrate as we've gone round, has survived almost entirely intact.'

'Just how significant?' one of the councillors asked.

'Of national importance,' Manners said, to a surprised murmur from all the councillors. 'The survival of a domestic chapel from that period with so many definitive features is itself a great rarity.'

'So it's a building we should be proud to have in our area, and one we should be encouraging a suitable use for?'

'Yes, indeed, councillor, that way its repair can be justified and helped by grants from public funds.'

'Surely there are better things to spend public money on than crumbling old ruins like this?' asked another acidly.

'I don't believe so,' Manners said. 'Such structures are a vital part of the history and culture of our area – and the council has a duty to ensure their future.'

'What arrant nonsense!'

'Now, now,' said Madam Chairman, 'Dr Manners is quite right to remind us of our responsibilities. And let's have a gentle reminder that we shall remain courteous to each other – and our officers – whatever our views.'

With that one exception, the committee showed strong support for the proposals. As this was their last visit of the afternoon, almost all stayed enjoy the warmth of the farmhouse and the tea Anna and Daisy had prepared.

After they'd left, Jonathan asked Tony how he thought it'd gone.

'Well enough,' he replied. 'You never can tell of course – they're under instruction to stay in listening mode, but they gave every indication they were right behind the scheme. Manners did us proud, didn't he? And the other officers are all for it.'

'Bit weird Penhaligan turning up though,' said Ted. 'And he didn't stay for tea.'

'He was pushing his luck just by showing,' said Tony. 'He'll have come along to sniff out which way the other councillors are leaning. It'll be interesting to see what happens when they report back to the council.'

◈

Jonathan and Tony both went to the meeting where the final decision was to be made.

'Look at that,' said Tony pointing to a hastily-written notice in the entrance foyer to the town hall.

'PLANNING COMMITTEE MOVED TO COUNCIL CHAMBER IN VIEW OF PUBLIC INTEREST IN APPLICATIONS BEING CONSIDERED THIS EVENING.'

'I guess we can expect more nonsense,' Jonathan, said, looking decidedly gloomy as they took their seats in the public gallery.

'The hoops have to be jumped through, I'm afraid,' said Tony. 'It's quite a turnout for a cold winter evening. Least it won't be dull!'

After the sub-committee reported favourably on their site visit, the officers recommended approval of the plans, with Dr Manners again giving his strong support. As Tony had predicted, most of the objections had been ruled out of order so couldn't be considered. That prompted outrage from the protesters, who to tried to shout down the proceedings, which led the chairman to threaten to clear the public gallery if there was any further disturbance.

Two councillors spoke against the scheme, rehearsing the familiar (and inadmissible) arguments of the objectors, one using colourful language to summon up the nightmare of 'feral teenagers from the slums running riot in peaceful Michaelchurch.'

His remarks succeeded only in irritating his fellow councillors, and when it came to the vote the plans were overwhelmingly approved with only two against.

Then something curious happened.

Horace Penhaligan, who had sat at the back of the committee since he wasn't a member, asked the chairman's permission to make a short statement – which was granted, but with obvious reluctance.

'Council just given the green light, so good luck to the Northcotts, I say.' He swept a mild gaze over the assemblage. 'I 'opes they makes a success of it. But the real answer to what we need down 'ere is proper investment, specially in the 'oliday trade. I 'appens to know of folks with loads of money who are looking to build these 'ere 'oliday villages in our part of the world. What I say is, the council should send a message to such folk, loud and clear, that we're open for business, and I 'opes we'll be seein' those kinds of schemes comin' in soon.'

He was heard in silence, the committee chairman clearly embarrassed and quickly moving things on to other business.

Jonathan and Tony left the meeting, the former mystified by Penhaligan's statement.

'Do you want to know what I make of that little speech?' said Tony.

'I certainly do, it's confused me.'

'These days, Penhaligan's all about development – he's the driving force behind the council's enthusiasm for overspill and the motorway, genuinely seems to think it'll be good for the area. Couldn't oppose our scheme without being accused of inconsistency, even though it's not in line with what he's really after.'

'God, I can't keep up with all this, Tony.'

'Cheer up, old thing! We've got something to celebrate – the Northcotts can now forge ahead. Now, let's go and get a pint, or possibly two!'

THIRTY-THREE

Late February 1969

For all Jonathan's concerns in the wake of Naomi's departure, the Broadhaven build had gone well and more or less to schedule. But, just as he felt he could afford to relax his guard, he had a call from Nigel Ashman asking for an urgent meeting.

'Sorry to get you over here so quickly,' Ashman said, 'only something's come up which is going to need both of us being on the same page if we're to handle it properly.'

Jonathan was suddenly on red alert. 'Oh?'

'The thing is, out of the blue, Walter Johnson's told me in confidence he thinks our main contractor's about to go bust.'

'Bloody hell, I don't believe it. That bunch was hand-picked by Naomi and they've been doing a brilliant job.' Jonathan's lips moved, silently, as he ran some calculations. 'By my reckoning there's only about ten to fifteen percent of the job left to do.'

'I know. And I don't begin to understand it either.'

'Did Johnson say why they were about to go to the wall?'

'He muttered something about cash-flow – and that he never thought they were up to the job anyway.'

Jonathan fumed in silence.

What a bastard! He'd have never wanted them because they weren't in on his little game.

'That's absolutely out of order! They've performed meticulously and met every deadline spot-on.'

'I agree, believe me,' Ashman said. 'But there's worse. Johnson wants me to replace them with a firm I've never heard of – says he knows their work and they can start straight away.'

'I bet they can – and I don't like the sound of this one little bit. For a start, have you ever known a good contractor who can start straight away? Of course you haven't, the good ones are always too busy.'

Ashman lowered his voice. 'I know, but what can we do? As Johnson keeps reminding me, we're up against a tight deadline from Whitehall, and we'll be penalised for any delay.'

Jonathan was in a dilemma. All his instincts told him this was almost certainly a stitch-up by Johnson and they should do anything they could to stop it in its tracks. But Naomi's words about playing the game long came to mind. Probably better to let this one run. He could enforce the proper standards for completing the project, and in the process perhaps pick up more evidence.

'OK, Nigel. Tell you what I suggest: let's interview this lot Johnson's keen on. We've got the whip-hand because I'm responsible for seeing the contractors meet the specifications, so we can always get rid of them if they turn out to be complete rubbish. But I'm not playing Johnson's game. I'm going to record my reservations about this turn of events, and I suggest you do the same.'

'I'm happy to do that. You can see what difficult position I'm in – my principal role is to ensure due process is followed. But I'm only on secondment.'

'I think it's wise for both of us to have put safeguards in place then.'

That evening when he got back to the mill house he set down a record of this encounter, adding it to the notes he'd already accumulated about the *Gazette's* campaign, Humphries' behaviour at the open meeting, and Penhaligan's strange little speech at the planning committee. He was musing about what he should do with all this, having still not had the contact from London he'd expected, when Sophie arrived home.

'Hello darling, still working?' she said, with more than a touch of irony. 'I need a drink, can I get one for you?'

'Hello Soph,' he said, scarcely looking up from his writing, 'yes please, thank you.'

She brought his drink, and hovered quietly for a moment at his shoulder.

'Thanks love,' he said, still scribbling, 'I'll be with you in a minute, just finishing something.'

'No surprise there,' Sophie murmured.

When he'd finished, he hurried through to the kitchen where Sophie was preparing supper.

'Sorry love,' he said, joining her at the sink, 'I was going to do that.'

She turned and looked at him, not unkindly but with more than a hint of sadness.

'I'm not sure you realise just how 'absent' you are,' she said softly. 'There doesn't seem to be much room for me in your head.'

She returned to the vegetables, but he slipped his arms around her waist and laid his chin on her shoulder.

'I apologise,' he said, whispering softly into her hair. 'I'm still just so worried. It's getting worse rather than better, and I've now got another crisis over at Broadhaven.'

'You seem to be bottling a lot up,' she said. 'Maybe it would help if you shared a bit more with me – I'm here for you.'

'I know you are, and I'm so grateful.' For a fleeting moment, he tightened his hold on her. 'Please bear with me a bit longer – the housing's nearly there now, and then I'll be shot of any involvement with the council, I promise I will.'

'I do hope so,' said Sophie gently, 'because I don't want to go on like this much longer Jonathan, I really don't.'

THIRTY-FOUR
Spring – Autumn 1969

At least all was now set for the future of Hall. It pleased everyone that the contract was awarded to Hocking & Sons, a long-established local building firm in the town. Work started at the beginning of March, the weather was mostly kind, and the builders made rapid progress. The Northcotts, thrilled to be seeing their plans turning into reality, were the most engaged of clients – especially Ted, who spent more time than was good for productivity chatting to the workforce about the technicalities of the job. Jonathan often found both him and Anna lingering late in the summer evenings' light, inspecting the day's progress.

Sophie's reputation had been growing steadily as she received glowing reviews for her fresh interpretations and accomplished technique in wood, stone and bronze. She began to win commissions from further afield, which took her to stay in parts of the country she hadn't known before. Often exhausted by the miles as well as the physical demands of her working day, she found it increasingly difficult to get back to the mill house every night. Despite her frustration over Jonathan's obsession with work, she didn't feel anything had really changed between them – she was still mad about him, adored his company, and delighted in their mutual interests.

As for Jonathan, Sophie's upbraiding had hit home. He was now determined to be rid of his pre-occupation with the council as soon as he could, and give Sophie the priority she deserved.

'You know I'm almost through with the housing project, thank God, and things are going so well here. I think Ted and Anna could cope for a few days without me. How about we find somewhere we could relax, get away from it all?'

'That's sweet of you, darling,' Sophie said, 'but you know how frantically busy I am just now – I can't afford to lose momentum.' Then, softly, 'but we'll have a break soon, I promise.'

He didn't push it – she'd been patient with him, and now it was his turn to be patient with her. Still, he couldn't help but feel a slight sense of disappointment.

'Then can I – at least – get supper for you?'

It was said with a smile, instantly reciprocated by Sophie.

'Always,' she said.

Throughout the summer, progress on the construction of the studies centre continued smoothly, and it seemed they'd easily meet their early October deadline. But then, out of the blue, a major problem cropped up with the roof of the granary. Dr Manners was called in again.

'It's no easy matter,' he said, after a thorough examination of the beams and bosses over the east end of the chapel. 'We'll need specialist craftsmen to preserve these carvings.'

Jonathan had difficulty getting hold of the right people, and when he did, they said they couldn't start until late November. It was difficult to put refurbishment on hold, but if they wanted the Centre to open on time – and if they wanted to appease the people funding the restoration – they had little choice.

Eventually the Rural Studies Centre, as it was now officially called, was ready to welcome its first guests. The Northcotts wanted no fuss but the government funders insisted, much to Ted's irritation, on an official opening. 'Important people' – of whom no-one in Michaelchurch had ever heard – arrived from London to give speeches.

'Like a secular baptism,' Leo said quietly to Jonathan, 'but without the freedom of the newly baptised infant to protest!'

The *Gazette's* reporter turned up as well, and the paper ran the story under the banner headline, 'CONTROVERSIAL HOSTEL FOR URBAN KIDS FINALLY OPENS.'

◈

That evening, after all the official guests had gone, Ted and Anna threw a party for their friends, including Leo, the Athertons, Tony and Jim, who'd supported the project throughout. Dr Manners was there was well, along with a couple of councillors who'd taken an interest since the beginning.

To Jonathan's delight, Sophie had also come back for a few days, as had Ted and Anna's children Nicky and Will – it was the first time they'd had time to meet each other properly.

'We've waited a long time for this moment,' said Jonathan, as he and Sophie found themselves briefly alone with them without their parents.

'Yes,' said Sophie, 'we've heard so much about you.'

'Oh God,' said Nicky, 'how embarrassing! Nothing worse than parents banging on about their kids!'

'Not at all,' said Sophie. 'All we hear is how your Mum and Dad are so grateful for all the support you're giving them.'

'Well,' said Nicky, who'd inherited her mother's good looks and ease with people, 'we've got a bit of a vested interest, haven't we? It's our future as well. And it's great to meet you too. Mum and Dad are always going on about how brilliant your scheme is Jonathan, and now we've seen it finished, we can see why!'

'Yes,' said Will, a more reserved character like his dad, 'we certainly can. We've felt a bit guilty about not coming back more often – but college life is pretty all-absorbing.'

'We just about remember that, don't we, love?' said Jonathan to Sophie.

'To be honest,' Nicky said, 'there were moments when we wondered whether they'd be able to see it through – but here it is, and we're so proud of them!'

Ted had spoken movingly during the private party about how the discoveries in the granary had inspired him and Anna to pursue their vision for the future of the farm, and how keen he was to see work on the granary completed as soon as possible.

'And then we'll have another even better party,' he'd added, lifting a glass with a smile, 'because we'll truly feel we've finally achieved what we set out to do.'

◈

The first school party arrived the following week.

'Makes me smile just to see how excited they are,' Ted said to Anna as they walked over to the Centre to be introduced to the children after supper on their first evening. The look on their faces when they got off the coach!'

'And the teachers too,' said Anna. 'They seem just as thrilled to be here!'

'Let's hope they have good weather for their stay – the forecast's not bad at all, cold and dry, just what we want this time of year.'

After they'd been introduced, some of the children came over to meet them.

'Do you really live here, Miss?' one of the boys asked Anna.

'Yes we do, as your teacher explained – we're the farmers.'

'Just the two of you?' said one of the girls, almost incredulous.

Ted and Anna exchanged amused looks. 'With a couple of others who help us run the farm, yes.'

'You're so lucky, we live in the sky,' said another boy. 'At home, we have to go miles to play football – but we could play anywhere here with all this grass around!'

'Well, perhaps not quite anywhere!' Ted said with a laugh. 'But yes, there's lots of space.'

'You can see how thrilled they are to be here,' said one of the teachers who'd come over to join them. 'It's all so unbelievable for them, living in tower blocks. We can't say how much this all means to us, teachers as well as the children.'

In the weeks that followed it was common for Jonathan to come back to the farm after a day's work and see the Studies Centre humming with activity, the buildings all illuminated, music drifting out across the farmstead, and children's voices hanging in the air until lights out.

'It's come alive again,' Ted told him one evening, 'and do you know what Jonathan? The great bonus is getting rid of that blessed generator – I can now switch the light on to go for a pee in the middle of the night without waking the whole place up!'

THIRTY-FIVE

Early November 1969

The annual carnival was another of the highlights of the year in Michaelchurch, and buoyed up by the successful start of the Studies Centre, Ted and Anna were more than usually keen to join the celebrations.

'Any chance Sophie will be back this weekend?' Anna said.

'Yes, she is,' said Jonathan, 'she's going to be working at her studio for a few days next week.'

'Would you both be free on Saturday evening?'

'I should think so, but I'd better check,' he said. 'Why do you ask?'

'Ted and I would like you to join us for carnival night. We always have a meal at The Castle, then we go to watch the carnival procession and the fireworks. So this year we thought you could be our guests, as a small thank you for all you've done for us.'

'That sounds great – and just up Sophie's street! I've been meaning to go since I got here but when the time comes round something always gets in the way.'

'Well, you can't really say you belong around here until you've experienced the carnival!'

◈

It was a crisp, clear evening when they drove over to the town – the first frost of winter was expected overnight. As they parked, they met a party of children Ted and Anna recognised as the latest group staying at the Studies Centre.

'Have a lovely evening!' said Anna to one of the teachers, who was keeping a close eye on her exuberant charges.

'We certainly will, Mrs Northcott, the teacher said, 'as you can see, we're all so excited – Billy please get back here – '

The party made their way to The Castle through streets already packed with eager crowds of onlookers.

'Just as well you booked,' said Arthur Kennall as he welcomed them. 'I'm pleased to say we're packed out tonight.'

'So we can see!' Sophie said.

'It's the one night of the year when the town lets its hair down,' said Arthur. 'Not surprising, since most of the pubs have been open all day! Now, let me show you to your table.'

They were given a place of honour in the bay window. 'Our little gesture for all you're doing with this Rural Studies Centre of yours.'

'Thank you, Arthur,' said Ted, 'we've appreciated your support all the way along.'

'Now,' said Arthur, 'you know we run our carnival night special menu this evening.'

'What's that?' Sophie said.

'Bangers and mash, of course!' Arthur grinned. 'But a bit special. It comes with bubble-and-squeak, onion gravy, and fresh vegetables.'

'Sounds delicious,' said Jonathan, 'and it'll help keep out the cold while we watch the procession!'

'Four of those coming up then,' Arthur said. 'Now, you enjoy yourselves.'

◈

Their hearty portions of The Castle's 'special' went well with the local cider. One of the advantages of dining at the hotel was the opportunity to watch the procession from the prized vantage point of the raised terrace at the front, so the party eventually togged up and ventured out into the cold night air.

The town's silver band led a steady flow of elaborately decorated floats, all bathed in glittering lights, representing an apparently random selection of themes: some deadly serious tableaux, others verging on slapstick, some depicting aspects of the town's life. Most were accompanied by blaring music, all of varying degrees of sophistication. By the delighted look on the faces of young and old as the floats passed, Jonathan suspected it captured the hearts of the whole town.

From their vantage point, Arthur's guests waited to see the poignant coda of this great performance: the emergence of the procession from the town as it wound its way down the hill towards the cattle market at the bottom, moving like a river of silver light until it slowly disappeared into the darkness.

'Fantastic,' said Sophie, 'what an absolute treat!'

'Hell of a lot of work, those floats,' said Jonathan. 'They're really only trailers aren't they?'

'*Only trailers*?' said Ted. 'Don't say that around here! Some folk work on them most of the year. There's stiff competition for the best float!'

'Come on,' said Anna, 'we're not finished yet – we've got to get off to the bonfire and fireworks on the Rec!'

'The Rec?' said Sophie.

'The Recreation Field,' said Ted. 'You know, where the football and cricket pitches are. They keep a special spot well away from the playing areas for the annual bonfire.'

The festive atmosphere continued around the fire long after the firework display had finished with a spectacular finale of a rocket fusillade fired from the tower of the castle.

'Let's head for home,' Anna said, 'we need our sleep.'

As they were leaving, they saw a minor scuffle between some youths at the edge of the field – shoving and shouting, soon broken up by a few more shadowy figures, before the noise faded.

'Too much booze too young,' Ted said, sounding weary. 'Can't hold their drink.'

A few days later in the office, Tony came over to Jonathan with the latest edition of the *Gazette*.

'Have you seen this?' he said, pointing to *Beachcomber's* column, run under the headline 'I TOLD YOU SO.'

'I don't believe it,' Jonathan said as he read on. *"It gives me no pleasure to report a brawl developed between local lads and youths from the recently opened hostel at the Michaelchurch carnival ...'* What's he talking about? There was no 'brawl', certainly not involving any kids from our Centre, they're all too young! And anyway, I know they were being properly supervised, they left when we did.'

'Jim tells me some of the black kids from the Centre were shouted at by a group of local yobs,' said Tony, 'and some other local lads had a go at the yobs.'

Jonathan let out a huff of breath in exasperation. 'Humphries at it again, the little rat. Trying to stir up trouble where there isn't any to suit his warped narrative.'

It was the sort of thing Naomi Walters had wanted to know, so Jonathan added another note to his dossier that evening.

THIRTY-SIX

24th November 1969

One miserable evening in late November, Jonathan hadn't long got back from work when he heard the familiar chug of the Land Rover coming down the track, considerably faster than Ted's usual steady pace. When it stopped outside, he opened the door – but to his surprise it wasn't Ted but Len who got out.

'Pardon me troublin' you, young man – could do with yur help if you don't mind.'

'Of course Len, what's up?'

'Anna's bit worried about Ted – 'e isn't back in from working out on the far fields, due back an hour or more ago. 'Tis a filthy night out there. Any chance you'd come along with me to look for 'im?'

Jonathan felt a strange uneasiness settle on him. 'Of course – anything I can do to help.'

Pausing only to don his waterproofs and boots and collect Cadoc, he climbed into the Land Rover. Len drove them swiftly out towards the furthest fields.

'What do you think's happened?'

'God knows. Most likely just Ted thinking 'e could do the job quick, then it not working out so easy –still at it now, shouldn't wonder.'

'Let's hope so. He shouldn't be out on a night like this.' There hadn't been a word about his heart since the last visit to the doctor, but still.

'True enough, and no, 'e shouldn't be. Don't mind sayin', 'e can be an obstinate old bugger sometimes.'

By now it was blowing a gale; they got mired in the sodden ground several times. Not unlike his first journey to the farm, in fact, in old Jim Jewell's Land Rover.

'Reckon we're 'bout where Ted've 'bin workin', goin' on what 'e said to Anna.'

Jonathan began to peer out of the window in earnest. 'What's that over there?'

The Land Rover's headlights picked out the familiar form of the tractor and trailer, the latter leaning over at a precarious angle.

'That's it, right enough – but can't see any sign of Ted,' said Len.

'Looks a bit hairy, that trailer.'

'Better us stop 'ere an' leg it over. Don't want this 'un to get mired down.'

'Good idea. I'll let Cadoc out. Go on Cadoc, find Ted!'

It was a command Jonathan had taught the dog early on and he rushed off, hunting round before he started barking excitedly.

Running over to where the dog was, their torches lit on Ted lying underneath the coupling between tractor and trailer, Cadoc licking his face.

'Oh God – Ted!' Jonathan slipped and stumbled in his haste to reach them – relieved as he and Len knelt down to hear Ted speaking quietly to Cadoc.

'Hello my old pal, what took you so long?'

'Ted, thank God,' Jonathan shouted against the noise of the wind and rain. 'Can you hear me? It's Jonathan and Len.'

'Am I pleased to see you…' Ted spoke quietly and slowly. 'Got myself in a bit of a pickle… my own stupid bloody fault really.'

'Stop blaming yourself,' Jonathan said, fear making his voice more firm than he'd intended. 'Tell us what happened and how you are.'

'Bloody rough… got these… chest pains… been lying here a while.'

'We need to get you back to the house,' Jonathan said – the man was soaking wet, and his hands cold when Jonathan took one. 'Don't worry now, Len and I'll get you out.'

With some difficulty they extracted him from where he'd fallen, then carried him back to the Land Rover where they wedged him between them on the bench seat.

'That bloody hydraulic linkage playing up again, Len… been meaning to see to it for ages haven't we? Trailer got stuck in the mud, tried to free it, felt it tipping over… the linkage had locked… tried to fix it… then got these chest pains...'

'Never mind that now,' Jonathan said. 'Anna will be so pleased to see you.'

'Hope so – but she'll be cross with me... told me I should have taken you with me, Len, because of the forecast…'

His voice was fading but they tried to keep him talking as Len drove, faster than was sensible, back to the farm.

Anna ran out to meet them.

'What's happened?' she asked, looking anxiously into the cab. 'Ted, love, what's wrong?'

'I've been better, sweetheart,' Ted whispered. 'I'm sure I'll be fine after I've warmed up a bit…'

'We need to get him to hospital, Anna,' Jonathan whispered. 'He's had bad chest pains and collapsed trying to fix a problem with the trailer. And he's been lying out in all this for a couple of hours.'

'Oh Ted,' Anna whispered as she climbed into the cab and cradled him in her arms. 'It's all right now, you're home and we'll look after you.'

'Keep him talking. Len, you stay with them while I phone for an ambulance,' Jonathan called over his shoulder as he jogged towards the farmhouse steps. 'Then we'll get him indoors, if they say it's OK to move him.'

When he telephoned he was assured an ambulance was on its way. They advised him to move Ted as gently as possible inside to the warmth of the farmhouse, get him out of his wet clothes, and try to keep him awake – he'd fallen silent, perhaps out of relief, but in the warmth of the farmhouse kitchen he gradually he began to respond to Anna's voice and even managed to thank Cadoc again for finding him.

It seemed an age before the ambulance arrived but they were all hugely relieved to hand the patient over into the crew's reassuring hands, Anna following in the Land Rover to the hospital in Broadhaven.

Realising there was little more they could do immediately, Len and Daisy locked up the farmhouse, and Len drove Jonathan home, promising he'd come over if there was any news during the night.

Jonathan poured himself a stiff whiskey. He longed for Sophie, but she was away in London for a few days. He cursed that he still didn't have a telephone – and cursed again when he realised he could have phoned her from the farmhouse. He felt a sudden surge of resentment that her growing success seemed to be taking her away from him – then scolded himself for being so self-centred on a night of such peril for Ted and Anna. All kinds of outcomes flooded through his head, each one somehow more dire than the last.

He poured himself another generous shot, and eventually a third, dozing fitfully in his chair by the open range. Waking in the early hours, he hauled himself up the stairs and fell into bed still fully clothed.

THIRTY-SEVEN

25th November 1969

The whiskey hadn't brought him any sleep.

Anna still wasn't back by morning. Jonathan called the office from the farmhouse, let them know he wouldn't be in that day, then screwed up his courage to phone the hospital. They told him Anna was still by Ted's bedside in the emergency medical ward, but when he said he was 'a close relative,' he managed to glean they were trying to stabilise Ted's condition. It was only marginally reassuring.

He then called Sophie.

'Hello stranger!' There was a touch of irony there. 'Early morning call, what a treat!'

'I'm afraid it's not. Something's happened to Ted.'

There was silence from the other end. When Sophie finally spoke, her voice was very low.

'Please tell me it's not too serious.'

'I don't know yet. He's in hospital and I'm waiting for news.' He then recounted the events of the previous evening.

'Good God, how terrible, I'm so sorry,' Sophie murmured. 'How awful for the dear, dear man – and for Anna. So lucky you and Len found him when you did... I wish I could say I'd come back, darling, but I'm stuck here for a few days.'

Jonathan bit his lip and tightened his grip on the telephone. 'Can't you get back a bit sooner?'

'I'm sorry, I just can't – I've got meetings every day, and an interview on Friday for this big commission I've been chasing. And over the weekend I've got to visit a foundry, which I hope to work with in the future.' He could hear the anxiety in her voice, but it only made him feel worse. 'But please call me as soon as you know anything.'

Jonathan went out to find Len and Daisy, who'd long since started tackling the morning routine, and relayed the news. His offer to lend a hand was taken up gratefully.

But though there was plenty to do, none of them could settle down to anything. Eventually Jonathan returned home to distract himself with work, but found that even finessing the final drawings for the granary raised only desultory interest.

In the late afternoon he was dozing at his drawing board when he heard the sound of a vehicle drawing up outside, followed by an urgent knock on the door. Suddenly fully awake, he found Anna already stepping inside.

'Anna, you look done in, come and sit down.'

She collapsed, wordlessly, into one of the chairs in the living room.

'Would you like a cup of tea, or something stronger?'

'Tea, thank you.' She pressed the heels of her hands against her tired eyes. 'I just can't say how grateful I am for what you and Len did last night. I'm sure it saved Ted's life.'

'It was only what any of us would have done,' Jonathan said as he put the kettle on. 'But how's Ted? I didn't get much out of the hospital when I phoned earlier.'

'I did get a message to say you'd called,' she said. 'I'm sorry I couldn't speak to you. I was so worried about Ted… his heart rate and blood pressure were all over the place, but he's stable now, thank goodness, and they told me to come home and try to get some sleep.'

'Have they said anything about what might have happened?'

'Not really. The initial diagnosis was a severe attack of angina – he told us he's been having chest pains for some time.' Her voice turned bitter. 'Typical man – 'working it off' he said – too busy to see a doctor – '

'I'll plead guilty to that.'

'Well, perhaps you'll take note,' she said with an unaccustomed snap in her tone. 'They think it's quite possible he's had a heart attack, so they're sending him to Plymouth or Exeter for further tests, and meanwhile keeping him under strict observation. No visitors except close family – Nicky and Will are coming down later this afternoon.'

Jonathan flinched. 'I bet he hates being banged up.'

'He does, but he's so weak he's sleeping most of the time.' Her tone softened. 'He just seems grateful to be alive. Everyone at the hospital is being so kind to him – and to me.'

'You will give him my love, won't you, and tell him I'll be in to see him as soon as I can?'

'I shall, and I know he'll want to see you. He was worrying how I was going to cope, so I said Len and Daisy would keep the show on the road. I hardly dare ask, given you're so busy yourself, but I was wondering whether you might be able to lend us a hand at weekends if we really get stuck?'

'I'd be more than happy to.'

'I've a feeling I'm going to need all the help I can lay my hands on in the next few weeks.'

They talked quietly until Jonathan noticed she was dozing. He let her be and went back to his drawing board on the other side of the passage, leaving the doors open so he could keep an eye on her. After more than an hour he saw she was stirring and went back to her.

'Sorry, I didn't mean to go to sleep on you.'

He laid a hand on her shoulder. 'You needed the rest.'

'Yes, I certainly did. But I'd better go back to the house and get something ready for Nicky and Will.'

'I can knock something up if you don't mind it simple. It would make me feel useful – I can't concentrate on work anyway.'

'Oh, would you, please? That would be wonderful.'

She rose slowly from the chair and, as if lost in her own thoughts, walked out of the door and climbed into the Land Rover. He watched her intently. Her bearing was upright, but she cut a lonely figure. Part of him wanted to run after her, put his arms round her, and reassure her how very much others cared about her and Ted. But he held back, knowing in his heart she needed to be alone.

He lingered on the doorstep in the gathering dusk long after her tail lights had disappeared up the track.

THIRTY-EIGHT
December 1969

For the next couple of weeks, everyone fell into the sort of routine which became a mutual comfort blanket. Anna would go to the hospital every afternoon with Nicky and Will, and Leo once or twice a week in his role as part-time hospital chaplain. Sophie eventually managed to get down from London for a few days, but wasn't able to visit Ted as it was still strictly 'family only'. Jonathan would drop into the farmhouse briefly every evening on his way back from work to get the latest bulletin. At the weekend he became Len's hired hand, doing whatever jobs needed attention. Somehow Len and Daisy managed to keep the farm going with extra help Anna hired in to do the milking, though they were all relieved it wasn't the busiest time of the year.

It was soon confirmed: Ted had suffered a heart attack and would have to stay in hospital while the medics decided on his further treatment. In the run-up to Christmas, he was finally allowed to have more visitors, though still on a restricted basis, and Anna reported that he wanted Jonathan to be one of the first.

As soon as he walked into the small ward at the hospital he saw Ted looking out for him.

'Hello Jonathan, Anna told me you'd be coming in this evening. I can't tell you how good it is to see you.'

He was smiling broadly and reaching out his hand, though it was a shock for Jonathan to feel Ted's hold so tenuous compared to the strong farmer's grip of old.

'Well, it's very good indeed to see you,' he said, forcing a smile. 'I can say with absolute honesty you're looking a lot better than the last time I saw you!'

Ted, who'd been lying on his bed, suddenly decided to sit up straight, as if determined to demonstrate his improvement.

'I guess that wouldn't be difficult. I was in a pretty bad way when you found me – don't tell Anna this, but I was starting to think my number was up. I'm only here because you and Len and dear old Cadoc came to find me. The quacks reckon if I'd been out there much longer I'd have died from hypothermia – they say it's lovely way to go but I don't want to try it just yet!'

'You'd have done the same for me or Len.'

'I'd like to think so. But I'll never be able to thank you enough.'

'The only thanks we need will be seeing you back at the farm.'

'I'm determined to do that – they say the patient's attitude makes all the difference. I'll do everything I can to get back to normal as soon as possible.'

'So how are you feeling?'

'A lot better than when I came in – the staff are brilliant, couldn't ask for more. Thank God for the National Health Service is what I say.'

'Have they said anything about your future treatment?'

'I'm told I'll need open heart surgery after Christmas.'

This was the first Jonathan had heard of it, and he feared the alarm must have showed on his face. 'That sounds a fairly major job.'

'The surgeon in Exeter said it's pretty routine these days – well, it may be for him but I'm not exactly looking forward to it. And to make matters worse, I've got to stay in here all over Christmas. Not a very jolly thought, is it?'

'We'll all come and see you,' Jonathan said, 'and it's a lot better than the alternative, isn't it?'

'That's what they say.' Ted gave a grudging sigh. 'And of course they're right. Apparently once I've had the op and a few months recuperation I should be able to return to a fairly normal life.'

'So, it's not so bad then, after all?'

'No, I suppose not. But it's very frustrating. It's such a bloody nuisance for this to happen just when the Centre's finally up and running – and we haven't even finished the granary.'

'Don't you worry about that. The most important thing is for you to make a good recovery. Things can wait a bit at Hall, till you're ready to enjoy them. Sometimes a dose of enforced rest can work wonders, I'm told.'

'Yes,' said Ted after a bit of thought and a few sips of water. 'I see you can put the building work on hold. But to be honest I'm worried about how Anna's going to cope while I'm all crocked-up.'

'She's doing fine – you know better than anyone what a capable person she is. Len and Daisy are being brilliant, we've got extra help in too – even I'm lending a hand when I can.'

'That's a great comfort to me,' said Ted as he lay back on his pillows. 'We're so lucky to have all of you around.'

He was speaking more slowly now, his voice dropping to a whisper as he closed his eyes. Jonathan, worried he'd stayed too long and overtaxed the man, got up to go. As he did so, Ted opened his eyes again, reached out for his friend's hand, and squeezed it gently.

'Thank you so much for coming… I'm sorry, I think I need some shut-eye now. Please, come and see me again soon, won't you?'

His eyes drifted shut and his hand relaxed as he slipped into sleep.

Jonathan stayed a little longer, holding on to his hand, looking at that familiar face and remembering all the times they'd shared since he'd happened on the farm on his first visit. It seemed a lifetime ago. And for the first time in years, he prayed: silently, for Ted, for Anna, and for a return to the life they'd come to share.

December 1969

◆

Ted was allowed home for Christmas on the strict understanding he was to continue to have as much rest as possible and not too much excitement. So the festival was celebrated in a more muted fashion. Nicky and Will came home for the whole holiday period, and Anna invited their special friends in from time to time if Ted felt up to it. When he did, he held court from his favourite chair in the kitchen near the range with Cadoc, now his inseparable companion.

1970

THIRTY-NINE
New Year 1970

Sophie stayed for a week over the holiday, spending most of her time in the farmhouse kitchen with Anna and Nicky, while Jonathan and Will helped Len keep the farm running. Ted made obvious his pleasure at being home among family and friends. His surgery was planned for the second week of the New Year and he was to return to hospital for tests a few days beforehand. The day before he went in, Jonathan called to wish him well.

'Thanks, Jonathan,' Ted told him. 'I'm anxious, I admit… but it's a price worth paying to get me back home and healthy.'

Late the next afternoon Jonathan was in the middle of a client meeting when Emma put her head round the door.

'Jonathan, apologies for interrupting, but I think you need to take an urgent personal call.'

'Yes, of course. Please excuse me for a few minutes,' he said to his clients, 'I'll get Emma to make you a cup of tea.'

At the reception desk he asked Emma who was calling.

'It's Anna Northcott.'

He froze. 'Thanks – I'll take it in the other meeting room, if it's free.'

He shut the door behind him and, after a momentary hesitation, picked up the phone.

'Hello, Anna.'

'Jonathan…' Anna's voice was broken by a loud sob. 'It's Ted – '

He felt his breath stop.

' – he's gone.'

'I'm coming straight back now,' he managed, not even sure how he got the words out at all. 'I'll be with you as soon as I can.'

Jonathan drove slowly back to Hall, taking the turns of the road automatically, trying to compose himself. As he turned into the farmyard, he passed an ambulance.

He pulled aside to let it pass, momentarily blinded by tears as he watched it disappear slowly up the lane.

Pulling himself together, he walked over to Len and Daisy's cottage to find out what had happened.

It had almost certainly been a second, and this time fatal, heart attack. They told him Ted had died in his favourite chair in the kitchen with Anna holding him and Cadoc's head on his lap.

'Where's Anna?' he asked quietly.

'In the kitchen,' said Daisy through her tears. 'Sittin' in Ted's chair.'

'Do you think I should go in now?'

'She said to say, if we was to see you, she wanted a bit o' time to 'erself – then to go in,' Daisy said. 'Why don't you 'ave a cup of tea and a slice of cake 'ere? You can be by yourself, 'cos we'm be needing to finish the milking.'

'Thanks – where's Cadoc?'

''E's still with Anna, she wanted 'is company till you come over.'

Though grateful for time alone, it was one of the longest hours of his life. He sipped his tea until it went cold, and stared at the slice of cake.

He spotted the telephone on the sill. He should call Sophie in London.

She burst into tears when he told her the news.

Finally screwing up his courage, he walked over to the farmhouse. He opened the door softly and entered the kitchen quietly, though Cadoc soon ran to him and put his paws on Jonathan's knee. From the doorway, he saw Anna slumped in Ted's chair, tear-stained and crumpled, with her eyes closed against the world.

After a couple of minutes, he cleared his throat.

'I just wanted to say I'm here, Anna,' he said softly.

She got up immediately and crossed the room, throwing herself against him. He held her tenderly, her tears flooding his shoulder.

'I'm so sorry to be like this,' she murmured.

No words came to him, so he went on holding her until she released him and returned to her chair. Then, looking at him for the first time, she spoke quietly.

'It's all been such a dreadful shock… I don't know what to say except I'm so grateful to you for coming over to see me. It's a comfort.'

'I don't know what to say either, except…' His voice broke. 'I can't begin to imagine the loss you feel… Ted was someone I looked up to… the most admirable of men, one in a million… I'll be here for you, if I can be of any use at all.'

'Thank you… Nicky and Will are due back any minute – they only went off a couple of days ago… and Leo's calling round this evening, bless him.' She rubbed her eyes. 'There's so much to do, I know I'll need to call in help… I don't need to tell you this because you know it, but…' Her lip trembled. 'Apart from being married to him all these years, he was my dearest, most wonderful friend…'

She'd struggled to say this, and now sank back into the chair, closing her tear-filled eyes as if to shut out everything except Ted's memory.

After a few minutes, Jonathan and Cadoc left silently – though he longed to stay and comfort her, he knew she was lost in grief.

FORTY

January 1970

The next few days passed in a blur of mourning. Even though the daily rhythm of the farm carried on, everything else seemed to be on hold. Jonathan called an immediate halt to work on the granary, and was circumspect about putting in an appearance at the farmhouse, leaving the family to themselves and working with Len and Daisy to keep things going. He had the fleeting comfort of Sophie's presence for a few days – she had come down as soon as she could but had to leave again to begin work on a large new commission.

A post-mortem was necessary, and delayed the funeral arrangements. Ted's heart, it turned out, would not have survived surgery. This was a slight comfort to Anna, that at least he'd died at home in the arms of the person he loved. When possible, Leo guided Anna and the family in helping to prepare a farewell for Ted that would truly reflect the man and the life. Rituals of death, Jonathan recalled the Abbot saying, were cathartic, and a necessary part of grief.

It was after one of these visits to the farmhouse that Leo dropped in on Jonathan. It was a pleasure to be able to offer the rector a drink for a change, and the offer was gratefully accepted.

'Would it offend you if I had a smoke?' Leo asked, settling himself into the chair Jonathan had offered.

'Not in the least.' Jonathan lifted his glass. 'I'll confess I've found a little more comfort in the whiskey bottle than I should these last few days.'

'Is Sophie not with you?'

Jonathan shook his head. 'She's starting on a big new job in London.'

'She's a good woman, that Sophie.' Leo took a long and meditative drag of his cigarette. 'I hope you don't feel I'm trespassing on our friendship, and I'd understand if this is too difficult… but I wondered whether I might ask you a bit about Ted.'

'Not difficult at all,' Jonathan said, despite the weight that seemed to suddenly assail him. 'It'd probably help me to talk, honestly.'

'Good. Of course, Anna – and Nicky and Will – have told me a lot, but I'd like to know how he ticked outside the family. I always found him a very private person.'

'Yes, Ted kept things to himself.' Jonathan spoke hesitantly at first, but the words became firmer as he went on. 'He was… a modest man, shy in some ways. Bit of a loner beyond Anna and the children, and a few of his farming friends.'

'But you'd got closer to him than most perhaps?'

'In some ways I suppose I did. Probably because I'm a bit of a loner too, as I'm sure you've clocked. I feel his loss dreadfully. We had a few conversations about what you and I might call the journey of faith…' Remembering Ted's snippy remarks about the soul he nearly smiled. 'Though he would never have put it like that.'

'Would it be an intrusion to ask the flavour of his thinking? I'm not asking you to disclose confidences, mind, just some sense of where he was on his journey.'

Jonathan rose to pour them another drink, and mused for a few minutes before responding.

How the hell do you summarise a life in just a few words?

'There was a real depth to Ted. He loved poetry, you know. Used to recite it to himself when he was working around the farm. He'd process a lot of things while he was out there. He'd never make a glib response – he'd listen, go away and turn it over in his mind – and then he might come back to the subject days or even weeks later with something worth hearing.'

Leo lit another Woodbine.

'That's just what I was looking for – and just what I thought he'd be like. I'm only sorry I never had that kind of conversation with him.'

'I'm sure it wasn't that he didn't warm to you – but he didn't care for 'the clutter of religion.' Got in the way of his 'wondering', as he put it.'

'I can understand that… but it's a pity nevertheless. I feel he and I might have got on rather well.'

'You would have. Look, I wonder whether one little story about him might be useful to you. You'll remember the protests at the public meeting about Hall?'

'I certainly do! Some of the stuff thrown around was pretty unpleasant.'

'It got him down for a while, but I ran into him out on the farm a few days after, and… he told me he'd had a sort of vision. He became convinced the granary could be a place of healing. He saw significance in its dedication to St Mary Magdalene because of her anointing Christ's feet, and he intended to put something back in the image niche to signify that.' The grief that came over him was less overwhelming than it had been, but no less pervasive. 'He believed that healing, in its widest sense, was what the Studies Centre was about.'

There was another long pause, then:

'That's perfect Jonathan, thank you so much.'

They sat in silence while Leo finished his drink and cigarette. Then, with a warm handshake but not another word, Leo rose from his chair and departed. Jonathan watched as his Morris Minor Traveller disappeared up the track to another solitary night in the rectory.

FORTY-ONE

Thursday 12th February 1970

The funeral took place on one of those February afternoons when the light never triumphs. An Atlantic gale swept in with unexpected intensity across the exposed coastal landscape, its power at once intimidating and cleansing. The wind bowed the bent trees even closer to the ground, while incessant rain drove rivulets across fields to their lower edges, where waterfalls cascaded over hedge banks and rushed down the lanes. It was as if even the solid earth was dissolving in grief.

Anna had asked Jonathan and Sophie to follow behind her and the children as Ted left the farm for the last time. The coffin came into view from the yard behind the house: borne on Ted's trailer, pulled by his tractor, driven by Len, and surmounted by a wreath of snowdrops. As they drove slowly through the muddy, flooded lanes, they noticed more snowdrops peeping from the hedgerows in defiance of the weather, as if to pay their last respects.

Jonathan suspected it would have surprised Ted to find so many friends gathered in the church. Leo conducted the service with sensitivity and grace, delivering a homily of thanksgiving for a life fully lived with Anna and the family. He mentioned Ted's love of Clare's poetry, in harmony with the natural world.

Anna bore herself with dignity until, in the snowdrop-flecked churchyard, Leo sprinkled the first handful of earth onto Ted's coffin. Then her tears mingled with the rain, as Leo invited everyone to drop a single snowdrop into the grave.

Afterwards, almost everyone returned to the farm for tea in the great barn of the Studies Centre, where tears gave way to the release of love and affection, the atmosphere gradually emerging from raw grief, through muted conviviality, to genuine celebration.

Going outside for a breath of air on the hill above the farm, Sophie and Jonathan smiled at the sound of laughter coming from the great barn. And when eventually they turned their gaze towards the sea, they noticed the sky had cleared to reveal a watery sun sinking below the western horizon.

'Your dad wouldn't have believed it,' Anna said to Nicky and Will as they all walked back to the farm for an early evening drink. 'That all those people thought so highly of him.'

'But he wouldn't have wanted to talk to so many people, would he, Mum?' Nicky offered a slight smile. 'He'd have found some excuse to go and do a job that needed doing!'

'You're right,' Anna said, a smile on her own face now. 'He'd wonder what all the fuss was about! But that reminds me, as Dad would have said: there's still work to be done this evening.'

'Mum, stop worrying!' said Will. 'Len and Daisy are coping with all that. Come on, you need to take it easy for the rest of the day, you've done brilliantly.'

'And so have you, my loves,' Anna replied, putting an arm around each of them. 'I'm so very proud of you, and Dad would have been too.'

Sophie and Jonathan watched silently as the family went back into the farmhouse, bound together in comforting embrace, before they followed them in.

FORTY-TWO
Early March 1970

As the days began to lengthen, everyone began to face up to life without Ted. For Jonathan, the immediate demand for his attention was the completion of his Broadhaven housing project. The first tenants had moved in at the beginning of the year, in advance of the official opening.

The scheme had received much praise in the national press. Whitehall was as keen as the local council to publicise what had proved a successful partnership, so the opening ceremony was quite an occasion. A large marquee had been erected on the green at the heart of the development. On the platform to do the honours was no less a figure than the Minister for Housing. She was joined by Horace Penhaligan as chairman of the council, Johnson the town clerk, Leo Colchester representing the community initiative behind the scheme, Caroline Atherton, Jonathan, and some senior councillors. The guest list included a wide range of other representatives of the local and regional community, with journalists from several of the national papers and the BBC and ITV.

'This government is proud to have been a partner in such a pioneering initiative,' the Minister declaimed, 'where we've proved that by working together with the community and its elected council, we can deliver public housing of the highest quality, fit for the modern age. We believe similar projects, based on this model, should now be instituted nationally. In declaring this development open, I want to pay tribute to you all for this magnificent achievement and convey the government's special thanks to the local council, and to the architects, Atherton & Green, for doing such a splendid job. And, most importantly, I'm delighted to be able to hand over commemorative keys to our first twenty tenants!'

Penhaligan responded for the council.

''Tis quite a day for us down 'ere, Minister. We'm not one of them 'uge councils up country, no, we'm quite a minnow. But we was real proud to 'ave been chosen to take on this project, and to 'ave delivered the goods. And to think government wants to use the experience we've 'ad 'ere to build schemes like this all over the country, that's going to make us prouder still. I also wants to thank everyone who made it possible, not least Father Leo Colchester 'ere and 'is 'ousing action group – 'twas their idea in the first place.'

Both speeches were received with warm applause, and the genial atmosphere was picked up as the drinks flowed freely in the reception which followed. To his discomfort, Jonathan was even glad-handed by Johnson, while Horace Penhaligan was positively effusive.

'Congratulations, young man,' he said, 'I 'opes you'm feeling proud of yerself – you should be, you'm the toast of this council for the grand job you've done f'r us. An' it's bought us a lot of credit in London too.'

'Kind of you to say so, Chairman,' Jonathan said. 'I have to say it's not all been smooth sailing, but we got there in the end.'

'Well done, Jonathan,' Caroline said, coming up to refresh his glass. 'This is *your* job, *your* success, you deserve to celebrate!'

'Thanks Caroline, but really it's me who should thank you for trusting me with such an important job.'

'I knew you'd deliver – it's raised the practice's profile quite spectacularly. Are you up for more of the same?'

'I certainly am,' he said, highly conscious of Penhaligan at his elbow. 'And next time I'll be more ready for the unexpected challenges – I've learned a few lessons along the way.'

'That's good. We're already getting enquiries from other councils about other schemes – and I'd expect even more interest after what the Minister said this morning.'

Jonathan wanted to say more, but realised this was neither the time nor place. As he turned to go and find Leo, there was a tap on his shoulder.

He turned to find himself facing Harry Humphries.

'Mr Lane,' Humphries purred, 'what a pleasure to meet the man to whom we owe this amazing achievement. Many congratulations.'

Jonathan was stunned.

What the hell does the smarmy git think he's up to?

'Thank you,' he said frostily, 'I wasn't expecting compliments from you.'

'No doubt, no doubt.'

Humphries' patronising tone and crocodile smile – and perhaps the drink in his hand – finally made Jonathan snap.

'I'm grateful for what you said, Mr Humphries, but it beggars belief you expect me to take it at face value.' He paused momentarily – now seemed the right moment to confront the man. 'Frankly, I regard it as plumbing new depths of hypocrisy to mouth those words when you've been the source of all the vitriol the *Gazette* has been pouring over this project all the way along!'

Humphries fixed Jonathan with a stare no doubt intended to intimidate, but which only irritated him further.

'You really shouldn't believe all you read in the newspapers, Mr Lane,' Humphries said. 'I might have penned the odd piece, but we journalists sometimes have to set up straw men to knock them down again – to further a bigger agenda.'

'I confess I don't understand your world, Mr Humphries. Cynicism seems your stock-in-trade, but I'd like to think people behave more straightforwardly.'

'Nothing wrong with being high-minded, but the world's a rough old place – survival of the fittest, dog eat dog, and all that.'

'That may be true of your world, but not mine,' said Jonathan, deciding to end the conversation and turning away. As he did, he felt Humphries' hand on his arm.

'I like your style, Mr Lane,' Humphries said quietly. 'Perhaps you're not interested now, but you might be in the future – I've got property interests all over the country, and I was just wondering whether you'd be interested in coming to work with me. I'd make it worth your while – it's very lucrative. Here's my card.'

Good God, the man's shameless!

'Thank you, but I'm very happy in my present position,' Jonathan said as he walked quickly away.

'Well done that man!' Tony was approaching with another glass of wine. 'You look shattered – can't take all the compliments, eh! Get this down you.'

'Thanks Tony, you'd need a drink if you'd been through what I've just had to endure!'

That evening, he made another long entry in his ever-expanding dossier – this time, he thought, with some critical evidence.

FORTY-THREE
Spring 1970

When at last the clocks sprang forward and the lighter evenings came, Anna's spirits began to lift. As she took her first tentative steps towards the new reality, she knew she must start making decisions about the future. But the immediate imperatives, like completing work on the granary, were now tangled up with a gnawing doubt.

Did she really want to carry on at Hall, without Ted?

One morning she answered a knock on the door to find Richard Forrester standing there. Though wary, part of her was intrigued by his sudden appearance.

'Please forgive the intrusion, Mrs Northcott,' he said. 'But… there were so many people around at your husband's funeral I didn't have a chance to pay my respects personally as I'd wished.'

Had he been at Ted's funeral? No… no, she remembered now, seeing him in the back. 'That's all right, Mr Forrester, I understand. I've got to get going shortly but do you want to come in for a minute?'

'That would be very kind.'

Anna showed him into the kitchen and towards one of the chairs around the table.

'I could offer you a coffee before I go out – I was just about to make one for myself.'

'If you really have the time, I'd appreciate that very much.'

Anna filled the coffee pot and brought it over to the table with two mugs and a jug of milk. There was an awkward silence between them as she poured the coffee, then returned the pot to the range to keep it warm.

'Do you take sugar, Mr Forrester?'

'Ah... no, no thank you, Mrs Northcott.'

'You really needn't have bothered to call, Mr Forrester, 'Anna said, feeling strangely clumsy and off balance.

'Oh, well… no, it's just… I wanted to say how much I admired your husband. He was such a respected figure in the area, yourself as well. And I suppose I didn't want you to feel, just because I'd voiced different ideas about development round here, that I didn't appreciate what a great vision you and he had for this place.'

Her shoulders tensed even as she gave him a gracious nod. 'That's kind of you.'

'And I also wanted you to know that, if I can be of any help, of any kind, in taking your project through to completion, I'd be happy to act for you – gratis, of course.'

'I'm not sure I follow you,' she said, tone slow and cautious. 'You'll know I'm in the capable hands of Atherton & Green.'

'And they're a very good outfit indeed. And Mr Lane is a talented architect. But I can also see this is a difficult time for you. Without wishing to cause offence, I was just wondering… whether you might be rethinking how to proceed – I mean, because of your changed circumstances. If you wanted to pursue other options.'

How often had she tossed and turned since Ted's funeral, thinking of exactly that?

'I'm not sure I understand what you mean,' she said. 'Since we last spoke, as you know, we've opened the Studies Centre.'

'And that's a remarkable achievement which deserves the warm reception it's received. But, if you'll forgive me for saying this, it's only realised a small part of the potential here. When we spoke before, I was talking of future possibilities on the distant horizon. But things have moved forward since then and – if I may cut to the chase – if you were open to exploring other options, I'm now in a position to secure you a deal which would not only make you comfortably off for the rest of your life, but your children as well.'

Anna was stunned. It sounded far too good to be true, but he sounded genuine enough. She got up and fetched the coffee pot back from the range, buying herself a moment before she responded.

'How on earth might that be? We've only got as far as we have after taking a lot of expert advice and hard negotiations with the council – and finding the partnership with government agencies to fund it.'

'Well, you remember I mentioned Hall would be ideal for a different approach to holiday development?'

'I certainly do. My husband wasn't very impressed.'

'I can understand that, and I can only apologise. I behaved clumsily. I should've come to you and your husband together – and what I said was premature and ill-considered.'

'Thank you for the apology. But what do you mean by 'premature and ill-considered'?'

'At that time my clients weren't sure the council would entertain what they had in mind. But they've changed their tune recently, and now they're now actively encouraging purpose-built holiday villages. So, if you were minded to sell, they're ready to make you an offer.'

'I'm not clear what exactly your clients would have in mind for Hall.'

'May I explain?'

'Please do.'

'What my clients are after is to create a complete holiday experience. Your farm is ideal because it's so close to the sea. A few of your fields are on, or very near, the coastline and would make a wonderful links – golfers love to play in sight of the sea. And in one of the sheltered valleys which lead down from here to the sea – the ones that are more or less invisible from anywhere – they would build a substantial development of proper cottages – like an estate village, with shops, swimming pool, and other facilities.'

'It sounds very ambitious. But in any case, you're forgetting the facts – we've already got the Studies Centre up and running with a fifty-year lease, and a working farm is a vital part of the package.'

'But suppose those facts needn't change.'

'What does that mean?'

'What if you were able to keep the Studies Centre and farm going alongside my client's development? They don't need anything like the whole farm – or Hall itself either – to realise what I've just outlined. So you could continue to live here, complete the repair of the courtyard ranges in due course, and farm the rest of the land as you do now, without a few of the less productive fields.'

'Surely that sort of thing wouldn't be allowed? We faced some pretty strong opposition to our proposals – all hell would break out to your sort of scheme.'

'I'm sure there would be protests. But the key thing is the council's change of heart. I was at the planning meeting when you got your consent, and I heard Mr Penhaligan say as much publicly.'

'And as a result, you think this place would go for a very good price?'

'Without question – three or four times what it would fetch just as a farm and Studies Centre.'

'Well, that's all very interesting.' Anna wrapped her hands around her mug. 'It's given me a lot to think about. My husband and I had a wonderful vision for this place which I'd like to think I might still be able to realise, in spite of all the difficulties I'm now facing. What I can say is I'll give careful consideration to what you've said.'

'Of course, I understand. I'm grateful you've allowed me the opportunity to air some ideas – which I feel are compatible with your vision. If, at any time, you wanted to take things further, please don't hesitate to call. Here's my card with my details – and I'm Ricky to my friends, by the way, as I may have mentioned before.'

'You did.' She rose and extended a hand. 'You'll forgive me if, in the circumstances, I can't quite cope with that at the moment. But I'd be happy to call you Richard, and for you to call me Anna.'

After he'd left, she decided not to go out as she'd planned. Instead, she topped up the coffee pot and sat mulling over everything he'd said.

It had shaken her up, she couldn't deny. She couldn't work out what Forrester was up to – and could never forget how much Ted had taken against him. But it would be foolish to dismiss his proposal out of hand – she needed to evaluate its possibilities.

Over the next few days – and nights – she gave herself time and space to take stock. For the first time since Ted died, she felt a little more like her old self. Forrester's offer had jolted her out of her immediate grief and forced her to accept that her future was largely in her own hands. She had always been the steadying force in their marriage, not as prone as Ted to sudden swings of mood – 'Why can't I keep a cool head like you, love?' Ted would often say as he emerged from another bout of introspection.

Though she still missed him terribly, she knew she had to move on.

She soon felt strong enough to talk to Jonathan, deciding she'd level with him about her dilemma before tackling Nicky and Will. Sophie was now staying in London for increasingly long spells, working on a prestigious private commission and chasing another major public one, which Anna thought opportune as she needed Jonathan to herself on this occasion. She asked him to supper one evening in late April when spring was finally in the air.

Jonathan arrived with Cadoc, who bolted through the door, sniffed around the chairs, then went to greet Anna enthusiastically. She seemed delighted to see them both, and gave Jonathan a warm hug. She'd already opened a bottle of wine, and they had a glass before they sat down and she put supper on the table.

'It feels so strange,' she said. 'It's the first time just the two of us have been here since Ted's funeral.'

'I keep expecting him to come in from the yard any minute.'

Anna smiled, though it was a melancholy look. 'I do that all the time.'

'He's very much still around the place, isn't he?'

'Always. And he'd be chivvying us to get on and make some decisions, so that's our agenda for the evening!'

'Ah, right… So you're beginning to think about the future?'

'I've thought of almost nothing else.' Dropping into an adjacent chair, she sighed and stared into her wineglass. 'I want to be honest with you Jonathan – I really don't know what to do. What Ted and I had planned – the whole thing was so much 'our' project, so much about us. Just at present I'm not at all sure I can carry on without him.'

'That's only natural – it's still early days.'

'It's blindingly obvious to me that things have to be different now – the only question is how different, and what's best for me, and for Nicky and Will. It's their future as well as mine I've got to consider.'

'Yes, of course. Presumably you've all been starting to think about that.'

'We have, and the kids have been great. As you know, it was always the plan for them to move back here, once we'd got a lot more income rolling in from the Studies Centre and we'd developed the holiday business further. But they're only part-way through college now. I wouldn't dream of putting any pressure on them to leave.'

'Have they said what they think you should do?'

'They want me to press on, because 'It's what Dad would have wanted,' and I'm sure they're right about that.'

She reached for the bottle, refilling both their glasses as they paused for thought. Walking away from the table with her drink, she stood gazing out of the window to the spring grass and lambs in the nearest field. It was some time before she resumed, but it was with a confidence Jonathan was surprised and pleased to hear.

'Strictly speaking, as my architect, can you tell me what I've absolutely got to do?'

'Well, you're still bound into a contract with the builders. There are the loose ends left over on the Studies Centre and the completion of the granary – those are the two things we really need to tie up soon. And then there's the second phase – the repair of the rest of the courtyard ranges and what to do with them. The grants for the granary have a clause that ties some of the funding to the future repair of the house within an agreed time frame.'

'Oh God, I'd forgotten about that. Well, I certainly want to get on and complete the granary. It's what Ted would have expected me to do first. Is there anything else?'

'No, that's about it.'

After a long pause, she turned away from the window and sat down at the table facing him again.

'There's something else I need to tell you, something that's been really bothering me the last week or so. And this may be difficult for you, because you're such a great a friend as well as our architect, but I don't know who else to turn to at the moment.' She laughed, a little. 'I'm almost embarrassed to tell you.'

'Whatever it is, I promise it will remain between us – and Sophie, if you don't mind?'

'Of course, and I do trust you both completely. Ted always said you were someone he always felt he could confide in, and you know how fond he was of Sophie.' She took a deep breath. 'The thing is, out of the blue, I've got the prospect of an astonishingly good offer for the farm.'

'I think I'm the one who's astonished,' Jonathan said, his equilibrium suddenly shaken. 'I'd no idea you'd put the farm on the market.'

'I haven't.'

'How have you had an offer then?'

As she recounted her talk with Richard Forrester she was acutely aware of Jonathan's obvious discomfort. After she'd finished, there was a long silence and she could tell Jonathan was struggling to find the right words. He got up and walked around, avoiding her gaze. Still unable to make eye contact, he was now the one looking out of the window.

'Thanks for being straight with me, Anna – at least I now understand why you're rattled by all this. Do Nicky and Will know anything about it?'

'No, I haven't told them – I'm pretty sure they'd see it as a betrayal of their Dad's legacy. So do I, in one moment – but then, at another, I see it as a way we could all stay on here. We'd have the funds for them to develop the courtyard ranges, and though the farm would be smaller, it would still be viable. And with their qualifications, they could well be part of running the Studies Centre.' Her blue eyes watched him closely. 'I hope you can see why Richard's offer is something I should explore seriously.'

'I'm trying my best.'

'Don't be too hard on Richard, he's very proper – curiously formal actually – and always behaves with courtesy.'

'I'm glad to hear it'

'You don't take to him?'

He turned from the window to face her. 'I'm sorry Anna, but I can't believe you'd be so naive. He didn't become a very successful property developer without being a very smart operator.'

Anna bristled, standing abruptly from the table, levelling a much hotter stare at him.

'And I can't believe you'd speak to me like this! I'm not some gooey-eyed teenager – what makes you think you've the right to make such assumptions? I'm perfectly capable of looking after myself. If I'm honest, I think you're jealous I'm even giving him the time of day.'

Jonathan was brought up short by her sharp retort. He realised he'd crossed a line, and had indeed let his jealousy show. An awkward silence followed.

'I'm sorry, Anna,' he said eventually, much more quietly. 'I was completely out of order, I want to apologise.'

'Thank you – but please don't ever do that again. You've got no idea how insulting it is for a woman to be told she needs a man to look out for her. I had Ted, but now I don't – and I'm going to do things my way in future.'

Another silence fell before they returned to their seats at the table, though their eyes were still rather more on the remains of their dinner than one another. Jonathan was unsure what to say, Anna was aware she'd come down on him harder than she intended.

'Look, Jonathan, I'm sorry,' Anna said after a few beats. 'You've always been such a rock to Ted and me, ever since you came into our lives on that wet February evening three years ago. The truth is I need your support more than ever – but at the moment, that means I need you to respect my decision to investigate all my options. I won't do anything stupid or impetuous, and I'll come back to ask for your advice on any course of action I'm seriously considering.'

Jonathan spoke quietly. 'As I said, I'm here for you Anna – and I hope you'll bear with me while I work my way through this one too… '

His voice trailed off to silence. Then, suddenly, as if on impulse, he got up.

'I don't know what more I can say at the moment, so I'll make my way home now. Thank you for supper – and for giving me such a lot to think about.' He gently clapped his hands, and a sleepy Cadoc rose at once from where he'd been curled up in Ted's old chair. 'Come on, Cadoc.'

Neither Jonathan nor Anna slept well that night.

FORTY-FOUR

Early May 1970

Sophie was also facing a dilemma. Working in London had enhanced her profile more than she could have hoped, and she had landed a major public commission: a sculpture in Richmond Park. Its subject was to be 'any aspect of human interaction with the natural world,' and was on a more ambitious scale than anything she'd previously done. With a sizeable advance for the project, she'd rented a unit on a suburban industrial estate as a studio, as well as a small flat nearby, so she could work seven days a week to meet a challenging deadline.

It was proving daunting, and there wasn't much room in her life for anything else at the moment, but she knew this was her big break. She did feel guilty about spending so much time away from Jonathan – ironic, because it had been his obsession with his work which had pushed her to focus on hers.

There was still no phone at the mill house. She supposed she could call the office, but she knew Caroline frowned on personal calls at work. That left them only letters – which wasn't a strong suit for either of them.

She decided to take the initiative and risk a call to Atherton & Green, choosing coffee time when she thought he'd most likely be free.

Emma put her straight through.

'Hello stranger,' he said when he heard her voice. 'You're still alive then?'

Nothing for it, I'll just have to throw myself on his mercy.

'Darling, I'm so, so sorry, I've been neglecting you scandalously.'

'I was beginning to think you'd left me altogether.'

She couldn't work out whether this was said with bemusement or censure.

'Well, I'm calling to see whether I can make amends.'

'Oh?' It pained her, how cool his voice still was.

'By coming down for a long weekend – if you'll have me of course?'

'When am I going to be granted this honour?'

'I was thinking the weekend after next.'

A pause, then, 'that would be so lovely, Soph.' To her relief, his tone had warmed considerably. 'I'm sorry, just surprised to hear your voice, I suppose... Of course it'll be wonderful to see you.'

Jonathan's enthusiasm was genuine. He'd missed her all the more now he was finally rid of Broadhaven and had not yet moved on to another major project. Though he was still haunted by the shady goings on, all that was – for now at least – at one remove. He needed to reset his relationship with Sophie, and finally had space in his head to do so.

The spat with Anna left him more upset than he first realised. It was ironic that until recently he'd enjoyed a close friendship with Anna and a loving intimacy with Sophie – now he felt deprived of both.

On Thursday of the following week, he heard the familiar screech of the Sprite's brakes announcing Sophie's arrival. He and Cadoc rushed out to greet her.

'God, Soph, am I glad to see you!' he said as he half hauled her from the Sprite and swept her into a tight embrace.

'Darling... Cadoc! I'm here, I'm really here!' Her words, and laughter, were muffled by his shoulder. As he reluctantly let her go, she looked around wide-eyed at the familiar scene, now bursting into late spring growth.

'It's lovely to see you, darling – and all this!'

'I can't quite believe you are here. It's been bloody ages – nearly two months!'

'I know, and I'm sorry. Darling, I'm dying for a drink.'

'Come on in – I've got a couple of bottles of your favourite white.'

Over one bottle before, and a second with supper, they caught up. Sophie's account of the demands of her current commission calmed Jonathan's fears about any other possible reasons for her long absence. She was struck by how much more relaxed he sounded now than he had over the phone.

Jonathan informed her – reluctantly – about Anna's apparent willingness to sell part of the farm for development, but didn't mention the current tension between him and Anna.

'I have my doubts about the credibility of the offer,' was all he said. 'But on the plus side, she's determined to finish the granary. In fact I think it means even more to her now.' Realising Sophie might be able to help smooth things over, he added, 'I thought of inviting her over while you're here, but wanted to clear it with you first.'

'I'd love that.'

Anna and Sophie were thrilled to see each other. Jonathan let them catch up over a glass of wine while he prepared the meal. He smiled as he heard Anna talking with such enthusiasm about the granary.

'And there's something I wanted to ask you, Sophie. You know that niche?' Anna's voice turned serious. 'What do you think about putting something back in it?'

Jonathan's ears pricked up.

'Well, that's an exciting idea – what kind of thing?' said Sophie.

'A figure – it was one of the last things Ted and I decided on.'

'Well, that's what the niche was for, wasn't it?' Sophie replied, leaning back in her chair and calling over her shoulder. 'What do you think Jonathan?'

He stepped back into the room. 'It's an interesting idea,' he said. Something about the way Anna broached it made him cautious – particularly about mentioning that Ted had already told him this.

'So what would it be?' Sophie asked.

'I was thinking about commissioning a sculpture, and I wanted your professional view.' Anna scooted forward, on the edge of her seat, blue gaze fixed seriously on Sophie. 'Ted wanted it to represent something of Mary Magdalene – of her warmth, openness, vulnerability, her wish to heal.'

'That makes such perfect sense,' Sophie said, 'don't you think, darling?'

'I like the idea very much,' he said, 'Now you've reminded me, I remember Ted talking about it – the dedication to Mary Magdalene. But it'd be quite a challenge for a sculptor.'

'Not too much I hope,' said Anna, 'because I've got another idea I'd like to run past you, Sophie. Is there any possibility you'd consider doing it?'

'Me?' Her eyes widened. 'That's... very flattering of course...' A long pause. 'But I'm afraid it's rather out of my range, and anyway, I'm up to my ears at the moment.'

Anna's shoulders dropped. 'That's a pity – is it the timing?'

'Partly,' Sophie said hesitantly. 'But mostly it's that I don't do religious sculpture.'

Anna broke into a broad smile. 'I don't want *religious* sculpture – sorry, perhaps I haven't been as clear as I should have been.' She was speaking quickly, and with an eagerness Jonathan hadn't seen in her for some time. 'I'm thinking something very free form, something which is true to the spirit of Mary Magdalene.'

For once Sophie seemed lost for words. Jonathan watched her closely: he could see a spark of interest growing in her thoughtful expression.

Eventually she spoke, quietly and seriously.

'In that case, I think I would be interested... Very interested indeed... Can we talk about it? It would be new territory for me.'

'For now,' Jonathan said, 'Why don't I refill our glasses, and we can drink a toast to 'The Niche'? Then I'll serve up!'

Jonathan and Sophie spent the next two days making love and walking the fields and coastal paths of the farm, easing back into the deep conviviality they'd felt between them since they met. On their last walk, they'd stopped on the shoreline and were standing side by side, skimming pebbles onto the calm sea.

'So, Sophie Ryder, what are we going to do?'

'Well, *there's* a question...' She sighed and flung a pebble hard; it skipped over the waves twice before sinking. 'If I'm honest, it'll be tough going for a bit.'

'More time apart?'

'I know we respect each other's work.' For a moment, she was silent. 'You're much further along the road than I am – I'm at the point when I need to devote myself to it, like when you were going full tilt at your housing project. Until I've got this commission cracked, I'm going to have to stay in town.'

'That could be months.' Even at his busiest, he'd still been there – now he wouldn't even see her face. 'And what are you going to do about Anna's commission? She'll want it done by the time the granary's finished.'

Sophie nodded. 'I've thought about that. I know the granary so well, and I'm confident I know what's in Anna's mind. So I can get going on that straight away – as a welcome relief from the Richmond Park beast – whenever I have a moment. I've got an idea, and I can work up a bit and send to Anna for comment quite quickly.'

'But it'll still be some time.'

'Let's think of it as a few weeks. It can't run into more than a couple of months, for both commissions.'

Jonathan realised he'd pushed as hard as he could. He let the stone he was about to throw fall from his hand and turned instead to hold her.

'Soph… you know I'm so proud of you. I'll never stand in the way of your ambition, even if I'm sobbing into my pillow here every night!'

'Get on with you,' she murmured, wrapping her own arms around his waist in turn. 'You've got lovely friends to keep you amused till I'm back.'

'I have… but we do need to sort things out.' She could hear the earnest, serious tone of his voice. 'We can't go on like this for ever, can we?'

Sophie pulled back, just enough to look him directly in the eyes, their faces only inches apart.

'No, darling, we can't,' she said. 'Why don't we agree to do exactly that when I'm finished with my current jobs? I mean, devote proper time and space to thinking about us.'

'Thank you.' He hugged her close and whispered in her ear. 'It's a deal.'

FORTY-FIVE

Late May 1970

Once Sophie returned to London, Jonathan couldn't help but wonder whether it might always be like this. He knew her work was everything to her, but she was also much more of a free spirit, willing to take more risks, always seeking new adventures. He felt a dullard in comparison – and couldn't help but feel bitter that all the confidence he thought he'd got back since Judith left him, Sophie had now taken with her.

Still, work must go on, for the both of them. He called on Anna to finalise the details of the granary, only to find her looking weary, and without her usual welcoming smile.

'Sorry, have I come at a bad moment?'

'Not really,' she told him. 'I'm just a bit up and down at present.'

'Would you have a few minutes to talk about the granary?' He lingered in the entry to the boot room. 'I can come back another time.'

'No, let's get on with it.'

They sat down at the kitchen table, and Jonathan showed her his designs for the new railings up the steps to the granary and the external door. She seemed content, so Jonathan moved the conversation on to the sculpture.

'Have you heard anything from Sophie?'

'Not yet – I didn't expect anything quickly. Has she said anything to you?'

'Only that she wanted to get an idea to you soonish, for you to mull over.'

'I could do with something to take my mind off things.'

Still feeling at a loss, he asked, 'Anything I can do?'

'No, thanks all the same. It's something I've got to deal with myself. I'm sorry, I'm not very good company at the moment.'

He excused himself on the grounds he had to get back to the office. For the next few days he kept his distance, and on the rare occasions they bumped into each other, he noticed she looked anxious and pre-occupied.

Just as he was beginning to despair, he came home from work to find a note from Anna on his kitchen table, inviting him for supper the following evening.

He was glad to get it, but the next twenty-four hours passed with some trepidation. Was it possible she'd changed her mind, and taken Forrester up on his offer?

As he reached the farmhouse, he saw the door from the yard – firmly shut the past few days – was open wide again, as it always had been during Ted's time. To his surprise, Anna greeted him with her old warmth, and as soon as they entered the kitchen she poured him a glass of wine.

'Come on in, I've got a bottle open and I'm afraid I've already started. I've got something to celebrate!'

'What can that be? There are quite a few options.'

'Guess.' She grinned as she poured him a very generous glass.

'I'm dreading what you might have to say, if I'm honest.'

Her features softened for a moment into sympathy. 'You really don't need to – it's something you'll be thrilled about.'

'Well, I'm certainly thrilled to see you looking so cheerful.'

'I'm sorry about how I've been – though I had my reasons. Anyway, I think I'm through it now, and out the other side.'

'Thank goodness,' he said, hoping he didn't sound too excessively relieved. 'But I still haven't a clue what you're on about.'

'Where's your imagination gone?' She clucked her tongue at him. 'I suppose I'll have to tell you. It's this.'

The table, as he'd noted, was laid for supper at one end but with a cloth covering some kind of object at the other. With a broad smile, she approached the other end and whipped off the cloth, revealing a maquette of a young female nude.

'There, now you know why I'm so excited – what do you think?'

He walked around the figure, studying it from different angles, absorbed in its simple beauty. It was some time before he spoke again.

'I think it's inspired. It somehow captures innocence, vulnerability and sensuousness all at once.'

'Yes, that's exactly it. Sophie's so clever, isn't she? She's written this covering note to explain what she's trying to do – shall I read it to you?'

'Please! I know nothing about it – Sophie's always strict about client confidentiality – and anyway, I haven't heard from her since she went back. Got her head down again, I suppose.'

'She does say she's up to her ears – which is why I'm so impressed she's found time to do this for me. So, let me read what she says:

'I've been turning over in my head what sort of age Mary Magdalene might have been. I think the general presumption is she would have been in her late thirties perhaps, been round the block a few times. But why does she have to be middle-aged? Why can't she be a young woman, who's lived a bit for sure, but who's still full of life's possibilities?

'I guess some people might find that rather daring – but it's got to be good, I mean, if it changes perceptions? That'd fit in with what Ted and you had in mind for the new use of the granary, wouldn't it?'

'Don't you think that's brilliant?'

'It is – perfect for a space for fresh thinking and new directions.'

Eyes sparkling, Anna moved towards the fridge. 'I've got another bottle, so we can refill our glasses and drink a toast to Sophie – and Mary Magdalene!'

She poured two more generous glasses.

'Now, I'd better get our supper out before I have any more wine, all this excitement is making me light-headed!'

For Jonathan – and, he sensed, Anna as well – the evening was a return to the friendship they'd always enjoyed. They talked with that easy intimacy which comes from knowing each other well. After dinner he felt bold enough to ask what had caused her recent worries.

'I'm sorry,' she said, 'but I really can't say at the moment. Except to say it was about feeling lonely, I suppose.'

'That's what I guessed – and why I wanted to help.'

They were standing at the sink, finishing the washing up. Anna turned, looked him straight in the eye, and put her arms out to him. He stepped into them willingly.

'I know you did – and I couldn't cope with you. You and Sophie looked so happy together that evening. I so missed Ted that night – and felt so alone when I got home.'

He felt a pang, he hadn't even considered that. 'I can see now it would have been so hard.'

She was still looking at him intently.

'What about you? Aren't you sometimes lonely down at the mill now Sophie's not around so much? Though Ted and I always used to say there was more than a bit of a loner about you.'

'That's all true enough. And yes, I've been more on my own recently than I want to be.'

'It's none of my business, but… is everything OK between you two?'

He hesitated. 'She's just so caught up with this commission – we agreed she'd stay away in London for the time being.'

'So we're both on our own.'

'I guess… at the moment, anyway.'

They held each other closer. He was aware that something had shifted, between them, in that moment, and very conscious of how lovely he still found her.

For Anna's part, there was a natural hesitation, a keen awareness of betraying her husband's memory so soon.

But then they looked into each other's faces and, quite naturally, their lips met. She felt his strength, he her softness, as their bodies pressed against each other.

Wordlessly, she led him upstairs to the bedroom he'd had on his first visit. Still silently, they undressed each other, slowly and lovingly, until they could wait no longer to fall into that huge four poster bed.

Gently but surely, she drew him to her.

They lay together all night, not wanting to be parted for a moment – whenever sleep overcame them, one would surface enough to reach out to find the other and they fell together again. Words had never seemed so superfluous, neither wanting to break the spell.

But all too soon, still wrapped in each other's arms, the familiar sound of the morning milking woke them. They looked at each other in the glow of the farmyard lights, kissed gently, and held each other tight.

'What have we done?' Anna asked softly.

'We've made love.' He brushed a few strands of blond hair out of her face. 'We both needed that, I think.'

'Yes,' she replied, 'we absolutely did.'

'I know you'll want to get on with the day now, but… I just wanted to say that was beautiful.'

'It was,' she said, still holding him close and looking at him intently. 'Let's not say anything more just now, though. Let's live this day to its fullest, enjoy every moment, and be glad we're alive!'

'Yes, let's do just that,' he said.

They washed and dressed quickly, then went down to the kitchen, where Jonathan made a pot of tea which they shared, smiling at each other across that familiar farmhouse table. Then she came round to his side, and they shared a brief embrace before she set off across the yard to begin the work of the new day.

Curiously at ease about what anyone might think of him leaving the farmhouse at such an early hour, he made his way back to the mill house, where he treated himself to a long and leisurely breakfast with Cadoc and a short walk, before eventually, and very reluctantly, driving to the office.

FORTY-SIX

2nd June 1970

Once the spell of the morning was broken, however, the day dragged for them both.

Anna was filled with confusion – she still desperately missed Ted and worried that, in her neediness, she'd taken advantage of Jonathan, who'd perhaps only wanted to comfort her in her bereavement.

Jonathan wondered whether he'd abused Anna's vulnerability, and certainly felt he'd betrayed Sophie. Several times he was tempted to call Anna, but decided against it – a snatched conversation would achieve nothing. Better to wait till they were face to face again.

In the early evening, Anna heard his footsteps coming across the yard, a bark from Cadoc, then a nervous knock.

'Oh you are silly,' she said as she ushered him in. 'Really there was no need to knock.'

'It's lovely to see you' said Jonathan cautiously. 'I wasn't really sure what to do.'

They kissed, but tentatively.

'Would you like a cup of tea?' said Anna.

'That would be good.'

An awkward silence followed, while Anna bustled about the kitchen making the tea. Once it was made and poured, they sat staring at each other.

'I need to say something about last night, and I'm sure you do too,' she said. 'Shall I start?'

He nodded.

'It was one of the loveliest times I've ever known,' she said, 'and you were absolutely right when you said we needed to. It meant so much to me.'

'It meant so much to me too.'

'And now I need to say something more difficult.' Anna took a deep breath. 'I've spent the whole day thinking about how to put this. You'll forgive me if it doesn't quite come out right, but I say it with love.'

Jonathan felt himself bracing for the worst. 'Of course I will.'

'Here goes then. I feel quite… unsettled… anxious, even. I shouldn't have given in to my feelings and led you on.'

He let her words fall around him, keeping his eyes engaged with hers.

'You didn't lead me on,' he said. 'You're a very desirable, sexy woman. You know I'm very fond of you – and I wanted to make love with you very deeply.'

'That's very flattering… but… please, hear me out.'

'Of course.'

'You're a very lovely man – you deserve love and affection and intimacy, and Ted and I were thrilled when you and Sophie got together. I wouldn't be able to forgive myself if I got in the way of that. And I need a clear head right now, to make decisions about the future. So, lovely as it was, we can't do it again. Ever. But it'll always be in my heart as one of the best things to have ever happened to me.'

It was some time before Jonathan spoke.

'I understand what you're saying,' he said slowly, 'because you must sense I'm all muddled up too.' Now it was his turn for a steadying breath. 'I want Sophie and me to stay together, but… I sometimes wonder whether she'll want such an earthbound plodder like me, when she's such so supercharged.'

Anna reached across the table, resting her hand on one of his. 'Maybe a high-voltage woman needs to be earthed from time to time?'

He smiled weakly. 'I've never thought of it like that.'

A long silence followed, until finally she got up, came over to him, and wrapped her arms round his shoulders.

'I've got a suggestion,' she said. 'Why don't we just make supper together, keep off the booze, and talk through a few more things?'

'That sounds good.'

The routine of making a meal together settled them, and it was afterwards with some reluctance they parted, and Jonathan and Cadoc dissolved into the night.

In their separate beds, which now felt worlds apart, they slept fitfully.

FORTY-SEVEN

3rd and 4th June 1970

Next day Jonathan determined he would lose himself in his new project – a housing scheme in Bristol – shutting out all thoughts of Anna and Sophie. It didn't really work, but when Jim Jewell called to invite him for a drink at The Castle, he relished the prospect of a convivial evening away from the mill house… and Hall.

Jim had asked Tony along too, and no sooner had the three of them settled themselves at their usual table than Jim opened up a familiar line of conversation.

'Couple bits of gossip on the development front that'll interest you both.'

'What would we do without your intelligence gathering?' Tony said, already puffing on his pipe.

'I don't know what I'd do without you both,' Jonathan said. 'You do realise, you two could've had quite successful careers as private eyes!'

'Ah, well, it's only what I pick up on my rounds,' Jim said, hiding his grin with a sip of beer. 'Anyway, the first thing is, Annie Webber told me that last week a couple of blokes turned up at her place. They weren't from around here and, when she asked them what they wanted, they said they'd been sorry to hear she'd lost her husband and were wondering if she was thinking of selling up.'

'Despicable,' Tony said. 'I bet she gave them short shrift!'

'Too right she did – she's as tough as old boots, that one. But before she told them to bugger off, she asked them what they might want the farm for – I take it they were sharp-suited types who looked as though they'd never set foot in a farmyard – and they told her they were looking at possible sites for a holiday village – 'very much the coming thing,' they said.'

'That's what Penhaligan wants everyone to believe,' said Jonathan. 'And it can't just be coincidence they were shooting exactly the same line as Forrester's been spinning to Anna Northcott. God, they're all scum.'

'Well, it's certainly clear evidence of what we suspected,' said Tony. 'I've heard a couple of similar stories from two of my other farmer friends.'

'Has Annie called the police?' asked Jonathan.

'Yes, she did, immediately,' said Jim. 'Though they couldn't see any offence had been committed, they said they'd have a word and warn them off 'intimidating behaviour'. Apparently they've been staying at the White Hart, which happens to be the favourite watering hole of one of our regular coppers – he recognised them from Annie's description.'

'Pity they haven't done the same with Forrester.'

'As it happens,' said Jim, holding up a finger, 'the other bit of news is about Tricky Ricky.'

'Go on Jim, spill the beans – what's he been up to now?' Tony asked.

'I happened to be in Broadhaven hospital yesterday evening to see one of my clients who's had an op, and who should be in the next bed but our mutual friend?'

'Nothing too trivial I hope?' Jonathan said, only half-joking.

'Actually, he's pretty crocked up,' said Jim. 'I only managed a quick word – he can't talk much at the moment – but I gathered he'd been walking the cliff path at dusk – quite near your place, Jonathan, actually – when he'd slipped and fallen down a steep slope, about thirty feet he thinks. Managed to crawl back up and made it home. Got a neighbour to drive him to hospital.'

'Bit stupid of him, walking the cliff path as it was getting dark,' Tony said.

'I certainly wouldn't try it,' Jonathan said, 'and it's very slippery at the moment after all the rain.'

'Something else,' Jim said. 'I'm only a vet, but I've treated lots of animals who've had that kind of fall. They usually end up having to be put down – broken legs or spine.' Another pause. 'Forrester didn't break any limbs. He's got concussion – that's why he was being kept in overnight for observation – and a few cracked ribs. But his face's a hell of a mess – broken jaw, broken nose, and two black eyes.'

Tony drew sharply on his pipe, and ended up coughing. 'You mean it looks more like a beating?'

'As I said, I'm not a medical man, but I'd bet on it.'

'I don't find the fellow easy, but don't wish him any harm either,' Jonathan said. 'If he's been done over, I wonder who did it and why?'

'Probably quite a queue!' Tony said.

'Too right,' Jim replied. 'I suppose it could be a falling-out among rivals.'

'Well,' Tony said, reaching for his glass, 'I guess he'll be out of action for a while. A suave operator like him won't want to be seen out and about in that state.'

'That's true enough,' Jonathan said, a little quickly. 'Now, I'll get the next round, and we can move on to more pleasant matters.'

He returned home shaken up by Jim's account, which had revived all his anxieties about sinister goings-on in the area. And, if Forrester had been attacked… Jonathan realised, uneasily, he'd be a likely suspect. He'd got a motive – Forrester's attempts to pressure Anna about the farm – and opportunity – he lived nearby and walked those paths daily.

What on earth would Anna make of the news?

He found himself hoping Forrester stuck to his line about slipping and falling.

But the next morning, Anna waved him down as he was passing the farmhouse on the way to the office.

'Have you heard what's happened to Richard?'

'Only last night in the pub,' he said, immediately assailed by an over-developed sense of guilt. 'Too late to call in on my way home, you'd gone to bed, I'm sure.'

'I probably had. I heard about it from the postman this morning – he'd seen Richard earlier when he dropped his post off, said he'd had a bad accident and only just got out of hospital. He looks awful apparently, face like a punch-bag.'

'Yes, I'd heard the same from Jim Jewell.'

'Do you think it was an accident?'

Jonathan hesitated. 'Seems a bit odd to have done such a lot of damage to his face.'

'That's what I thought. I gave Richard a ring just now and he sounded rough. Insists it was his fault, shouldn't have been so stupid walking the coast in the dark.'

'Why on earth was he out walking the cliff path at that hour anyway? Lucky he didn't do himself more damage.'

Anna paused. 'Have you got time to stop in for a few minutes? There's something I need to tell you.'

'If it's quick – I've got a meeting at ten o'clock.' He turned off the Volvo's engine and got out of the car. 'This is all very mysterious.'

'I don't know how to put this,' Anna said as soon as they were settled at the farmhouse table, 'because I'm worried you'll think badly of me.'

'I promise I won't, Anna, whatever it is.'

'You'd better wait till you hear what it is first.' She grimaced. 'What's happened to Richard may be my fault.'

'Don't see how that could possibly be the case.'

'You might if you hear me out… remember when I went all quiet on you? Well, the truth is Richard's called round a few times recently. He's proving to be a good friend – but I promise, just a friend.'

Jonathan coloured up.

'FOR GOD'S SAKE, ANNA!' he blazed. 'You might have told me you two had got it together before we fucked each other!'

'HOW DARE YOU!' Anna fired back. 'I didn't tell you because I knew you'd lose it. If you weren't so bloody jealous and hostile to him I'd have told you straight away – '

'Oh really?'

'YES, you idiot!' she shouted. 'UNLIKE YOU, he appreciates I'm barely keeping my head above water!'

The silence that followed was broken only by some rather hard breathing.

'All right,' Jonathan said, holding his hands up in a pleading gesture. 'So why on earth do you think his 'accident' is anything to do with you?'

'If you'd not so rudely interrupted me, I was trying to explain.'

'OK, OK. I'm really sorry.'

'I didn't want gossip going round about Richard and me, which might have happened if his car had been seen coming here or parked in the yard. So he agreed to walk over and back by the cliff path – he'd been here earlier the evening he had his accident.'

'It sounds as though he's been coming quite frequently.'

'For heaven's sake, Jonathan!' she said, raising her voice again. 'If you want it straight, it was precisely to avoid you being like this I asked him to walk over. If you'd seen his car in the yard, you'd have put two and two together and made a hundred. Let me remind you of what I said last time – I'm a grown woman and I don't need you acting like an over-protective father of a teenage girl.'

There was a long silence while Jonathan struggled to get control of his anger.

'I was only trying to look out for you.'

'Well stop – I don't need 'looking out for,' as you so patronisingly put it. Why don't you grow up and try to get your head round what might have really happened to Richard?'

Another silence followed. At some point during their shouting match they'd both stood up, but now Jonathan sat down with his head in his hands.

'I'm sorry,' he said. 'It's been... difficult. I've got this wrong, apparently... So what do you think happened?'

'If I'm honest, I'm sure Richard was attacked, though he's probably so shaken up he won't admit it to anyone just now.'

'How can you be sure?'

'One of the reasons he's been coming over here is he suspected his house was being watched and his car followed – he thought it was much more difficult for someone to trail him if he was out walking the cliff path. So it also suited him to come on foot.'

'Do you know why anyone would be watching him?' He recalled what Jim said about Annie Webber. 'Assuming it wasn't the police... '

'It definitely wasn't the police. He'd told me he'd had notes put through his door, left on his windscreen – warning him to leave off property dealings in the area.'

A good ruse to get her sympathy, thought Jonathan, though he was chastened enough not to voice that suspicion. And anyway – when he thought about it rationally, at least – he realised it fitted into the pattern he, Jim and Tony had speculated about, and for which this could be another bit of hard evidence.

'I hope he's kept those notes,' Jonathan said. 'If it turns out he was attacked, he'll need something to show the police... Look, Anna, I'd better get off to work now, I'm already late for my meeting. But I'm sorry if he's been given a beating, I wouldn't wish that on anyone. And I apologise again for being jealous and stupid, please forgive me.'

'I shall – but please keep your word this time, and never do this again.'

'I give you my word, Anna.'

With that he got back in the Volvo and drove off, much chastened.

FORTY-EIGHT

Second week in June 1970

Though he couldn't be sure his memory was entirely reliable, Richard Forrester did now remember being hit from behind – which was why he'd initially reasoned he must have slipped, hit the back of his head as he went down, and blacked out. The more he mulled it over, though, the more he realised his other injuries were unlikely to have been caused by a fall.

He decided to let Anna in on his thinking. He'd been getting out on short walks but was anxious for his own safety, living on his own in a relatively remote spot. And he wanted to keep out of the public eye till his face had healed up. So he asked Anna if, as part of his recovery, he could drive over to Hall occasionally to do some light tasks needed around the farm.

She'd agreed immediately, knowing Len could always use another pair of hands. She'd sometimes offer him a cup of coffee or tea after he'd finished – in fact she began to look forward to his visits, feeling increasingly at ease in his company. She'd mentioned this to Jonathan because she wanted to be open about it, but also to demonstrate she knew her own mind. He hadn't been best pleased, to say the least.

'Hello Anna, it's me again I'm afraid,' Richard said tentatively when she answered his knock on the door. He still looked as if he wasn't entirely sure of his welcome – or was just checking the coast was clear of Jonathan.

'Come in Richard, please – did I spot you giving Len a hand in the tractor shed today?'

'Yes, I rather enjoy tinkering with engines, good fun, and it keeps my mind off other stuff.'

'Do you fancy a cuppa?'

'Please, if you can spare the time.'

'Your face is healing up nicely, now all that bruising's starting to fade.'

'Yes it is, thank goodness.'

She had made a cherry cake earlier, and they had a bit more time to talk while they sampled it. As they did, Anna decided to level with him about Jonathan's prickly reaction to his offer. He responded with a sigh and shrug of the shoulders.

'Par for the course, I'm afraid – it's ironic really, architects and property developers need one other, but many architects tend to view everyone in my line of business as wide-boys, utterly unscrupulous, and only interested in as much profit as possible.'

'That's true of some developers, isn't it?'

'Of course it is, as I've found out to my cost. In fact there's some unsavoury characters from the London area apparently operating round here now. But we're not all out to make a quick buck.'

'I'm beginning to realise that. It would be quite a shock to Ted to hear me say that, he tended to take the same line as Jonathan.'

'I'd picked that up.'

She went over to the range to refresh the pot. After she returned to the table and refilled their cups, she returned to her line of questioning.

'Can I ask what you honestly think about the Studies Centre?'

'I've always thought it was an interesting concept,' he said, 'right from the start when you had that open evening to launch it. And now it's up and running I think it's great – it's really brought new life to the area, just the sort of thing we need.'

'I still worry a bit about the hostility it whipped up.'

'More the hostility other people whipped up, surely?'

'I suppose so. But it wasn't nice, and it really upset Ted.'

'Pretty much inevitable, I'm afraid. In my line of business, I'm always up against the fact most people are, at best, ambivalent about change. Most of those who've moved into the area don't know anything about country life – and those who've only lived in the country have absolutely no idea what life is like in our cities now.'

'Have another slice of cake.' Heartened by his response about the Studies Centre, she now moved to the critical question.

'In your heart, Richard, do you think your client's ideas about new holiday villages could be a good thing in themselves, other than bringing in huge profits to the developers?'

'I'm not sure about huge profits,' he admitted. 'The holiday business can be pretty fickle. But yes, I think there's potential for community good. You might even argue they could help rural and urban England reconnect again – as the Studies Centre does, but in a different way.'

'I suppose so.' She was half ready to be convinced, half sceptical, and fully conscious of what Ted would have thought.

Richard had finished his cake and pushed his chair back from the table.

'I read history at university, so tend to the long view,' he said. 'You get periods of prosperity and expansion followed by stagnation and decline, followed by recovery, followed by another downward spiral, and so on. We've been on the downward path for a lot of this century, but now we seem to be on the up again – about time too, a quarter of a century on from the end of the last war.'

'Ted always saw the history of Hall like that,' Anna said, gazing into her mug of tea. 'Though he had his glass-half-empty moments, he was always looking forwards, not backwards… that's why we took the risk of developing the farm in the way we have.'

Richard slowly rose, smiling a little.

'Then perhaps our world views aren't as far apart as they've sometimes seemed.'

Anna got up too, anxious to get over another point before he left.

'I'm still not entirely sure… But I'm seriously considering your offer. I've talked to Nicky and Will about it, and they want to take a bit of time to go into the implications with various advisors – which surprised me, I thought they'd dismiss it out of hand.'

Richard had almost reached the door, but turned round, smiling broadly.

'Good for them. Now, just take your time, all of you, there's no need for you to rush into a decision. And, I say again, I only want the best for all three of you.'

FORTY-NINE

17th and 18th June 1970

Jonathan knew he'd handled his most recent exchange with Anna badly. Though he wanted to put things right, he couldn't see how – he daren't broach the subject of the farm's future again, and all he could do now was wait on the family's decision. At the same time, he was exasperated by the lack of contact with Sophie – they hadn't spoken for a month now – and in his gloomier moments wondered whether it might be all over, despite her promises. On top of this personal angst, he was rattled by the attack on Richard Forrester and mystified about what it might mean.

'Jonathan?' Emma was peering round the door. 'Will you take a personal call?'

'Who is it?'

'I don't know – a man, who won't give his name or even say what he's calling about. When I pressed him all he would say was that it was a private matter.'

'That's a bit odd.' Jonathan rose from his drawing board. 'Tell you what – is one of the meeting rooms free? Give me a minute and I'll take it there.'

He descended the stairs, closed the meeting room door behind him, and took a deep breath as he sat down and picked up the phone.

'Hello, Jonathan Lane speaking.'

'Good morning, Mr Lane.' The voice was friendly enough, but professional. 'My name is Probert – Detective Chief Inspector Probert.'

Jonathan froze. What on earth could this be about?

'I'm afraid the name doesn't ring a bell, Chief Inspector,' he managed, after more than a moment's hesitation.

'It wouldn't, sir, we haven't met. The thing is, I was wondering whether you could spare me an hour of your time in the next day or so – absolutely nothing for you to be worried about, more a question of a quiet chat between us on a matter I think you'll find of interest.'

'Well yes, of course – but it would help me to have some idea of what that might be.'

'I'd rather not say on the phone, sir, if you don't mind. But as I say, you've got nothing to worry about. I appreciate this is an unusual request – and I'd quite understand if you'd rather we came to some other arrangement – but I'd value your time, and your discretion. Perhaps my sergeant and I could call on you at home? I understand you live in a fairly remote spot where we wouldn't attract attention.'

The fact the police knew where he lived only increased his agitation, but he decided to play along for the time being.

'Yes, it's a bit out of the way.'

'That's all to the good, then. So, when would suit you, sir?'

'Let me check my diary with reception. I'll be a minute.'

Better get this over with sooner rather than later, he thought, whatever it was. After peering at Emma's office diary he found he was free the next day. He jogged back to the conference room.

'Hello Chief Inspector, would tomorrow morning about ten o'clock be any good for you?'

'That would suit very well, sir.'

'Good. Do you need directions?'

'My sergeant says your place is marked on the O.S. map, so we should be able to find you easily enough. We'll see you at ten then.'

He put the phone down and drew breath.

Bloody hell, what on earth's going on? He figured it must be pretty serious if they'd put a Chief Inspector on it. Then his throat seemed to close up – God, it couldn't be about Forrester, could it?

Jonathan spent a restless night, his fevered imagination running through unpleasant scenarios. When morning came, he found himself watching the clock nervously, fidgeting until it was time for his visitors to arrive.

On the dot of ten, an unmarked saloon car pulled up in the yard. Cadoc dashed out to meet the new arrivals, sniffing the air and investigating unfamiliar scents. Out of the passenger door stepped a large, comfortable-looking man in late middle age – just as Jonathan had imagined him from his voice on the phone – while out of the driver's door came a smartly dressed young woman. As they walked towards the house, Jonathan gaped – the smartly dressed woman was more than familiar.

'Hello Jonathan,' Naomi Walters said brightly, 'sorry about the shock, but it's good to see you again.'

'Naomi? What on earth – '

'Detective Sergeant Walters, strictly speaking, Mr Lane,' said the policeman, advancing towards Jonathan with outstretched hand. 'And I'm Detective Chief Inspector Probert.'

Both officers produced their warrant cards.

Jonathan was momentarily lost for words.

'Well, I'm… very pleased to meet you, Chief Inspector... and I'm pleased to see you too, Naomi, of course… or should I call you Sergeant?'

She glanced at the Chief Inspector, who waved a hand in casual assent.

'That's absolutely fine with me,' she said. 'We'd like our little chat to be as relaxed as possible.'

'And this is Cadoc,' Jonathan said in slightly apologetic tones, as the dog continued to snuffle their shoes and eventually placed muddy paws on Probert's knee.

'I love dogs,' said the Chief Inspector, bending down to give the enthusiastic spaniel a scratch between the ears. 'The wife and I've got a golden lab back home – he's company for her when I'm away, which I often am in my line of work.'

'Cadoc's a great chum to me,' said Jonathan, warming to the Chief Inspector's affability. 'Well, do please come in. Would you like some coffee?'

'Thank you, sir, that would be very welcome,' Probert said as Jonathan ushered them both through the front door and into the sitting room. 'Nice spot you've got here, tucked away from the world.'

'Yes, it suits me very well.' He had to bite back a fumbling string of assurances that he simply liked the country, and his seclusion was in no way a cover for anything suspicious. Instead he busied himself at the range, fetching the coffee pot and a couple of mugs.

'Help yourselves to milk and sugar,' he said, as he brought everything in. 'There's a slice of cake too, if you'd like…' He added that last with slight hesitance, not wanting to be seen as currying favour.

'Rather,' said the Chief Inspector. 'Never can resist cake, can I, Sergeant?'

'No sir, that's very true,' Naomi said with a practised smile.

'Now,' said the Chief Inspector, 'I expect you're wondering what this is all about.'

Jonathan's heart was pounding.

'I think that's the understatement of the century, if you don't mind me saying, Chief Inspector. I've had a sleepless night I don't mind telling you… Asking for a secret meeting in my own house – and you, Naomi, turning up as a police sergeant! That takes the biscuit.'

'Perfectly understandable you should feel like that, sir, and I apologise that it was necessary,' said the policeman calmly. 'Let me try to explain.' The Chief Inspector settled back in his chair. 'I'll level with you straight off: we're from Scotland Yard's Serious Fraud Squad, and we're investigating a suspected criminal conspiracy involving nationwide corruption. It's a complicated case with several intersecting lines of inquiry, but we'll do our best to paint the general picture for you, and then explain why we need your help.'

'I see,' said Jonathan, recalling Naomi's last words before she left Broadhaven.

'For some time we've been investigating an outfit, based in London and the South East but with tentacles all over the country, which procures contracts for public sector development. Nothing wrong with that, of course, but this lot land a suspiciously large proportion of such contracts. We're on to serious wrong-doing in the way they operate – improper use of influence, backhanders, intimidation, etc. We think it also involves bribery of some elected councillors and officials.'

'The sort of thing that got you the push from the council for being too nosy about,' Jonathan said, looking to Naomi. 'I have to say, it's worried me ever since.'

Naomi looked to Probert.

'Go ahead, Sergeant.'

'That's exactly right, Jonathan. Back then, what I told you was almost all true: I was seconded from London, though not from Whitehall. I was with the Fraud Squad, working undercover. Our investigation was in early stages, and we were beginning to look in detail at a range of different councils to see if we could find common factors in the awarding of contracts. I was rumbled just as I was beginning to get my teeth into some meaty evidence. But, as I promised you I would, I've continued working on the case from London, co-ordinating evidence from other colleagues working across the country.'

'I can imagine when you join up all the dots it's a big operation,' he said. 'But surely, it's all small beer and bit-part players down here? Like our modest little housing scheme.'

'Far from it, sir,' Probert said. 'What's going on hereabouts is proving the key to unlocking the whole conspiracy.' He paused, helping himself to another slice of cake. 'There's a lot of money on the line: lucrative property speculation around the new motorway, promise of new towns and overspill, and then there's private sector development, these 'holiday villages' and the like. It adds up to potentially very rich pickings.'

'And it's got much more intense now the motorway is under construction,' Naomi said. 'We think the conspirators assumed the far south-west would be a pushover for their operation: gullible rustics, easy to roll over. They couldn't be more wrong, as we're assembling the evidence to prove.'

'I can see better how it all connects, but I'm still wondering what use I can be.'

'Ah,' said Probert, 'time we got round to that. Any chance of another coffee, please, sir? And would you mind if we stepped outside for a breath of fresh air, sir, while you're doing that? It's such a beautiful morning.'

'Not at all.'

He welcomed the short break, and as he returned to the range with the coffee pot, he spotted Probert through the window, having a quick smoke as he and Naomi walked around the yard talking quietly to each other.

'So,' he said when he took the refilled coffee pot back to the sitting room, where his visitors had since returned to their chairs. 'How can I help?'

'I gather from my sergeant that you agreed before she left to keep an eye out for any suspicious activity?' Probert said.

'Yes, I did. I've compiled a dossier, actually… various bits of information which you may or may not find useful.'

'That's brilliant Jonathan, I told the Chief Inspector we could count on you – would you be happy for us to see it?'

'Yes, of course. I'll fish it out now and you can take it with you.' He went off into his study and returned with his folder. 'Here it is – would you like a flavour of what's in there?'

'If it's no trouble, sir,' said Probert.

He gave them a brief summary of what he'd accumulated: Penhaligan's curious antics, not least over the council's sudden enthusiasm for new holiday villages; Harry Humphries' speech at the public meeting about the Studies Centre and his role in the hostile campaign run by the *Gazette* against that and the public housing project; Humphries' brazen effort to recruit him; the suspicious behaviour of Walter Johnson over tendering and contracts; the cack-handed attempt to intimidate Annie Webber; property speculators sizing up farms for development; and Forrester's activities, including his offer to Anna to buy up Hall for development as well as his 'accident'.

'This is just what we need,' said Probert, looking through the dossier and noting how each entry was meticulously recorded with date, time, and place. 'Ever since Sergeant Walters had to be recalled, we've kept a discreet eye on the goings-on around here, and what you've described corroborates what we've gleaned from other sources. Anything you've got on the activities of Mr Johnson, Councillor Penhaligan, or Mr Humphries will be especially useful. Humphries is most certainly a person of interest, as his name crops up in several of our other investigations.'

'Can I ask a question, please?' said Jonathan. 'Is Richard Forrester's accident news to you?'

'I can confirm Richard Forrester is also a person of interest,' Naomi said. 'We're aware he's active on the property development front, but so far we've got no evidence to connect him to any of this suspicious activity. We had heard he'd 'taken a tumble' while out walking on the cliffs – all I can say is that if it turned out to be an assault, that might have a very significant impact on our inquiries.'

'Intimidation is one of the hallmarks of this mob,' Probert said. 'If we could pin a charge of GBH, or even something more serious on one of their thugs, we'd probably be able to tie it back the big boys back in London running the show. That would be a real breakthrough for us.'

'I see,' Jonathan said. 'Well, I'll certainly let you know if I hear anything more about Forrester – and anything else of course.'

'Good,' said Probert. 'Now, that's probably more than enough from us for now. You've already been of great assistance to us, sir. Here's my card with our phone number, and if you hear anything you think might be of interest to us, give me or Sergeant Walters a call. And keep all this to yourself for the time being, if you don't mind.'

'Yes, I certainly will, of course. It's been a very interesting morning.'

'Thought you'd think so, sir. And thanks for the coffee – and cake!'

'Thanks, Jonathan,' Naomi said, with a broad smile at last. 'It really is good to see you again. And thanks for the refreshments too.'

As they got back into their car and drove off, Jonathan collapsed back into his chair, with a surge of relief and reassurance – relief that he wasn't being held accountable for anything, but more than that, it was good to know his suspicions had been well-founded.

FIFTY

21st and 22nd June 1970

Though Anna was pleased Jonathan now seemed prepared to give Richard Forrester the benefit of the doubt, she knew there was a long way to go if she and Jonathan were to find a way back to their old ease with one another. She missed their friendship – but she also needed his professional advice, more than ever now she and the children were looking seriously into the pros and cons of Richard Forrester's offer.

Somehow, she had to resolve the impasse between Richard and Jonathan.

She briefly considered inviting them both over for a meal, an idea she'd flagged to Richard, who seemed relaxed about it. But she knew Jonathan would need time – and more evidence – before he'd take to Richard. Sometimes – in that respect, anyway – he reminded her of Ted.

So she hit on another idea. Given that Richard had begun to recollect some of the details of his attack, she reasoned it would greatly enhance the credibility of his story, not least in Jonathan's eyes, if he'd go to the police and come clean about it.

To her surprise, when she put this to Richard, he agreed immediately.

'Stupid of me not to have done it before – but I wanted to wait till I was back to my old self. If I could use your phone, I'll ring the police now and see if I can file a report this afternoon.'

'Go ahead. You know where it is, in the hall passage.'

She watched as he went off to make the call, busying herself in the kitchen as she strained to catch a few murmured fragments of the conversation. After a few minutes he returned.

'All settled. I'm going over to Broadhaven at four. I think you're right, it could make a difference as to how Jonathan sees me.' His tone turned wry. 'Can't do any harm, certainly.'

'That's brilliant, Richard, I'll tell him this evening when he calls for milk on the way home.'

'Probably even better to wait till tomorrow morning on his way to work – then I can phone you later to let you know how I got on, and you can tell him that too.'

It was, however, much later than she'd expected when Richard eventually called.

'It was all a bit curious really,' he told her, 'they seemed to be expecting me.'

'Well, the rumour mill's been running full tilt about what happened to you. The police will have picked up on that, I'm sure.'

'I suppose so. Anyway, the duty sergeant was very interested in what I had to say. I gave him those threatening notes I'd been getting and told him all I could remember about what happened on the cliff path. He asked me to draft a statement, including the names of the medics who treated me at the hospital and anyone else I'd spoken to about the incident. I suppose, given my delay in reporting it, he wanted to pin down when I changed my story. So they're going to talk to the medics and you as well, I'm afraid, because you're the only one outside the hospital I've told about it.'

'That's all right. I can corroborate a lot about how you were after the attack and the way your memory's gradually come back.'

'That'll be very helpful.' There was a long pause, Anna pressed the phone more tightly to her ear. 'But something strange happened, which is why I've been so long in calling you.'

'Which was?'

'They asked whether I'd have time to speak to a more senior officer, a Detective Chief Inspector, I think they said he was. He seemed a nice enough fellow – went over the same ground with me, and said he was going to do some follow-up work on the case because it might have links with other inquiries they were making.'

'Did you tell him your suspicions about those other dodgy characters operating in the area?'

'Oh yes, he was very interested in that – and my notes. He said they could turn out to be important evidence.'

'That all sounds good.'

'It was. Except the Chief Inspector told me, in a friendly way mind you, to watch my back – 'don't take any unnecessary risks, and don't walk the cliff path on your own for a bit,' which I found a little disconcerting.'

'That's only what I've been saying, isn't it?' Anna rolled her eyes; one day, maybe, she'd meet a man who had any concern at all for his own health and safety. 'How much of this do you want me to say to Jonathan?'

'Good question. Not all of it – I was told to keep quiet about the wider investigation. I think just stick to the bits about me going to the police and them taking my story very seriously.'

'I will.'

Next morning Anna waved Jonathan down as the Volvo chugged down the lane past the farmhouse.

'Can you come in for a moment? It's important.'

'Yes, of course.'

He parked up and they went into the house.

He was relieved she seemed more relaxed, and more like her old self as they sat at the table opposite each other.

'I want things to be right between us again,' she said as she set the coffee mugs down on the table.

'I do too, Anna, I really do.'

'Good. Then I think you'll be interested in what I've got to tell you. It's about Richard. And before you say or think anything, I want to say I realise he's been a big part of the problem between you and me recently.'

'Yes, I agree.'

'So, when we last talked about all this, you admitted you didn't wish him any harm and would be very sorry if it turned out he had been attacked.'

'I did – and I would.' Jonathan gave her a cautious look. 'Given you told me he'd been on the receiving end of threatening notes, it seemed the most likely explanation. I couldn't understand why he seemed to be pretending it had been an accident – '

'He wasn't pretending, Jonathan – he was badly concussed and it'd played tricks with his memory. But as he's recovered, he's now clear he was attacked pretty viciously by two men, first from behind with a blow to the head, and then when he was on the ground with kicks and punches.'

He'd made some jokes about it, but the prospect of actual violence – that someone he knew, even if he didn't particularly like them, had been savagely beaten… the very idea caused him to recoil.

'Poor fellow – he could've been killed. He must go to the police.'

'He already has, yesterday afternoon. They're taking his story very seriously – he wanted me to tell you that – and he gave them all the notes he'd kept. But they also want it kept quiet for the moment while they follow up some leads.'

'Of course, I'll keep it to myself.'

Jonathan rose, taking a slow circuit around the room, peering out of the window before coming back to his chair.

'Look, Anna,' he said, 'I'm really very grateful, to both of you, for telling me this. You're absolutely right – it's been my view of Richard which has fouled things up between us.'

'I've hated how at odds we've felt the last few weeks.'

'So have I. I owe you both an apology. I've been pretty insensitive about what a struggle it must be for you without Ted. And I think I've got it seriously wrong about Richard – about the kind of fellow he is, and his offer on Hall.' Finishing off the last of his coffee, he laid a hand on hers. 'Now… high time I got off to work. But again… thank you.'

FIFTY-ONE

Late June 1970

Jonathan felt a cloud had been lifted. Things between him and Anna were on the mend, and what Richard told the police tied in with the wider picture they'd painted. Richard was in the clear, in his own mind at least, and Jonathan felt he could regain a proper perspective on the future of Hall.

Now all he needed was for him and Sophie to sort themselves out.

He'd been agonising over whether to come clean with her about what had happened between him and Anna. In his heart, he felt he must, but what would she think of him? Not much, he suspected – who'd want to stay with a creep who'd taken advantage of a lonely widow and a mutual friend?

◈

Back in London, Sophie had been totally immersed in her work for weeks. The Richmond Park bronze had been a nightmare – two large sections had required recasting at the last moment. But now, apart from its installation, it was almost done. Somehow, she'd also squeezed out enough time and space to finish the Mary Magdalene figure. Now her thoughts could finally return to her future.

She adored so much about her life in London, the sheer buzz of it, the feeling she was where it was all happening. And here, she was best placed to win more work – when she compared it to staid, small-town living in the far south-west, she found that wanting. And, lovable though Jonathan was in so many ways, he was rather staid too – did she really want to hitch her star to a provincial architect in a small rural practice?

And there was another complication, this one wholly unexpected.

She and Esther Gracie had seen a lot of each other now they were both living in London. Esther was pursuing a career in painting and, in order to earn a few pennies, had agreed to model for Sophie. She was brilliant, able to hold a pose for ages. And one day Sophie had a flash of inspiration – why not use Esther as the model for her figure of Mary Magdalene?

Esther had been taken aback.

'I don't understand – surely I'm too young? Mary Magdalene was much older.'

'She's mostly been seen like that. But I see her as much younger, someone in her early twenties like you. She's a mixture of innocence and knowing, for sure, but still full of wonder about what life will bring.'

'I can see I qualify for the innocent bit,' Esther said with a laugh, 'but I'm not sure about the knowing! What do you need me to do?'

'Well, like you've done for me several times now: posing for an hour or so at a time while I draw and sketch you. I'd pay you well.'

'Sounds easy enough.'

'There's just one thing. I'll need you to model completely nude this time.'

'Oh, I see – can I have a think about that? It would be rather different from my sitting for you till now.'

'I'm not asking any more than your models do in your life classes at The Slade,' Sophie promised. 'And we can be here in the flat rather than the studio – it's a bit too cold to be standing around there without any clothes on!'

'That's certainly true! ... All right, I'll give it a go.'

It proved a good move. Esther could hold exactly the standing pose Sophie wanted, and sculptor and model soon relaxed with each other.

They'd work for an hour, take a break, then resume for another hour. Sophie was pleased with her progress and Esther was pleased with the images Sophie was creating. An easy intimacy developed between them and, if they were working in the evening, they got to share supper and an occasional bottle of wine.

'I'm just coming over to adjust your hair,' Sophie said, on one such evening, 'if that's OK.'

'Yes, of course, it's got a bit longer than I like it.'

'It's lovely… I only need to push it back a bit so it falls in a slightly different way.'

As she adjusted Esther's hair, she found herself stroking her neck and shoulders. She saw Esther was smiling.

'That feels nice,' she said softly.

They were standing very close to each other. Tentatively, Esther put her arms around Sophie's neck, and Sophie's hands began to caress. As she did, Esther drew Sophie's body to hers and their lips finally met.

'I think it's not fair you've got your clothes on,' said Esther, in between their lingering kisses.

'We can soon put that right!' Sophie said, with a wide and knowing smile.

For the next few weeks, they were lovers – thrilled to find such joy in each other, neither having ever contemplated such a possibility before. But soon they were forced to confront what the future held. Esther was about to take up the scholarship she'd been awarded to study painting in Paris in early September. And now the lease on both London studio and flat were ending, Sophie needed to decide whether to stay in London, move back to the far south-west – or go somewhere utterly different.

With great reluctance – but a mutual agreement it had been life-enhancing – they agreed to end the affair, vowing to remain the closest of friends.

Sophie felt she'd been brought down to earth with a bump. She had to get a grip, and knew that had to be as much about Jonathan as anything else. She wasn't certain she'd ever tell him about her and Esther – there's a good reason why some things are best left unsaid. She'd been on a high, absorbed in her work, and carried away by the sensuality of not just Esther, but the piece itself. Now, for all her frustrations with Jonathan… though she didn't regret the affair itself, she felt deeply troubled about the way she'd treated him.

She determined to go down and see him. She had a gold-plated pretext, because she had to deliver the Mary Magdalene figure for the granary's opening anyway.

Once again, the constraints of Jonathan's office set useful boundaries. She made the call with some trepidation, wondering what sort of reception she'd get.

'Sophie,' he answered with no trace of his usual boyish enthusiasm, 'what a surprise.'

'Hello, darling, I'm just crawling down the phone with apologies for my bad behaviour.'

'Well, I have to admit I was beginning to wonder whether I'd ever hear from you again. You've gone completely silent for weeks.'

For the first time, she felt a tinge of guilt.

'I know. I don't want to make excuses, but that big job turned out to be a bugger towards the end –and I've been racing to finish the piece for Anna as well. But I've treated you very badly, I know, and I'm just so sorry.'

'Well, thank you for saying that. I have to say I am a bit confused.'

'You mean about us?' There was a long silence. 'Look, I know you can't talk in the office. Can I come down and stay so we could talk properly?'

'Why does that phrase always sound so ominous?'

That hurt her. 'I didn't mean it to be.'

'We did agree when you were last here it can't go on like this for ever, so maybe now is a good moment for us to have that proper sort out.'

'That's what I want, darling.'

'Good. So when are you thinking of coming? Anna's been asking me whether you'd finished her figure.'

'I've finished it. So I thought I could bring it down with me – and maybe we could install it together?'

'Yes, of course I'd be very happy to – it's come to mean so much to all of us.'

'What dates can you manage? I'll fit in with you.'

'I'm free almost all of next month. Why don't you call Anna and find out what would suit her?'

Sophie got on to Anna straight away.

'Hello Anna, Sophie here. I'm sorry to have been an age getting back to you.'

Anna was momentarily taken aback to hear Sophie's voice – and more than a little anxious about what Jonathan might have said to her.

'Hello Sophie, good to hear from you,' she said, more tentatively than she intended. 'I was beginning to think you might have forgotten me now you're so much in the public eye.'

'I'm really sorry Anna, should have kept you more in the picture.'

'It's all right. Jonathan mentioned you'd expected your Richmond Park job to be tough going. But how are things going with my little figure?'

'It's finished! I'm calling to arrange a time when I can bring it down.'

Anna relaxed. Either Sophie was just being utterly professional, or Jonathan had said nothing. 'Wow, how exciting! I can't wait to see it. When can you come?'

'I might come and stay with Jonathan for a couple of nights the week after next. It'll take a bit of time for me to install the figure in the niche, of course, so we'd need to put aside a few hours of a day to make sure I get it right for you. So you could choose any day in the middle of that week.'

'That would be wonderful. Given we're so near midsummer, I thought we'd have a small lunch party in the granary to celebrate the installation – just the family and a few people who've been close all the way along. Then, after we've eaten and everyone's got a glass in their hand, I'd ask you to unveil it.'

'I'd regard that as a real privilege.'

'Let me make a few phone calls and I'll get back to you. We're talking about the week beginning the sixth of July, aren't we?'

'Yes. I'll keep it completely free till I know what would suit you best.'

FIFTY-TWO
8th July 1970

Sophie drove down on the 8th, the day before the planned unveiling, leaving London early and arriving in the late morning. Though they'd both sensed the tension between them over the phone, it was different face to face. They held the other's gaze, smiling broadly, then threw themselves into each other's arms.

'It's so good to be here,' Sophie murmured.

'It's so good to have you here,' Jonathan said. 'Fancy a coffee?'

'That would be a lifesaver. But...' She pointed to a large package strapped into the passenger seat of the Sprite '... then we'll need to get on. Young Mary M's been sitting patiently for hours and she needs to find herself a niche!'

After swiftly downing their coffees, Jonathan followed Sophie over to the farmhouse where Anna was waiting.

'Sophie, it's so good to see you!' Anna said. 'I can't wait to see the real thing!'

'Well, here she is, sitting in the car.'

They carried the carefully wrapped figure up the steps and placed it on the floor of the granary. Sophie loosened the protective layers, and silence fell as Jonathan helped her lift the figure into the niche.

They stood back, waiting for Anna to speak.

'I'm sorry about this,' she said, wiping her eyes. 'You're so talented,

Sophie. I'll never be able to thank you enough. Ted would have adored it. Don't you think, Jonathan?'

'I do,' said Jonathan. 'I love the way you've used the grain of the wood to express the flowing curves of her body. You've somehow managed to make her chaste and sensuous. And the face is just perfect – serene but with the wide-eyed wonder of youth at what life might hold.'

'I've really only been finding her beauty in the wood,' said Sophie.

'You're too modest Sophie. It's your idea – and your skill as a sculptor – which brought her to life,' Anna said. 'It's just what I wanted – and Ted would have wanted too – for the granary's new lease of life.'

'I'm glad you feel she suits – I have to say I am pleased now I see her in place! I'll need to settle her in properly so she's firmly fixed.'

'Why don't you do that after we've had some lunch? You could surely do with a bite to eat after driving all the way down this morning? Come on, I've got something ready. When we're done this afternoon, I'll come over and cover her with a lovely gold cloth I've found for the unveiling, but let's leave her in peace for now – she looks entirely at home already!'

After they'd finished the installation, Jonathan and Sophie went for a long walk in the warm July sunshine, conscious of the need to have the 'proper talk' they'd promised. The familiarity of their surroundings and their engagement in a common task had recovered something of their old intimacy, and to Jonathan, the moment seemed right.

'I haven't seen your Richmond Park piece, Soph, but in my humble opinion Mary Mag is the best thing you've ever done.'

'Do you know, I think it is too? There's a lot of my life in that piece.'

'It's a remarkable interpretation. In fact there was something about it I couldn't quite put my finger on – a kind of familiarity.'

'That's very perceptive of you.' She smiled, but it didn't quite touch her eyes. 'Why don't we find somewhere to sit and enjoy the view? – it's so blissful in this summer sun, and that cooling sea breeze is lovely too.'

They climbed up the cliff path for a short distance and found a grassy bank with a wide ocean view.

'Can we be honest with each other?' said Sophie as they settled down shoulder to shoulder.

'It's time we were, I feel.'

'I'll cut to the chase then. I've been thinking about the future. I didn't realise how much I missed life in the big city… I kept thinking it would probably be better be for my career… and I'd started wondering about us, too. To be blunt, I wasn't sure I was ready to commit.'

They were both looking out to sea.

'You're a freer spirit than me, Soph. I think I know where this is going.'

'Can you?'

She'd turned to look at him, and he to her.

'I was almost ready to stay there,' she said quietly. 'But the second I was back, I knew this was where I want to be. I've realised that, all the time I was working in my studio in London, my heart was here, with you…'

He saw she was smiling, the old mischievous Sophie smile. And, after a while, he smiled back.

'That's good to hear.'

'So… I've said my bit. I need to hear where you are, Jonathan.'

He returned his gaze to the waves, glittering and tipped with foam as they rolled in towards the shore.

'I've been a mess, Soph. It's partly been about you and me, of course, but other stuff too. It's been doing my head in – and it's made me doubt my own judgement. And I got close to believing it might be all over between us.'

'Darling, it would help me – and maybe you as well – if you opened up a bit more. Do the personal bit first,' said Sophie tenderly.

There was a lull in the warm breeze, and for a moment the whole world seemed to have gone still and quiet.

'I never told you the whole story about Judith,' he said at last. 'We were fellow students at architectural school, planned to set up practice together – our life was all mapped out. You have to understand… I really believed that.' He paused. 'She dumped me for one of our lecturers who had his own, very successful, practice. It crushed me completely. I started second-guessing everything, Soph, myself included. Looking back, I'm sure all that pushed me towards the door of the monastery.'

He finally risked a sidelong glance at her, but all he saw in her face was love.

'That makes so much sense.'

'When you disappeared for ages,' he said, 'I started slipping into not believing in myself again. I'd been so wrong, once already. What if I was wrong again?'

'*You're not*,' she said, smiling. 'But I can see why you might think that, I really can. You might not believe in yourself, but I believe in you!'

'And I believe in you too, Soph, absolutely, passionately – as someone I can be myself with,' he said.

'So, we're a mutual admiration society!' She laughed. 'Now, what this about 'other stuff', as you put it?'

'I'm sorry… I've probably bored you to death with the shenanigans about property development, but...'

'I thought you were getting a bit obsessive about it – to the point it took you away from me.'

'I can see that now. But I'd good reason to worry, because much of what I suspected looks as if it's true. I can't quite say why yet, but the police are now involved.'

Her eyes widened. 'That's good, isn't it?'

'It is. But I got the personal and professional completely confused, and made all the wrong calls. For a start, I was far too protective of Anna.'

'You thought she couldn't manage without Ted.'

'I know that was wrong. But I was also jealous – that she was giving Richard Forrester the time of day. And worse, I thought he was involved in all this dirty dealing, which I'm now sure he isn't.'

'I was jealous of your closeness to Anna, you know,' she said. 'Even before Ted died.'

'Was it that obvious?'

'Yes, it was. I tried to ignore it, but it pissed me off pretty badly.'

Jonathan knew he had to come clean. He stood up and paced around for a bit before coming back, this time sitting down opposite her.

'Soph, there's something I need to tell you which might change everything.' He took a deep breath. 'Anna and I… we've been to bed together.'

Sophie jumped up and took several rapid steps away.

'No wonder you didn't call me all those weeks,' she said, her low voice now rising rapidly. 'Good God, Jonathan – you might at least have had the courtesy to tell me before I saw her this morning!' She wrapped her arms tight around herself and turned away.

'It wasn't like that, Soph, it really wasn't,' he said, head down and rooted to the spot.

When she finally turned she was shaking with anger. 'So what was it like then? Were you… God, I don't know if I want to hear this… were you fucking each other in our bed at the mill house?'

'No,' he said, firmly. 'It was just the once, at Hall – and we both agreed it couldn't happen again. It's not a defence, but the truth is I thought you'd gone for good. But I immediately felt I'd betrayed you – as did Anna for betraying Ted's memory. And she's desperate not to hurt you, or get in the way of us being together.'

She seemed to crumple as she sat down well away from him, still staring at the sea. 'I don't know what to say.'

'Well then, would you let me say one more thing?'

He looked pleading as Sophie glanced at him sharply.

'Ever since then,' he said, voice strained, 'I've realised just how much

I love you, and how important you are to me. I don't want to be with anyone else, honestly I don't, Soph.'

Sophie continued to contemplate the sea and the sky. It was ages before she turned around to face him again, eyes nearly overflowing with tears.

'I'm sorry I shouted at you,' she whispered. 'Please forgive me.'

'I'm the one in the wrong.' He wanted to move close to her but found he couldn't, the hurt in her expression pinning him to the spot. 'It's me who needs your forgiveness. You've done nothing wrong.'

She shook her head. 'But I have done.'

'What are you talking about?'

'I'm a coward and a hypocrite because I'd decided not to tell you about it. But I must now.'

He finally decided to move over to be next to her. 'Then tell me,' he said gently, reaching out to find her hand and grip it tightly.

'You know you said there was something about the figure which was familiar but you couldn't quite pin down?'

'Yes.'

'That's because I used Esther as my model. And to cut a long story short... she and I slept together, several times.'

Jonathan was stunned into silence, but felt Sophie grip his hand more tightly. She eventually continued.

'It only lasted a few weeks – then we both decided it couldn't continue. I don't know why it happened really, except, perhaps... well.' She gave him a sad smile. 'We were lonely.'

He took ages to find any words, but eventually whispered, 'we've both messed up, then.'

'I don't know whether you'll still want me. But, just like you said, it made me realise how much I do love you.'

They were leaning into one another now, Jonathan's arm around her shoulders.

'We've managed to hurt each other pretty badly, haven't we?' said Jonathan.

'We have – but, against the odds, maybe it's helped.'

Sophie stood up and held out a hand, drawing him up. They held each other close.

'Please let me say one more thing, and this really is the truth,' said Sophie, looking into his eyes. 'I'm glad you told me – both about Anna, and about how much you love me. Not just because it propelled me to come clean about Esther – but – for the first time ever, I think I've seen a glimpse of the real you. I see the flesh and blood Jonathan, the one who messes up just like me and the rest of the world, not the buttoned-up monk. And I love you so much the more for that.'

'That's much more than I deserve, but thank you.'

'I could say exactly the same, couldn't I? Oh, for God's sake, enough of all this angst – let's go back to the house and open a bottle of wine – or two!'

FIFTY-THREE
9th July 1970

In the early morning, Jonathan went down to make mugs of tea. When he returned, he sat on the bed as Sophie slowly stretched herself awake in the morning light.

'What a wonderful night,' she murmured, still blinking sleep from her eyes.

'It was bliss.'

He nursed his warm mug, waiting until Sophie was ready for hers.

'Come back to bed and cuddle me,' she said.

As they lay together, sipping their tea, they talked about the day ahead.

'This is where it all comes back together,' Jonathan said.

'I hope it's not too hard on Anna,' Sophie said. 'There'll be so much of Ted around today. We've got to make it special for her, and Nicky and Will.'

'I know we shall,' said Jonathan.

Anna had invited only family, close friends, and some of her and Ted's most steadfast supporters, including Dr Manners, Professor Evans, and Audrey Elkins – Esther had been asked, but she'd already left for Paris to begin her scholarship. Sophie was quietly relieved.

Once all her guests had gathered and were milling about in the middle of the granary, Anna stepped towards the niche and cleared her throat.

'Thank you all so much for coming,' she said. 'It's a very special day for us at Hall. We've waited a long time, and we've had our setbacks, but I hope you'll think it's been worth it. Nicky, Will and I want this to be a celebration. So what we're going to do is let you enjoy your drinks for a bit, and then I'm going to ask Sophie to unveil her sculpture. It was something Ted and I decided to commission before he left us so suddenly – and it turned out to be one of the last decisions we made together.'

'It's like a wonderful extended family!' Leo said to Anna as they mingled with familiar faces, including Caroline and Oliver, Tony, Jim, Annie Webber, and Len and Daisy.

'I kept it small,' she said, 'because I think that's what Ted would have wanted – you'll no doubt remember how he used to bang on about the 'Grand Opening' of the Studies Centre!'

'Well,' said Leo, looking up approvingly at the restored mediaeval roof, 'the craftsmen have certainly done a great job, don't you think, Dr Manners?'

'Oh yes indeed, it's exemplary, Father.' He beamed; quite an odd expression on the normally serious and sombre man's face. 'And of course, it's such a privilege to meet my mentor, Professor Evans, at last!'

Eventually Anna called for silence, and Sophie made her way to stand beside Anna near the niche.

'This has been such a special commission for me,' Sophie said. 'It honours Ted, the man who first saw how this old granary could play a special role in the continuing life of this ancient farm. He found great significance in the dedication of the mediaeval chapel to St Mary Magdalene, a woman whose life was turned around by love, acceptance and healing. Anna asked me to try to express something true to the spirit of Mary Magdalene in this figure, which now takes its place in the niche here – originally made to house a devotional figure. I just hope you'll think I've done it justice!'

As she took the cloth away, there were cries of applause and delight from the guests. It was left to Leo, whom Anna had asked, to respond.

'This is not a moment for more words,' Leo said. 'It is a moment to be still and reflect, to give thanks for Ted's life, as well as his and Anna's vision – and Sophie's skill in helping realise that vision. So, let's spend a minute or so in silence, to gaze on her representation of the spirit of St Mary Magdalene, and wonder at the simplicity and freshness of her interpretation... And commend this place as a still point in a turning world for all who cross its threshold in the years to come.'

Sophie had told Jonathan she'd need to return to London soon afterwards, though she seemed increasingly reluctant to leave as afternoon slipped into evening. She eventually loaded the car, but lingered by the driver's door as they held each other close.

'I'm sorry I've got to go so soon, darling,' she said. 'We could have done with a bit more time.'

'I suppose so, but we did and said what we needed to, didn't we?' said Jonathan. 'And ended up in a good place.'

'Talking of places, one thing we didn't touch on,' Sophie said. 'The leases on the London flat and the studio expire in a couple of weeks, and I gave up my Broadhaven pad earlier in the summer. I'm going to have to find somewhere to live, and a bigger studio down here now.'

Jonathan knew this was the golden moment.

'Why don't you just come back here? For good, I mean?'

'Do you really want me here?'

'Of course I do. I told you – we told each other really – we're in love. And that means being together, doesn't it?'

'We did… and it does!' She held him for a moment at arms' length and gazed at him with those huge brown eyes.

He clasped her tight.

'Off you go then.'

She opened the car door, stood by it for a second or so, then turned round to face him.

'I've got a better idea,' she said, shutting the car door firmly. 'I'll leave in the morning!'

FIFTY-FOUR

10th July 1970

At the granary party, Caroline had invited Jonathan to lunch at Tremaine the following day. As he drove through the gates into the park he recalled that delight on his first visit, a sense that he was entering a magical other-world. Now, it felt different. Sure, the fallen trees and bramble-clumped fields lent an air of picturesque disorder, as if the park had absent-mindedly fallen asleep… but tumbled walls, roofless buildings, and broken fences spoke of a more profound decay. This was the twilight of the Athertons' centuries-old stewardship of their ancestral estate.

Oliver greeted him, and they all lunched in the vast old kitchen at the rear of the house. Their conversation ranged widely, and as the meal drew to a close Caroline suggested she and Jonathan should go for a walk in the park.

'Now, Jonathan, as you know there's no such thing as a free lunch,' she said as they roamed the shady, overgrown grounds. 'I want to talk about the future of the practice. The thing is, Tony's told me he wants to retire next year – he's well over his three score years and ten, you know.'

'That'll be a huge loss to the practice,' Jonathan said, 'and to me. He's been a real mentor.'

'I know he has – and he'll be a great loss to me too. As you know, he's the only partner I've ever had, so I need to ask myself whether I carry on solo, or look for a new one. We've built up a good reputation for a small firm in this part of the world, and I'd like to expand a little.'

'I'm full of admiration for the way you run things,' Jonathan said. 'And if you're asking my opinion, I think you should definitely be looking for another partner.'

'But it has to be the right person,' she said. 'Someone younger, energetic, and fully engaged with our sort of work.'

'I can see the problem,' said Jonathan. 'But it's worth advertising, and seeing who turns up.'

'I don't think so,' Caroline said. 'I've come to a decision.' She'd stopped and was looking straight at him. 'But it'll need your agreement.'

'I'm not sure my views are all that significant,' he said, pleased but very awkward and taken aback.

Caroline shook her head, amused. 'I wondered whether you'd consider coming into partnership with me.'

A few silent seconds passed.

'Well,' he said after he'd recovered his breath, 'that's… not what I was expecting.'

'Let's walk on while we talk about it,' said Caroline. 'I've sounded out Tony, of course, and he's all for it too – he's got great respect for you. And equally important, he feels it would go down well with the rest of the office.'

'Forgive me, Caroline, I'm just not sure what to say,' Jonathan replied with caution. 'I'm surprised – and very flattered of course – but a partnership in Atherton & Green isn't something I'd ever considered. Would you mind if I took a bit of time to think it about it?'

'Of course you must. It's a big decision for both of us.'

They continued to speak at some length about the pros and cons of Caroline's proposal. Eventually she suggested they should make their way back to the house.

'Let's have a cup of tea before you go,' she said. 'There's something else Oliver and I want to share with you.'

They took tea back in the kitchen.

'You've become a good friend,' Oliver said. 'And you don't need us to tell you that keeping Tremaine going has become a bit of a battle – one we're losing. The house and estate need so much investment, which we don't have the resources to meet any more. Keeping it going by ourselves is beyond us, so we have to find some way of lightening the load.'

'I've always thought it amazing you and Caroline are so committed to Tremaine – your deep love for the place, and your family's history here,' Jonathan said.

'It's kind of you to say so,' Oliver said. 'But family history can easily become a millstone around one's neck – it can drag you down and prevent you from facing up to the future. So we're thinking of making a radical decision.'

'Not selling up, surely?'

'No, certainly not that,' said Caroline. 'But we're going to move out of here and live at Endscombe, a Victorian shooting lodge you won't have seen – it's further into the estate, quite modest, at least compared to this place, and much more manageable for us.'

'What would happen to this house?'

'We don't know yet,' Caroline said. 'We're following up a couple of promising possibilities – which come from the opening up of this part of the country by the new motorway.'

'I'm just beginning to get my head round what all that's going to mean,' Jonathan said.

'One of the things it does mean,' said Oliver, 'is that big organisations are looking to relocate their London HQs down here, at much reduced costs and with the opportunity to give their employees a better quality of life. We've had a couple of enquiries asking whether we might be interested in putting Tremaine into that kind of market – one on behalf of an internationally renowned agricultural research institute, which could be ideal for us.'

'How would that work?' asked Jonathan.

'They'd fund the major repairs and bring the place into full use again,' said Caroline, 'as well as restoring the gardens and parkland. And crucially, of course, they'd have the acreage they needed for their research purposes, leaving us to continue to farm most of the estate.'

'We'd give them a long lease,' Oliver said. 'So we'd have an income which we can invest in the rest of the estate. The tenanted farms need just as much investment as the main house and park.'

'It sounds exciting. How far have you got?'

'We're in the early stages,' Oliver said, 'but it looks promising – they're very keen. We haven't told anyone else – you know how the rumour mill gets going. We'd be grateful if you'd keep it to yourself just now, though you must share this with Sophie, of course.'

'Well, thank you for taking me into your confidence. I will tell Sophie – she'll be back from London permanently later this month.'

'It was good to see her yesterday,' said Caroline. 'She's been away for so long, and I haven't heard a word all that time she's been in London – she's OK, isn't she?'

'Well, it's been a testing time for both of us. But, fingers crossed, once she's back, we can make some decisions. Not the least of which is her finding a new studio – now she's doing much bigger pieces, she's going to need rather more working space.'

'I think her Mary Magdalene figure is inspired,' said Caroline. 'I'm sure she'll go from strength to strength – I'm so proud of her!'

'So am I.' He smiled. 'Look, I think I ought to be getting back to the office, there are a few things I need to do before close of play today. Thank you both for your hospitality once again. And, Caroline, I promise I'll mull over your offer very carefully and come back to you as soon as I can.'

Back in the office, Jonathan couldn't wait to share his news with Sophie. He found one of the meeting rooms vacant and called her at her studio.

Please let her be there – I need to know what she thinks!

He was in luck.

'Hello darling! You've caught me at the right moment – just made a cup of tea.'

'Hello my love, can you talk? I've got some amazing news.'

'How exciting. Shall I try to guess?'

'You could, but you'd never get it.'

'Go on then, tell me.'

'Caroline's offered me a partnership!'

There was a squeal of delight from Sophie. 'Caroline always said you were a star, and now you're going to shine alongside her!'

'So you think I should accept?' Jonathan said, laughing along with her.

'Are you mad? Of course you should, it'll be wonderful for you – and for us too, especially now I'm coming back for good!'

'I can't tell you how good it is to hear you say that! Because I feel exactly the same.'

'Don't delay too long in getting back to her – maybe just long enough to convince her you're taking the decision very carefully. She'd want that, wouldn't she?'

'She would, and I promised I'd do exactly that.'

FIFTY-FIVE

11th and 12th July 1970

Saturday night, unusually warm for an English summer, without a breath of a breeze.

Jonathan couldn't sleep.

His mind was churning with excitement. He'd seen his move west as a time to sort himself out, but he'd never imagined all this: a partnership, a life with Sophie, and some treasured friends.

He got up before sunrise, and went about the morning rituals of washing, dressing, and walking Cadoc. Watching the sun peep over the sea's horizon, he found himself seized by the need to fall to his knees with thanksgiving – a need that had only ever surfaced fleetingly since his time in the monastery, and often on a Sunday morning – which, he now remembered, it was.

He reached the Square in Michaelchurch a few minutes before eight o'clock, the tolling of a single bell urging him on through the churchyard and up to the church porch. He paused at the door, conscious of the significance of the moment. Turning the old handle as gently as he was able, he stepped inside, the nave cool and still in contrast to the warmth outside. There was no sign of life, so he made his way through that glorious rood screen into the more mysterious ambience of the chancel. All the rich decoration, exquisite woodwork, and golden altar were richly illuminated by shafts of sunlight piercing through the Morris & Co glass… a transport into the numinous.

He knelt and prayed.

Opening his eyes and discreetly surveying the scene, he saw a modest congregation scattered among the choir stalls. He recognised most of them from the comings and goings of daily life in the town. But there was one surprise among them: Richard Forrester.

The church clock struck the hour, and Leo, robed in a Trinity green chasuble, emerged in near silence from the vestry, a server preceding him. They reverenced the altar before observing a few moments of silent prayer.

Leo began the liturgy, its cadences and rhythm unifying the intentions of this disparate group of humanity. For Jonathan, the familiarity was comforting, dissolving all his worries, the cause of so much grief over the years. It felt like a homecoming.

When the liturgy ended, Leo and the server returned to the vestry as quietly as they'd come. The congregation slipped away to resume their lives, unhindered by small talk, just a word of greeting or a nod and a smile. And it was a smile exchanged between Jonathan and Richard which finally offered the opportunity of a breakthrough.

'Hello Jonathan,' Richard said. 'At last we find ourselves in the same place.'

'Hello Richard. Yes, we do – and it feels good.'

'You'll forgive me for thinking we've avoided each other for far too long.'

'Then perhaps you'll forgive me for thinking I've been responsible for that,' Jonathan said. 'You may think this is a bit odd in view of all that's happened, but… I'd like to buy you a drink sometime soon.'

'I'd like that very much.'

They shook hands, and went their separate ways.

FIFTY-SIX

15th July 1970

Jonathan was at work when Emma summoned him for another personal call – from 'that man who wouldn't tell me his name.'

Jonathan felt his heart racing.

Kidded yourself you're OK with all this stuff, didn't you?

'Morning Chief Inspector,' he said when he picked up the phone, 'how can I help?'

'Morning Mr Lane. We've had a couple of developments. Could you spare us another hour of your time…. sooner rather than later?'

Jonathan was outside pulling up weeds from the garden with Cadoc when he heard the car approaching.

'Afternoon Mr Lane,' said Probert as he and Naomi got out of their car. 'Good to see you again.'

Jonathan straightened up and brushed off his hands. 'Good to see you too, Chief Inspector, and you, Naomi. Do come in, I've already put the kettle on.'

Once tea and cake were served, Jonathan sat right on the edge of his chair, unable to contain himself to pleasantries any longer.

'So, what's cropped up in your investigations, Chief Inspector?'

'Well, you were very helpful last time we spoke,' Probert said, 'so we wanted to ask for a bit more of your assistance. We've two significant developments – I'll let Sergeant Walters start because she's the one who made a bit of a breakthrough.'

'Last Saturday night,' Naomi said, 'our uniformed colleagues at Broadhaven were called to a pub. The landlord had told two pretty unsavoury characters they'd had a skinful and he wasn't going to serve them again. They turned nasty, he asked them to leave, they refused, and when he tried to eject them they resisted. The locals joined in and quite a brawl developed.'

'So far, normal Saturday night in Broadhaven,' the Chief Inspector said, looking rather weary as he helped himself to another slice of cake.

'When our colleagues arrived,' Naomi said, 'this pair tried to resist arrest. So they were cuffed and taken to the station, which is where it got interesting. They started shouting their mouths off in the cells – 'Do you know who we are?' and that kind of thing, which as you can guess, always gets us going.'

'I can imagine it would,' said Jonathan.

'So,' Naomi said, 'when the duty sergeant said he hadn't got a clue who they were but he'd be pleased if they could tell him because he needed to make up the charge sheet, they said 'All you need to know is we're close friends of Harry Humphries, he'll hear all about all this and he'll see us right.' The sergeant thought that would be of interest to us, so I was asked to interview them. They were pretty unpleasant but they described themselves, in the presence of the duty solicitor, as 'close business associates' of Humphries. They said a lot more, but that'll do for now.'

'Of course,' said the Chief Inspector, 'when they'd sobered up, they denied saying any such thing, but we had it down in black and white. Turns out they're from London, as we'd suspected, part of the same mob we've been investigating over fraudulent property development in other parts of the country. Bottom line, it was enough for us to get a search warrant for Humphries' office and home, which is turning up some very interesting material. We've already interviewed him under caution.'

Jonathan knew this was indeed a breakthrough.

'That's great news,' he said. 'You seem to have cracked it – seems like you won't need me now.'

'On the contrary,' the Chief Inspector said, 'your assistance is crucial. We're now able to prove that the information you've accumulated here ties in with the bigger picture – and will be vital evidence when we bring charges against Humphries and his associates. We've had good general commentary from the source Sergeant Walters recruited, but we need the specifics only you can provide.'

'I don't suppose you're able to tell me who that source is?'

'I'm afraid not, for the moment, sir,' Probert said. 'It's important to our investigation to collect as many independent strands of intelligence as possible and see where they converge. We'll need you as one of our key witnesses when we get this to court. Because the trail we're following may start from here, but it leads us directly into the wider conspiracy we're now near to cracking.'

As Jonathan sipped his coffee, he realised there was one name he hadn't heard in some time. 'Where's Penhaligan in all this?'

'He's been a fool, certainly, a pawn in a much bigger game, but not much more than that,' said Naomi. 'The crucial link between Humphries and the council turns out to be Johnson, the town clerk.'

'It's how this lot operate,' said Probert. 'They recruit a useful idiot, an apparently respectable local figure – Johnson, in this case – convince him that over the years he's helped many a dodgy customer make a pile of money through the planning process, and persuade him to join their game.'

'So, even though Penhaligan's behaviour could look suspicious, he's in the clear?'

'Most likely. We'll run a few more checks,' Naomi said, 'but we've found no evidence of his involvement so far. Whereas we've got evidence that Johnson's been taking backhanders for years, which is why the same firms kept on getting all the council jobs.'

'That's quite a relief,' Jonathan said. 'A lot of people around here would find it difficult to believe Penhaligan was mixed up in such shady business.'

'If he's guilty of anything, it's being naive,' said Naomi, 'and not asking enough questions.'

'Humphries is a master of deceit – expert in laying false trails to cover his tracks,' Probert said. 'For all his ranting *against* development – he's actually up to his ears promoting it, all over the country.'

'How on earth does that work?' said Jonathan, feeling an innocent in a world he never wanted to inhabit but had been forced to visit. 'Surely he's only damaging his own interest?'

'His role is to smoke out likely opposition by playing devil's advocate in his newspaper articles,' said Probert, 'which he can do because he's a national name. Then his lot can neutralise it with backhanders, intimidation, and the rest.'

'God, this is all too much for me, I'm afraid.'

'That's all right, sir,' Probert said, 'we needn't burden you with any more this afternoon.'

'Except you said there were a couple of things you wanted to update me on. I assume that was the first. What's the other one?'

Probert snapped his fingers. 'Indeed, there is another line of inquiry that's proving fruitful. Tell you what, sir, it's a bit of a cheek, but is there any chance you might stretch to another brew before we get on to that? Give me a chance to nip outside for a quick smoke.'

Jonathan welcomed the pause in the conversation, and took his time brewing up the tea as he watched the officers walking around outside, no doubt evaluating the progress they were making with him.

They settled down again.

'Now,' said Probert, 'I expect you'll want to know what progress we've made with Mr Forrester.'

'I certainly would.'

'Well, we now know for certain it was an assault – and a vicious one,'

Naomi said. 'Mr Forrester came to the station and made a statement to that effect and the Chief interviewed him later the same day. He was concussed after the attack, which is why he'd initially assumed it must have been an accident. I checked with the hospital and with Mrs Northcott, who he said he'd seen several times since the incident, and they both confirmed every detail of the account he's now given us.'

'I did know he'd been to the police, from Anna Northcott, but your confirmation is very welcome,' said Jonathan. 'Have you got any further with the attack itself?'

'Untangling the different threads is proving a challenge,' said Naomi, 'but we believe the assault is connected to the wider conspiracy. We've done a few more background checks on Forrester and, as far as we can see, he's absolutely clean. He is connected to major national property developers, but they're all very much above board and with good reputations.'

'So what's the link between the assault and the wider conspiracy?'

'It's Mr Forrester's misfortune to be extremely good at his job – which is why this outfit wanted him out of the way so they had a clear run down here,' said Probert. 'We've got proof from tapped telephone calls that the attack was ordered by Humphries himself, and organised by Johnson.'

'Were the thugs who beat him up from London too?' asked Jonathan.

'They could have been – this gang usually hire in heavies from outside to do their dirty work,' Probert said. 'But we'll find out – we've got recordings of their telephone conversations, and they made various threats to Mr Forrester during the assault, so we're hoping he'll recognise their voices in due course. And we've also got sightings of the same men drinking in other pubs in Broadhaven.'

'Well, that's all quite a lot to take in,' Jonathan said. 'But I have to say I'm mightily relieved.'

'We understand that,' said Naomi. 'I involved you right from the start, so we're very grateful to you for sticking with it – and for what you're still prepared to do for us.'

'We are indeed,' said Probert. 'But let's talk about something more pleasant while I finish this tea,' said Probert. 'England doing OK in the Test, aren't they? At least they were when I last heard before we came out. Marvellous thing, the wireless, always have one back at the station – completely against regulations, of course.'

Though it was late, Jonathan had to get back to the office to collect some papers for a site meeting first thing in the morning. He met Tony coming out as he was going in.

'You doing overtime, old thing! Actually, you look rather pleased with yourself. I'm just off for a jar with Jim in The Castle – care to join us?'

'Yes, thanks, Tony, I think I will, I'll just nip up and collect some drawings.'

'Good, then we'll go straight over, and you and I can talk over a little matter of mutual interest in strict confidence. Jim said he might be running a bit late.'

As soon as they arrived at the pub, Tony insisted on buying the first round.

'Here's to the new partner!'

'Steady on, Tony, I haven't accepted yet! But thanks for your endorsement anyway.'

'But you will accept, of course? Take it from an old 'un, chances like this don't come along more than once in a lifetime.'

'I shall, Tony, but for God's sake don't say a word till I've told Caroline.'

'You'll be bloody good at it, and it'll be just the right balance in the practice for Caroline – I couldn't wish for a more promising successor. Ah good, here's Jim – don't worry old thing, mum's the word.'

FIFTY-SEVEN

7th July 1970

Leo had noted, with more than passing interest, Jonathan's appearance out of the blue at the early Sunday service. He'd long since learnt to assume nothing about such sudden manifestations – people might have a thousand and one reasons for suddenly turning up in church. Often it was a one-off, and the person would never grace the pews again – visitors, perhaps, or newcomers looking around to see what might suit – and finding it didn't. Occasionally it was a signal of something deeper, a significant moment in a spiritual search.

Leo felt he'd never really worked Jonathan out – annoying, because he was usually good at that kind of detective work. Maybe he was missing London – it must have been as much of a culture shock for Jonathan to land up in Michaelchurch as it had been for Leo himself. But the young architect had settled in well, and people had taken a shine to him. Perhaps it was an affair of the heart – though he and Sophie seemed so right for each other. Or could he have come to a bump in the road on a journey of the soul?

Leo decided to satisfy his curiosity and have him over for a drink.

⟐

They sat with Cadoc in summer evening warmth on the rectory's south-west facing terrace, beneath its graceful if dilapidated veranda, sipping their whiskey and gingers, with Leo puffing contentedly on a

Woodbine. They talked mostly about the life of the town – Leo was practised at letting people find the right moment to open up, and eventually his guest was ready.

'Leo, can I run something past you, in confidence?'

'If you think I could be of any possible help, of course.'

'I've come to one of those forks in the road. I think I know what I want to do, but it'd be good to rehearse it with you, you've become such a trusted friend.'

'Then tell me about it.'

'Caroline's offered me a partnership – and I'm going to accept.'

'Congratulations! I think most people had assumed you were Tony's natural successor now he's retiring. But why does choice come into it? You said you're going to accept!'

'I suppose my only doubt is that I never expected to stick around here too long – I came because I wanted somewhere I could sort myself out.'

'And have you?'

'Yes, I think so. I've found a stability which has surprised me – different from anything I've ever known.'

Leo waited in silence, giving Jonathan a moment to gather his thoughts.

'A lot of it is because I've found a soulmate in Sophie,' Jonathan said eventually. 'We've had our struggles – she's been away so long – but she's now going to base herself with me at the mill house, for the long term. And she's thrilled by my being offered the partnership.'

'So she should be! I think you're good for each other, you know. I shouldn't really say this, but I can't tell you the number of times I've thought to myself when couples come to be married 'Well, that's never going to work!''

Jonathan laughed. 'I'm not sure we're anywhere near the altar yet, Leo!'

'No, no,' Leo said hastily, 'I'm sorry – I didn't mean to imply any such thing. I suppose it's just that I've grown to have some sense of when two human beings complement one another.'

'Well, that's very good to know – Sophie thinks the world of you.'

'And I think very highly of her. Now, let me refresh our glasses before you carry on, I sense this is the kind of discussion best had over a stiff drink.'

On the long trek to the kitchen for fresh supplies, Leo mused that Jonathan hadn't yet offered a clue about what was really on his young friend's mind.

'So,' he said on his return, 'I can't see you've got any problem with Caroline's offer.'

Jonathan accepted his drink and nursed it for a few sips.

'No, I haven't really. I suppose it's only what we've often talked about – everything in this part of the world being in flux. I find it unsettling to see everything dissolving before my eyes just as I discover how wonderful it is.'

'How often, just when we sense how perfect things are, we also come to realise that it won't last,' Leo said. 'How fleeting and transient life is.'

Jonathan nodded.

'But there's something else. I realise I've made serious misjudgments about people. You'd be shocked by some of the things I've discovered.'

Leo laughed as he took another pull of his whiskey. 'Would I really? People in my line of work become pretty familiar with human frailty.'

Jonathan chuckled too. 'Sorry, I guess you're pretty unshockable. The thing is, I've found what really happened to Richard Forrester.'

'Oh?'

'He was beaten up to frighten him off his patch. The police think Harry Humphries is one of the main players in the wider conspiracy, but sadly our own council's involved as well. For a long time I wondered whether Horace Penhaligan might be the link, but that was another one of my misjudgments – he's clean. In fact, all the evidence points to Walter Johnson.'

'I wouldn't shed any tears if Humphries was brought to book after all the harm to other people he's done in his nasty rag over the years,' Leo said. 'And it wouldn't surprise me to know Johnson had his hand in the till. I found him duplicitous when I was chairing the advisory board.'

'It worries me I got Horace so wrong.'

'Horace is his own worst enemy: too inclined to court popularity, and too disinclined to ask awkward questions about things which need interrogating. But Citizen Pen's a good soul, if a rather canny one, who's done a lot for the area over the years. Now, can I gently steer you back to where you started?'

'Sorry, I've been far too caught up in all this for my own good – which is really what I wanted to say, I suppose.'

Leo let this remark hang in the air while he lit another cigarette, the match hissing as it sprang to life.

'Well then, let me take you back to Richard – can I assume he's another of your 'misjudgments'?' He shook out the match and took a long drag, letting out a long stream of smoke into the evening air. 'When I saw him in hospital, he told me it could have been a lot worse.'

'It sure could have been. And I've been so prejudiced against him.'

'I'd picked up on that. Not unconnected with wanting to protect Anna?'

'Yes… and I'm sorry to say, there was more than a dash of jealousy there. I'm ashamed of myself… I only came to terms with this on Sunday, seeing Richard in church. I realised how good it was we were both there. We spoke briefly as we left, and we're going to have a drink together soon.' He paused, and his next words were slow and quiet. 'A wonderful calm came over me afterwards… and it's still with me.'

'I thought it entirely right you were both there,' said Leo.

'Is Richard a regular?'

'He is. He's a good soul too. He's mentioned several times how much solace he gets from visits to the holy well near you – you and he have more in common than you think.'

'I'm beginning to see that,' Jonathan said. Then, suddenly, 'if you don't mind, Leo, I feel this is the right moment to come clean about something in my past I've wanted to tell you for ages.'

'If you think it would help, of course.'

'Would you believe I spent a couple of years in a Benedictine monastery?'

They'd been sitting alongside each other, but now Leo turned and looked directly at Jonathan, a slow smile breaking across his features.

'I would believe that, Jonathan, and I mean that as a compliment. There were some pointers, or so I thought, particularly your familiarity when we touch on spiritual matters, which we sometimes have.'

'I've wanted to tell you for ages, but couldn't bring myself to, for some reason.'

'You were waiting for the right moment – and I believe you found it,' Leo said quietly.

'Thank you. It's important to me that you know – I haven't told anyone else, except Sophie.'

There was a pause while both men drew breath and nursed their drinks.

'Now, since we're exchanging confidences,' Leo continued eventually, 'I want to ask you something – which I hope you don't think is impertinent.'

'Never, you're too much of a gent.'

Leo laughed. 'I wouldn't be so sure about that. But how did you come by all this information about what's been going on?'

Jonathan shifted uneasily in his chair, momentarily regretting he'd poured it all out.

'I really shouldn't have told you. But you've been straight with me – so I think I should be with you. And I know you keep confidences.'

'If I didn't I'd soon be out of a job,' Leo said, smiling.

Jonathan smiled too. 'OK then. Between you and me, I've been helping the police with their investigation. They want evidence about anything I've picked up about this whole business. As you can imagine, I've got quite a lot of material which they say will be significant when the case comes to court.'

'I imagine it would be.'

'Apparently someone down here's been acting as lookout for the police already, so they've got a good handle on what's going on. I'm pretty sure the source will have vetted me too, before I was approached. I've racked my brains to work out who it might be, but I'm stumped.'

Leo's kind eyes narrowed in amusement. 'May be I can help you.'

'How?' Jonathan sat up straighter. 'You know who it is?'

'He's sitting right next to you.'

There was a stunned silence. Then, throwing himself back in his chair till he almost went over backwards, Jonathan burst into laughter.

'Of course – the utterly impeccable source! No-one else has his finger on the pulse like you. I reckon Jim Jewell and Tony aren't bad either, but you're in a different league. So you knew about the 'in strictest confidence' stuff all along!'

'You'll forgive me, I hope, for stringing you along a little. Remember I got to know Naomi Walters when I was chair of her advisory board. Shortly after she left, she telephoned me to reveal her true identity and recruited me to keep a discreet eye on development activity in the area. We've kept in touch ever since.'

'You always said she was a rare talent.'

'And I was right, wasn't I? Our Detective Sergeant Walters will go far. One other thing – am I right to assume you haven't told anyone else, except Sophie perhaps?'

'Absolutely, yes.'

'Good. Because the uncomfortable truth is that we're both involved, albeit on the margins, in a very dangerous game. That said, the police are clearly making very good progress, so we won't have to put up with the cloak-and-dagger nonsense much longer.'

'That would be such a relief.'

Jonathan sighed and rose to his feet; Leo followed suit.

'On that note, it really is time for Cadoc and me to wend our way home. Thank you, Leo. I can't begin to say how much I've valued our time together this evening. It's helped sort my head out…'

'Nor me, Jonathan. We have a lot in common, don't we!'

'Not least that we're both coppers' narks!' He chuckled. 'Come on, Cadoc!'

Leo watched as Jonathan left the rectory until he disappeared from view, walking like a man much more at ease with himself.

FIFTY-EIGHT

17th July 1970

Dusk

As he left the town, Jonathan paused to take in the familiar panorama of the warm, still evening: the land falling gently towards the sea; the coastal paths he walked with Sophie and Cadoc; the tapestry of small fields knitted together by deep lanes he could now navigate effortlessly; farms half-hidden down mysterious hedge-lined tracks; the Bible Christian chapel standing stark against the sky at that isolated crossroads; the towers of two neighbouring churches, squatting low and sturdy against Atlantic gales… and in the distance, the sea, tranquil as the fading light blended blue-grey waters with the softer, lighter line of the horizon, grey heaven streaked with hints of red and gold.

For all its serenity, he knew this was not a landscape of innocence. What was so easy on the eye had been hard-won by generation after generation of farmers, perennially resilient. They faced up to whatever market, government, or the weather threw at them – the endless rain and mud of winter, the vagaries of the growing season, fickle harvests. But on such grit was this landscape built and sustained.

He now understood the rawness in Clare's poetry, as he too saw a landscape of lost certainties, and the stirrings of a revolution. So much had been turned upside down in the three short years he'd been here. Ted's death had been a brutal but necessary lesson that stability was as elusive in the farms and fields of the south-west as it was in the metropolis. Even the Athertons' struggle to keep up appearances at Tremaine was coming to an end – and in a few years, when Leo retired, his rambling rectory and wonderfully unkempt garden would be gone too.

He turned and gazed inland. Somewhere over the eastern horizon, construction of the last leg of the new motorway had begun. What would be sailing down those tarmac rivers as they snaked their way through this secret country? Substantial new, and much-needed, investment, said the politicians, bringing thousands of jobs and creating a vibrant economy – nothing less than the revival of a rural England so long unregarded.

But he understood, now, the inevitability of all this – and also the fear of change it brought with it, hastening the demise of a world he'd so recently discovered. Might this quiet dreamy landscape dissolve into a nightmare of agribusiness, leisure parks and golf courses, tin sheds on 'industrial estates' at the edge of every settlement? All the lovely crooked lanes replaced by straightened roads to speed people faster to nowhere in particular?

He left the lanes to take the footpath across the fields.

He counted his blessings. He'd come as a complete stranger on a cold wet night in winter, and was quickly made to feel at home. He couldn't possibly then have imagined the turn of events, some the cause of so much happiness, others so much angst – nor the irony that, having never intended to stay, he might now spend the rest of his working life here. Most of all there was Sophie, who'd helped him to imagine life's possibilities again.

He stopped at the field gate just above the farm, drinking in the scene as daylight faded into dusk. The lights of the Studies Centre reminded him what a transformation they had wrought. He lingered before making the final descent, walking the very same route he'd stumbled along the first evening he'd arrived three years ago. Then, as now, the light in the farmhouse kitchen was on. He caught a glimpse of Anna standing at the window, head down washing up, but she hadn't seen him in the gathering dark and he walked straight on towards the mill.

Dusk, 17th July 1970

As he reached the point at which the track descended steeply down the valley side, he rejoiced in his good fortune. The route was familiar and Cadoc was quickening his pace, excited by the prospect of home and supper.

As he neared the house, Cadoc, now well ahead, started barking wildly. Rounding the final bend, he saw why – there were lights on in the house.

I can't have left them on this morning. And the door's open, and that's jazz I can hear – that's the Sprite parked up outside!

Cadoc had run inside, beating Jonathan by quite a few yards.

'Soph,' he cried out as he followed in, 'what a wonderful surprise!'

She was on her knees, laughing as Cadoc attempted to wash her face with his tongue. 'Hello darling, yes, I thought I'd be early for once! Come here,' she said, getting up and moving towards him, 'I need to give you a huge hug!'

'I can't believe you're here!' he said as he wrapped her up in his arms.

'Well, darling, you'll just need to get used to it,' she said. 'Remember – I'm back for good this time!'

Acknowledgements

As in most fiction, some of the material in these pages is drawn from life lived. For it has been my good fortune to have spent over half a century – in various guises - exploring farms, houses of every scale, churches, estates, and small market towns all over south west England. Almost always, and whatever the purpose of my mission, I have found a warm welcome. So, first and foremost, I salute the stewards- for that is how most of them see themselves - of these wonderful places because they are the heroes who sustain this ancient ladscape and its deep-rooted society and culture.

That said, I must make explicit that all the characters and events described here have only ever existed in my imagination. But I hope readers familiar with the south west may feel some affinity with the fictional places I have conjured up as the setting of my story.

Many friends and colleagues have, often unconsciously, helped this endeavour on its way. I owe special thanks to Chris Bryan, Diana Marriott, and Marion Sankey who were burdened with reading early drafts and who all made helpful critiques. Chris also set me on the path to fictional redemption by introducing me to Shannon Roberts of *The Editorial Department* in the USA. As my editor, she has helped immeasurably to transform my raw material into the finished product. I am also grateful to Richard Crangle for his thoughtful copy editing which further polished my narrative.

I have been very fortunate in working once again with Andy Jones of *Topics – The Creative Partnership* who, with meticulous attention to detail, has designed the book and overseen its production through to publication. And my wife Chrissie and daughter Rachel have patiently sorted out my perennial battles with the digital world.

Finally, I owe the atmospheric illustrations in this book to the kindness of Val Organ – they are drawn from the Devon and Cornwall sketch books of her husband Robert [Bob] Organ. My dedication of this book to his memory reflects my gratitude for his painterly opening of my eyes to the immersive beauty of this small part of the world. Bob never took it for granted – and nor should we.

Peter Beacham
Advent Sunday 2023

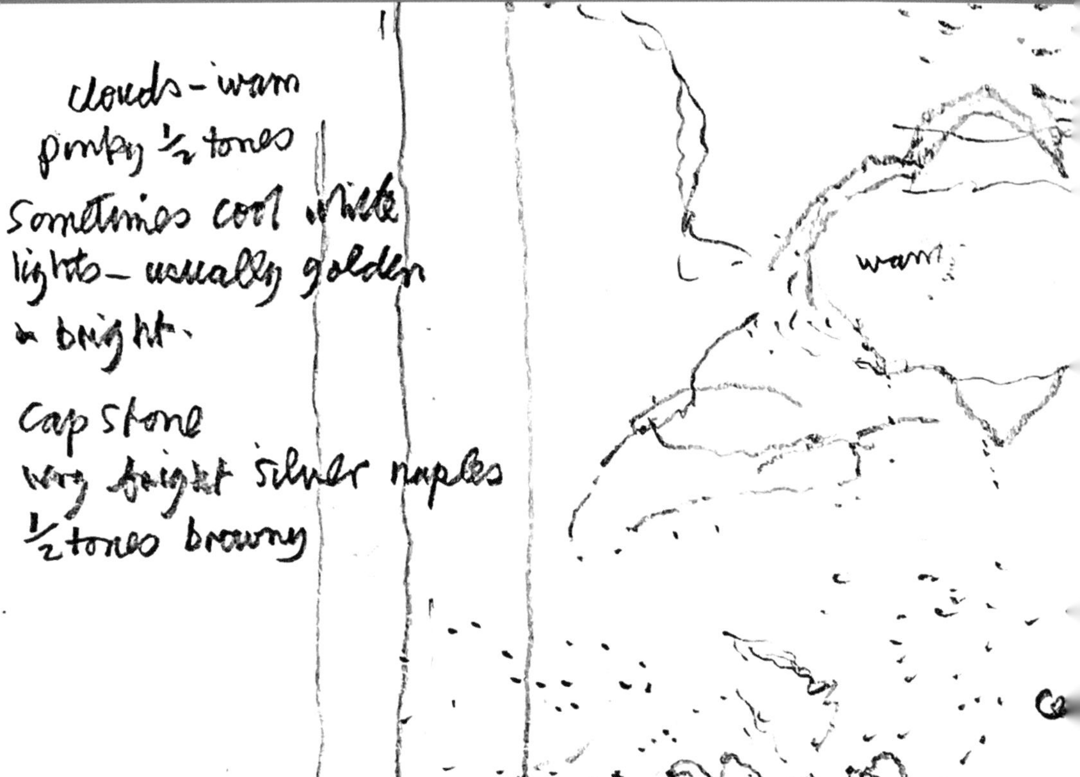
clouds - warm
pinky ½ tones
sometimes cool white
lights - usually golden
& bright.
cap stone
very bright silver naples
½ tones browny
warm
violet

vivid
pink

About the Author

Peter Beacham was born in Somerset, and has lived in Devon almost continuously since 1967. He has been a passionate advocate for the fragile beauty of the buildings, settlements and landscapes of the south west throughout his working life. His previous publications include *Down the Deep Lanes* [1999], with the photographer James Ravilious, about rural life in North Devon and beyond, and the revised edition of *Cornwall* [2014], with Nikolaus Pevsner, in the internationally acclaimed *Buildings of England* series.

Above: *A sketch portrait of the author* by Robert Organ.